KATHY TYERS

FIREBIRD

BETHANY HOUSE PUBLISHERS
MINNEAPOLIS, MINNESOTA 55438

Published by Bethany House Publishers
A Ministry of Bethany Fellowship International
11400 Hampshire Avenue South
Minneapolis, Minnesota 55438
www.bethanyhouse.com

Printed in the United States of America by
Bethany Press International, Minneapolis, Minnesota 55438

ISBN 0-7642-2214-7

To a blue-eyed, mostly Irish storyteller
who thinks I believe he's a Kansas farm boy—

Pro drummer by five, dressed unwilling
like Little Lord Fauntleroy, long curls and all—
but later, a hot cornet and an alley-cat keyboard—
And in between, a young test pilot measuring his airspeed
by the notes that the wind whistled between his wings;
He crashed a tractor in midlife, but stubbornly lived
and then walked when they said not to count on either—
An accomplished dentist and computer trailblazer
who grows orchids and onions and hundred-pound pumpkins
(and planted the Shasta Jazz Festival).

When the saints march in, may he be in that number.
H. Chester (Chet) Moore—I love you, Poppa.

KATHY TYERS is a bestselling author in the ABA market with earned degrees in microbiology and education. A classically trained flutist turned folk artist, she regularly performs folk music with her husband and also plays with the Bozeman Symphony Orchestra. She and her husband make their home in Montana and have one son.

ACKNOWLEDGMENTS

Thanks for critique and encouragement to Kathy, Lisa, Julie, Janna, Martha, Matthew, Karen, Chris, Eddie, Dr. Bob, Jane, Marlo, Maureen, Marjorie, Jo, Linda, Vance, Sharon, Wynne, Basia, George, Gayla, Kevin, Mike, Michele, Tana, John, Sylvia, Jane, Diann, Chris, Sigmund, Clint, Andrew, and Bob.

Special gratitude to Robert C. Mathis, General, USAF (Ret.) and founder of the Eagle Mount recreational therapy program (for your technical advice and encouragement); Harry P. Mathis, Chaplain Major, USAF (for spiritual support, insight, and the Academy tour); Major Diann Thornley, USAF Reserves (for inspiration and suggestions); and William D. Woodman, Captain, USN (Ret.), submarine officer (for your tactical, management, and protocol suggestions and the tour of your awe-inspiring boat!).

Deepest thanks to Steve Laube—and most of all, to Mark.

The best words on these pages belong to all of you . . . and to One who has given me the desires of my heart (Psalm 37:4). Inconsistencies, impossibilities, and weak wordings are all mine.

CONTENTS

In this whorl of imagined star systems,
God created not Earth but different worlds.

One world's people lived by false doctrine and death.
Light-years away, faithful exiles awaited
the Messiah of all creation.

On a third world, they met.

PRELUDE

Lady Firebird Angelo was trespassing.

Shadowed by her friend Lord Corey Bowman, she squeezed and twisted through a narrow, upright opening between two dusty stone walls. She'd paced off twenty meters in silence. Her eyes had almost adjusted to faint gray light from ahead and behind. Growing up in this palace, she'd explored it thoroughly and cautiously during her childhood. She hadn't tiptoed between these particular walls since she found the gap, four years ago, when she was fifteen. If she remembered right, then in ten meters more—

Something rattled behind her. She froze. If anyone caught her and Corey this deep in the governmental wing, they could be done for. *Powers help us!* she prayed silently.

Slowly, she turned around. Corey crouched three meters away. He pointed at a loose stone and cringed a silent apology.

Time hung suspended, like a laser satellite passing overhead. They waited motionless, hardly even breathing.

Evidently, the Powers weren't feeling vengeful—if those supernatural guides even existed, which Firebird had started to doubt. The soft voices behind the curved inner wall kept droning on, incomprehensible from this point in the hidden passage.

Firebird crept on.

The rough partition on her left enclosed an elliptical chamber. Inside, the highest council in the Netaian planetary systems held its conferences.

Firebird had heard whispered rumors among other cadets at the NPN Academy: that the Netaian Planetary Navy planned to hold military exercises in Federate space, or that an attack was imminent—Federate or Netaian, depending on who had heard whom—or that secret weapons were under development. None of her instructing officers had acknowledged those rumors. They kept their cadets working in blind, busy ignorance.

But this morning, staring out a classroom window-wall, Firebird had seen a silvery shuttle with Federate markings emblazoned on its underside decelerate into Citangelo spaceport. According to a hasty check at her desk terminal, the queen's Electorate had immediately closed this afternoon's session to observers.

Maybe the Federates were protesting those rumored maneuvers, as she guessed—or trying to head off an open confrontation, Corey's assumption. Someone had to find out, on behalf of the second-year cadets. If a war broke out, they'd be in it. During an afternoon hour reserved for studying, Firebird had sneaked home with Corey.

Ahead, light gleamed into their passage through an inner-wall chink. The palace's builders, three hundred years before, had been more concerned with elegance than security. During her privileged childhood, Firebird had found many odd niches in this historic building where walls didn't exactly meet, or where they came together at peculiar angles to create blind passageways. Palace security should have sealed every breach that gave illegitimate access to the electoral chamber. They'd missed this one.

On her next birthday, Firebird would be confirmed as a short-term elector. That was her right, an honor she would receive as an Angelo. Then, she would tell the House Guard and the electoral police about this passage.

But no sooner.

She reached the chink and peered through. Inside the grand chamber's red walls, lined with portraits and gilt bas-relief false pillars, the Netaian systems' twenty-seven electors sat at a U-shaped table that surrounded a small foreign delegation.

Firebird glimpsed the rest of her family. Her oldest sister and confidante, Carradee, sat beside the gilt chair of their mother, Siwann, a strong monarch who was already much more than the traditional electoral figurehead. Beyond Carradee lounged the middle Angelo sister, Phoena, the "beauty of the family" and Siwann's obvious favorite. Though taller and lighter haired than Firebird, Phoena had the same delicate facial features and large, long-lashed dark eyes. They'd often been mistaken for each other, to the disgust of both.

Five strangers stood below the U-shaped table's open foot. The two who'd stepped forward wore dress-white tunics and carried recall pads. One addressed the electors in clipped Old Colonial, the language of most colonized worlds in the Whorl's great half circle of stars. "... as a surtax only on nonessential goods," he declared, "such as ..."

What was this, a trade delegation?

Phoena exchanged disdainful glances with the trade minister, Muirnen Rogonin. Maintaining an indolent slouch, Rogonin—the jowly Duke of Claighbro—flicked two fingers toward the man who'd spoken. "I would see no reason to levy a military assessment against a well-defended system such as Netaia, Admiral. Your logic is flawed."

Admiral. Maybe their business wasn't entirely trade, then—

Corey nudged Firebird from behind. "Hey," he whispered.

Reluctantly, she rolled away from the chink. She pressed against the inner wall, listening closely.

In recent decades, the Federacy had consolidated twenty-three star systems in the local spur of the galactic arm. Netaia, isolated at the Whorl's counterspinward end, had resisted confederation. Despite tight governmental control over their lives, most Netaians lived in proud and comfortable, if xenophobic, prosperity ... so far as Firebird knew.

As the debate continued, she gradually concluded that the Federates did in fact want to set up a trading protocol. She glowered into the darkness. For this, she'd risked death?

Predictably, the noble electors—the heart of Netaia's spiritual and political power, which Firebird's family served as standard-bearers—were mouthing the same isolationist policies she'd heard all her life. Rogonin's voice rose, boasting about Netaia's high culture, its superbly terraformed ecological diversity, and the absolute lack of necessity of trade with any other planetary system.

All true, Firebird reflected with casual pride. Netaia was a wealthy world with rich resources.

She glanced at Corey. He stared through the chink, his oval face lit softly by fugitive light. Black haired and freckled, he was broadening into manhood, but they never had—never would—become romantically involved. Both were wastlings. Both would die young, as the Powers had decreed for most of these third- and fourth-born noble children. Firebird and Corey had made a pact, years ago, not to make that fate any harder on each other.

She jabbed his midsection. "My turn," she mouthed.

She pressed her face to cold stone and looked enviously on the five Federates. The thought of so many worlds, so much knowledge, frustrated her. She only would see the Federate systems as a military pilot, if at all.

Behind the two ambassadors, an honor guard stood at stiff attention, two armed men in ash gray and one in vivid midnight blue. Ash gray was for Tallis, the Federacy's regional capital. Midnight blue. . . ? Firebird frowned. She ought to remember—

Realization hit her like a laser blast. Midnight blue designated Thyrica. That was only a minor Federate system, but a few Thyrians were genetically engineered telepaths. Was this man one of them, and a spy?

Alarmed, she leaned toward Corey to whisper.

The Thyrian guard turned his head and looked straight at her.

Firebird's jaw dropped. She hadn't made a sound! Her pulse accelerated as the Thyrian stepped back from his formation to touch the arm of a red-jacketed electoral policeman. He whispered into the red-jacket's ear, and as he did, she caught a sparkle at the edge of his right shoulder, where the telepaths wore their gold insignia.

She flung herself away from the wall. "Corey, they spotted us!" she whispered. They must move fast . . . and separately. Because she was an Angelo, she stood a better chance of surviving arrest. "Get out the underway," she ordered. "I'll go back through the palace."

As Corey dashed toward a boarded-in cellar hatch, Firebird squeezed back through the narrows. Trying to run silently, she dashed to the passage's end and scrambled up a stone partition. She rolled onto a crawlway, groped for the board they'd left loose, and whisked it aside, then peered down into the public-zone maintenance closet.

So far, so good. The closet was dark. Heart hammering, she lowered herself through the impromptu hatch and then cracked the hall door.

It swung out of her grasp, seized from outside. A massive black-haired man backed across the marble hallway, covering the closet with a deadly service blazer. Kelling Friel, captain of the electoral police, recognized Firebird at the same instant she recognized him. "Lady Firebird," he growled, replacing his blazer in its holster.

She stood a moment, collecting her breath and her wits as she straightened her red-collared Academy blouse. The electoral police carried special authority over Netaia's small wastling class. Firebird had learned years ago—the hard way—that redjackets only honored regal manners, which they encouraged. A few wastlings eventually became heirs, so they all had to be trained, in case they survived to head their families.

She nodded a solemn greeting. "Good afternoon, Captain," she said. "It's only me."

He stepped into the closet, peered into the dark gap in its ceiling, and then frowned. "I think, my lady, that you'd better come inside." He swept a muscular hand up the passway.

Into the chamber? A cold weight settled in Firebird's stomach, but she had to obey. She walked beside him toward the chamber's gilt doors.

Ten powerful families governed Netaia, guarding its traditions of faith and authority. Representing the ancient and holy Powers—its state religion—to the common classes, those ruling families religiously controlled their heirs. Third- and fourth-born noble children could live only until their eldest brothers or sisters secured their titled lines' survival. Then the young wastlings were ordered to seek honorable ends to their lives. Outranked, outnumbered, and constantly chaperoned by electoral police, they had little chance of escaping that sacred duty.

Even earlier, an offensive wastling could be severely disciplined. Fifteen-year-old Lord Liach Stele had faced a firing squad two years ago for incorrigible behavior. Firebird had never liked Liach, but—required to attend his execution—she'd watched with sickened pity and damp palms. She too had been disciplined. Last year, an Academy senior had caught her practicing docking maneuvers on off-limit flight sims. For her punishment, the redjackets had injected her with Tactol, a sensory hyperstimulant that made every sight, sound, odor, and movement torture for an hour . . .

. . . and then they'd locked her back inside the simulator. Despite the excruciating sensory overload, she'd flown the preprogrammed mission with furious determination. Her all-Academy record still stood.

She wiped her palms on her uniform trousers. Friel's decorative sword harness jingled as he marched her through the chamber's double doors and up toward the U-shaped table. A second red-jacketed electoral policeman fell into step on her other side. Firebird drew a deep breath. Trying to look both submissive and innocent—although she felt neither—she looked up at her mother.

Siwann rose from her gilt chair. An unadorned coronet rode squarely on her coifed hair. With her tailored scarlet dress suit, the effect mimicked a formal portrait. "You have been spying, Firebird," she said. "Alone?"

Firebird was too proud to lie, but she never would've betrayed another wastling, particularly Corey. She stalled for his sake, glancing sidelong at her escorts in their long, gold-edged crimson coats. If she'd been three years younger, she might have tried to kick one of them. But since then, her oldest sister had married and borne her first child. Firebird's life expectancy had already shrunk.

Carradee looked down from the table, biting her lip and raising both eyebrows. Their middle sister, Phoena, merely smirked.

Captain Friel gripped Firebird's arm through the long auburn hair she wore loose over her shoulders. "Answer Her Majesty," he ordered.

Gambling on a few more seconds for Corey, she glanced at the Federates instead. They'd stepped aside, waiting to resume negotiations. The slim Thyrian stood apart from his muscular colleagues, almost as if they answered to him, despite their weathered faces. He looked the youngest, with a straight chin and vividly blue eyes. He stared at Firebird so intently that for an instant, she imagined she could feel his scrutiny. He wore that gold star on his shoulder openly, either flaunting his identity or at least refusing to disguise it.

We see you, she challenged him silently. *We know what you are. Go back where you belong.*

Captain Friel tightened his grip. Firebird faced her mother again and silently prayed to the Powers that the Electorate wouldn't try to impress the Federacy by executing her for espionage. "Your Majesty," she said, lowering her eyes and hoping that by now, Siwann would want to get on with business—or with refusing to do business—and that Corey would've escaped. "I apologize for interrupting. I promise not to observe you again. Ever."

The queen stood, visibly evaluating Firebird's breach of conduct. "This is my youngest daughter," she told the Federates. "She has a history of playing hide-and-search in the palace. I assure you, she is no threat to this meeting's security. However," she added, raising her voice, "you are too old for games, Lady Firebird. You will not be dismissed with just an apology."

Firebird's stomach knotted.

"Friel?" Siwann's voice echoed off the red walls, black marble floor, and domed ceiling. "She will show you her spying place. See that it is made inaccessible."

The captain touched his cap in salute. "Any further orders, Majesty?" he asked blandly.

Firebird met her mother's cold stare. This time, she didn't beg the Powers for mercy. She'd been caught, and she faced the consequences. Phoena's smirk broadened.

"Tactol again," the queen ordered.

Friel grasped Firebird's shoulder. She marched out, breathing slowly and deeply, maintaining a dignified brace until the massive doors boomed behind her. Then her shoulders relaxed. Someday, after Carradee and her prince secured the Angelo inheritance with a second child, she would kneel at the foot of that gold-rimmed electoral table to receive her geis orders. Compared with that virtually inevitable sentence, one miserable hour was nothing. She'd survived Tactol before.

Still, maybe she could distract Captain Friel. "That one's a spy," she muttered ominously, pausing in the great hallway. "The guard in the dark blue tunic."

"We know," Friel answered. "They're going directly back to their shuttle. They won't see anything they can't image from orbit. It's another spy who concerns me now. You."

She followed Friel back up the passway, disgusted. Five years from now she would be dead, guilty only of having been born after Phoena . . . while Phoena still sat on the Electorate, steering Netaian policies. The Powers had decreed their birth order.

Friel paused outside the hall closet where she'd emerged. "Show me your—no. Come this way first. You'll remember this better if we stop in my office."

Firebird's poise slipped at last. Shivering, she resisted the childish urge to plead for a reprieve. She had only one irrational fear, but the redjackets had found it. Injecting instruments—intersprays, sub-Q and intramusc dispersers, and old-fashioned needles—terrified her.

And it had been a trade delegation.

Friel motioned her through an open door. She squared her shoulders. At least Corey had escaped. She wouldn't cringe, wouldn't cry. Wouldn't react at all, if she could help it. She might be only a wastling, but she was an Angelo.

CHAPTER 1

WASTLING

maestoso ma non tanto
majestically, but not too much

A Netaian year had passed since Firebird's first brush with the distant, powerful Federacy.

"... but the phase inducer—*here*—bypasses the third subset of ..."

Firebird dropped her hand into her lap, unable to concentrate. She leaned away from the table and gazed up at a crystal chandelier that lit the palace's private breakfast hall, and she let her mind wander far from the Academy scanbook that glowed on her viewer. In a week, she must be able to reproduce that schematic for a senior-level exam. But tonight, she would appear for an interview with the queen.

In the year since she'd been caught spying, the Netaian Planetary Navy had carried off those rumored maneuvers in Federate space, drawing only a strenuous protest. Her mother's electors had tightened their grip on both high- and low-common classes. Carradee's little daughter had charmed the palace household, and Phoena—

Phoena burst through a swinging door. "You nearly got yourself taken to see Captain Friel again last night," she chanted to Firebird.

Phoena hadn't changed a hair.

Firebird watched over her empty breakfast plate as her middle sister paced the table's length.

"I can't believe you'd be so stupid." Phoena seized a chair across from Firebird and rang for service. Her spring gown shone by morning light, and when Firebird glanced from Phoena's sparkling earrings and necklace up to the chandelier, she couldn't help comparing. As an Academy senior of noble family, Firebird had been allowed to move back to the estate for her final semester. It wasn't far from campus, and this still was her home, for a few last weeks.

"Countervoting the whole Electorate?" Phoena went on. "With a unanimity order? What's the matter with you? Have you forgotten your place?"

This year, Firebird also had learned that her music—she played the high-headed Netaian small harp, or clairsa—was a passport into the common classes. In quarters of Citangelo that Phoena never had visited, she'd heard ballads that should make any elector nervous. After three hundred years, Netaia was beginning to chafe under the Electorate's absolute rule and its grip on the planet's wealth.

Firebird faced her sister squarely. "You know what I think about your basium project. If I had to do it again, I'd still vote my conscience. You're not expanding our buffer zone. You only want a threat, a show of power."

"So you said." Phoena buffed her nails on the sleeve of her gown. "We heard you clearly yesterday."

Firebird laid her palms on the scanbook viewer. "You got your commendation, didn't you? Twenty-six to one."

"One." Phoena lifted an eyebrow. "In your position, I think I'd be trying to live awhile. You're lucky the redjackets haven't already wasted you. Wastlings who countervote don't last. You're only in there for show, you know. For your *honor*," she mocked.

Firebird curled her fingers around her viewer. "There's no *honor*," she echoed, mimicking Phoena's tone, "in threatening worlds that would rather trade with us than attack us." Phoena's project was secret, and no commoner knew of it. Still, Firebird had used her vote to express her people's earnestly sung longings to live in free, fair peace.

"You never should have had electing rights to begin with," Phoena retorted.

The door swung beyond Phoena. Firebird fell silent, toying with her cruinn cup. Carradee pushed through. A servitor-class attendant followed the tallest and eldest Angelo sister. A deep green robe draped Carradee's form, now swollen with a second pregnancy.

Firebird's life expectancy had almost zeroed.

"Carrie," Firebird murmured as the crown princess sank into a cushioned chair held by the servant. "You look exhausted."

Carradee sighed and splayed her fingers on her belly. "With the little one's dancing all night, it's a wonder I sleep at all. And I'm so worried for you, Firebird. Why must you try so hard to throw away the time that's left to you?"

Phoena leaned back and fixed Firebird with dark eyes.

Easy for Phoena to smirk now, Firebird reflected, but it hadn't always been that way. Phoena had been born a wastling. Firebird was three at the time and Phoena six, both beginning their indoctrination into their holy destiny, when their second-born sister had been found smothered. Investigation had implicated the programmer of Lintess's favorite toy, a lifelike robot snow bear, but—as with the death of their father years later—Firebird harbored suspicions about Phoena that she didn't care to voice.

She watched the scarlet-liveried servitor hurry out. "How can you condone fouling a world, Carradee?" She spread her hands on the tabletop. "Aren't some things worth standing against?"

"But, Firebird—oh!" Carradee grimaced and stroked her stretched belly. "I'll be glad when this is over."

Firebird bit her lip.

Phoena seized the opening like a weapon. "Five weeks," she crowed. "Then there'll be a shift in the family."

Carradee turned pale gray eyes to Phoena in a mute reprimand. Firebird snapped her viewer off. "I'll have longer than that. They'll send me with the invasion force. I would love to fly strike, just once. And I'd rather die flying than . . ." She bit back the comparison. Another wastling had gone recently in a suspicious groundcar accident, but her grief still was too fresh to expose to Phoena. Lord Rendy Gellison had wanted badly to live, had lived hard and wild.

She shook her elbow-length hair behind her slender shoulders and stood to leave. Phoena's breakfast arrived, carried by a mincing white-haired servitor. Netaia's penal laws supplied the noble class with hereditary laborers, who lived caught between the fear of further punishment and the hope that exemplary service would win freedom. Some of the finest musicians Firebird had known, and some of the kindest people, had been servitors.

She snatched up her scanbook and swung out the door. Phoena called after her, "I'll help put the black edging on your portrait."

Firebird paused in the long private hallway to gather up more Academy scan cartridges. As she pocketed them, she shot a wistful look down the gallery, past spiral-legged tables weighted with heirlooms, to the formal portrait Phoena had mentioned: she'd been sixteen and star eyed when it was painted, absorbed in her piloting and her music, years away from this shadow of impending death. The scarlet velvette gown with white sash and diadem made her look queenly, but the artist had painted a mischievous smile between brave chin and proud brown eyes. A scarcely tangible sadness in those two-dimensional eyes always haunted Firebird. Did other people see the flaws in her mask of courage?

She straightened her brownbuck flight jacket in front of a jeweled hallway mirror. *Well*, she told her reflection, *there's an advantage to dying young. People will remember you as pretty.* Humming a defiant ballad from the Coper Rebellion, she dashed off for the Academy.

If Firebird had been born an heir, she'd have had a hard choice between the Citangelo Music Conservatory and the Planetary Naval Academy. She loved flying, though, and had trained hard to develop from a skillful pleasure pilot into a potential naval officer. Noble families considered their wastlings' training as investments in Netaia's glory. When her geis orders came, she'd pay back that advance by making her own contribution to Netaia's greatness, whether or not she approved—or survived—the invasion.

Morning classes were unexceptional. After lunch, she almost crashed into Corey in a passway crowded with cadets. "Easy, Firebird." He stepped back, and his grin faded. "What's wrong? Phoena again?"

"Of course," she muttered. "And Her Majesty, tonight."

"Oh, that's right. I forgot." Lord Corey had taken a surprise growth spurt this year. Pursing his lips in sympathy, he palmed the door panel.

They entered a hushed briefing room. This would be a two-week, special-topic session. These top cadets had waited all term to meet a civilian instructor who'd come in midwinter from the Federate world of Thyrica. Vultor Korda had turned traitor and fled to Netaia, which appalled Firebird: Loyalty was a discipline the Netaian faithful, even wastlings, didn't question. Worse, he was known to be one of the shameful Thyrian telepaths.

She and Corey slipped into adjacent seats and loaded their viewers as the little man scuttled in. Physically, he looked anything but powerful, with a belly that strained the belt of his brown civilian shipboards. His complexion was the fragile white of the academician or the UV-allergic spacer.

Last year, Firebird had learned that his kind descended from a civilization from far above the galactic plane. In a grand bioengineering experiment, they had destroyed their children's genetic integrity . . . then they'd almost annihilated themselves in a horrendous civil war. Only one sizable group of these "starbred" was known to have survived, a few religious mendicants who'd fled the distant Ehret system. They'd made planetfall on the Whorl's north-counterspinward edge, at Thyrica.

Instead of depopulating Thyrica, though, the Ehretan group had adopted strict religious laws to control their powers. Quickly they proved to the Federacy that they were absolutely undeceivable. Since then, they'd insinuated themselves into Federate diplomatic, medical, and intelligence forces.

Maybe one day, they'd bring down the Federacy as their ancestors destroyed Ehret. *Someone should write that song,* Firebird mused.

Standing at his subtronic teaching board, Vultor Korda twisted toward the quarter-circle of seats. "So," he said, "you think Netaia can take Veroh from the Federacy? I happen to think you have a chance."

Corey fingered the edge of his terminal and whispered, "Slimy."

Firebird nodded without taking her eyes off Korda. He struck her as the arrogant kind who compensated for weakness with meanness. His type would deliberately downgrade others—particularly a woman near the top of her class. She shifted uncomfortably.

"You've heard of the Federacy's starbred forces," Korda continued. " 'Sentinels,' they call the trained ones. As officers, you'll be more likely to encounter them than your blazer-bait subordinates will. By the way, you won't find a more self-righteous, exclusive group if you see half the Federacy—not that it trusts them. Common people fear what they can't control."

One student protested, "But aren't you—"

Korda waved a hand, dismissing the objection. "Yes. I'm Thyrian, and starbred. But I'm no Sentinel. No one tells me how to control my abilities."

Firebird went rigid. If Korda had such abilities, had he influenced the dangerous decision to attack Veroh? Could he have gone to some of the electors, even to Phoena, and convinced them to try this?

She frowned. Maybe he'd pushed an elector or two. But Phoena's proposal to take Veroh, and Siwann's endorsement, fit their lifelong, belligerent pattern—

Siwann. A tiny time-light blinked on her wristband. Fourteen hundred. She could relax; there was plenty of day left. Vultor Korda launched into a rambling tale of his testing and training under Master Sentinels, then their history.

Then the briefing room went dark. Korda pressed a chip stack into the blocky media unit at midboard, then faced the class. "My topic is Sentinels in military intelligence. If you think you see one of these people, in battle or otherwise, shoot first and make sure of your target after he's dead. Assume you won't get off a second shot. Some of them can levitate your side weapon from the holster."

Firebird's memory served up a year-old image of the electoral chamber. She hadn't seen any levitating, but she'd certainly suspected that Thyrian guard.

A life-size holographic image appeared over the media block. Rotating slowly, it portrayed a handsome black-haired woman who apparently stood taller than half the men in Firebird's cadet class. "This is Captain Ellet Kinsman. She's stationed at Caroli—which governs Veroh, by the way—and rising fast in the ranks. We rate the starbred on the Ehretan Scale according to how strongly they've inherited the altered genes. We're all mixed-blood now, but Kinsman comes from a strong family. She's seventy-five Ehretan Scale out of a rough hundred, which means she can do over half the tricks the original Ehretans could've. You don't want to get near a person like that. Fortunately, you probably won't encounter Kinsman. She processes information that others collect. Desk worker but still dangerous. Memorize the face, if you have enough room in your memory."

Firebird was already memorizing. The woman resembled her first flight trainer, high in the forehead with a long, aquiline nose. Kinsman's uniform, vividly blue-black with no insignia except a gold shoulder star with four beveled rays, fit Firebird's recollection . . . almost. Something had been different.

The image blurred and vanished. Next appeared a man, older, also black-haired. "Admiral Blair Kinsman is her cousin. Based on Varga. The throwback of the family, about a twenty-five Ehretan Scale. I think he can nudge a few electrons along a wire, if it's early in the day. . . ."

Distracted, Firebird missed several sentences. So they had different skill levels. Where did that put last year's alleged honor guard? She'd finally guessed how he had spotted her; she must've sent off a blast of dismay when she realized just what he was—

"Now, this is trouble." The admiral disappeared in a cloud of static. A younger man's figure materialized in his place, and Firebird gaped. This was the guard! In the chamber, she'd had no time to stare. She did now. Average height, not overly muscled, with hair that was the light russet brown of exotic leta wood. This image's eyes were lost in shadow, but she hadn't forgotten that ice-blue stare.

"This is Wing Colonel Brennen Caldwell," Korda announced. "He's stationed at Regional Headquarters, Tallis, but as a member of the Special Operations force"—Korda scratched the initials SO onto the teaching board—"he has no permanent base. Don't even get close enough to recognize him. He scored an ES ninety-seven, and they haven't had one so high in a hundred years. See the master's star on his shoulder? Eight points, not four."

She nodded. That was the difference. . . .

"Supposedly, Caldwell's the first strong-family Sentinel the Federacy has considered for real rank. Military Sentinels pretend they don't want authority, but the situation is more complex than that. Remember our violent history." Korda paused. "The Federacy uses us, but it's afraid of us. Anyway, Special Ops rotate between fleet and special assignments, so they only serve part of the time with a regular unit."

They'd sent a Special Ops officer here, with a trade delegation? In that case, she—and the electors—had badly underestimated its importance. There'd been a highly skilled telepath in the heart of the Netaian government that day. A shudder flickered down her spine. She wondered what kind of data he'd taken back to Regional HQ, Tallis.

"He's cute," whispered Lady Delia Stele to no one in particular.

Not "cute," Firebird thought, *but compelling—*

Korda flung out both arms. "If that's all you think about, Stele, get out of here. Out! My time is valuable, and I won't waste it on giggly wastlings that anybody can play with but no one will ever marry."

Delia's face, so prettily circled in blond hair, was a study in humiliation. Other cadets glared. Firebird angrily rose halfway out of her seat.

Korda brought up the lights and swung his arms again. "Go ahead, hate me. I can feel it. But I'll be alive next year and most of you will be dead. I only had an hour today, and it's up. But come back tomorrow and I'll show you some things that could give you another week or two." He dove for the exit.

When Firebird saw that Delia was being consoled by several girls (and, Powers bless him, Corey's twin brother, Daley), she slipped out into the passway and headed for the parking garage and her skimmer. For all his sliminess, Vultor Korda had given her a good deal to think about. It roiled in her mind during dinner, which she took alone in her suite.

Telepaths, here. Then and now. What did Korda do when he wasn't teaching? Had the Federacy suspected, over a year ago, that Netaia was moving toward a military invasion? If so, what kind of hair-trigger watch were they keeping on the Netaian systems?

She would mention that to one of the marshals.

After calling her personal girl to remove her leavings, she retreated from her parlor to her music room. A long triangular case lay on her carpet below the studio's window. Carefully she drew out her clairsa. A master-maker's work, its long leta-wood arches had been carved with a pattern of linked knots. Twenty-two metal strings reflected the dying daylight to shine brassy red through her hair's dangling strands.

She spent the hour that remained before her interview cradling it, seated on a low stool with her transcriber running. She was writing a song, one that might be her last.

Almost ninety years before, another queen's wastling had survived to mount the throne. Lady Iarla had set a standard Firebird hoped to match. Manifesting all nine of the holy Powers—Strength, Valor, and Excellence; Knowledge, Fidelity, and Resolve; Authority, Indomitability, and Pride—but also a remarkable compassion, Iarla was a respected figure in Netaia's recent history. The melody Firebird had composed for this ballad was musically solid, and the chords stirred her longings even on a hundredth run-through, but words just wouldn't come. She'd hoped to pass this song on to her friends in downside Citangelo before she left for the invasion.

Then again, there'd been a time when she'd secretly hoped to repeat her great-great-grandmother Iarla's climb to glory. As Carradee's second confinement approached, Firebird had abandoned that hope—but just as a few defiant tunes kept the Coper Rebellion alive, Iarla's name couldn't die as long as someone sang it to honor her.

After four attempts to rhyme a second stanza, Firebird gave up in disgust and ordered the transcriber to shut itself off. She returned the clairsa to its soft case before changing into a fresh Academy uniform.

Flecks of dust had settled on her ornate bedroom bureau. She needed to call Dunna back in to give the suite a good cleaning. Slowly she turned around as if seeing her marble walls and costly furnishings for the first time. Bunking in a cramped Academy dorm had changed her perspective. These elegant rooms had been Iarla's, too. That had always been a point of pride to Firebird. To be Angelo was to be proud.

With dignity that masked her apprehension, she swung down the curved staircase and across an echoing foyer toward the queen's night office.

Siwann had made this appointment weeks ago, which didn't suggest a matter of personal warmth. Loving moments between them had been rare—not that Firebird expected warmth from her mother. No parent could invest her emotions in a wastling child. It was safer to let servitors raise them and redjackets train them.

For two centuries, wastlings had provided Netaia with some of its most notorious daredevil entertainers and naval pilots. Some were heroes in history scanbooks, but unless an older sibling's tragedy elevated them to heir status, none lived past their early twenties. Any who recanted allegiance to the holy Powers and refused their geis orders disappeared, or had fatal accidents, like Lord Rendy Gellison. Firebird wondered sometimes if some who'd vanished had fled the Netaian systems and begun new lives elsewhere. She knew one who'd made the attempt. She had helped. Naturally, she had never heard from him, nor from the high-common-class woman who'd gone with him, but she thought of them occasionally. Had the redjackets found and killed them after Firebird and Corey reported them dead in space, or had they vanished effectively enough?

Her role in the plot nagged her conscience. Aiding their flight had been her one deliberate breach of the rigid, sacred Disciplines. If those holy Powers truly judged the dead, she had doomed herself to linger in the Dark that Cleanses, a purging place where disobedience would be burned from her soul . . . unless the Electorate ordered her to sacrifice herself for Netaia's benefit and glory.

As it would.

Still, she'd enlisted willingly. A soldier's death would cancel all her infractions. She only wished she were bound for a war in which she could give herself gladly, instead of this raid to help set up Phoena's despicable secret project. Rumor made it an environmental weapon that could poison whole regions of a targeted world.

A House Guard admitted her. At the night office's center stood a crystalline globe, grown at zero-g into an incredible likeness of her home world and lit from inside by a white everburner, but Firebird had passed it so many times that it had lost its power to impress her. Beyond it, Siwann sat as stiffly as her bust in the Hall of Queens, erect in a flawlessly tailored black suit. One hand swept a platinum stylus along her desk's inset scribing pad. Siwann had been striking in her day and was rarely caricatured, even by her enemies, except for her lofty haughtiness.

She looked up. "Sit. I'll be with you."

Firebird complied with her usual twinge of awe. Her Majesty's antique leta-wood desk loomed in front of a window draped with shadowy curtains, creating the illusion of tiers of red wings. Gilt-lettered ancient volumes, bound with animal skins, stood in dignified rows along two walls over files of chip stacks, data rods, and scan cartridges. Firebird occupied her waiting time trying to second-guess the Electorate. Would Netaia be preparing to invade Veroh for its unique minerals if the electors had ratified that trade agreement last year? Metal and mineral production and trade, like most Netaian industries, were regulated by electoral underlings. Surely, if Phoena had wanted basium, she could have bought it from the Federacy, if Rogonin's cartel hadn't kept offworld trade strictly illegal.

Siwann switched off her scribing pad at last, then took a white envelope from a drawer and flicked its corner. "Firebird, we have something for you."

"Yes, Your Majesty?" Firebird leaned forward carefully in the massive chair, keeping her posture correct. A graduation gift from Siwann? Unlikely, but possible.

"You will be commissioned next month. Assuming, of course, that you complete your classes."

"That's right." She hoped her mother was joking, or maybe the queen didn't follow her wastling's academic career with the same interest she'd shown in Carradee and Phoena. Firebird, already guaranteed an honorary captaincy as a wastling, had pushed that to a first major's commission with her class and flight evaluations. Top marks on Korda's seminar would win her a special commendation, too. She meant to try for it.

"You're aware that you then will be a first major."

"Yes." Siwann knew! Firebird felt the skin around her eyes wrinkle with smile lines. "My flight trainer tells me I'll be assigned to Raptor Phalanx with a flight team of my own choosing."

"We're glad it makes you happy, Firebird. That makes it easier for us to give you this, as the Disciplines demand." She handed the envelope across her desktop. Firebird fingered it open and found a white paper packet. "Anyone in a combat situation risks capture," explained her mother. "As a first major, you could be a candidate for a particularly thorough interrogation. Think what that would mean to Netaia." She ticked off details on her fingers as if summing up a criminal case; and Netaia's penal system, like its state religion, made few allowances for mercy. "You have been privy to the electoral council for nearly a year. There is your Academy education. Your knowledge of Angelo properties. Military facilities. Defense procedures."

Stricken, Firebird slipped the small packet back into the envelope and let it drop into her lap. She'd held death on the desktop. Her fingertips tingled. "This is poison?"

"You will keep it with you at all times, beginning here and now. For your sake, we hope that you will go out with the navy and finish your days in some exciting episode. We would be proud to see you named in Derwynn's new history series. But if ever it becomes obvious that you cannot avoid being taken prisoner, then your Resolve to use this may be the most important weapon you have carried into battle." She emphasized Resolve, one of the Powers, with regal deliberation— and then dropped her habitual royal plural. "Must I make myself clear, Firebird?"

"Not your orders, Majesty. But—"

"Captain Friel assures me you keep all of the Disciplines and the Charities, and I am glad. Besides guarding your place in history, the Powers will welcome you gloriously into true bliss if you keep this last obligation."

Swallowing a qualm of guilt, Firebird bowed her head. She'd irrevocably broken the Disciplines, helping Jisha and Alef escape. "I understand," she murmured. "But tell me what this is. How it will . . . kill."

"The vernacular is Somnus." Siwann slipped back into the lofty voice that she used at weekly electoral Obediences, when she read from the Disciplines. "It suppresses the involuntary nervous system. Taken orally, it will induce unconsciousness in about five minutes, irreparable brain damage in about fifteen, and finalize in twenty, without discomfort. Your aunt Firebird took it when Carradee was born, as did our mother the queen when we were ready to rule."

Firebird nodded slightly. Such was the duty of a Netaian queen, and she knew about her namesake. The elder Lady Firebird hadn't even waited for the Electorate to issue her geis, but had gone to her suite, eaten a slice of her favorite cream pie, and then poisoned herself as soon as baby Carradee was declared normal and healthy.

Carradee's first little daughter was normal and healthy, too. Firebird loved her as much as she envied her. Princess Iarlet, now three years old, was a beautiful, flirtatious firstborn.

Firebird tucked the packet into her breast pocket. "I shouldn't need this, madam. I intend to have the fastest striking team in the Planetary Navy."

"Fine words for a pacifist."

Didn't Siwann understand? Firebird would never slaughter civilians, but she longed for fame and glory—to let Strength, Valor, and Excellence shine in her actions. "I'll go, Majesty." Firebird rested her hands on her knees. "I know what my orders will be. Just see that they put us on a military target run, not a civilian one, and I swear I'll do my best for you."

"Yes. You will." Siwann's posture softened infinitesimally. "You always do, don't you?"

Grateful for the crumb of royal recognition, Firebird nodded. "Thank you, Mother."

Abruptly Siwann pushed back her chair and stood. "Little Firebird. Come here."

Firebird stood up, unsure of her mother's intentions. "Majesty?"

"Here." The queen flicked her hands. "Come to me."

Hesitantly, Firebird made the circuit of the massive desk into Siwann's outstretched arms. Only when she was not ordered away did she return the embrace.

"My baby," Siwann crooned. "My bright baby."

They swayed back and forth, Firebird holding tightly with painfully stiff shoulders. She didn't know how to react. This outpouring of sentiment made her feel guilty, as if she were taking something from Siwann that rightfully belonged to Carradee and Phoena.

Just as suddenly and inexplicably as she'd called her close, Siwann pulled away. She flicked both hands brusquely. Firebird was dismissed.

CHAPTER 2

COREY

affettuoso
with warmth

The empty foyer lay quiet. As Firebird hurried out of her mother's office, a puff of warm air danced through monolithic doors from the colonnade. She accepted its silent invitation and walked out into a clear summer evening.

She wandered downhill, numbing her dismay with the fragrance of formal flower gardens and a breeze that rustled long, glossy leaves on the drooping fayya trees. Where her path crossed a bridge over an inlet of the second reflecting pool, she stopped and leaned over a railing to throw path pebbles at goggle-eyed skitters. The palace gleamed white behind her, columns and porticoes of semiprecious stone coolly reflecting soft garden lumibeams. She tossed a pebble idly. Two green-gold fish flitted forward to nip at the sinking stone. The tiny packet that would probably kill her felt heavy and huge in her slim breast pocket.

She'd lived well, she reminded herself. This year, training at the Academy, she'd traveled the solar reach and visited Netaia's buffer systems. She'd had good friends, both noble and common, including some of the best musicians in all three systems. *Plop!* went another pebble. Carradee had been especially gracious. Although besieged by her suitors, Carradee had put off marriage longer than anyone would have expected, had even given Firebird a kind of posterity by naming her firstborn for Iarla, the queen Firebird admired. When Iarlet had been born, Netaia had rejoiced, but dread had settled in Firebird's heart. Soon, another little princess would push her down the succession to the deadly fifth position, and the geis order would come.

Though it couldn't be said out loud, Firebird believed she would have made a more capable monarch than either Carradee or Phoena. She desperately hoped Netaia would remember her that way, and for the courage . . . the Indomitability . . . with which she faced her fate. *Plop!*

She truly was proud to be an Angelo. Three hundred years ago, Netaia had thrown off an invasion from outsystem. Declaring martial law and banding together under the Angelos, who declared themselves limited monarchs, the ten noble families had restored order from anarchy and industry out of planetwide devastation, and they'd elevated reverence for the Powers to an official state religion. The invasion was history, but just as Netaia's distrust of offworlders never had ended, neither had the aristocracy's religiously and judicially enforced stranglehold on its people. Loyalty to the state, and to its noble electors, remained every Netaian's highest duty. That system concentrated vast wealth where it could best be wielded to preserve independence.

Plip! Another pebble disappeared in murky water.

Phoena could marry next. She could have no children, but she would be spared. Firebird bristled, recalling her sister's cruel words over breakfast, and looked skyward.

That bright yellow-orange star was Veroh, target of the pending invasion. Veroh's proximity, and its orientation ninety degrees from Netaia's two buffer systems, made its conquest a logical step in expansion. But though the regime intended to occupy and hold Veroh, its immediate goal was Veroh's basium ore, which the Electorate wanted for the research of Dr. Nella Cleary.

Cleary had come from Veroh, offering talents in strategic ordnance research in return for absolute secrecy—and a price. In personally meeting it, Phoena had startled many electors by exercising a royal prerogative with Siwann's blessing, and had made Cleary the wealthiest commoner on Netaia. Cleary's project would require quantities of basium, a heavy-metal compound mined nowhere in the Netaian systems. Basium had few industrial uses and barely supported Cleary's mining family, but Cleary had developed a way to give it strategic value. If Siwann and Phoena had their way, Netaia would never again need to lower itself by negotiating with the Federacy. *Plip!*

Fortunately, Veroh stood out almost as far toward the tip of the largely Federate Whorl as Netaia itself, hopefully too far for a strong military defense to be economically feasible—*plop*—or so hoped the Netaian marshals. *Plunk!* According to recent intelligence, the Veroh system had only a small self-defense installation and ten support depots. The Federacy was obviously lax. If enough basium concentrate could be seized, the mission would be declared successful, but they would try for conquest. Netaia must grow or stagnate. The invasion would be under way ten days after commissioning.

Firebird would probably die there.

And then?

She stared into the murky water. She'd pondered the written Disciplines for years, but they were vague on the subject of life after death. She had no trouble imagining the terrible purging that might claw her spirit as she served her allotted years in the Dark that Cleanses. She'd probably imagined it too many times. But she'd never adequately imagined bliss, the state of utter joy that she hoped was her ultimate destiny.

She found the Powers themselves hard to imagine, too. Named by an ancient Netaian religion, these nine qualities supposedly enabled the nobles to rule. They existed beyond any person or persons, though, and so—she'd been taught—they could be addressed as gods. They were actually more real than gods, because they were visible. They showed themselves in electors' lives. Their written Disciplines demanded acts of obedience and charity, but as Firebird understood them, the Powers were nothing like . . . persons.

If they existed.

At least it was allowed to have doubts, so long as she never mentioned them. Posterity and the Powers would judge her by all she'd accomplished, not by the depth of her certainty. They demanded obedience, not faith. If Firebird believed in anything, she believed in Netaia and its people. All of them—noble, common, and even the servitors. For them, she was willing to sacrifice herself.

Then what if the Powers didn't exist?

She fingered her pebbles uncomfortably. Then when she died, she would be dead. At least she would never see Phoena again.

She flung a pebble as hard as she could. It bounced off the lawn on the pool's far side.

West of Veroh, the Whorl stars became thicker. Dimmer, more distant than Veroh, she picked out a yellowish spark: Tallis. On Tallis IV, a planet she would never see, the Federacy had established a Regional capital. Nine major civilizations, in two Whorl regions rich with G-spectrum stars, lay under covenance to the Federacy.

Independence made the Netaian rulers proud. Too proud, maybe. Proud enough to attack Veroh, only a protectorate of Federate Caroli, but the treaty ties were there. Firebird hoped the Federacy would let Veroh slip into Netaian hands.

Or did she?

She glanced east. Netaia's second smallest moon, Delaira, crept slowly up over the treetops. Tiny Menarri would soon follow, chasing Delaira in the orbit they shared, sometimes approaching, sometimes dropping back, but never overtaking its larger, sparkling sister.

Firebird felt that way, following Phoena forever, doomed by her birth order. . . .

Splat! went the rest of her pebbles into the water. She climbed the green lawn between drooping fayya and majestic leta trees and stepped up onto the colonnade. Between high white walls and fluted columns, a sentry paused on his rounds. She returned his salute, then went in to bed.

Vultor Korda made the following day's extended session intensely practical. After displaying several more holograms, he shut off the media block and said, "The Sentinels have developed a technique you need to experience. It gives them a critical edge in intelligence gathering. They call it mind-access interrogation."

Out the corner of her eye, Firebird saw Corey scribble on his recall pad.

"It doesn't damage the subject the way psychophysical methods can do, but it's more effective. A Sentinel can send something they call an epsilon carrier wave inside your mind's alpha matrix, where your thoughts and your feelings arise. He can find out anything you know, if he has enough strength and can plant a relevant suggestion.

"To resist, you must concentrate on something totally irrelevant— your boot heels, or maybe your girl friend. Then you have to hold on like grim death when your mind starts to wander. Because it will.

Someone else is trying to direct your thinking. Let's show how it's done, Angelo."

Firebird stiffened. The idea of linking minds, with Vultor Korda or anyone else, repelled her. But she couldn't escape without being cited for disobeying an instructor.

Korda sank onto Corey's desktop. With a slim white hand, he turned Firebird's chin toward him. "Don't be scared, Angelo. That gives me a headache. Look at my eyes. I'm going to be trying to find out your favorite color."

She blinked at him. His eyes were totally irrelevant brown. The sensation started subtly, like pre-nausea prickles at the back of her throat, and then she felt the essence of another person approach, deep beneath her external senses, on a level of awareness she'd never known existed. That other's presence struck her like a stale odor or a string out of tune: it was *wrong*.

"Colors," he whispered.

Suddenly she was panicking, and she saw her best clothes, all crimson.

"That was easy. Red, isn't it? You'll have to be quicker, Angelo. Can you do better, Parkai?"

As he moved on to other cadets, demonstrating and berating, Firebird's hand crept toward the deadly packet in her breast pocket. *Why should I bother to try?* she wondered. *If I were captured, I'd be unconscious before anybody could touch me.* But she coveted that commendation. One day, it would be part of her legend, her own . . . short . . . ballad. She scrutinized each demonstration, scheming how to resist better than anyone else.

In the afternoon, he came back to her. "All right, Red Bird. What's your middle name?"

Staring boldly at his eyes, she stopped down her awareness to a horrendously tricky passage from a clairsa etude she'd recently memorized. Notes danced in her mind as the prickly wave smacked her and ebbed away. Minor chord . . . it had three accidentals . . . descending run . . . arpeggio, two octaves . . .

The wave fell again with more force, and the distasteful otherness cracked her concentration. "Elsbeth," Korda crowed. Firebird opened her eyes to see him backing toward Corey with an odd look in his eye.

"Thought you were doing well, didn't you?"

"That is the idea, though?" she asked. "Or did I do something wrong?"

Korda ducked his chin and frowned, studying her. "No, nothing wrong. That's a fair start. We'll try advanced techniques later." He turned to Leita Parkai and said, "Your turn."

Two weeks later, on the day after commissioning, the Netaian Planetary Navy held its traditional officers' ball. With the final flurry of Academy graduation finished and her commendation won despite Vultor Korda's badgering, Firebird intended to dance. She'd let the palace tresser tame her auburn mane into a ladylike coif, smooth to the crown with the back curled stylus-tight, and then she'd carefully pinned two new ruby rank stars onto the collar of her cobalt blue dress blouse. The marquis-cut stones framed her throat with glimmering light. Her regulation dress shoes concealed a little sharpened stick she'd tucked into her instep, for the sake of an old game. Maybe she could catch Corey off guard one more time, later on.

Nursing a goblet of wine punch and stopping at each group of partygoers, she worked her way down the main ballroom's black marble floor. Tonight the long crimson window curtains were overhung in cobalt blue, and most of the formal furniture and statuary had been moved into storage to make room for dancers. At its far end, a small orchestra filled the dais. Liveried servitors wandered through the crowd dispensing wines, sweets, and steaming, spicy cruinn.

Before she could dance with Corey, she would have to pay her respects to each of the other electors, the marshals, and nearly all her superior officers, all the while watching for heirs with hazing on their minds. Two of her friends had developed ugly, mysterious red blotches on face and throat after talking with Phoena. If those swollen weals felt as nasty as they looked, they would make the uniform's snug collar feel like a garrote.

Major—she was a major now, a career-grade officer! Her fingers stole up to touch one rank star, to assure herself it was real. The music rejoiced with her, a sweep of strings and brass that sang in delight. Dreamily she gazed out over the dance floor and caught sight of Phoena in the arms of a tall, black-haired new officer. . . .

Corey! Firebird halted in midstep. Phoena's hand rested lazily on Corey's shoulder, and she wore a saccharine smile. In Corey's expression Firebird read resigned patience.

A tall couple swept between Firebird and Corey. By the time she caught sight of him again, the dance set had ended. She rushed forward, seized his arm, and pulled him into a crowded corner.

In his fresh haircut, Corey seemed impossibly tall and broad shouldered. Firebird jostled him deeper into the noisy mass. "Did Phoena do anything odd? Quick!"

He shrugged. "She was friendly. That's about as odd as your sister can get."

A passing group drove them closer to the wall, and Firebird guarded her sloshing cup. "What did she do?"

He shrugged and wrinkled his freckled face. "She commented on my haircut—she and everyone else—but she actually played with it."

Seizing Corey's shoulders, Firebird worked around behind him and pulled him down low enough to examine the base of his neck.

A cloth square, almost invisible against his skin, clung just below his hairline. Firebird tore it off and dropped it on the floor.

Rubbing the bared spot, Corey turned around to her. "Skin patch?"

"Absolutely. That's what got Daley and Tor. You may be fine if we got it off in time, but—"

"I will be fine, Firebird. She wouldn't dare debilitate commissioned officers." Corey's black eyes brimmed with mischief. "Too bad you wasted it. I'd like to see your sister in spots. I wonder what she's saving for you."

"So do I." Firebird tapped one foot. "And I wonder where she's carrying them. Surely not next to her skin."

They'd been working sideways out of the congested area. Firebird broke free, pulling Corey along by his hand. "Watch her if you can. I have to make about six more duty calls."

He leaned down and kissed her cheek. "Good luck, Major. And thanks."

She gave him a quick thumbs-up and then recollected her dignity. Devair Burkenhamn, the navy's massive first marshal, stood alone a few meters away, nibbling a pastry and watching the richly dressed dancers.

He'd been her strategies instructor, hard but fair, a high-common-class officer who treated noble wastlings precisely like the other cadets. One of Netaia's aging few who couldn't tolerate the implant capsules that preserved an appearance of youth—and which a wastling never would need—he wore a fringe of silver hair around the back of his skull, far above her eye level. He was a huge man, all muscle. Firebird still wondered if they'd redesigned the tagwing fightercraft's tight cockpit to let him squeeze inside.

"Sir." She saluted, then raised her goblet toward him. "Good evening to you, and my thanks."

He returned the salute and her smile. "Congratulations, Major. Perhaps later you would dance with your marshal."

"Of course, sir." *Major*—he'd said it! She sipped her punch to keep from grinning foolishly. "I have worked for yesterday for so long, I'm astounded to find myself on the other side of it."

He nodded, looking venerable. "Your mother. Give her my respects."

"I will, sir. And my regards to your family." Small talk. She hated it. She wanted to ask, *Have you accepted my flight-team list?* But tonight wasn't the time.

From behind the marshal's bulk, Phoena stepped up. She tapped his elbow. "I'm glad to have caught you together. Firebird." Phoena nodded a mannerly greeting. Her spectacularly interwoven hair and kaleidocolor gown didn't distract Firebird from the narrowing of her eyes that typically presaged some new cruelty.

It might be nothing, Firebird reminded herself. *Get it over with, Phoena.*

Burkenhamn bowed from the waist. "Your Highness, ever your servant."

"Ah," said Phoena, and the bodice of her gown expanded. Body heat, Firebird knew, created the chromatic changes in the fabric—golds, greens, and intense shades of pink. "Thank you. I have a bothersome problem." She traced saffron colorbursts on a sleeve with one fingertip. "It seems that Lady Firebird might not be eligible to accept her officer's commission after all."

"Your Highness," said Marshal Burkenhamn. "Please explain."

Phoena skewered Firebird with a condescending smile and turned sideways, wedging Firebird out of the conversation. "Oh, it may be nothing. Before I forget, has your daughter's mare had her . . ."

Small talk again. What was she working up to? Firebird studied the back of Phoena's hair as her sister prattled on. Several bright clips held the knots in place, and in a pink one . . .

Firebird spotted the patches, hidden precisely where Phoena's habitual primping gesture would put them in her reach, in the lowest hair clip. They looked loose enough to fall free without attracting attention. Gingerly Firebird raised a hand.

At that moment Phoena spoke her name again. "At any rate, it seems there has been suspicion cast on my little sister concerning the deaths of Lord Alef Drake and a commoner named Jisha Teal, last year at about this time."

Momentum carried Firebird's hand forward to pluck out the patches, but her breath caught as Phoena's words registered. Suspicion? What had been found? One patch stuck to her fingers as Phoena stepped back to include her again. Inspired even through her dread, Firebird dropped all the patches into her punch cup and swirled it, remembering one of Phoena's favorite minor indignities.

And Phoena snatched the cup. "Thank you for sharing, Firebird. I was so thirsty." She drank half and then continued. "She and Lord Corey Bowman reported them dead, you'll remember. I'm certain there should be an investigation. I'd have come sooner, Marshal, but decided to save it for tonight. Firebird hates childish pranks, but traditions are important. This seemed an acceptable compromise."

Phoena drank deeply again, but Firebird's moment of revenge was ruined. She felt as if the blood had drained out of her upper body, leaving her with leaden legs and a nonfunctional brain. Because heir limitation was decreed by the Powers, assisting flight was apostasy—a capital crime if the offender belonged to a noble family. If convicted and executed, Firebird would lose her chance to die in battle and redeem herself for eternity. Of course Phoena would save her coup for tonight.

Burkenhamn's massive shoulders pulled back to attention. He bowed again, eyeing Firebird ruefully. "You place it in my hands, Highness?"

Phoena shrugged. "I wouldn't involve underlings in a charge against any member of my family."

"Thank you, Highness. I shall see that all is done for the glory of Netaia."

Phoena curtsied as Firebird clenched her jaw. At that moment His Grace the Trade Minister, Muirnen Rogonin, touched Phoena's shoulder. Nearing sixty, Rogonin had black hair that showed no gray and never would. Fleshy jowls filled out his facial skin and masked any wrinkles his youth implants couldn't arrest.

"Highness, would you honor me with—" His eyes narrowed between folds of flesh. "Highness, are you all right?"

Phoena's entire face was flushing, the shade deepening every second. She touched her left cheek, where a red weal rose visibly, then pulled her finger away as if burned. As she plucked out the pink hair clip, she made a strangled sound and glared at Firebird. "Where are they?" she demanded.

"Oh dear," Firebird murmured as Marshal Burkenhamn extended a solicitous hand to the princess. Another weal was coming up at the base of her throat. "What is it in the air tonight?" Firebird backed away, raising her voice. "Everyone's breaking out!" Nearby heads turned. Someone on Firebird's left snickered.

Phoena threw down Firebird's punch cup, splashing one gawking bystander, and seized Rogonin's arm. Holding a hand over her face, she pulled the duke toward a freshing room.

Firebird saluted Marshal Burkenhamn and then fled back to Corey, while gossip wafted the report of Phoena's humiliation throughout the ballroom.

Firebird and Corey retired outdoors very late. Menarri and Delaira dimly lit the palace grounds, gleaming on the meandering pools and a fayya glade below the colonnade. Along its edge Firebird walked slowly, deep in thought. Every new officer present had congratulated her for scoring on Phoena and wished her luck in the investigation— as had several high commoners, on the sly. Her popularity comforted her.

Proudly she lifted her head, certain that Alef and Jisha had escaped. If Phoena could've reported their arrest, she would have done that—

and public suspicion that Firebird had foiled the redjackets would only enhance her legend someday. She honestly didn't think Burkenhamn would order her interrogated. He respected his wastlings. For months, Firebird's common-born friends had urged her to vanish like Alef and Jisha, but she'd refused. She'd chosen the path of Valor and Pride, Fidelity and Resolve. She wouldn't change her mind now, at the end.

Especially not after yesterday's ceremonies. At last, Netaia had honored her.

Beside a fluted column, Corey vaulted down from the long, bright porch. Firebird silenced thought to listen to the fayya leaves' unending rustle and the *swish-plop* of night-feeding skitters, and joined him. The grassy slope yielded beneath each step, but she kept her shoes on. Although Citangelo's winter would come without her this year, not even for bare feet on the fragrant summer lawn would she dishonor her new dress uniform.

Corey halted under the dark foliage of a fayya tree and turned to gaze down at her. He looked so serious that she almost decided not to go for the stick in her shoe.

But would she have another chance? Leaning forward as if footsore, she reached down and swept up the stick. "Score." She flicked a gold pin on the front of his uniform. "Wake up, Corey."

His mouth crinkled. "Oh, Firebird. That old game."

"Old game," she echoed. "You were glad we'd played it the night Daken Erwin tried to cut you up."

"All right." He reached for her with one hand. "You caught me off guard. Your point. But do you remember the score?"

Oddly, she did. She'd consistently doubled his points over the years at the wastlings' dueling game, but she decided not to remind him. She slid a hand along his shoulder and down one arm, flicking his sleeve stripe. The taller he grew and the more his face matured, the harder she found it to honor that non-romance pact. "Nice suit, Captain. You look your age tonight." Even in midnight shadows, the slick dress fabric gleamed.

Corey didn't seem to be attending. "You too," he murmured absently, staring across the park behind her. "Well," he sighed, "we've arrived, haven't we? 'We who stand on the edge of battle,'" he quoted from the commissioning ceremony. "The victims have come of age.

We're ready to be sacrificed, so the others may prosper."

Firebird stepped back, frowning, arms hanging at her sides. "Corey? That's not like you."

He sighed and caught her hand again. "Firebird." She heard unusual sadness in the way he spoke her name. "Usually it's all right. I'd like to go out with a roar, and I'll never need a vanity implant. But . . ." His eyes fixed on the lake again. "I'd rather live. Wouldn't you, really? Marry . . . raise a . . ." He pressed his lips together.

"Family?" she supplied disdainfully.

"Yes," he whispered. He squeezed her fingers, and his gaze came back to hers, uncannily sober for Corey Bowman. "A family, Firebird. I like children."

She stood silenced by the yearning in his voice and a lump that rose in her throat. For an instant, she entertained the forbidden notion. To be represented among those future generations, not merely honored by them, would be sweet. Would their children have had black hair, or auburn. . . ?

She strangled the thought. She couldn't alter heredity. She'd been born an Angelo, not a commoner. A year from now, she would be dead, even if she betrayed her destiny. Why not die heroically instead? That should take her straight into bliss—and history. "Children are for heirs." The words came out more bitterly than she'd intended. She shook herself inwardly, and the mask of self-control settled back into place. "Corey, you're only hurting yourself," she declared. "You know better. And why tonight? Tonight we should just be happy. We did it." She pressed against him, and his hands locked behind her back. A minute later she felt him relax. His familiar, man-scented warmth made her drowsy and comfortable as she rubbed her cheek against the front of his tunic. "Do you know," she murmured after a while, "the one thing I'm going to regret?"

"Mm?" His sharp chin shifted on top of her head. "Now who's doing it?"

She stared over his arm into the distance, toward a starry darkness the garden lumibeams never would touch. "I would've liked to have seen the Federate worlds. Imagine the night sky on Tallis, Corey. Stars everywhere, huge, bright stars. Yellow, red, white . . . Veroh will be a good trip, and farther outsystem than most people ever travel, but the

Federacy has so many worlds. I would've liked to have seen them all."

"Of course," he whispered.

"Corey." She slid a hand onto his shoulder. "I do wish . . ."

A flock of nocturnal cardees flew low over the fayya tree, twittering protest at the first pale light appearing over the walls of the palace grounds, and then stillness returned. Firebird held tightly until the melancholy mood passed.

Corey shifted. "Tired?"

"No," she said. "Yes. No." She pushed away. "Let's go in and see if the orchestra has fallen asleep."

CHAPTER 3

VEROH

duo alla rondo
two players alternate carrying the melody

A week after the officers' ball, Firebird reported to Marshal Burkenhamn's office. His aide told her that the investigation had fizzled due to lack of evidence. Phoena's announcement had been a hazing prank after all, a shrewd guess. Burkenhamn apologized personally, but Phoena's influence had earned Firebird's four-ship flight team a place on the first attack wave, a position supposedly assigned at random because of its high risk.

Phoena always was impatient to finish a task, Firebird thought wryly as she ran a spot-checking hand under her tagwing fightercraft's fore wing, one huge golden dart among dozens below the lights of the carrier's number six hangar bay. *But in this case she's only given me what we both wanted.*

Three days after Burkenhamn's apology, Firebird had stared down into the wrinkled red face of a new princess and heir, Kessaree Nyda Laraine Angelo. That infant would live now, and so Firebird must die.

Close behind her, her crew chief in gray coveralls clutched his pocket recorder and called up components for her final checkout. Seventeen minutes remained before launch for attack. The carrier would return to normal space in ten minutes, and in fifteen drop slip-shields over Veroh II.

"Starboard laser cannon," he called.

She caressed the barrel, set close to the fuselage under the fore wing. Finding no external imperfections, she peered into the focusing lens. "Go," she answered, trying to sound detached. Even a mostly honorary first major shouldn't be too excited.

"Shield antennae, particle and slip."

This was it! No longer practice but a check for battle, and she was glad she'd always trained in the way she intended to fight. This felt as automatic as tying back her hair.

She stroked the little projection antennae. They felt secure. "Go," she answered.

"Starboard thrusters."

She moved aft to the second starboard wing, which swept out from the fuselage precisely where the fore wing ended.

The checkout ran perfectly. As she struggled into her life suit just before mounting the cockpit steps, she caught sight of Corey—Captain Lord Corey Adair Bowman—dangling his helmet from one hand and saluting from the stepstand alongside the tagwing behind hers. Mounting the next ladder in line was his brother Daley; behind him, Delia Stele. Firebird waved and climbed aboard, then checked her console.

Seven minutes until launch. . . .

Through the pale blue sky they dropped in final deceleration. The four tagwings made a loose tetra formation on Firebird's main screen, just close enough to support and cover each other. On her display's holographic targeting map, route/risk data for her first assigned target gleamed steadily. Firmly harnessed against her inclined seat, she braced mentally for real combat and gave an order. "Delia, take the generators. Daley, field projectors. Corey, cover me across midline."

The sleek tagwings paired off to strafe the mining colony's support depot, one long squeeze of her side trigger.

A light on her left bluescreen caught her eye—two lights—eight— Verohan interceptors soaring south across the flats, beyond her line of sight but clear marks on her beyond-visual-range BV board. "Twenty-four, we have company," she warned. "Eight bogeys at two-six-six."

An energy-field projector far below and behind exploded, spewing metal fragments into the atmosphere. She gripped her throttle rod as adrenaline made her shout, "Nice shooting, Daley! Now, let's say hello. Pull in. Max shields." She touched a control to extend her energy shields as Corey and Daley pulled in at right and left, low. Delia took the tetra's high slot position.

Firebird concentrated on her BV display, then line-of-sight. The moment the interceptors came into range, they fired laser cannon, but the tagwings' overlapped shields deflected the energy. "Half-eight left . . . now!" directed Firebird. The tagwings looped bubble-down beneath their opposing marks, came up behind, and gave chase. Those old-line atmospheric interceptors, just as awkward as she'd been instructed to expect, split left and right. The Netaian fightercraft followed in loose pairs.

"No cockpit shots," she ordered. "Let them eject if they can. Careful, I don't read particle shields." Every interceptor destroyed cleared the way for the invasion force.

Left hand on the ordnance board, she shot a bull's-eye pattern of ranging bursts while braking to stay above her hindmost enemy's tail. Had the interceptors scattered, she might've had a real fight. These pilots clung together like banam fruit on a tree, keeping their atmospheric shields overlapped. *All they can really do against better ships*, she reflected, smiling. She fired again. An interceptor fell out of formation, wing shattered on its axis, just beyond the shield overlap that had protected its fuselage.

Just like on the simulator. Still in ideal position, she fired once more. Another interceptor veered away. "Overlap's gone," she called. Corey and Daley took the enemy wingmen, and Firebird watched, satisfied, as Delia scored last. The final interceptor pilot ejected from a smoking craft.

"Now let's finish that depot!" Though her flight gloves dulled the touch, she fingered a star on her inner collar as she brought the tagwing into a tight turnabout. If this went on, she might last long enough to win another pair of the glittering insignia and promotions for her friends.

In her earphone, Delia cried, "I'm right above you, Major!" as she dropped back into slot position of the broad tetra.

Soon the depot was glowing rubble. Firebird circled her team to be certain its warehouses' contents were burning.

At that moment, a voice rumbled in her helmet. "Raptor Phalanx, this is Command and Control. We have a stage one alert. We're confirming three Federate cruisers breaking slip-state just inside Veroh III's orbit. Continue operations."

Squill! she exclaimed silently, dismayed. So much for strategic speculation. "Too distant to defend?" And how in Six-alpha had they gotten here so soon?

Something had tripped the hair-trigger watch. With superior Netaian technology and armament, losses had been light. Even Veroh had suffered little damage under the circumstances.

But the Federates' technological edge was assumed in all drills. With the odds more equal, advanced Federate craft against Netaian numbers, the battle could turn grim.

No more mercy shooting. She tried to steel herself. She'd taken her geis at Kessaree's birth, but Delia, Daley, and Corey had no such orders yet. Maybe she could find a way to obey hers and protect them at the same time.

Furthermore, Federate reinforcements couldn't reach this planet for some hours. "Twenty-four, let's take our next target." She touched a cross-program control, sending route/risk data.

"What do we do when *they* get here?" Daley asked.

"Depends where we are. If we can, we'll run for those mountains and lose them in the canyons." A range of glowering pinnacles bordered the red plain. The four golden darts soared toward Firebird's next target. *One more . . . good*, she observed, a weaponry storage dump. They'd burn it before the Federates could use it.

At attack velocity, they covered the distance in minutes. Before surface defenses could get a bead on them, the formation transmuted into a horizontal line. One pass, and those defenses were neutralized. Firebird wheeled the line and returned at ninety degrees from the first pass, targeting three poorly camouflaged armament warehouses.

She ran a loving eye over her control panel. Flying this advanced short-range attack fighter in real combat had been as satisfying as she'd dreamed it would be: watching the horizon spin around her, pressing deep into her seat as ion-drive engines responded to stick and throttle.

Two industrial targets later, Corey spotted them: "Marks at oh-eight-six-five!"

Her BV screen picked them up in another instant. "Roger, Corey. Oh-eight-six-five." Six of them were coming in from Corey's side, two pairs and two loose wingmen. And the speed! These were no Veroh interceptors. "Twenty-four, max shields. Let's run for it." *All we can really do against better ships*, she reflected, pursing her lips. Still at strike speed, her escorts—her friends—roared back into tetra formation. The pinnacles loomed closer, nearly filling Firebird's field of vision, as six ominous pips advanced across her BV board.

In the foremost Federate craft, her opposing strike leader gave an order. "Intercept range, ten seconds. Delta Six, drop out and check on the colonists. Call Med Wing if you have to." One wingman peeled away. Five elegant black Federate intercept fighters streaked on after the Netaians. "Energy wedge. Standard intercept. Commence fire on my mark."

Firebird needed maneuvering speed, but she didn't dare push for it. Once the pursuers came into firing range, only overlapped slip-shields would cover the tagwings' critical spots at engine ports, where the escaping gases' heat warped each single shield. Overlapped flight was slower, but as long as the Federates' lasers were off wavelength from the Netaians' shields, Firebird could hope to turn the counter-attackers into prey.

She could see them when she craned her neck, narrow wings perched aft of their long, sleek fuselages, black as jet, flying tight to maximally overlap their shields and firepower. That close, they made a tempting target. She armed a missile and initiated a turn.

They opened fire.

Delia, in high slot position, saw what Firebird could not: All five Federate ships trained their cannon on Corey's fightercraft, at right wing low, where his starboard engine port lay on the unsteady edge of shield overlap. And, incredibly, the shade of those beams began to change.

"Twenty-four," Delia shouted, "they're tuning those lasers! If they hit on our shield wavelength—"

At that instant, Corey's ship exploded with a flash of fusion fire that quickly fell behind.

Delia's anguished voice announced it. "Corey's gone!"

For a moment, Firebird went blind. She couldn't believe or even understand that her best friend had died between two of her heart-beats. She cried denial, though her boards confirmed the gap in formation where Corey had been.

The pursuers roared overhead, gaining altitude, circling tightly to set up for a second kill. The maneuver gave her precious seconds, another chance. She veered back toward the canyons. There, her pilots could split and dodge and maybe trap those Federates.

But why had they overflown? Why hadn't they simply kept firing?

Delta Leader was starbred. Besides his Thyrian ancestors, he descended from Ehretan telepaths who'd reached Thyrica from far north of the galactic plane. Ten seconds ago, a mental shriek had pierced his personal static shields and splintered his concentration. It hadn't originated in his own mind, but in one of those Netaian tagwings.

But that was almost impossible.

He glared at his glowing sensor screens. "Delta Flight, cease fire and pull up."

Normally, he couldn't sense any individual's feelings over that range, even one in emotional extremity. Personality factors must've matched him to this man like a transmitter and a receiver on the same frequency. Even among other Sentinels, he rarely found this kind of connaturality, that deep like-mindedness that led to real brotherhood.

By standing orders for a situation he'd never thought to encounter, he couldn't target that pilot.

But maybe Delta Flight could take him as a resource . . . or even, eventually, a recruit.

He overflew the tagwings and circled high, studying his fleeing enemies through a visual screen skewed far from the horizon by his high-g turn. With most subjects, his best quest pulse over such distances would catch only intense, uncontrolled—

There it was. The lead fightercraft echoed with the anguish he'd sensed.

"We want the number one," he transmitted. "Alive. Delta Three, get high. Relay his catchfield coordinates as soon as I read them. We target the others only if we have to." Another ship veered away, climbing furiously. His compatriots dropped, following in formation as Delta Leader nosed into a precipitous dive.

Firebird's grief became heart-wrenched relief when the Federate fighters pulled up. That turned to terror as they started their second dive.

"Delia, pull into right wing! We need full overlap on those rear shields or we're all dead!"

In close triangle formation, the 24th Flight Team fled for the pinnacles.

Delta Leader plunged groundward, now entirely satisfied as to which Netaian pilot he wanted. *We have a surprise for you*, he thought at his unknowing enemy . . . *mercy*. "Come in high and scatter them," he directed. "Stay with the leader. Chase him out into the open. We'll get a clear fix for the catchfield."

Daley's voice squeaked on the intersquad frequency. "Firebird, they're coming down right on top of us!"

She made a hasty decision just short of the peaks. "Cadence starboard. Go!" One by one, the tagwings sheared under, looping back barely within overlap range. "Heading eight-zero!" she called, and she pulled away at a sharp angle from the pursuers. Her wingmen followed. On the sims, that maneuver would've easily shaken off a pair of Verohan interceptors.

But the Federates kept closing with absolute accuracy. *They're good*, Firebird admitted. Though catching up faster than when they'd taken Corey, they were still holding fire.

Corey . . .

Did they mean to break up her team?

Blast Phoena and her secret project! What a wretched thing to die for—

But it was time. She would give Corey the highest possible tribute and die with him. Her lead position made her the likeliest of a scattered flight team to be chased, especially if she braked for one second. That might help Daley and Delia escape.

"Twenty-four, I'm going to dive. Split nine-zero port and nine-zero starboard on my mark. Maintain full velocity and shake those birds. Get back to the carrier if you can."

"Right, Major," Daley's voice choked.

He knew. He'd take his own geis someday. She kept her voice calm and officerlike. "Daley, you're in charge. Give Carradee . . . my best. Three seconds." She inhaled with a sense of utter unreality. This was only a role, one she'd rehearsed for years. "Go!" she shouted with a plunging, twisting turn away from her wingmen. She cut in her thrust inverters, and her velocity indicator spun down. Daley streaked on to the west, Delia to the east. Once clear of them, she nosed toward the highest pinnacle and shut off her brakes.

Delta Leader smiled behind his visor as the tagwings scattered. "Let the wingmen go," he said.

Firebird checked her display. Good. All four remaining adversaries had locked on to her. Things were happening too quickly now to let her think beyond the moment. At attack speed, her impact should explode her ship and catch theirs in the fireball. She wouldn't feel a thing.

Wait for me, Corey!

She switched off both shielding systems and directed the generator's full output into her engines, accelerating her dive yet more. An alarm light pulsed on her display.

"Delta Three, stand by: point . . . six . . . two, eight, dropping fast. Get him."

A staggering force flattened Firebird against her flight harness. Rattled, she checked her controls. Everything read functional, but she was decelerating hard.

Seconds later, the velocity indicator plunged past zero into the negative range. She was going backward!

Realization slapped her as limp as a dead skitter. Somewhere above, a Federate starship had projected an electromagnetic snare, a catchfield, down into Veroh II's atmosphere. The field had seized her tagwing and was drawing it back into space, toward the Federate ship itself.

She maxed her engines, wrenched the throttle rod in all directions, even tried redirecting her brakes.

Nothing.

She glanced up into pale blue sky and trembled. Her mother's voice spoke from the back of her mind. ". . . If ever it becomes obvious that you cannot avoid being taken prisoner . . ."

Firebird slumped. The packet still lay in her breast pocket.

She hesitated. She'd done everything as ordered, except for that final obedience. It was too late to change her mind. Whether or not there was a bliss, she owed this to Netaia. Her young life had ended.

But with or without the Powers' endorsement, death was a terrible mystery. That blackness seized everything and gave nothing back. She faced it now with a painful abundance of time to consider what she was about to experience.

Irreparable brain damage . . .

There'd be no discomfort. Her mother had promised.

She brought her craft back to the horizontal and shut down its engines, one last act of respect for the tagwing she'd longed to fly into battle. Then she slipped off her right glove and fished out the packet.

She tore off a corner with fumbling hands. Inside, she found a gram or so of tiny white crystals. She hesitated, wishing there were some quicker way to have done with dying. Waiting to fall unconscious would be horrible, each breath a last sweet sip of life. Her handblazer would be hard to reach, though, in the cramped cockpit, and when it came to the choice, that didn't sound any more pleasant.

Wasn't there some escape? Did she really want to die? No! She did not! But capture would be far worse.

Still she waited, not wanting to waste a minute of life if she had only minutes left. The altimeter read higher and higher, and soon she spotted the Federate cruiser against a starry background, looming nearer as the sky darkened. Her ventral screen showed a lone intercept fighter like a black shadow below, circling and slowly climbing. Following her to her doom.

Whoever he was, he'd beaten her.

Stung, she pulled the mask away from her helmet, toasted her unseen adversary with the packet, and tipped the crystals down her throat.

They tasted like salty metal and burned all the way down. With her mask off, the cockpit air already seemed thin. "Done, Your Majesty," she said aloud. Then she bowed her head, shuddered, and breathed slowly.

Nine minutes later, a second catchfield landed Delta Leader in a minor docking bay aboard the Federate cruiser *Horizon*. The space door shuttered closed. Atmosphere swirled in, then techs and carrier crew. Near the inner bulkhead, the golden tagwing rested on another receiving grid.

Eager to face his prisoner eye to eye, he jumped from his ship and hurried to the captured fightercraft. The Netaian hadn't sprung his cockpit. As a deck crewer sprinted alongside and activated the external cockpit release, Delta Leader drew a shock pistol and held it ready.

The bubble swung upward. The hunched shape inside didn't move. "Unconscious?" guessed the subordinate.

Delta Leader holstered his pistol and leapt up onto the forward triangular wing of the golden dart. Unconscious, he confirmed, and barely breathing. He pulled off the pilot's gold flight helmet.

A long tail of dark auburn hair fell free. This was a woman! He inhaled sharply. White paper fluttered beside her gloved hand. "Call Medical," he cried, grim-voiced. "Suicide attempt."

As the crewer barked into an interlink, he unbuckled the Netaian pilot, lifted her, and jumped down onto the glossy deck, still cradling her against himself, noting the flashing officer's stars, the absence of ID plate, and then her petite, lovely face: small nose, delicate chin, softly flushed cheeks. Brushing soaked auburn hair from her forehead, he knelt and steadied her on one knee. Besides his standing order and the lure of her mental cry, she was a valuable prisoner. This was a high-security matter. He didn't need to hesitate.

Guide me, he prayed hastily. Closing his eyes, he turned inward for his epsilon-energy carrier, then reached out with it to slow her frantically pumping heart as it spread poison through her body. She slipped into tardema-sleep. The medical crew arrived, and he held her there, near death itself, as they readied an ultradialysis unit. One tech cut the heavy outer life suit from her arms and upper chest. He was exquisitely aware of her will, fighting his for the right to escape into the void. The alpha matrix of her personality brushed his own, passionately determined to excel . . . but poised to sacrifice her life.

Two med attendants lifted her out of his arms onto their stretcher, then went to work. Blood-cleansing equipment hissed as it activated. He relaxed his mental stance. The foreign officer rose to normal unconsciousness and her pulse pounded again, rushing poisoned blood to her vital centers but also into four clear catheter tubes at her wrists and her throat, and then into the filtration system. He gripped her forearm. Three meds in yellow tunics watched their instruments. A red light flashed at one corner of the console.

It stopped.

He pulled back his hand. She was out of immediate danger. One attendant turned to him. "She'll need at least an hour on full filtration, sir. We'll take her to the med deck."

Abruptly, weariness caught up with him, and he wondered if the battle had ended. He didn't doubt that the Netaians would be repelled. It was only a matter of time, and maybe soon he could shorten that. Rubbing his face, he said, "Get her under a restraining field before she wakes up. Don't cancel that suicide watch."

Two attendants steered the stretcher away. He stared until the little group disappeared into a corridor.

That face. He knew that woman.

He commandeered an invigorating cup of kass and reported to the command bridge.

"We've taken a prisoner, General Frankin," he announced over a second cup. "First major's insignia. Tried to kill herself when she knew we had her."

"Herself?" echoed General Gorn Frankin, an ebullient acquaintance from Caroli. "They send women on the attack phalanx?"

"They sent this one."

"Took her yourself?"

He nodded.

"I assume you had reason. Do you want to interview her yourself, too?"

"Yes."

That was exactly what he wanted.

CHAPTER 4

SENTINEL

allargando
slowing, increasing volume

As Firebird slowly climbed back to consciousness, she reached out eagerly for sensations, curious about the afterlife. Finally, she'd put her ordeal behind her.

The muffled sounds around her seemed odd, though. Something swished past quickly. Something else clattered. And she ached everywhere, particularly her shoulders. If this was an afterlife, it wasn't the bliss she hoped she'd just earned.

She tried to bring up a hand to rub her eyes, but her arm wouldn't move. Cautiously she opened her eyes and saw a low white ceiling. Something started to beep softly.

Did she . . . could she lie in a restraining field, with a facial-movement sensor?

Unfamiliar medical-looking machines surrounded her. A med attendant gowned in soft yellow walked over and reached down out of Firebird's view. The beeping stopped. Her left leg jerked involuntarily as the restraining field released her.

"Sit up, please, Major," directed the attendant in a vowel-heavy accent.

This was a Federate ship!

The attendant supported her elbow as Firebird pushed up off the hard mattress. Walls wheeled around her. She sat still and let her head droop. While waiting for the bulkheads to settle down, she struggled to recall being taken aboard. How could she be here? She'd done everything as ordered. When she swallowed, her throat still burned. She reached up to touch it and found a short, rough strip of tape on the side of her neck . . . then another, at the other side, over her carotid arteries. Numbly she glanced at her wrists. They too were bandaged with tiny, almost invisible strips.

She guessed then what they'd done to her. She'd waited too long to open the packet. This was her fault.

The attendant stood in front of her. "Do you want something to eat?"

Firebird nodded. She waited warily on the edge of the bed, hoping the attendant would leave for half a minute. There must be something in this medical suite that was long and sharp and deadly. Horrified by the implications for Netaia of her capture, she must finish what she'd attempted.

But the woman turned to a servo on the nearest wall, assembled a tray, and handed it to Firebird. She accepted a hot cup of some sort of broth and several soft objects with a texture between bread and crackers. She ate slowly, still a little shaky, and cautious for aftereffects of the poison—which a victim generally didn't need to know, and she'd neglected to research. The broth soothed her throat.

"Enough?" asked the attendant.

Firebird handed back the empty tray. "Thank you."

"All right. Relax for a bit. I need to watch your vitals."

Firebird slumped back down onto the hard surface. She had only two options, suicide or escape. But how? A lean, gray-uniformed man stood at the sick bay's closed door. His breast insignia dispelled her last doubt. That stretched-out parallelogram, with its long red and blue triangles set back to back and edged in gold, was the Federate slash.

Powers help me, she begged. *Get me out!*

Delta Leader strode up a narrow corridor of the starship, carrying his recall pad under one arm. The meds had demanded a two-hour wait for the Netaian major's systems to clear the last toxin. To make any difference in the battle still raging below, he needed to begin soon.

His fellow pilots hadn't quite believed this call-up to Veroh, but he had. After studying the Netaian Electorate in action, he'd predicted this confrontation.

But not the connatural prisoner lying in sick bay. No data on her would go on record yet. He used a special secure shorthand to jog his trained memory. For deep class-three access work, he must first establish an alpha-matrix framework—decode her systems of mental association. Then he could collect every shred of useable intelligence.

But he already guessed that her personality patterns would prove starkly familiar. That cry of grief couldn't have reached him unless she were utterly connatural with him, with her mental functions closely matched to his own. This would be a quick, efficient frameworking.

He passed six pilots wearing Carolinian khaki. They turned and stared. Accustomed to stares, he searched his recollections for clues to his prisoner's identity. Their meeting must've seemed inconsequential. His visual memory was excruciatingly accurate. . . .

As he turned up the medical corridor, a young woman's face finally filled the blank. She wore a dust-smudged cadet's uniform and stood flanked by arrogant, gaudily dressed guardsmen. Though her raised eyebrows and slightly pursed lips suggested meekness, her emotions flamed with defiance.

He frowned. Surely this wasn't his prisoner. That cadet wouldn't be an officer only one year later.

But she'd been the queen's daughter. Entitled, maybe, to preferential promotion, the same way he was as a Master Sentinel.

Whoever she was, Frankin waited on the bridge for information.

The guard in gray finally turned aside for a moment.

Firebird rolled off the bed and sprang toward the door's opening panel, but her legs wouldn't move quickly.

The guard seized her wrist. "None of that, Major," he said firmly. "Unless you'd rather be put on muscle relaxants." He nodded at the yellow-gowned med, who reached for an intramusc injector.

"No . . . that won't be necessary." Firebird's voice shook, though she tried to control it. "No."

Just as the guard let her go, the door slid open. Firebird lunged. She made it through, and she'd almost dodged the first man outside in the passway when her legs buckled, utterly nerveless this time.

The lead Federate caught her by an arm and a shoulder and steadied her upright. "No," he said softly. "Don't do that."

Looking up into startlingly blue eyes, she had an instant of mindless, delighted recognition. It was the Thyrian guard!

Then she heard Vultor Korda's voice echo in the silent corridor.

*Wing Colonel Brennen Caldwell. . . . Don't even get close enough to rec-
ognize him. . . .*

Firebird cast a frantic glance up the passway. Two guards in Tallan
ash gray stood with shock pistols trained on her.

"Come back inside," Caldwell ordered. Though she had no intention of obeying, her legs walked her back through the sick bay's metal
door. Korda had explained, but never demonstrated, Sentinel voice-
command.

The door slid shut, closing her inside with Wing Colonel Caldwell,
the med attendant, and her original Tallan guard. She braced herself
against the bed where she'd wakened. This couldn't be happening!

Caldwell set a recall pad on a lab bench, keeping his other hand
slightly upraised. He still wore the vivid midnight blue of Thyrian
forces. On his right shoulder, as in the hologram, she saw the eight-
rayed gold star. When he lowered his free hand, she felt the ethereal
cords on her body drop away.

She clenched her own shaking hands. Did he remember her, too?

He dipped his head slightly. "Wing Colonel Brennen Caldwell, of
Thyrica."

She avoided his stare. Korda had warned, *Guard your eyes! A Sentinel can use them as doors into your mind.*

After she'd stood still for almost a minute, silently begging that
inanimate door to open once more, he said, "Please sit back down,
Major. I must ask you some questions." His vowels sang strangely in
her ears.

Standing stiff legged, she compressed her lips.

The guard paced back to the door and stood there unmoving—
probably trained not to hear, either.

Caldwell raised his hand a few centimeters. "Sit down, please," he
repeated.

Though she tried to stay upright, her body obeyed him again.

Colonel Caldwell sank onto a stool that the med assistant slid up
to him. "Now," he said, "sit back, Major . . ." He hesitated. "Angelo?"

Firebird glanced at his face, horrified.

"Lady Firebird," he said softly. "We've met."

Powers, no! If he knew her, soon he'd know everything. Her heart pounded, a great weight jumping in her chest as she perched on the edge of that hard bed. That bed with its restraining field . . . and even as she watched, the med readied a life-signs cuff, to monitor her body's responses to interrogation procedures. There'd been a short but tough class on this kind of thing in her senior year.

"How long have you been in service, Your Highness?" Caldwell pushed his stool back half a meter, a gesture she supposed was intended to calm her. "Last year I thought you were only a cadet."

It seemed a harmless, even friendly question, but she could guess at his motive: get her talking, start her remembering things. She shook her head.

"I see."

She eyed his booted feet, planted firmly but casually on the deck. Soon they'd move, and then it would start.

"Sit back, then, Highness," he said, but he didn't command. She found that she could stay upright, so she did, clenching her jaws and gripping her thighs.

"Lady Firebird, please. I'd prefer not to force your defenses."

"I'll give you nothing willingly." She swallowed hard.

The booted heels came together under his knees. "Then sit back," he said, regaining that queer tone of voice, and she swung around to recline. Immediately she found herself frozen again. "The restraining field is only to help me keep my mind on my work," he intoned as the med secured the life-signs cuff around her arm. "I'm not going to harm you. Don't be afraid, Major."

If only she were just a major! She could move only her head. She turned it away.

After another minute's wait, he spoke again. "How long have you been in service, Lady Firebird?"

She pressed her eyes shut. This was the real thing, a terrifying variable Vultor Korda had never introduced in his classes. She called the difficult etude into her mind and focused on it with performance intensity, waiting with the fringe of her attention for that revolting, prickly feeling to begin.

But Vultor Korda had barely started Sentinel training. Brennen Caldwell had won a master's star. Vast weight pressed her toward the deck, driving chinks in her defenses. She accelerated the etude, making it harder to follow, demanding more concentration.

Unexpectedly, the weight lifted. "Someone has breached you before this."

"What?" escaped through her clenched teeth.

"Who trained you in access resistance?" When she tightened her jaw muscles, he went on. "I'm sorry for your sake that they did. That will only make this more uncomfortable."

She stared at a metal ceiling panel. "I have a conscience."

"You've satisfied any reasonable conscience. You tried to crash into a mountain. Then you poisoned yourself. You followed orders, Major Angelo. How long have you been in service?"

She lay stubbornly silent.

"All right," he said softly. "It's your duty, of course. Keep me out for as long as you can. Although . . . it would be more comfortable for you if you'd look this way."

She shut her eyes tightly.

The weight fell onto her again. She bound herself round with a supreme effort of concentration. For long, desperate minutes she felt like a stone on the seashore, trying to hold back a tide that rose swiftly to become a storm surge. She was drowning in darkness, terrified to breathe.

A wave fell that was sharp and warm. She ducked beneath it, rolling inward and aside, and gasped for breath. It fell again, tumbling her headlong. She flailed in the deep. Again. This time, a current propelled her toward rippling light and the piercing sense of another person's presence. She gasped, recognizing her peril. The Sentinel had breached her mind's outer defense. But she still might evade him. She called into her mind her most compelling composition—Iarla's song—but uncannily, her memory sprinted down the long stairway from her practice room toward the electoral chamber.

He'd taken it there. She fled outdoors, toward the gardens, but her thoughts shifted again, to the military, to her commissioning ceremony. She cowered inside the brass band's music.

The Sentinel forced her awareness wide open. Huge, long-faced Devair Burkenhamn bent to pin the second ruby star to her collar, shook her hand, and presented her Academy certificate. She read and reread the special commendation, deeply gratified. At one corner was lettered the commissioning date.

The vision vanished. Limp and disoriented, but shivering with indignation, she roused herself.

Her tormentor exhaled. "You realize I cannot go on that way. Surface access is gentler, but as you see, it can be complex and time-consuming. I have orders of my own."

She looked hastily away from his face. He wore no holster, but a glance at his left wrist confirmed that he—like the big Tallan guard—was armed. Korda had told them about the Sentinels' ceremonial weapon, the crystace.

She was doomed to fail, to betray her people. All of them. A tear rolled from her eye. She couldn't wipe it away, and it trickled toward her ear.

"Perhaps you'd answer this question for anyone, Your Highness. What do your friends call you?"

"Firebird," she choked. "And you had it right before. It's 'Lady,' not 'Highness.'" He brushed away the tear, the touch startling her into volunteering, "It's an awkward name."

"Not so awkward," he said soberly. "I'm called Brennen, or Brenn. Would you do that? Even though . . . this is my duty?"

She wished the outworlder would treat her like an enemy, so she could hate him more deeply. "You must be joking," she grumbled.

"No, Firebird."

Though she stared at the ceiling, from the corner of her eye she saw him take up a stylus and reach for that black recall pad he'd laid down. "You have courage," he said as he wrote. "I respect that."

She swallowed a trace of salt water that had run into her throat.

"Relax now. I will go gently if you'll let me."

She turned her head and tensed up.

He sighed softly. "All right, then. Charna, please dim the light."

The med waved at a panel. She seemed to vanish, leaving only a small luma burning behind Caldwell's left shoulder. Nearer and stronger drew the alien presence, pounding Firebird's awareness like a falling torrent. Inexplicable lights flashed in the dark sick bay. She flung herself against them, trying to fight her way free, to awareness of anything but that invader, but bit by bit he beat down her resistance until all thought was pinned and restrained.

His voice seemed to come from inside her. "Open your eyes." She could no more disobey than cease to exist. The shadowy ceiling reappeared.

"Watch my fingers," he directed softly. Two fingers of his left hand hovered over her face. They seemed to shine in the dim light as he swung them slowly across her field of vision, and back, back once more, then far to one side, and back again. When abruptly he dropped them, her dazed glance was snared by his eyes.

They were brilliant, azure blue. Her last defenses crumbled like seawalls of sand.

For several minutes, she felt only pressure. Then her mind raced out of control, dizzying and sickening her, first to the Planetary Naval inventory, then ship by ship all that she knew about their armament and defensive hardware. Schematics and illustrations and memories of qualifying flights spun by. She'd been allowed to study most of them. Wastlings didn't survive to face . . . this.

It stopped. The Sentinel turned aside, and she was herself again, exhausted by useless resistance. How could she stop him now? He wrote rapidly on his pad, then touched a final panel. Addressing a wall interlink, he said, "Transmitting." The recall pad ticked an ominous rhythm. Her heart sank. She urged her bruised memory toward Vultor Korda's special session. He'd taught them to concentrate on nothings, blank their minds of anything that truly mattered. If only she'd known nothing about—

As the thought rose, her interrogator seized it. He homed on Dr. Nella Cleary, the co-workers D'Stang and Parkai, and Phoena's passionate calls for the Electorate to support her secret project. Firebird struggled to break the Sentinel's control. She writhed against his restraining field. "No," she pleaded.

When at last he told the med to bring up the room light, she felt as limp as if she'd flown a mission helmetless and unharnessed. He left her under guard to sleep for a while, and returned a few hours later with a small breakfast.

He wasn't settling for the data it would take to win today's battle. He wanted all that she knew.

Humbled but rested, Firebird was freshly determined to resist, knowing now that she couldn't succeed by strength. She relaxed her defenses and let him pass through, watching from a distance as he called back memories of electoral Obediences and secret meetings.

When he moved her focus toward their discussions of planetary defense, she began her resistance. She called up the passionate *intermezzo* of an orchestral suite she loved, bass, tenor, and treble strings soaring together like the skyward rise of sweet flight. Sensitized to his focal point, she felt him touch the music. Effortlessly it swept him along with her, back to neutral ground.

He withdrew roughly.

Disconcerted, she shook loose of the music and the warmth she'd sensed as he flew alongside her. When she could think clearly again, she opened her eyes.

He'd slid his stool back several meters. "Very good." His voice, though not angry, sounded tired and peeved. "You surprise me." He stared at her for quite a while without attempting access again. Then he shifted his stool. "Mind access almost invariably causes revulsion, even nausea, and a clear sense of foreignness. Do you feel those signs?"

Recalling the sessions with Vultor Korda, she grimaced. "No. None of them."

He made a few aimless-looking marks on the recall pad, set down his stylus, then scooted closer and raised his fingers again. "Watch," he commanded.

But she'd finished cooperating. He took no more information on Netaia's main bases until he'd exhausted her again, and then he scanned her mind like a data stack, without drugs or intimidation, and for all her resentment she was glad he didn't need them, for he could have terrified her. Surely by now he'd discovered her irrational fear of injecting instruments, so commonly used by the redjackets and in Netaian interrogation. Firebird's efforts to desensitize herself had only made it worse. She guessed the sick bay's compartments held dozens of the ghastly things.

He soothed instead, flooding her raw nerves with warmth that carried a faint, smoky-sweet savor. Vultor Korda's mental touch had sickened her. This felt like being plunged into a warm ocean permeated with incense.

Forced backward and forward in memory, she lost track of time.

At some point, as he sat writing on his recall pad, she tried to guess what a Sentinel could've been and done in the Planetary Navy and the advantages it would've given Netaia.

"I wish you were Netaian," she groaned, meaning nothing disloyal.

"And I wish you were Thyrian. Look this way."

At the next respite, he shocked her with the suggestion that she ask for asylum. Netaia never offered haven to military prisoners. Evidently the Federacy followed a different prisoner-of-war protocol, because he pressed the suggestion four more times. Eventually he switched off his notes and leaned against the lab bench. "I'm sorry, Lady Firebird. Forcing a mind is tiring for both involved."

It was over, then. Over . . . and she'd survived it. She had never felt so ashamed.

He touched a control, and the restraining field collapsed. She stretched stiff joints and muscles.

"I will no longer listen in on your thoughts. You are a sovereign being, and I'm sworn to honor your privacy except when ordered otherwise."

Yesterday, being called "sovereign" would've made Firebird smile. She glanced at the door guard, then faced Caldwell quietly, miserably.

"You should also know," he continued, "that of all the people I have accessed for the Federacy, I've never met a person of your abilities who was so determined to throw away her life. Who exactly did you mean to die for, Lady Firebird?"

An intelligence officer, offering sympathy? She clenched her hands. "I was born to serve the holy Powers. That is our way."

Rotating his stool, he set his recall pad on the lab bench behind him, and then he said somberly, "You've questioned their existence for years. You certainly don't love them."

Firebird glared. Unfair! He knew all her doubts now, all her weaknesses. "They require obedience. Not faith. Definitely not love. They rule through us."

His voice softened. "You intended to die for something you don't love?"

No, not sympathy. He was still interrogating. "It was for Netaia," she said angrily. "To keep from . . . this." *Finish your job, Sentinel. Dispose of me.*

"I understand that. Not your allegiance to gods you don't believe in."

She fingered the tiny red scar that had already formed on her wrist. "Then you probably have no religion, sir."

He raised a dark eyebrow. Then she remembered his ancestry, and the "mendicants" who'd fled Ehret's destruction.

"I'm glad you failed." *To die*, she understood. He still held his stylus in one hand. He tapped the lab bench. "You could still be a help to us. And to yourself."

Firebird refused to react. She didn't want asylum. She was Netaian; she was Angelo. "I have no hostage value, Colonel. I am 'geis,' to be finished. They gave me a death order when I dropped to fifth in the succession."

"Why?" he demanded.

"Because I'm a—"

"Why, by all that's sacred to either of us, do your people kill extra heirs? Why not simply disinherit them?"

"Oh. Now I see what you're asking." She clenched both fists in her lap. This was an unexpected privilege. She'd never hoped for the freedom to explain this as she truly saw it, especially to an enemy officer. It certainly wasn't current intelligence. "We call it a religious obligation, but it didn't start that way. About two hundred years ago, a pair of younger heirs—disinherited under the old custom—led an uprising that nearly succeeded. They were popular," she said, raising her chin, "unlike the ruling regime. The Coper Rebellion was a blot on our history." *Our official history, anyway.* "After it was quelled, the custom was changed. By electoral decree, which gave it the Powers' endorsement. We punish some crimes to the second and third generation. This one, apparently . . . forever."

He shook his head.

Her hopes had died, but her loyalty hadn't. "Flying in a combat squadron was one of my life dreams, Colonel, but I was assigned to the first attack wave to die. First line, right into the defenses, is a common use of wastlings when they have us to spend. If we succeed, we win lasting acclaim. If not . . . ." She shrugged. "We die well. 'Only as one obeys at the highest cost to oneself,' " she quoted the Disciplines, " 'can one escape the Dark that Cleanses and go straight on to bliss.' "

He frowned, but his eyebrows lifted as if he pitied her.

"Besides," she muttered, "no drone can take out defenses as effectively as a trained wastling pilot."

Bowing his head, he steepled his fingers. Somewhere nearby, a faint mechanical hum changed pitch. "Would you like kass?" he asked.

Firebird shook her head. He touched a control above a servo cubby beside his recall pad. A minute later he pulled out a steaming cup, drained it, and keyed for another. She wrinkled her nose at the Tallan tonic's strong, bitter smell.

"We cannot ignore Netaia any longer," he said. "We need someone who can advise us, who understands Netaian mindset and policies."

"You know everything I do now. What more do you want?"

"I know what you've seen and done and felt recently," he agreed, setting down his cup. "But the will that controls your decisions is not mine to direct. I don't even understand it.

"As we face each other now, the Federacy might respond to a situation one way, while your electoral regime might do something completely different. You could anticipate them. That might help us avoid costly mistakes. Unnecessary deaths," he added.

"What are you suggesting?"

"That you advise us, Lady Firebird. Your loyalty is to your people, not the Electorate."

"I can't betray either of them." She turned away, grimacing. "As if I hadn't already. If Netaia is destroyed in this war, one Netaian will be responsible."

"You don't understand at all, if you believe we would do that. We will never destroy a people . . . not even in war," he added after a pause she understood too well. Shamed by all she'd guessed about Nella Cleary's basium research, she shook her head.

"Are you aware of the greed and deception and the monolithic arrogance that has surrounded you all your life?"

Firebird's cheeks flushed. He might've been quoting her own stunned thoughts when she heard her first suppressed backroom ballad.

Actually, he'd probably done just that.

"Changing that regime could bring freedom and advancement to many Netaians, whatever their history. But, Firebird, I understand your reluctance—if not your actions." He walked away, hands clasped behind his back. "Maybe in time you'll reconsider."

She couldn't keep still. "You're speaking of my family, Colonel. I chose to accept what I was born to become. What do you know about that kind of honor? You're Federate."

"Federate I am," he said softly, "but first, I am something else."

The concept shocked her. Did these Thyrians put their religion before their government?

"Under normal circumstances," he said, "you might have been held under cold stasis until hostilities end, but I wish to treat you differently. As I said, I'm willing to sign asylum papers. Let them be under another name, if you can't come to us openly. Let them be temporary, if you aren't ready to commit yourself. But you need time. You cannot make such a vital choice without adequate information."

Firebird gripped the bed's metal edge. "Thank you, sir," she insisted, "but I still want no more than death with honor. I'll be glad to have it over with."

He drew up sternly. "That's a lie."

"That is obedience," she snapped. "I'm a criminal now."

"You've done nothing wrong," he argued. "If you won't accept asylum, I have to lock you down. I'm sorry. The brigs on this ship are even smaller than the cabins. But you will be anonymous. I can do that for you. Try not to think like a wastling for a few weeks."

She glared. "Are you listening to me think?"

A smile softened his eyes and then vanished. "No. It's an unmistakable sensation, and I don't think you'll forget it. But I'll never force access on you again, unless security is again at stake."

Maybe. But obviously, here as in the electoral chamber, he read her emotions like a scanbook. At every change of her mood, he responded.

"You suggested another name." She sat rigidly, aware that she'd lost another battle. "Make it a common one."

He curled his fingers under his chin. "Marda," he said softly. "No. Mari. Popular, but pretty enough to suit you." He dropped his hand and let his glance linger. "You like it."

She frowned at the door guard, a new one.

"He's heard nothing," Caldwell said. "Now choose a solid Netaian surname. You'll be a political refugee, I think."

Firebird lowered her voice. "Sir, I'm no refugee. I'm a prisoner of war."

He looked at her steadily. "Would you prefer that status?"

She couldn't believe the Federacy offered a choice . . . or was this special treatment from Wing Colonel Caldwell? Netaia kept its war prisoners on subsistence rations, or else had medics cold-stase them. Civilian prisoners, especially political ones, could be transferred to better quarters.

And she was so tired.

"No," she murmured, staring at the deck tiles. "I wouldn't. I . . . appreciate this."

"Then First Major Lady Firebird Angelo," he said softly, "has just vanished."

With a promise of anonymity her only remaining possession, Firebird stepped into a shipboard holding cell about two strides across and watched another dark door slide shut. Sick bay staff had exchanged her cobalt blue shipboards and ruby officer's stars for a green worker's coverall. A servitor's uniform.

As the tide of battle turned over Veroh, Firebird fell onto a rock-hard cot, curled into a fetal ball, and cried bitterly.

CHAPTER 5

MARI

meno mosso
a little less quickly

With a full division of the Federate fleet defending Veroh and a suddenly heavy string of losses, First Marshal Burkenhamn elected the route of discretion and recalled his forces. Firebird wasn't told, but she guessed it. Within a day, another uniformed Sentinel released her from her cell. Anyone who noticed them saw only a small worker-class woman with a long auburn braid that hung over her green coverall and a dark-haired Thyrian who followed protectively.

An atmospheric shuttle, a flattened oval with stubby delta wings, lay against *Horizon* like a yeast bud on its underside. A lift shaft dropped Firebird and her escort from the cruiser's lowest level into a shuttle corridor. They followed a waist-high trail of tiny red lumas to a private cabin.

The Sentinel, First Lieutenant Jonnis Mercell, secured the lock and waved her to an isolated window seat. Mercell looked younger than Colonel Caldwell, with a round face and curly hair. Eyeing his four-rayed star insignia and wondering how their talents differed, she buckled a black harness across her lap and shoulders. Shortly, their shuttle and four others pulled clear of *Horizon* and drifted toward Veroh's main settlement, Twinnich.

Ten flights of sleek black intercept fighters and a trio of tiny messenger ships escorted the shuttles. As they glided toward the red plain, Firebird withdrew into a contemplative haze and stared out the viewport. Her mind and memories still felt raw, almost bruised.

And what about Daley and Delia? Had they been imprisoned too, or killed, or were they on their way home?

As for Corey, at least he'd died instantly. He'd never had to kneel before the electors, between two redjackets, and receive the hated geis. Her chin quivered at that humiliating recollection. Her chest ached with grief.

Jon Mercell leaned toward the oblong window panel. "There." He pointed. "That would be Twinnich."

She followed his gesture, out and down, as the shuttle banked. Twinnich sparkled like bright children's blocks scattered around a cylindrical bin. A slight movement of Mercell's hand focused her attention back inside the cabin. His tunic's deep blue sleeve had risen far enough to reveal one end of a weapon sheath.

He reached across casually to pull the sleeve down and covered the crystace.

Once again she heard Vultor Korda's voice.

"Hollow handgrip, activator stud. Ehrite crystal inside the grip." The slouched little man had straightened enough to sketch on his teaching board with one fingertip. "The crystal is priceless, and even crystallography hasn't explained the chemistry. Imbedded in the handguard is this sonic mechanism. You can hear it if you're close. Like one of those little bugs that flies into your ears . . ." He appeared to grope for the name.

"Bloodletter," Daley offered from his seat behind Corey.

"Yes. Sounds like that. Now, do all you children know why ice floats?"

Corey rolled his eyes.

Korda didn't miss a beat. "That's right. It's lighter than liquid water. Less dense. The molecular bonds in an ice crystal expand when it freezes. Activate a crystace and the same thing happens, only more dramatically. As a certain resonant frequency is sounded, the crystalline bonds lengthen along their beta and gamma axes, and you've suddenly got a crystal as long as your arm, three fingers wide, and with two cutting surfaces exactly one atom thick at the edge. That's sharp."

"So you need a twinbeam blazer," suggested Corey. "Sir," he added, imitating Korda's unflattering tone.

"Hardly. The refractive properties of ehrite scatter cohesive laser waves into harmless beams of light."

"Where are they made?" Delia twisted a blond curl around her ring finger.

"They're not. The Ehretans brought them. Apparently the crystace was invented as a shipboard weapon before the Ehretans developed variable-power energy guns."

Firebird spoke up. "Does the crystal have fracture planes? How can you fight a man carrying one?"

"You can shoot him before he knows you're there."

"Anything else?"

"You might try a shock pistol if you're fast, or a sonic disruptor. But for that, your chance of tuning in the resonant frequency is about as good as hitting one of your moons with a rock. The pitch varies from crystal to crystal."

Speaking of shock pistols . . .

Firebird glanced down to Mercell's holster and confirmed that he carried one of those instead of a blazer. They suspected she'd try to escape, and they were determined not to kill her if she did.

"This'll be your defense base, then?"

"For a small force."

"What about the fleet?"

He flicked one hand in a dismissive gesture. "Sorry. Can't discuss that."

Not that she'd expected it. "Then why are you holding me planet-side?"

"Colonel Caldwell wants you there."

That sounded out of character for an intelligence officer. Surely his job was finished. "Don't tell me he's giving orders."

Mercell half smiled. "He is now. They've given him command of the groundside peacekeeping force."

Shocked speechless, she stared out the window again.

A command. They'd rewarded him well.

The shuttle touched down in a shady half-dome landing pod. Mercell let the other passengers debark, then led her through a clear-roofed passage onto a walkway that swept them toward the central tower. Inside, the complex was aging under colonial neglect. Derelict papers and containers, probably dropped in the initial terror of the Netaian attack, were everywhere. Even the tower had a shabby, ill-cared-for atmosphere, as though people who worked or lived there hoped soon to collect their fortunes and move on.

A pitted steel elevator door ground open. The cubicle held a silent old couple wearing shapeless gray coveralls, and two boys midway through their teens in torn and faded short pants and sweat-stained shirts. Firebird stared at the door as the others left two by two. Finally, the door opened on the fifth floor below ground. Mercell touched her shoulder.

A battered brown administration desk stood in this tiled passway. Two men in limp blue uniforms, one tanned and reed-thin with a long, sour face, the other pale skinned and only slightly heavier, slumped behind it. As the elevator grated shut, the pale man snatched a scan cartridge from a tri-D viewer's program port. His darker partner hurried around in front of the desk, carrying a camera recorder and a recall pad in sun-spotted hands.

"Mari Tomma?"

Firebird nodded stiffly, noting as she did that the detention guards avoided approaching the Sentinel too closely. She could sympathize.

The dark man glanced down at his recall pad while she eyed his nameplate, which read Tryseleen. Like the underground passway, he seemed to be aging, declining under a too-long tour of duty. "We didn't get her rank or status in your transmission, Lieutenant."

"She has none."

She envied the Sentinel's ability to lie so smoothly.

Tryseleen took her right hand by her wrist, spread her fingers, and held it against the recall panel. His tan, callused hands scratched hers.

"Mari Tomma." The pale-skinned guard grabbed his colleague's camera and pressed the exposure release without warning. "Have I seen you before?"

Her heart sank. Had she been recognized again? Braiding her hair had been the only feeble disguise she could manage with materials at hand. She studied the grimy floor while Tryseleen finished tapping side panels on the registry. Then he handed it to her for confirmation.

She and Colonel Caldwell had orchestrated a careful harmony of truth and invention. This registry listed her name as Mari Aleen Tomma. That, of course, was wrong. Birthplace Citangelo, Netaia III,

Netaia Systems (Independent)—correct. The age looked wrong, but she'd forgotten the conversion factor into Federate annual units. She skipped height and weight to confirm her alleged offense, which had been listed as "political." That wasn't so far afield. But the baldest untruth was her military rank, where Colonel Caldwell had entered N/A.

She nodded.

The short man snatched back his registry pad and strode off down the corridor's left branch. It took Firebird a moment to realize she was expected to follow.

This underground cell had mottled gray walls and smelled vaguely stale. The guard shut her in without instructions, leaving her to examine a network of blemishes that stained the gray floor. At least here she could take several steps. She tried the cot and found it slightly softer, too. Cautiously she lay back and gazed up at a cracked gray-green permastone ceiling.

Were the Powers utterly powerless? This was completely unjust. How could one battle shatter her dreams, kill her dearest friend, and reward her interrogator with the command of a peacekeeping force?

In a stark but private bunk room twelve stories above the detention center, Brennen Caldwell sipped from his half-empty kass cup, grimaced, and thumped the cup onto his desk. It had gone as cold as Thyrian rain.

How long had he stared at that wall?

He cleared away mental images that had held him hypnotized, pushed back his stool, and spun it to face out into the bunk room. Part of the inner-tower security quarter, it had no window, though the walls had been painted off-white to reflect as much light as possible. On the only furnishing other than this data desk, a low cot, his midnight blue duffel lay open.

He should unpack and then stow it to keep moving, keep from staring like a night-slug. A leg muscle twanged as he stepped off the stool.

Only a small, clear packet remained at the bottom of the carryall. He frowned. Evidently he'd unpacked so mechanically he'd forgotten. Through the packet's wrap, gold gleamed. Brennen focused a flicker of epsilon energy into one hand and called the packet to his fingers, then rubbed it thoughtfully. Years ago on Planetfall Day, the quiet commemoration of his Ehretan ancestors' arrival on their world of exile . . .

. . . His memory shifted. His older brother, dark hair still uncombed at breakfast, stood over him as Brennen fumbled to unwrap a small package. (A glimmer of little-brother adoration glowed, and the grown-up Brennen savored it. He hadn't let it pass his trained emotional control in years.) The medallion fell free, a bird of prey plunging with wings swept back almost far enough to touch each other. Delighted, young Brenn held it up in the bright light of his mother's kitchen. On an impulse he flung it high and called, "Fly!" The golden bird hovered for a moment over his outstretched hand. His mother covered her mouth. His father blinked rapidly. "Put that down!" his brother exclaimed. "You can't do that!" The medallion clattered onto the table. . . .

Both brothers had tested for epsilon potential three autumns later, though at twelve Brennen was much younger than the usual applicant. Tarance had tested respectably, particularly in carrier strength, but Brennen was inducted into college on the spot.

. . . Brennen, slightly older, sat with Master Keeson in college. Head back in a comfortable chair, he struggled to focus static from a tightly modulated epsilon wave between emotion and his awareness. The target sentiment: that burning ache of Tarance's rejection. . . .

Brennen set the medallion on a corner of the gray Verohan data desk. Tarance had abandoned their mutual ambition to travel the Federacy, had gone into psi medicine and bonded a wife of appropriate family, while Brennen finished his schooling. Graduating early, Brennen had risen through the lower ranks of Thyrian forces and then vaulted into Federate service. Before Brennen won the Federacy's Service Crest at Gemina, Tarance had fulfilled a higher obligation. He'd fathered three children, fresh heirs to their small but ancient family's holy promises.

Brennen's own romantic dream, of bonding the perfectly connatural woman within a week of finding her, had faded when he hadn't found her among the women near his age in the starbred families. His enthusiasm had shifted to his career as his twenties passed.

He touched the medallion's beak. It pricked, even through its wrapper. He wore no jewelry but his master's star, but he'd carried this memento wherever the Federacy sent him.

His data desk still displayed a page of pale blue characters on a deeper background. He shut it down.

As on that morning with Tarance, how life could change in an instant!

Guarding his emotional threshold, he let the new memory return.

. . . Body steady, mind focused for work, he sat aboard *Horizon* with his prisoner humanely restrained. Ignoring her painful terror, he focused his carrier, made the breaching plunge . . . and failed. Astonished, he made a second effort, then a powerful third.

Braced for suffocating otherness, he found only warmth. As he worked his carrier deeper, her presence grew even more compelling. The interrogation had taken hours to complete, hours, deep in that tantalizingly connatural matrix. . . .

He'd never anticipated this, not even from the power and appeal of her mental cry over Veroh. Her new pseudonym helped his subconscious to separate the identities: Firebird Angelo before that plunge into warmth, Mari Tomma after, and himself, still free . . . but changed.

A provincial aristocrat, sworn to serve unholy Powers? Fine traits, most of them, but not to be worshipped.

Some life events are not in your control. Shamarr Lo Dickin, his father in faith and his sponsoring master, spoke from another pool of memory. *Even you, Brennen. You can refuse to walk any path, for your will and rewards are your own, but some fates will find you.*

Still he recoiled. For years, he'd begged the Eternal Speaker to send him a mate. Could Firebird Angelo—undeniably lovely and fully, deeply connatural, but scarred and tormented—be his answer?

Surely not. He of all people must not join himself to a woman who worshipped false gods. And their connaturality—the deep likemindedness of compatible personalities—didn't require him to set aside his highest priority. Firebird . . . Mari . . . had no inkling of the web of identity, duty, and ambition inside him.

But she'd torn that web apart. Despite her insane belief system, she'd understood and obeyed one of its few truths: self-sacrifice, the determination to serve at all cost. Moreover—he smiled, recalling one final memory he'd observed—she'd found him appealing, at least in a poor quality holo.

. . . Soaring music of winds and strings captured his attention, sweeping him off focus of the interrogation. Her deepest feelings resonated with his own. . . .

Not for years had any subject broken his concentration during the deep class-three access of an intelligence-rated prisoner. What were the odds against their having met in battle and then in person? Thousands, tens of thousands to one?

Odds meant nothing in eternity.

Some fates will find you. . . .

Caught. These new memories wouldn't fade or lie down under a sediment of daily experiences, not if he lived for a century. Nor would her other memories, now his own. They were wastling memories, deep scars left by the nobility's heirs and her fierce longing for fame. She would rather have died than survived to meet him. She still might suicide, to satisfy the terrible guilt that her beliefs and this twist of events had heaped on her.

He forced down the visions, disrupted his emotions, and sank staring, visually and mentally blank, onto the edge of his cot.

Holy One, I've made mistakes before. But this couldn't be your answer!

That evening Tryseleen finished his guard shift by escorting Firebird from her cell to a wide observation deck. Semi-circular and covered with brown viewing glasteel, it commanded a view over Twinnich toward distant gray mountains. Shabby furniture stood in groups, but after she'd passed the door guard, the only signs of life were a dusting of litter and one man, who turned toward her as she stepped off the lift. He stood precisely in the setting sun, so she couldn't see his face, but she recognized Colonel Caldwell's body type and posture.

Out of the sun. He would've made a good pilot.

She wondered if he'd sensed her entrance. Defensively she muted her thoughts as he left the window and crossed to the doors, finally stepping into plain view. His hair, just too dark to be blond, almost touched the high collar of his tunic.

Tryseleen drew up to a stiff salute. His faded blue uniform looked slightly more dignified on straightened shoulders. "You sent for Miss Tomma, sir."

The Sentinel saluted with rather less flair, extended a hand, and introduced himself.

As Tryseleen answered, he gripped Caldwell's smooth hand with his callused one. "Koan Tryseleen of Caroli, sir. Recently of Veroh."

"How long have you been here?"

"Six years, sir. Welcome, sir. We were cert'ly glad when you all turned up. Looked like we were going to be Netaia's next royal buffer system."

Caldwell's glance flicked toward Firebird.

Yes, she grumbled silently, though he'd sworn he would no longer listen in on her thoughts. *That's what they would've been.*

He turned back to Tryseleen. "Off duty now?"

"Yes, sir."

"Would you have an hour to do me a favor?"

Tryseleen, who'd slouched, straightened back up with what Firebird read as pleasure. "I think so, sir."

"I understand Twinnich has a resource center. Would you withdraw five or six good cadet-level scan cartridges on Federate history and a viewer?"

"Of course, sir."

"Bring them to Miss Tomma when you come on duty tomorrow morning."

"Very good, sir." Tryseleen cocked an eyebrow at Firebird. She glanced toward Colonel Caldwell, trying to project her discomfort with Tryseleen's presence.

Caldwell nodded. "That'll be all, Tryseleen. Thank you."

The dark guard strode out. Firebird wandered to the spot where Caldwell had stood, and she gazed out over scattered low outbuildings. Below the sky, now a regal shade of purple, the settlement glimmered with lights, yellow and white on a hodgepodge of quonsets and bunkers.

Caldwell followed. He sat down against the back of a threadbare blue lounger.

She turned to him. "Thank you for the books, sir," she muttered. "And congratulations on your command."

"My name is Brennen." He matched her low volume. "I wanted to ask if you were being treated well."

"Better than I could've expected," she admitted, wondering what he really wanted. More information, no doubt.

"I'm aware that you know little about the Federacy. You shouldn't reject us offhand."

"I'd like to know more about other worlds," she admitted, "other people." Overhead, familiar constellations were appearing in oddly skewed shapes. She looked at . . . Brennen, he wanted to be called, though he hadn't corrected Tryseleen. He stared at a nearby hangar. Surveying his new dominion? "So," she said, "you're not counter-attacking yet."

"No." His voice, she noticed incongruously, was mellow but not deep. He'd sing tenor, if he sang at all. "Our mission was to defend the colonists, not to discipline your navy. I don't think Netaia will re-peat its mistake."

"Not with your fleet still insystem," she suggested.

Instead of agreeing, he watched a small civilian craft touch down near the hangar.

His silence seemed to imply that the fleet had left. What if it had withdrawn back to Caroli, or Ituri, or wherever that division was based?

Uneasy, she eyed the sky over those distant mountains. Netaia's humiliated marshals would be maintaining close surveillance. If the Federate division had dispersed, she would bet her life—whatever it was worth now—that they'd turn back the strike group and attack Veroh again. She wondered if Caldwell had catalogued that assumption.

Half her mind laughed bitterly at the thought that he might've missed something. The other half, after reminding her this was pure speculation, worked mercilessly onward.

If somehow she were retaken by Netaia, she'd be executed as a trai-tor . . . which now she was. She'd never forgotten watching Liach Stele collapse in front of that firing squad.

But did she have the courage to ask for the only real alternative?

She shot Brennen Caldwell a guilty glance. He perched loosely on the lounger's back, hands on his knees, following that small craft as it taxied toward a brightly lit hangar.

Maybe he truly wasn't listening. "Brennen," she began. Pleased to hear her voice coming out boldly, she plunged ahead. "I'm grateful for the . . . status you've given me, but after all you've taken, you owe me something. I want the dignity of dying peacefully. I cannot live with the shame of treason."

His smile flattened. "Mari Tomma," he said slowly, "I must tell you three things. First, I'm amazed that the Netaian government is willing to waste someone of your talents, and astounded that you're willing to comply. Sometimes an officer finds it necessary to disobey an order that contradicts all reason.

"Second, you want to be admired." The frown lines softened on his forehead. "Of course. Your people owe you honor already. And there are other kinds of honor, which you've never experienced.

"Finally." He flexed his hands and lowered his voice. "I don't have the authority to sign a capital order on someone of your . . . social rank."

"Who does?"

"The regional council, at Tallis." He challenged her with a pointed stare.

She spoke right through it. "Would you ask them for authorization?"

"Don't even request it."

"Then give me a blade. I know how to use it."

"No," he said.

Her nerve failed. She sighed. "What will my people think of me?"

He laid a hand against the waist-level windowbar. "Your fighter," he said softly, "was launched from *Horizon* on autopilot near the place where you were captured, and targeted with an incendiary. Most of it burned before impact. So you truly have disappeared, Mari. You're free. Your people think you've died, just like . . . Alef and Jisha."

Firebird let the shock charge through her as a four-ship Federate patrol screamed overhead. Free . . . truly? Free to keep living and learning, free to dream—

Caldwell fingered his cuff tab.

No—she mustn't surrender! All her life . . . except that once . . . she'd kept the Disciplines and the Charities. She couldn't falter now. Never again. "I don't want your pity."

"You don't want to die," he pressed. "Your Powers demand obedience, but this practice of heir limitation goes beyond thinking submission. How could any civilized family raise a child for slaughter? Look what it's done to you."

She shifted her feet but met his stare. How dare this man, a common-born offworlder, challenge the Powers and insult her family?

"Once, you hoped to become a leader of your people. Now you mean to be a martyr. You think of death and dying when you could serve, could build, could govern.

"You love music, too. Don't you realize what a gift you have? At the least, as a performer you could bring pleasure into hard lives. Perhaps you could lead a . . . a cultural exchange that would bring your people into Federate prominence.

"But look at you. You're young, lovely, and talented. But 'wastling' is branded across your mind," he finished, plainly exasperated, "and you're proud of it."

"Of course I'm proud of it." She hated his shallow praise even more than his pity. "My honor is at stake, Brennen Caldwell. I insist on obeying my orders, just as you followed yours by interrogating me."

He rose from the lounger, scrutinizing her. "As matters stand, you could effectively vanish. If I sent your request through channels, it would destroy your anonymity, whether or not they granted authorization to execute."

"I'll take that risk."

"It would also end your freedom."

"I've never been free," she muttered. That had only been a terrible temptation. At best, she still was a civilian-rated prisoner.

His jaw tensed, and he closed his eyes. He appeared to be struggling with the decision . . . or was he consulting his Thyrian equivalent of the Powers? If so, she had a chance. He'd claimed to serve them— it—whatever it was, above his Federate government.

"All right," he said at last. "I'll write a request."

She felt her eyes widen.

He walked to a deep black chair and picked up a recall pad, then returned to where Firebird stood. Drawing a stylus, he wrote quickly. He signed the pad and then handed it to her.

She read carefully. It was apologetic and lacked command, but amazingly, it was what she'd requested. "When will you send it?"

"I'd prefer to dump it."

She remained silent. She didn't need an enemy's sympathy.

"Immediately, if that's what you truly want," he said at last.

"That's what I want."

His eyes accused her. She too knew she'd lied, but she clung to the knowledge that only this action would satisfy the Powers and her guilt-wracked conscience.

Frowning, Brennen touched in a numerical code and then hit the SEND panel. The pad clicked for two seconds. That data would travel out with the next scheduled messenger ship, still the fastest means of intersystem communication, until someone developed a way to extend the range of faster-than-light DeepScan com waves. It would reach Tallis in just a few days.

Firebird sat down on the back of a soft chair, considering while the night deepened. She'd settled matters as well as she humanly could, and Brennen Caldwell had done as she asked, against his expressed preference. Placated, her conscience sent her groping for some way to thank him.

What if Netaia did return, trying to destroy Twinnich or, more likely, to take enough basium to finish Cleary's research? The elimination of a Master Sentinel might be a significant accomplishment for Netaia, but if she told him that he was vulnerable to a second attack—if he made sure the Federate division stayed in Verohan space—then the threat of Cleary's allegedly ultimate weapon would come to nothing.

Imagine! Even if the Federacy executed her, she might stop Phoena's research. Fate, or the Powers, had placed her at this pivot point. She cleared her throat.

Brennen glanced at her.

Treason! screeched her conscience. *You promised the Netaian marshals absolute loyalty. You swore an oath. This man, this genetic freak, you owe nothing . . . unless you turn traitor.*

She bit her lip and looked away.

The lift doors opened, and a man in pale blue stepped off. "You're needed, Colonel Caldwell," he said.

Narrow eyed with frustration, Brennen beckoned the door guard. "I'm sorry," he murmured as the Verohan approached. "I must get back to work."

He raised his voice and ordered the guard, "Escort Miss Tomma back to detention."

CHAPTER 6

STRIKE

subito allegro
suddenly fast

In the elliptical electoral chamber on the Angelo palace's ground floor, Count Tel Tellai excused himself from a knot of his peers who were discussing the military invasion. Their talk had degenerated into an argument comparing Netaian and Federate armament. Critically Tel examined a portrait of his ancestor, Count Merdon Tellai, which hung between gilded false pillars on the wall's rich red backdrop. Several shadows seemed poorly placed, and the rendering of the nobleman's diagonal blue sash was clumsy. The brushstrokes, too, seemed . . . hesitant. It hurt his dignity to see his family badly represented.

Surreptitiously, Tel glanced down and smoothed his own sash. Ever conscious that his body had given up growing before he had, Tel understood the importance of appearance. Today his tailor and dresser had chosen a suit of elegant amber sateen. The shade caught the gold veins of the chamber's black marble floor. He looked as if he belonged here.

Satisfied, Tel backed against the chamber's inner wall, between a pair of chairs embroidered with the Drake and Rogonin crests, and craned his neck in search of Princess Phoena. Though he was eight years younger than Phoena, he now was the head of his family, and eligible to approach her. To marry a second-born who ranked him as Phoena did, Tel would have to give up his right to bear children for the Tellai name, but that didn't matter. His wastling brother would rejoice . . . and Phoena fascinated him. Besides, he was a count now, with more prestige than many closer to her age. Unquestionably, Phoena noticed rank. His electoral seat, midway up the inner branch of the table, lay apart from the Angelos on the center section, but maybe someday he'd sit higher, a member of the inner circle.

The gilded doors blew open. Phoena, gowned in pale orange, stepped between door guards. Without waiting for a lull in conversation, she cried, "Any word from the forces?" then swept forward. The sight of her blasted all daydreams out of Tel's mind. Orange—the color of Excellence in Netaia's heraldry—brought flame into her chestnut hair. If ever he found the courage to ask her to sit for an informal portrait, he'd suggest she wear exactly that shade.

He took another step away from the other electors and lifted a gloved hand, trying to catch her eye. "Your Highness."

He had to call twice before she walked his way. The hem of her gown whisked over the floor, and her plunging bodice floated on perfect skin. Tel coughed, unsettled by the sight. "Highness . . ." He paused, catching a breath of woody perfume.

Beside one of thirty false pillars, she stopped and arched her brows. He adored her regal impatience.

"We've received a DeepScan transmission from just outsystem," he explained. "Our forces were initially turned back, but—"

"Firebird? What word of her?"

The poor little wastling. Tel frowned, unable even for Phoena to hide his compassion. Around them, conversations droned on, and he knew that the others cared as little as Phoena that a delightful woman had left them forever. Maybe as he matured, he'd develop a firmer attitude. "They identified her craft—downed. Lord Corey and Lady Delia are missing as well. But with the distances involved, communications are dreadful."

"Downed?" Phoena's dark eyes sparkled. For the first time in Tel's experience, her poise slipped enough that she bit her lower lip. "Are there any other details?"

Her excitement encouraged him. "There was little left but the transponder, Highness. The fightercraft burned almost completely."

Her long lashes fluttered. "Thank you, Tel. That's what I wanted to know." She gathered her skirt, intending to brush past him, toward her seat.

"Highness, wait!" he cried. "There was good news as well. Our retreat wasn't pursued. Reading their weakness, we turned again. The basium . . ."

She seized his arm. "Little cousin, you have a marvelous sense of priorities. Powers bless you." Finally she seemed really to see him, as a fellow elector instead of the boy he'd been. "Are you interested in our research, Count Tellai?"

He rested his free hand on the gilded arm of a chair and tried to strike a strong pose. "I see in it two strokes of genius, Your Highness. One Cleary's, in discovering the, ah, basium principle. The other is yours, of course, in bringing her here. My interest in your mysterious secret is keen, yes."

Phoena gave a rising, tinkling laugh and released his arm. "Everyone wants to know my secret, Count Tel, and it is worth keeping. Within months, we will have power to spare, and the Federacy won't dare dream of subjecting us to any compromise. But until then, I do need support. Quiet support." She shot a glance up the table at Princess Carradee, who'd paused to speak with another nobleman. "There are some, Tel, who are having second thoughts. Who—" She seemed to catch herself before saying too much.

Hastily he murmured, "Highness, you must count on me whatever the circumstances. My house always has looked to the Angelos. I shall look always to you."

She smiled slightly, perhaps remembering her father—Tel's great-uncle. Tel's sire—her father's brother's son—had been more hard-hearted than Prince Irion Tellai-Angelo, but he hadn't deserved violent death. The murderer, a disgruntled overseer of their Tiggaree holding, had been executed under torture by the Enforcement Corps, and his family members (those who could be found) sentenced to ten years in dark Hinanna prison, then reduced to servile status for the maximum three generations.

A high-toned bell echoed off the white ceiling. Silenced by the call to order, Tel bowed to the princess. She extended a long, perfect hand. Earnestly he took it on his palm, closed his eyes, and touched his lips to her fingertips.

Brennen walked a zigzag pattern across the command post. Half enclosed by an L of glasteel windows, it had large viewing screens to fill in the panorama's missing sides. At its heart stood a transparent cylinder just over waist high and two meters in diameter. Inside that tri-D well, a relief-figured red sphere mapped Veroh II's surface. Four radio and laser-pulse interlink transceivers followed the well's curve. A ceiling map displayed the stars near Veroh, glimmering faintly above a conference table surrounded by rotating stools.

He walked the pattern again, internalizing every monitor's location. From any point along a captain's walk behind the controllers' stations, he could see all the data he'd need if this force saw further action. From one dead spot near the windows, he could see none of it, only the tri-D well. At any other place, he'd have partial vision.

With that done, though his legs still felt restless, he sat down at a monitor to evaluate his personnel, intelligence, matériel. Contingency plans. Fallback positions. The controller on duty bent over her own console, avoiding his glances.

He found memorizing easy. He needed only to focus his epsilon carrier through his memory and let lists scroll past. Evaluating those resources, though, and planning a defense if that proved necessary, would take concentration. He'd never headed a force any larger than Delta Flight. In the days to come, he must inspire confidence among Verohan men and women. He must know Veroh's defenses, including this room, better than he knew Thyrica's.

The Federate fast track, a system of rapid promotion that was an honor in itself, demanded a defensive major-command assignment without much risk of combat before his next advancement. Here it was, though he hadn't expected it so soon. It would've given him a chance to hide Firebird from the Federacy, for a time—until she'd demanded those papers.

What had she meant to say?

He pushed away from his viewer and eyed yellow-gold Netaia, bright in Veroh's dusty evening sky. Danger had throbbed in her emotions, there on the observation deck. Some specific fear had risen from her past to menace her, and maybe unfortunately, he hadn't found any reason to access that memory. She'd crept to the edge of allowing him inside her defenses and then fled in shame. Had she almost accepted asylum?

Chaos take that twisted, guilt-sick sense of honor! It anchored her to Netaia—

He paused. Did he mean that? Shouldn't she obey the highest law she knew, for now?

Carefully he reviewed the message he'd sent Tallis. Certainly he'd justified the request poorly, but his having sent it would buy her several days to reconsider her fate, meanwhile proving he understood her greatest desire: to show herself faithful, loyal even to death. Regional command would protect her, even from herself, once they knew she was in Federate custody. They would call her to Tallis, and possibly reprimand him for having kept her back. He knew the regional councilors slightly from several brief appearances, during which he'd kept closely attuned to their emotional states, but he'd never violated his codes by attempting even a shallow access. Of seven, he could count on three to show compassion under all circumstances. They would spare her life. But for what future?

A high cloud blotted out the yellow-gold star. He turned from the window, shaking his head. What good were his abilities if he couldn't ease her mind open, show her the false assumptions behind her harsh, legalistic beliefs . . . and then truth?

But that use of epsilon power was strictly forbidden. For the first time, he understood why the urge to guide others could've tempted his ancestors to their downfall. It had been an utter violation of free human will.

A young corporal in Tallan gray appeared alongside him, saluted, and dropped a scan cartridge on his desk. Brennen nodded thanks. The viewer glowed silently, reminding him that although Firebird's military duties might have ended, his hadn't.

Firebird awoke rested, realizing that in the night, her mind had settled the question that had kept her awake for so long. Completion of Cleary's work could cause Netaia's destruction, if the weapon were used, and if the Federacy took appropriate vengeance. In the end, nothing mattered more than her people's welfare: neither her death, nor treason, nor wanting to repay Colonel Caldwell for honoring her wishes. When the guards brought breakfast, she asked them to call him.

Within minutes the gray door slid open. Caldwell entered, clean-chinned and uniformed in crisp contrast to her wrinkled coverall. He strode directly to her side and trapped her eyes. "Good morning,

Mari," he greeted her gravely from an arm's length away.

The name caught Firebird by surprise. He didn't need to call her that in private.

"Did you change your mind?" he prompted. "About termination?"

"No. But I must . . . tell you something." This was harder than she'd expected. Much harder. She was about to pass information to the enemy. "You must watch—" She faltered, stepped back, and then started over. "One objective of our attack was to load enough pure basium to finish Dr. Cleary's research."

He nodded gravely.

"If . . . your peacekeeping force were the only Federate strength in this system," she said carefully, "then we'd come back to try again, if not by stealth, then by force. I can almost guarantee that we'd strike here first, at Twinnich."

His dark eyebrows lifted. "You're saying you would expect an attack here, if the fleet has withdrawn."

"I would," she managed.

"Probability?"

Firebird considered the commanding officer that Marshal Burkenhamn had sent, a ranking aristocrat with a noble's attitudes. "Ninety percent," she admitted.

He turned toward the door, then glanced back. As he stared at her face, she felt that smoky flicker touch the fringe of awareness. "Why did you tell me this?"

Firebird wanted to look away, but she couldn't, and suddenly she doubted her motives. Enemy or ally, she didn't want this man dead. He'd shown himself worthy of respect by sending that termination request. She felt no compulsion to speak, but she understood that he'd reject any attempt to fool him.

"The . . . basium project," she said carefully. "I don't like unlimited warfare any more than . . . than I think you do."

"I know that." He touched the locking panel. "But there's probably not much time." As the door slid away, he paused. "Firebird—Mari," he corrected himself oddly, "you, of all people anywhere, are in the best position to fight deployment of that weapon."

"I realized that last night."

"Maybe that's worth living for. If nothing else is."

She smiled wanly. They'd found grounds for agreement at last.

Later that morning, dark-tanned Koan Tryseleen brought a handful of scanbook cartridges and a lap viewer. "I cleaned the file," he commented dryly. "The super wanted to know if my kid was failing school. I don't have a kid." Fingering the brightly labeled cubes, he read her their titles. "*Systems of the Federacy. Federacy of the Free. Transnational Government.* You won't find any of these on Netaia."

Firebird loaded the top cartridge and spun its pages through the viewer. No pictures but plenty of footnotes. It had the look of an Academy text. "Do you know if any of these are particularly good?" she asked.

"No idea. Wait, this looks like one I had. Long time back."

"Well, thank you." She popped out the first cartridge and scrolled another. Glorious tri-Ds and large lettering—junior school history with a patriotic slant.

"Study hard." Tryseleen locked her in again.

Was this how Vultor Korda's treachery began? she wondered bleakly. But she'd always been a voracious reader and student. For hours, she compared indexes and contents. This was the other side . . . from the other side. She read until her eyes ached.

Brennen woke with the memory of a horn blaring in his ears. For an instant he struggled to identify this sterile room. Where. . . ? A luma pulsed on the far wall over an interlink speaker. Fully awake a second later, he sprang off his cot and touched the luma before the klaxon could screech again. "Caldwell."

"Large slip-shield zone approaching, sir. Netaian approach vector."

Too soon! The division had dispersed after repelling Netaia's attack, just as Firebird had suspected. At least he'd left Twinnich on stage-two alert before he turned in. "Call stage three. I'll be right up." Brennen cut the interlink, zipped into a clean uniform, and took a minute to wash his face. The tingle of depilatory soap helped make up for his shortened sleep. After drying, he stood motionless, composing his inner energies, focusing his spirit. *Guide us all. Keep me on the Path today, and save life.* Then he sprinted out.

Controlled chaos filled the com room—now a war room—and the ancient interlink didn't help. Dropping into his chair, he pressed a panel on the command display.

"Central," said a feminine computer voice.

"Caldwell speaking. Call up another pair of controllers."

"Sir."

He glanced at the tri-D well in the room's center. Only a few bright speckles, friendlies, hovered over the red topo globe. That would soon change.

On his left, a com tech in Tallan gray sat drumming his fingers on his board. Brennen created an energy flicker and dissipated his epsilon shields, a cloud of mental-frequency static with which he constantly and automatically wreathed himself to escape the assault of others' emotions. Chaos blared on that level, too, the nearby tech's anxiety welling over all else.

Brennen cleared his throat to catch that Tallan's attention. "Get me DeepScan to the outsystem scouts. Channel F."

"Sir." The tech's relief at finding something to do leaped out from the background buzz. Brennen's static shields sprang up again. The emotional noise cut off.

"DeepScan, sir," called the tech.

Brennen picked up a headset and clipped it on. "Outsystem? Give me status on that slip zone."

In ten seconds a distant voice hissed in his ear. "Now passing orbit nine, sir."

"Begin regular reports when it reaches six."

At least the Federacy now knew that Netaia had less accurate sub-space scanning, and that the approaching force wouldn't spot his scouts, nor Federate reinforcements, if they came in time.

Thanks to Firebird.

He glanced at the dead spot in the room that he had found earlier. Here was a chance to bring his best resource close enough to access on a moment's notice, and show her respect at the same time. It would be highly irregular. . . .

Holy One, would it be right?

He clenched a fist, debating . . . then reached for the interlink.

"Central."

"Detention desk, please."

Firebird hadn't dozed long or well when footsteps awakened her. Disoriented, she sat up on her cot and clutched her thin blanket. A masculine silhouette blocked yellowish light in her cell's open door.

"What is it?" She recognized the faded blue Verohan uniform, though not the man wearing it.

"We're under attack," he answered with thinly covered hostility. "You're Netaian?"

"Yes—"

"I have orders from Colonel Caldwell. You're to be allowed uplevel."

This is it! she thought with a thrill of fear. She jumped off the bed, smoothed her rumpled coverall, and hastily braided her hair.

"Don't get any wise ideas." He unhooked a singlet wrist restraint from his belt and let out a meter of cable, then linked it around her right wrist. "If the colonel trusts a Netaian observer, he needs a psych exam."

Cabled to the guard's heavy belt four minutes later, she stepped from the lift . . . not onto the quiet observation deck she expected but into a room vibrating with activity.

Four transceivers were manned. Controllers curtly relayed reports along the line, onto an overhead star map and into a tri-D well.

She gaped.

"This way," the guard said firmly, positioning his bulk to block her view of the controllers. He led her along a projection wall toward a broad observation window.

She couldn't believe this. On Netaia, even a civilian who accidentally reached an active command center would be instantly imprisoned.

Well . . . according to Verohan records, she *was* a civilian. And imprisoned.

That didn't explain Caldwell's reasoning.

"Sit down." The guard waved her to one of two stools that had been moved near the window. "Move off that stool and you won't move far." He touched the shock pistol on his belt.

"Understood," she said softly.

She craned her neck. From here, she could see nothing that even suggested a security rating, as hard as she tried. She could barely make out the tri-D well. It looked alive with glowing blips, red and gold, that must signify attacking and defending ships.

Brennen Caldwell stood just beyond it, speaking rapidly into a collar mike. He spared her a glance and a nod and went on issuing orders. Golden sparks scattered in the well. As far as she could tell from this distance, Caldwell was arraying his squadrons planetwide but with a treble concentration near Twinnich, to hold off precisely the attack she'd predicted.

He'd done a remarkable job, finding her this spot. She could see the well and the windows. Nothing else.

So she searched the sky for moving pinpoints of light. Those would be the attackers' fightercraft. So far, she saw none.

But she was glad to be above ground. *If Twinnich goes*, she reflected, *I'll die here with the Federates.* She surveyed the heart of the room, enemy headquarters. That Thyrian with the star on his shoulder was her enemy.

Why did she keep forgetting that?

The answer came easily, from another corner of her mind. *Because he has treated you with respect. More than your own commanding officers ever showed. Because he values you . . . alive.*

And she did want to live.

Hours of tracking crawled by. Patterns changed in the tri-D well as scouts' reports returned. The navy had reappeared out of slip-state at some distance from Veroh's surface. As the swarm of red blips started its series of deceleration orbits, Firebird tensed in memory. She'd made that approach so recently. Five days ago? More? *Skim lower to lose speed, but don't overload the heat shielding. Pass again, thicker atmosphere. Eyes on screens for defensive countermeasures.* There had been few. That approach had thrilled her.

This one was agonizing. Now she sat shackled to a target, a colonial outpost that had probably sent a messenger fleeing for reinforcements as soon as she warned Brennen Caldwell. Furthermore, if the Federates hoped to hold Twinnich, they must kill Netaian pilots. Daley might be out there, and Delia.

A small man in quicksilver gray hurried around the controllers and pulled up a third stool. Before he spoke, he too scanned the black sky.

There still was no sign of the attack force. In the well, it was in its second orbit and approaching the near side.

Then he cocked a bright brown eye at them. "Vett Zimmer of Tallis," he offered. "Messenger Service. Looks like an exciting day."

"Right," growled the guard. "I'm Deke Lindcra of Kilworth, here on Veroh. My friend"—he ran a hand up the cable—"is Mari Tomma of Netaia."

"Oh!" Vett Zimmer drew up a bit and spoke more formally. "You're a prisoner, Mari?"

"Yes. They're being gracious enough to let me observe, instead of waiting below."

"Caldwell," Vett guessed. "Right?"

Firebird glanced at Brennen's back. He peered into the well, tracking incoming ships.

"You'll hear disturbing things about his kind," the messenger captain continued. "But him, I like. About time they gave him a command—but I'll bet fifty gilds he's going to be absolutely dying to be in the air."

"Oh?" Did he hope she'd predict Netaia's strategy? Not for a chatty Federate messenger! "So he flies? I'd assumed he was Intelligence." Assumed. Ha.

Then she remembered the way he'd come out of the sun in the observation deck.

"Both." Vett kept talking. "Special Operations. Those SO people get called off their regular assignments whenever they're needed."

"He's a pilot, too," she repeated. Why should that matter? Then she remembered seeing six black shapes through her cockpit bubble, hearing the shock in Delia's voice. Corey! Could Brennen have. . . ?

She hung her head, unwilling to convict anyone on supposition.

Someone had killed Corey, though. Some Federate, who might still be here.

Evidently she really had been in love with him all along.

Enemy headquarters . . .

Everything suddenly grew still. Brennen turned toward a transceiver, and a voice filled the room. Firebird knew it. Count Dorning Stele, CO of the invasion force, was Delia's elder brother and heir of his house. "Veroh, this is Count Stele, Prime Commander for Raptor

Phalanx. Give me your commanding officer," he barked.

"This is Veroh," Brennen answered into his tiny collar mike. "Colonel Caldwell commanding. Break off your attack, or you will be liable to the most serious consequences. I repeat, break off, Count."

Stele spoke again. "Colonel, we will receive one negotiating party of your top people to discuss your surrender and reparations for damage suffered by our navy. You have ten minutes in which to launch a negotiators' shuttle. We will guarantee the safety of those negotiators only."

Firebird clenched her jaw. Dorning Stele had testified against his own brother at Liach's geis trial.

Brennen leaned onto the console. "Count Stele, this base now accommodates a Federate peacekeeping force. Any hostile action on your part will be answered by the Federate fleet upon your home system. I repeat. Any hostile action on your part will be answered by the Federate fleet upon *your home system*."

"You will be unable to send for additional ships, Colonel," sneered Stele's voice. "We guarantee the safety of one negotiating team. We grant the rest of Veroh no such promise. You have nine minutes in which to launch your shuttle."

So you can shoot it down, Stele? Firebird wondered.

Scarlet blips kept advancing in the tri-D well, with the majority overpassing Twinnich just to the north. Nine minutes crawled by, and then Stele spoke again. "Colonel, your time is up. Have you no one whose life you value enough to send us?"

As he spoke, a Netaian squadron that had trailed the others roared over Twinnich. Federate intercept fighters pursued, and groundside guns finally roared to life, but the overflight, only a hand slap, baffled Firebird.

A different speaker buzzed in an erratic speech rhythm. Brennen made a twisting hand signal to a controller. "Zeta Four. Can I have that again?" he asked his pickup mike.

Silence. Brennen leaned down and did something Firebird couldn't see. A static-charged voice cackled from a large room speaker, ". . . fifth series of battle groups on a five-two heading and the last one due eastward."

In the well, the crimson swarm was dispersing unexpectedly into smaller clusters.

Firebird leaned forward, listening intently, but no more information came. This wasn't the attack she'd expected! Twinnich should be the main target. It was virtually the only military strength in the system.

Brennen spun toward her and lifted his hand. She clutched her stool, clinging to balance as she found herself command-paralyzed and then accessed again. Her memory raced back to briefings, to strategy classes under Stele and Burkenhamn and her other commanding officers.

By the time Caldwell let her go, everyone watching had seen his attention to an alleged civilian refugee. Her guard eyed Brennen, then her, and then drew back to the end of his cable, as if making sure he'd be out of range of any future mind probe. The enthusiastic messenger captain eyed Firebird with bright-eyed curiosity, almost envy. She blinked, struggling furiously to restart her own thoughts.

Brennen turned back to the well.

So this was why he'd brought her into the war room! Would he also betray her presence to Dorning Stele, in spite of his promises? He'd lied on her behalf. Maybe he'd lied to her, too.

Firebird stared angrily at the line of his jaw, which was stern like that of a gamesman who couldn't play until his opponent revealed a strategy. The red speckles were far spread now, sweeping in twenty arches toward nightside as morning light grew in the war room.

A scout transmitted another report. "Twinnich, this is Tau at nine-seven by two. The settlement at one-oh-six has been bombed. Looks like a flasher. I can't get any closer for the dust and the rem count."

Her Verohan guard sprang to his feet, cursing.

Firebird gasped. Her own flight had overpassed that community, a hydroponics plant and a few settlement domes. It had no military significance. Surely it hadn't been flash bombed. Photo-enhanced weapons were forbidden by treaties even Netaia claimed to support. She'd known they were in the arsenal, as weapons of last resort, but she'd had no idea they'd been loaded for this invasion—and these were civilians!

Brennen's eyes caught hers again in the midst of her stricken thoughts. This time, she willingly showed her surprise and horror as he probed for the grim weapons' specs.

He studied the tri-D well, then redeployed a squadron. The Planetary Navy's twenty attack groups could sweep Veroh clean of life before converging on Twinnich. Brennen scattered six squadrons into pairs and sent them to intercept the Netaian advance, but as the Federates spread out to join battle, satellites continued to beam images of settlements bombed to dust clouds, life and structures wiped from Veroh with callous, methodical deliberation. Within hours, Veroh II could be open-air uninhabitable.

Had Dorning Stele planned this massacre all along? Had Marshal Burkenhamn, who Firebird admired for his integrity, authorized it?

Brennen called for a civilian com frequency and ordered every settlement within transport distance evacuated into Twinnich's shielding zone. Soon after that, one controller tuned in a Federate pilot on intersquad frequency, who'd come upon an NPN battle group and found himself outnumbered ten times. "Heavy bomber," he announced, then called off a string of range and bearing coordinates. A controller acknowledged. The pilot continued, "Cover me, Three."

Anxious silence filled the war room. Somewhere, two Federate pilots were taking on twenty tagwings escorting a big loadship.

"Look out, boss, he's dropped a drone."

"I'm on it."

Firebird squeezed her eyes shut, but she couldn't escape the mental image: Some Netaian bombardier sat at station in that loadship's bomb bay. Someone else who'd trained at the NPN Academy, who knew as well as Firebird the long-term effect of each deadly drop.

Could she have done it, even following orders?

She envisioned the warhead's steering rockets igniting, the Federate pilot chasing, his wingman covering him with a cone of laser fire, trying to give him hope of destroying the drone at high enough altitude to spare the targeted settlement.

She barely breathed.

In the war room they waited, but there were no more transmissions from those pilots.

Firebird's Verohan guard cursed again, clenching both fists.

"Attack pairs." Brennen's voice rose crisply. "Random scatter. Pull back. Re-form your squadrons at nine-oh degrees from Twinnich."

CHAPTER 7

STALEMATE

ritardando
gradually slackening in speed

The long Verohan day-cycle passed slowly, every hour bringing a wave of terrorized refugees and a few degrees' retreat toward Twinnich. When Deke Lindera was replaced by another guard, Vett Zimmer took a sleeping capsule and went for some rest. Firebird ate in her tightly guarded corner, but she scarcely tasted the food. Twinnich's particle-shielding dome might protect it from missile attack and radio-active debris, but that was no guarantee against a laser strike, and so many attacking ships swarmed on all sides that a shield overload looked bleakly certain, unless the perimeter could be held at a distance.

Near dusk, Vett Zimmer returned and took a shift wearing the guard belt. The horizon flashed with missile hits and laser cannon fire. Before long, heavy bombers would break through and begin to launch drones.

Firebird deliberately caught Brennen's glance. He was pacing now, with eyes that looked dark, and she knew he shared her grief for the massacred civilians. She spread her hands and shook her head, a help-less gesture. He acknowledged with a nod.

A series of day-bright flashes wrenched all eyes to the westerly projection screen. Another flight of Netaian drones had found targets between Twinnich and a distant mountain range. As the bombs' rumble reached Twinnich, the jagged horizon disappeared behind a rolling dust cloud.

No more refugees would arrive from that direction.

Firebird felt a hand on her shoulder and spun defensively around.

"Don't you want some sleep?" Brennen asked softly as he dropped his hand.

"No." She had to say more. "I'm sorry, Brennen," she murmured. "I never dreamed."

"I know." His forgiving tone wounded her as no rebuke could have. He strode away.

"Look at him," Vett whispered. "He is *dying* to be out in the thick of it. And he can't leave his post."

Firebird smiled ruefully. Maybe a command wasn't such a handsome reward after all. His frustration showed in clenched hands and the set of his jaw.

Stars came out, only a few of them bright enough to pierce the wild interplay of light in Twinnich's smoky sky. In the well, Federate ships scattered, regrouped, and picked off tagwings here and there. Once, Firebird heard the transmissions from a Federate squad that vaporized a pair of drones released by a distant bomber. It seemed as if she were watching a band of children hold off armed giants.

But before long, she realized that she'd seen the Federates score several kills, while not one intercept fighter had fallen since they pulled in to defend Twinnich.

She too longed to seize her tagwing's controls. A triangle of blue-hot engine lights roared overhead, and she watched with passionate envy. Chained, with nothing to do but watch, she felt a traitor to Netaia, and to the Federates a barbarian. She avoided Vett's casual questions until a horrendous, roaring shriek startled her eyes upward. Expecting a bomb, she found herself witnessing the immolation of an entire Netaian flight team, as the tagwings followed their lead pilot directly into the particle shield. It vaporized them, lighting the sky field.

Daley? she mourned. *Delia?*

At last, Dorning Stele apparently came to the conclusion Firebird had drawn hours earlier. The defense of Twinnich was too well coordinated to break. Shortly after midnight, the Netaians withdrew into orbit, settling for a stalemate and a siege.

Brennen finally passed command to a Verohan officer. Sweat soaked and whiskery, he smiled wanly as controllers congratulated him. He snatched a meat pastry from the conference table on his way to the window. "Captain Zimmer, are you willing to try to slip for Ituri? If that other messenger didn't make it, we haven't got a chance."

"Of course." Vett pulled off the guard's belt and held it up, raising both eyebrows.

"I'll bring in a staff guard. Look, Zimmer, I'm not ordering you out. Your chances are almost nil."

"I didn't hear that." Vett's buoyant salute so resembled Corey's—the very last time she'd seen him—that Firebird swallowed hard.

"Thank you." Brennen clapped his shoulder. Vett scurried off.

Two controllers were replaced by a fresh pair as Brennen sagged onto the stool beside Firebird's.

"Your people must've done some spectacular flying," she murmured. "We're still here."

He offered her half of his pastry, and she took it gratefully, too tired to argue.

Shortly after another Verohan guard took the stool beside her, Vett's little messenger ship roared off the breakaway strip. Fifteen minutes later, his dot in the tri-D well vanished in a circle of scarlet blips. She clenched her hands. If this went on, she would burst into tears. The Planetary Navy coiled just out of reach, a venomous snake gathering itself to strike again. Outside, on the dome that shielded Twinnich, ashen fallout slowly settled.

Brennen brushed crumbs off his lap. "I need sleep and so do you," he said bluntly. "I'm taking you back down. Belt," he told the guard. As the Verohan undid the belt's clasps, Brennen raised his voice. "Central? Page me if anything changes."

Cabled to Brennen, Firebird stumbled into the lift cubicle. While they rode, he stared silently at its door. Beside the guards' desk, he released her wrist restraint and removed the belt. Handing them to Deke Lindera, he turned away.

"Colonel. Could I talk to you for a minute?" she called.

His shoulders rose and fell in a deep breath. "All right," he replied without emotion, and he escorted her up the passway to her cell.

If she was exhausted, he must be half dead, but she desperately needed to speak. "Brennen, I can't be a part of that. The ones who ordered that attack aren't my people. The pilots and crews—the ones who went out to fight and die—I still believe in them. But not the Electorate. Not the marshals. The butchers," she added bitterly, rubbing her chafed wrist. "Flash bombs. On civilians."

"What are you saying, Mari?" He sat down on the foot of her cot.

"I think," she began, and then she choked. She tried again. "Brennen, you've been . . ."

No more words came. Sobbing, she buried her face in her hands.

At a hesitant touch on her shoulder, she raised her head to see Brennen, standing and looking down with something in his eyes she hadn't seen before. Gone was the power of command. In its stead was a depth of understanding she'd known only in Corey.

Corey. Dead, as she deeply wished she were.

She fell against Brennen, clutching him and crying. His arms gathered her in as they might hold a child, and he stroked her shoulder with one hand.

Slowly, her tears subsided. Her pride revived, though, mortally wounded. She'd made an idiot of herself in the arms of a Federate colonel, a genetic oddity. What depth would she reach next time?

His grasp loosened as suddenly as her emotions changed. Forcibly reminded of his starbred empathy, she wrenched out of his warm grasp. She hated herself and his humanness. "I wish you'd move me uplevel," she lashed out. "Then, when they break through and flash Twinnich, at least I'll die fast with the rest of you. Do you really think you can hold them off?"

His stare remained compassionate. "The fleet will come. Soon enough, I hope. But I'll find you better quarters as soon as I can."

"The fleet will come," she mocked. *Come on, Sentinel! Since you're human, get angry!* "But meanwhile, Netaia raids the basium mines. They can—"

He shook his head. "Not now. We've made contingency plans. I cannot tell you why, but the mines won't be taken."

Too relieved to fight on, she asked, "But what happens to me if your fleet comes and they won't issue those termination papers?"

"I've given that serious thought. Mari . . . would you want to go home?"

Firebird blinked, passed a hand over her aching eyes, and then shut her gaping mouth. She could return voluntarily. She could face the electors and proudly tell them she'd come back to meet a Netaian fate on her home ground. "You'd let me?"

"Would you go, if I could?"

They'd like that, she reflected grimly. *They love to punish people.* "They want me dead," she reminded him.

"Yes."

Of course he knew. "It doesn't matter. Here or at home, I'm condemned."

"I doubt any Federate termination papers will come at first request, if that's your concern. You're valuable . . . to us."

Firebird interlocked her fingers and squeezed tightly. Could she really choose to live among the Federates, whom she'd been raised to despise, instead of facing the sacrificial death that would satisfy the merciless Powers and their blood-lusting electors?

After what she'd just seen, was there any question? She'd hide on Tallis, or Caroli, or somewhere in deep space, before letting Dorning Stele enjoy watching her die, the way he'd leered at his brother.

"No," she murmured, "I couldn't go home. What they did here was wrong. I want to live. A little longer, at least."

He stood against the far wall, unmoving, unthreatening. "May I take you into protective custody?"

"That makes me sound helpless."

He rubbed his rough chin and nodded.

"Under the circumstances, I suppose I am." She looked down at the cot. She ached to fall onto it. "But what if that authorization to terminate comes through?"

"I don't give the order. Particularly if you've requested asylum. You still haven't," he reminded her.

"All right," she said numbly. She took a deep breath of stale air, and then she spoke the treasonous words. "I'm officially requesting asylum, Colonel Caldwell."

He paced toward the gray metal door. "I'll be back in a minute."

"Oh, Brennen, it'll wait for the morning." She sank onto the thin mattress.

Inside her doorway, he stopped. "I don't want to risk waiting. This won't take long."

He returned carrying a recall pad. She read it carefully, battling to concentrate, to simply stay awake. For three standard months, she would be quartered and cared for, and granted diplomatic immunity, by the Federacy's Tallis Region. During that time, Wing Colonel Brennen D. Caldwell would answer for her safety, and when the period ended, other arrangements would be made. There was a place to record date and time with her own hand, so that if the document were ever published on Netaia, then the Electorate, the marshals, and her mother would know she'd signed only after the slaughter at Veroh.

"So if Twinnich falls and I survive," she observed, "this will record my protest."

"I'll get you a microcopy to keep with you, in case that happens." He drew his stylus from his left cuff and signed the pad.

She'd unbraided her hair while he was gone. It fell over her shoulder as she signed below him and pressed her thumb to the recall panel, confirming her signature. "Thank you," she mumbled.

"I'm glad I can offer it." Against the gray walls his midnight blue uniform looked almost black, and so did the circles under his eyes.

"Are you as exhausted as you look?" he asked.

Aren't you? "I haven't slept well since . . . before we left Netaia," she confessed.

"May I—I could help you with that, if you'd let me."

She eyed him warily. "Sleep only? Nothing else?"

He shook his head. "Nothing else. I promise."

She shrugged permission. He walked forward and gently placed his fingers over her eyes.

All fear and tension dropped away, leaving her too deeply relaxed to wonder what he'd done, or how he'd done it.

"Good night," she whispered. Irresistibly, her eyelids dropped. That was no genetic freak, she reflected in the last uncontrolled instant before she fell soundly asleep. That was a most exceptional man.

CHAPTER 8

REBEL

tempo giusto
in strict time

Firebird was roused midmorning by the pale guard. Fast advance ships of the Federate fleet had arrived from Ituri. She watched from the same stool as before, while Brennen ordered a sortie that caught Netaian attackers between jaws of titanium and steel. Most of the Netaians survived to flee Twinnich. The controllers cheered, but Firebird was achingly aware that it was only a foretaste of things to come. Netaia had used flash bombs on civilians. It was one thing to accept sanctuary for herself, another to consider the kind of retribution Federate technology might inflict on her home world. Her own people.

Brennen left after the battle. From that alone, she knew the defense of Twinnich was over. Little else would be done until more Federate ships reached Veroh. Firebird asked her guard to take her below.

Several of the Second Division's ranking commanders had come ahead with the advance detail. It was late afternoon in Twinnich when Brennen boarded the officers' frigate, a heavily armed, roomy but fast ship.

General Gorn Frankin of Caroli seized his arm at the airlock and pulled him bodily down the dark corridor toward a galley. "Brennen Caldwell! We thought you'd been swizzling killcare when that troop request came through, and I don't mind telling you, if it'd come from anyone else, we'd have sent the psych team instead of warships! What kind of fools attack a peacekeeping force? The clincher was that weird termination request. Was that the pilot you interviewed?"

At a gray galley table ringed with fellow officers, Brennen took a chair. Another Sentinel sat among them, Captain Ellet Kinsman, and he sent her a quick unspoken greeting. She returned it with a burst of feelings, relief foremost among them, but out of respect to the others present, neither added the subvocalized words of mind-to-mind speech.

"Then when we saw Veroh was under attack again," added another officer, "and how hot the atmosphere was, we were afraid they'd dusted you all. I'm with General Frankin. What's going on?"

Brennen accepted a staffer's cup of kass with thanks. "First, I have to know if I worded that termination request weakly enough to have it denied."

"Denied?" Frankin sat down, running one hand across his thick shock of hair. "Shredded!"

Brennen smiled into his mug.

"How in Six-alpha did we get a member of the royal family in custody?"

He explained, beginning with the first battle of Veroh and concluding with Firebird's request for asylum, and when he finished, they were silent. Lowering his static shields, he observed their reactions.

Ellet, tangibly surprised and concerned, spoke first. "You can quiet me if I'm out of line, Colonel, but what do you intend to do with her?"

Yes, what? "I'm waiting for orders. I've only just convinced her she doesn't need to die." *Thank the Holy One!*

"We have no orders for her disposition." Ellet tossed her head, and her chin-length hair shimmered. "What if she's sent back to Netaia?"

"Firing squad, I think." He'd thought hard before offering to return her, down in her cell. If she'd chosen that, his follow-through might have cost him, too—a court-martial.

Instead, just as he'd hoped, she'd repented. She'd distanced herself from her own forces with sincere remorse. He'd rejoiced on the run, bringing back that recall pad before she could change her mind.

"They're that sort, are they?" asked Ellet.

He nodded. "An incomprehensible penal system has propped up their government for decades."

Frankin, tangibly pleased, bounced a fist off the tabletop. "I don't imagine she's anxious for publicity, but think what an advantage she's given us. Maybe now we can settle down those people. So far, Netaians don't strike me as rational people."

"You accessed her?" Ellet asked.

Brennen nodded.

"Is she rational?"

Irritated by the scorn in her voice, he shot her an unguarded glance. He and Ellet shared a faith and a culture, but he didn't like her inflated sense of importance.

She strengthened her own shields, drew up stiffly, and watched his eyes.

Frankin stood. "Caldwell, before we go on, Regional sent you something." He picked up a folded, heatsealed paper from the table and passed it across. Brennen had barely pulled open the seal when Frankin announced, "We've all had crazy experiences with the time lag in communications. Our Sentinel friend commanded the defense of Veroh as a wing colonel, but when Regional found out I'd given him the command, they made him a field general. And I say, well deserved. Congratulations, Brennen."

Holding back a startled smile, Brennen shook Frankin's hand. Then he finished scanning the paper. It offered terse congratulations, the advancement in rank, and a significant pay raise.

The other officers murmured good wishes. Ellet Kinsman's epsilon sense fairly glowed with approval.

One step closer to the High command, he told himself. He tucked the paper into his pocket, briefly wishing he could've worn his new rank's triangular insignia on his collar, like Frankin. A Sentinel could wear only the star.

"Netaia, then." Frankin waved at the nearest bulkhead. A three-dimensional projection of that star system sprang into existence: one major world, two others designated *C* for "colonized," and several deep-space modules. "Full demolition of military resources, and this quarter of the Whorl will sleep easier. General Caldwell, your access intelligence will be critical."

General Caldwell. He liked the sound. He rolled it through his mind once more, then focused on the war. This would mean new responsibilities. "It's all on cross-programmable record aboard the *Horizon*," he said soberly.

"We requisitioned *Horizon* when we heard about your data," Frankin agreed, "but we had no idea your source was this good. The rest of the division should get here in another day. I'd like to speak with Her Highness before leaving Veroh."

Brennen cleared his throat. "Be careful. We still can't rule out suicide. Lady Firebird knows what that data she gave us will mean to Netaia, and she has a capacity for loyalty under circumstances we'd consider impossible. She . . . needs to be shown a worthier cause," he added.

Despite his objective phrasing, Ellet flashed with a jealous horror that he felt plainly.

"Very well . . . General," said a smiling, oblivious officer on his left. "Have you any other advice in dealing with this woman?"

So Ellet had read him correctly, interpreting his concern for Firebird as a personal hope. "Since you asked my advice," he said, "I'd transfer her to Tallis. As quickly as possible."

Firebird spent that day studying *Federacy of the Free*. Brennen Caldwell's likeness in Unit 78 startled her, an old tri-D of a nineteen-year-old second captain they'd decorated for leading a daring raid. Spying a birth date, she did the numbers mentally: He was seven Netaian years older than herself. By this account, just as Vett Zimmer had claimed, he'd been Academy-educated as a fightercraft pilot.

Even as she read from a suspicious mental distance, this Federate history intrigued her. She already knew its beginning, because Netaia had suffered the same catastrophe. Four hundred years ago, Sabba Six-alpha—a binary star between the Whorl's Tallis and Elysia regions—had evolved with only a few months' warning into something that still baffled astrophysicists. Without going nova, it started to spew radiation and high-energy particles in decades-long spurts. Space-faring civilizations were chased to ground for over a century, and much information technology was scrambled or lost. During that long disaster, while advanced civilizations deteriorated all over the Whorl, the Netaian aristocracy had repelled those marauders from out-Whorl space, consolidated power, and then saved Netaia's culture and industry by reviving predisaster technologies.

But as the radiation storms began to subside, the Federate worlds had reestablished free commerce and unrestricted research. According to this account, the Federacy claimed to be primarily a trade and mutual defense organization, founded on justice for all classes, respectful nonaggression between self-governing peoples, and a refusal to unnecessarily deprive anyone of life or liberty.

Firebird glanced up at the cracked ceiling and sighed. Maybe the truth was more complex than this junior-school oversimplification, but she would've gladly served such a government. Years ago she had grieved for her innocence when experienced electors finally bullied her into believing that common people couldn't be ruled by the ideals of her favorite ballads, but only by Strength . . . and the other eight Powers. Her mother had actually tightened the penal system. According to Netaian policy, the Federacy would have to be just as oppressive as the Electorate, or worse, to maintain its grip on so many star systems.

Maybe the electors were wrong. This government didn't claim to be "gripping" at all. The Federate fleet had let the NPN retreat unassailed from its first attack on Veroh. And hadn't Brennen Caldwell, the only Federate she knew even slightly, treated her decently when he could've been arrogant and cruel?

If the electors were wrong, then either the Powers were mistaken, or else they only existed as personal attributes, not as gods. If that were the case, then Firebird Angelo had sacrificed herself for nothing.

Nothing but Netaia. That was some comfort.

Uneasily, she popped out the scan cartridge. The truth couldn't be this simple. There were usually contingencies.

She was struggling through the preface to *Transnational Government*, a weighty volume on the Federacy's sociopolitical-economic structure, when Brennen came into her cell carrying a sealed parcel. He looked like a lord in dress whites. They carried no insignia or decoration but the Federate slash and his Master Sentinel's star.

"Your uniform." He laid it on the cot. "The officers who came with the fleet have arrived planetside. They want to discuss that termination request."

Enough history, enough theory. Her life was at stake. "What will they do?"

"Just talk. They've been in contact with Tallis."

"Does . . . everyone know I'm here, then?"

"Only Regional command and these officers. But they want to discuss making the announcement."

Which would destroy the sweet legend that she'd died a hero. It was false, anyway. Firebird tore the seal on the parcel. "All right," she said. "I'll just be a minute."

She dressed hurriedly but carefully. Early this morning, Brennen had sent down a microcopy of her asylum document, mounted on a plastene card. She slid it into the breast pocket that had once held a white packet, a promise of safety replacing her promise of death.

Official again in cobalt blue with rubies glittering on her collar, she found herself standing straighter than she had for a long while but profoundly uncomfortable. She'd been thinking treasonous thoughts this afternoon, and she'd accepted treasonous amnesty. Forcing a comb through her long hair, she greeted her reflection in the cracked mirror: *Welcome back, Firebird. You were always the rebel of the family at heart, even when you obeyed them.*

She left her hair loose this time.

Brennen stepped back in. The corners of his mouth twitched into a smile that reminded her she was safe, for the moment. "I feel like an officer again," she said. "Almost."

"You look it." He motioned her to lead him down the passway.

At a long table in a small conference room, five more officers in white scrambled to their feet. Undeniably nervous among so much Federate authority, Firebird still felt flattered that they'd met her in dress uniform. She came to attention.

"Your Highness." The nearest man extended his hand.

She clasped it boldly. He didn't look as if he had brought her a death warrant. "Thank you, but that's not my title," she corrected him gravely. "Lady Firebird is correct, or Major Angelo."

"Please, then, sit down, my lady," he suggested.

She took the vacant chair at the head of the table, one self-conscious soldier in cobalt blue facing six in Federate white.

Brennen introduced the officers, but they seemed a blur. The nearest, General Frankin, did nearly all the talking. "I'm not sorry to report that the Regional council didn't authorize your execution, Lady Firebird. General Caldwell says you have now applied for asylum."

General Caldwell.

She shot him a glance. He smiled faintly.

Of course they'd promoted him. He'd held a major command. Battling down her jealousy, she answered with care. "What Netaia did here lies heavily on my conscience, sir. I want to help ensure that this basium project will not be developed, as much for Netaia's sake as for yours." From their lack of reaction, she assumed they'd been told about Cleary's research. Brennen must've released that intelligence. Frankin and the other three men looked thoughtful, although the woman Sentinel—as Firebird stretched her memory, she recalled Captain Kinsman from Korda's holograph—scrutinized her, and even Brennen, through narrowed eyes.

Brennen. A general. Unfair, unbelievable.

But at least he wasn't promoted posthumously.

"We are aware of the basium project," announced Frankin. "We share your determination to see it thwarted. From here, we will proceed to demilitarize Netaia. I say this without malice, Lady Firebird, but your navy will be badly outgunned."

"I understand," she answered, wishing she didn't.

"Do you understand that your name will likely be used in negotiations?" Frankin asked.

This was the price she would pay for survival. Her people would brand her a traitor. Aching, she looked to Brennen. Suddenly his promotion didn't matter at all. He nodded, arching an eyebrow in sympathy.

She focused on Frankin again. "How will you use my name?"

Frankin laid both forearms on the black tabletop. "Your people should know you are safe. Their impression of the Federacy is in transition. We cannot ignore your navy's challenge to peace, but our goal is long-term mutual respect. We will strike quickly and mercifully and then allow your people to return as soon as practicable to home rule.

"We've received your claim that you have no worth as a hostage," he went on, "but be assured, the Federacy takes no hostages. Your presence among us is of great importance because our treatment of you will surely influence the Netaian public, as will your request for asylum."

They cared what the *public* thought. "I hope so," she admitted, "but that will not affect the Electorate."

"You also remain a source of advice and information."

Remembering her interrogation onboard that Federate cruiser,

Firebird looked hard at Brennen. He returned this stare frankly. He—or another Sentinel—might be ordered to question her again.

So maybe she'd learn to resist. She lowered her eyes. "You'll tell the Electorate that I asked for amnesty?"

"Only in context of the full account, including your final heroic actions as a squadron leader, and what General Caldwell has called your 'astonishing' effort to resist mind-access."

What? Had she almost succeeded? She glanced to Brennen for confirmation. Again he nodded. The chill on her heart thawed slightly. She turned back to Frankin. "Where are you sending me, then? Netaia will seek my execution."

"We'd prefer to see you transferred to protective custody at Regional command on Tallis. I hope you'll find that acceptable."

"I'm in no position to object." Inwardly she sighed. She would see Tallis after all.

Four of its walls, anyway.

"Very well, then. We'll meet again, Your Highness. Thank you for cooperating."

She winced at his choice of words. *Collaborator!* she berated herself.

Brennen led her away. Once the lift doors closed, she murmured, "General. Congratulations, Brennen."

"Thank you." She heard satisfaction in his voice.

"Expected?"

"Not quite so soon."

Plainly, though, he was on the fast track of promotion.

Down at the battered brown jailer's desk, he asked her to halt. "Gentlemen, this officer has accepted asylum and will be traveling to Tallis shortly. Please see that she's treated with respect."

"Sir?" Koan Tryseleen's rangy body straightened.

"Her name is not Tomma. I apologize for deceiving you, but it was done in the best interests of the Federacy." He glanced at Firebird, who stood at loose parade rest. "This is First Major Lady Firebird Angelo, the queen's third daughter."

Tryseleen and his pale associate drew away as though Brennen had announced she had a communicable terminal disease.

She believed that she did. It was called treachery.

Brennen inclined his head toward her end of the corridor. When the door had ground shut behind them, he took her right hand and pressed her fingers. "I'm going on with the fleet as soon as I can pack, and I won't have time to say good-bye later."

"To Netaia?"

"Yes."

In the yellow light, she looked up into his face, finding it hard to imagine that she would be living somewhere in this vast Federacy, but he'd be elsewhere. "Thank you, then. Watch out for yourself."

"I will." He studied her eyes. "You still feel guilty."

"Terribly."

He shook his head. "You've done nothing wrong. You obeyed your orders and more. Please, Mari. Reconsider your . . . deities. There's a higher call on your life now."

Why did he keep calling her that? She clutched his arm. "And please, don't . . ." She choked. How could she plead mercy for Netaia's forces, after Veroh?

His answering expression would haunt her for weeks: lips straight and bland, stress lines crowding his eyes, and a lift to his eyebrows that might have been sympathy or regret, or even pain.

"Be careful," she managed, ". . . General."

He took two steps through the doorway, turned, and saluted her. The door slid shut.

CHAPTER 9

NETAIA

marziale
martial, marchlike

Too many details needed final attention before Brennen could leave Twinnich in Gorn Frankin's hands. He eyed his shorthand notes. Since this job was no longer simply a peacekeeping command, Frankin—with experience on Caroli's board of protectorates—had the seniority and experience to get the Verohans back on their feet. In retrospect, it almost seemed odd Frankin hadn't taken the original command.

He was glad he'd been ordered out. From memory, and his brief data-collecting mission years ago, he was starting to grasp the Netaian mindset, but now it seemed urgent to know the place in his own flesh. He wasn't quite certain why.

He didn't like assigning Ellet Kinsman to escort Firebird to Tallis, but he had no other qualified woman to send. He had worked on and off with Ellet. About a year ago, she'd offered to exchange a connaturality probe, as unmarried Sentinels could do. He'd declined . . . maybe too politely.

Now he would have to rely on Ellet's vesting vows to keep her from deliberately shaking Firebird's fragile independence. Ellet's loyalty to the Sentinel kindred and her racial pride must make her a teacher, and Firebird's curiosity must cement their relationship.

He wished he could confide his true feelings to Ellet. He'd grown weary of living alone, when most Sentinels shared every emotion with a bond mate; but Ellet's first reaction to public events, without fully knowing his heart, had warned him away again. To Ellet, any outsider was suspect. Inferior.

As if Ellet had caught his thoughts, he felt her step into the com center. Looking up, he imagined Firebird, with her delicate face and long, hot-colored hair, next to Ellet, whose strong nose and slightly concave cheeks represented classic Thyrian features. At his own height and a little more, Ellet would tower over Firebird.

"When do we slip?" she asked, casually resting one hand on his desk. ". . . General?"

He couldn't help smiling slightly. "I'd like you on escort duty, Ellet. Would you take Lady Firebird to Tallis?"

An upside interlink buzzed nearby. Brennen made certain a com tech caught it, then turned back to the other Sentinel. "Minimal security detention," he explained.

Ellet's epsilon cloud had thickened. "Tallis is a choice assignment, but I've been working as Frankin's admin counselor. Don't you feel I should go with him?"

"Frankin will stay on Veroh. He'll have good counsel from Twinnich staff."

An aide hurried past, balancing a tray of kass cups. Brennen watched Ellet without communicating, each wreathed in static no outsider would discern and through which no emotion would pass.

Her face had gone blank. "Something is wrong, Brennen. Would you show me your feelings for her?"

Sentinel ethics dictated that he must grant such a request, and Ellet would need some assurance if he wanted this time to go well for Firebird. He cleared his outer shields and raised feelings that shouldn't distress Ellet: pity, understanding, optimism. Ellet's feathery touch, connatural enough to caress although the otherness felt distinct, swept over his surface emotions.

She pulled back and stood tall. "Brennen, be careful."

Ellet doubtless guessed more than he'd shown her. They both knew he could conceal some emotion under inner, deeper shields she wouldn't even sense. "I am always careful, Ellet."

"Very well," she said softly. "The girl has been through torments, and she could make the Federacy a valuable resource. I'll try to educate her."

"Thank you." Absently he tapped the desk. "I will ask for a full report."

"You'll have it."

Within a day, the rest of the Second Division reached Veroh. A shuttle picked up Firebird, Ellet, and a few other passengers and streaked on to Tallis. From another, Brennen boarded the Federate cruiser *Corona*. Half an hour later the division slipped, bound for Netaia.

The officers met after dinner on *Corona*'s bridge. Admiral Lee Danton, the only Second Division fleet officer to have risen through diplomatic channels, stood at one edge of a tri-D projection of the Netaia system. The tri-D's glow seemed to deepen the cleft in Danton's chin, and it set lights in his sandy hair. Inside a projected sphere, tiny gold and scarlet ship-images stood out against the orbits of Netaia's five stony inner planets.

"So the main strike," Danton continued, "will be the largest division of our forces. Smaller groups will deploy as follows. I'll keep *Corona* just outsystem and ensure the Netaians receive no reinforcements—"

Brennen glanced up.

"What, General Caldwell?"

"Sir, they have no outsystem allies."

"They could hire Geminan mercenaries. *Elysia*, with escort," he continued, "to orbit with and isolate the primary intersystem relay station. CNC One, Colonel Nikolas. You'll be on board *Elysia*. Deng . . ."

Leaning against a table-level communications console, Brennen waited out the other tactical assignments. A systemwide strike would require several CNCs, Colonial Neutralization Commanders, but Brennen didn't expect to miss the main battle. He wasn't surprised when Danton called his name for a job he didn't really want.

"*Horizon*, main planetary assault. Field General Caldwell, Atmospheric Commander." He looked up from his recall pad. "General Caldwell, I want you on the main attack with that target data. We do appreciate your understanding of Netaian affairs and locales."

Brennen nodded, frowning. He'd had a major command. He'd fly a bridge from now on, not an intercept fighter. He probably had more combat experience than any other officer here and knew more about Netaia, but the AC would direct the assault on Netaia itself. Today's action would be a kind of warfare he detested, a punitive strike.

He'd been decorated during that kind of battle at Gemina. The

Federacy always practiced restraint, but he wouldn't enjoy this assignment. His force would square off against Netaian combatants trying to defend their own bases, their own people. He was glad Mari didn't know what he had to do.

Mari—oddly, in his mind, "Mari" was the woman he knew. Another woman, Firebird, had tried to die for Netaia's glory. She was changing . . . he hoped.

Minutes later, Danton dismissed his staff. General Gulest Vanidar of Tura, the swarthy officer who would command *Horizon*, caught Brennen's glance and beckoned him over. "You'll be on my boat, then." Vanidar's accent, cultured with a slight drawl, suggested a classical education on Elysia, capital of the other Federate region and HQ of Federate High command. "I've never worked with a Sentinel."

Brennen shook his head. "Don't expect anything unusual. Not unless something comes up."

"No . . . telepathic orders across the bridge?"

Brennen shook his head. "I wear a mike like anyone else, General Vanidar."

The firm set of Vanidar's jaw softened slightly. "Then I look forward to working with you."

Bemused and slightly depressed, Brennen searched out his cabin, though a casual friend invited him to join a group for Carolinian dagger play in the R&R center. After Veroh, he needed some uninterrupted rest.

Someone else would lead Delta Flight, he mused as he pulled off his boots. He'd clung to his wings longer than normal, thanks to his SO status. But now—with this promotion—the Federacy finally had invested too much in him to risk him in battle anymore.

This would be strange, though.

He slept a full eleven hours before the attack force's final rendezvous, during which crews were transshipped for battle. The rest of Delta Flight shuttled to a huge fighter carrier escorting *Horizon* while Brennen familiarized himself with a new list of squadron commanders, including his former wingman, the new leader of Delta Flight. Brennen sat beside Vanidar when the battle group accelerated back into slip-state, making its final jump to Netaia.

Count Tel Tellai sat flipping the ends of his blue sash, waiting with twenty-six other men and women around the gold-rimmed electoral table. A tense, garbled outsystem message had interrupted this last afternoon session of the week. It would take several minutes for the electors' DeepScan request for a repeat to reach the system's fringe.

Irritation lines did nothing for Princess Phoena's features. Today she wore a snug, iridescent shipboard-style suit that touched several of propriety's limits, and jewels to cover what it did not. Crown Princess Carradee, in conservative mauve, merely looked concerned, and tailored Siwann held herself with utter calm.

He dropped his sash ends and emulated the queen. He should consider the report his holdings manager had sent up this morning, regarding how a recent early frost might cut profits—

The media block at center table hissed. "Repeating previous transmission. A report has come in from the Veroh strike force, Operation Pinnacle, dated four days past. Our forces had driven back the enemy to Veroh's main settlement and there established a state of siege."

Tel crossed his hands on the smooth, cool table. On his left, Muirnen Rogonin gave a satisfied sigh.

"Concern was then growing, however, regarding an apparent slip-shield zone approaching Veroh from out-spinward. Contingency alert was recommended, allowing for communications lag."

Tel furrowed his brow. Bad news?

First Marshal Burkenhamn stood. His cobalt-blue-swathed bulk seemed wasted on a man who didn't need size to command attention. "Contingency plans have indeed been drawn up by my staff. Our forces are standing alert." The marshal's rich voice heartened Tel. "And let us remember that a slip zone can exist merely as a lingering radiation echo from the great catastrophe, bouncing out of the Whorl or its Eye. That, of course, is our best-case scenario."

"And the worst?" The queen remained as collected as statuary.

Burkenhamn raised a finger. "Because no such slip zone has been observed near the Netaia system by our sensing stations, we assume Netaia is safe for the moment, even if the Federates have sent a force to retake Veroh.

"It is, however, conceivable that Veroh could be already retaken. A force large enough to achieve that could advance in this direction.

Because of the buffer systems' location ninety degrees from Veroh, we would have little warning, if any, of an attack. This is—"

Burkenhamn tapped the table to silence a whisperer at the outer branch's far end. "This is, I remind you, merely a worst-case scenario. Let us remember that the Federates hesitated to approach our system at the moment classic strategy would have suggested they strike."

Tel understood less than half of that.

Siwann raised an eyebrow. "Continue."

Burkenhamn bowed from the waist. "Let us then turn to the possibility of Veroh having been finally subdued by our forces—"

Again the media block buzzed, cutting him off.

"Outsystem report," said the clear, nearby voice. "DeepScan channel three. This is a new report. May I broadcast direct?"

"Certainly," Siwann snapped. Silence fell. Tel found himself holding his breath.

The distant voice babbled, all pretense of poise gone. "Subspace wake, passing deep-space module two. Alert. Very large subspace wake—"

Even Tel knew what that meant . . . many ships had entered the Netaian system!

Burkenhamn and Siwann fell on their communication terminals. Carradee's fingers splayed on the tabletop. Phoena clenched a fist and bit down on her thumb, keying furiously with her other hand. Tel wanted to hurry over and stand by her, protect her, but he sat welded to his chair.

Countdown to launch commenced. Brennen had conferred with squadron commanders—selecting primary targets, establishing refuel and re-arm procedures and contingency plans for possible enemy courses of action. Within minutes, *Horizon* would exit slip-state for normal space. Vanidar sat surrounded by junior officers, reviewing *Horizon*'s own maneuvers and defense plans. Brennen's monitors gleamed with maps that covered both of Netaia's major continents and the sketchy base data Firebird had remembered. Refueling information was one thing; energy-shield wavelengths would've been infinitely more helpful, but she'd had no need to know those.

He felt restless, fidgety. In vivid memory, he was elsewhere:

Helmeted, harnessed, and linked to life support, he had waited inside the cockpit of his intercept fighter. Behind, cabled one after another in a deep chute on the carrier's belly, sat the rest of his flight. Inside other chutes waited more pilots. He'd boarded hours ago, strapping down before the carrier began maximum deceleration, and then slept while he could.

"One minute to normal space reentry. Three minutes to launch. Activate generators."

Brennen obeyed the voice in his helmet with one pull of his gloved hand, then keyed over to intersquad frequency. His inclined seat started to vibrate. Lights sprang to life on the board. "Delta Leader, generator check."

"Two, check."

"Three, check . . ."

The carrier shuddered. Drop point: He'd ridden it twenty times from the cockpit of a carrier fighter, but it still made him nervous. A drop-point malfunction could strand carrier, fighters, and pilots in quasi-orthogonal space.

Seconds continued to melt off on his console chrono, still cross-programmed into the carrier's main computer. He gripped stick and throttle and cleared his senses one by one with focused bursts of epsilon energy.

The carrier's slip-shields dropped. The computer kicked his docking cables free. He pulled back his throttle. The chute rushed by—dropped away—and his overhead screen lit with stars. A reddish sphere lay ahead, growing visibly. With the momentum from the carrier as well as his own thrust, he carried enough velocity to make the crossing in minutes.

"Shields up," he called; then, "Deuce flight."

Five blips shimmered on his rear screen, jockeying into pairs.

He shook loose of the memory as drop point shuddered the ship, and he formed a silent prayer. *Guide our hearts, guide our hands. Show us mercy and help us show it.*

And wherever Mari is, Holy One, go with her.

As *Horizon* reentered normal space, surveillance screens lit all over the bridge with current data. Mari's was a wealthy world, with rich cities and fertile land masses, but its leaders were greedy for more. Did they know they couldn't win? Better for them if they surrendered quickly . . .

"General Caldwell," snapped Admiral Danton's voice in his left ear.

Brennen wore a collar mike. "Caldwell here," he answered.

"Confirm launch?"

Brennen touched up the carrier's frequency and consulted its main computer. "All fighters launched," he said, barely keeping the wistfulness out of his voice. "No malfunctions."

Within three hours, two of Netaia's seven main land and ice military bases were gone, and its auxiliary spaceports were following. The NPN was utterly outgunned, though its three sea bases might hold out indefinitely. Brennen was redirecting squadrons north toward the Arctica ice base when an alert light flashed on his main deployment screen. He slapped the response panel. "Caldwell," he said.

"Sir, it's a transmission from downside. Holding for you, at General Vanidar's request."

Brennen looked over his shoulder at Vanidar's command chair. Vanidar's voice rumbled in his earphone, "Transmit." After a short pause, he continued. "This is Federate Cruiser *Horizon*, Major General Gulest Vanidar commanding."

"General Vanidar," said a distant voice, "this is Count Dorning Stele, Second Marshal of Netaian Forces. Request cease-fire and negotiations."

"We will negotiate only one conclusion, Count Stele," drawled Vanidar. "You are to surrender. Unconditionally. Do you copy?"

"Copy," Stele responded, but he gave no further answer. Brennen imagined the electors that Firebird remembered, gathered in fancy dress around their ornate table, dithering while they tried to bully their armed forces.

Maybe those without military obligations had fled to country estates.

A squadron commander's voice spoke in Brennen's other ear. Until the cease-fire had actually been called, his job was battle management—and until necessary, Count Stele didn't need to know his location as AC. Brennen touched a panel that sent targeting data down to the squadron leader.

"Affirmative," Stele finally came back. "I am authorized to offer surrender."

Two junior officers cheered. Brennen touched on a com frequency. Two minutes later, he'd diverted the northbound squadrons. By then, Stele and General Vanidar were discussing time and place. They settled on two hours—here, on board *Horizon*—Stele in an unarmed civilian ship, with minimal escort.

As soon as Vanidar cut the transmission, though, Brennen spoke to him on a secured frequency. "General, one caution. Don't trust Dorning Stele. He commanded the Veroh massacre." *And*, he recalled, *consigned his own brother to the execution block.*

Vanidar rose out of his chair. "Thanks for the reminder, General Caldwell. We'll arrange an extra-secure reception."

Brennen waited on the control bridge for Landing Bay Four as Stele's craft slowly approached, pulled in by an auxiliary catchfield. The Netaian ship's exterior looked esthetically sleek, lacking shield projection antennae or weapons ports. A scanner alongside the visual screen confirmed no shipboard weapons, nor even energy shields. It was plainly an elegant civilian shuttle.

Up a corridor behind Brennen's right shoulder, Vanidar and his staff had assembled in a conference room. An extra security contingent, ten guards in Carolinian khaki, waited inside the bay's control bridge with Brennen, along with normal security and maintenance personnel, as the huge space door slowly drifted open. Three of the security people had brought in a weapons scanning arch, which stood at the base of the half flight of stairs outside this vacuum-secured bridge.

If Stele were sincere, this meeting would end the fighting and begin Federate occupation of Netaia. Brennen would like nothing better.

The passenger craft settled onto a receiving grid. The space door slid shut. Normally, the main airlock would be disalarmed and unsealed as soon as the bay held air.

Brennen had ordered it to remain sealed until he gave the order. Some weapons, some explosives, no scanner could pick up.

"Count Stele, this is Airlock Four," he said. "Please wait for security precautions. These are for your protection as well as ours."

"Roger, Airlock Four," clipped a voice Brennen now recognized as Stele's pilot. "Waiting for security."

"Go," Brennen said aside to the Carolinian security crew. They hustled down the half flight of steps and out into the bay. He followed, watching closely. Several crewers formed an honor-guard line along the little ship's hatch. Two others, moving more circumspectly, circled the craft to look for anything blatantly suspicious. The last three steered their scanning arch to a spot between the ship and main airlock. Brennen took a position behind the scan unit.

As the only Sentinel on board, he'd be a final weapons detector. The Netaians could conceivably bring low-tech weapons through a scanner—only fools would try to carry metal-frame blazers or shock pistols, so he doubted they'd try that. But no potential assassin should be able to hide his intention. This time, Brennen had to thank the college's policy makers for his unadorned uniform. The simple midnight blue painted no "Atmospheric Commander" target on him.

Just a "Danger! Telepath!" target, he reflected.

When all seemed secure, he nodded to the security crew's chief, who'd put on dress whites to serve as Stele's escort to the conference room. The chief signaled a communications tech up in the command post.

Ten seconds later, a hatch slid open.

Two crewmen in cobalt blue stepped off first. Then came Stele. He ceremoniously whipped off his hat and clutched it under one arm, half bowed, and accepted the security chief's offered hand. The chief motioned him and his crew toward the honor-guard line, which would steer them to the scanning arch.

Count Dorning Stele's posture remained stiff and straight. His nattily tailored uniform bulged halfway up his chest, suggesting a girdle.

And what else? Brennen wondered. He diffused his epsilon shields as the little procession approached his scanner. Four more Netaian escorts followed Stele, who stepped boldly to a table that had been moved alongside. Arching his neck to look down on all Federates, Stele ceremoniously drew and surrendered a gleaming full-dress dagger. Then his sidearm, an ornamental blazer.

Leaving all six of his escorts behind, he marched through the scanner.

It came up clean. Stele turned back toward his escort.

This was the critical moment. Brennen stepped up and tapped his shoulder. "My Lord Count," he said.

Stele whipped around. Brennen looked into hard brown eyes. There was no time to probe, only to check Stele's emotions.

Stele's mental state hummed with suicidal determination.

Brennen reached into his left cuff for his crystace.

Stele turned again. "Now," he shouted, thrusting his right hand through his uniform's front seam.

Instantly Brennen caught him in voice command, freezing him with his hand inside the breast panel. Stele resisted hard, struggling to pull his hand free.

"Security," Brennen shouted.

Two Carolinian guards hustled up. "Explosives check," Brennen ordered. He heard shouts behind him. He couldn't turn to assist until he'd disarmed Stele.

The Carolinian drew a tiny laser knife and slit both sides of Stele's breast panel. Beneath the cobalt blue fabric, he did wear a girdle, or something like it. Small, heavy-looking packets bulged beneath and alongside it. Another security tech hurried up. Brennen focused an access probe and made a fast, deep breach. "Keep his hand on that detonator," Brennen ordered. "Tape it there if you have to, until it's disarmed. If he lets go, it explodes."

Then he looked out into the bay.

Beyond the weapon scanner, three of Stele's crewmen had drawn twinbeam blazers. Another hurried toward the outer bulkhead, carrying an archaic hunting pistol, a projectile weapon fully capable of holing a ship's hull. Two Carolinians sprinted toward him.

Two—no, three—Netaians lay sprawled on the deck, felled by Federate shock pistols. But two Carolinians also were down. Out in the bay were four large, blocky starter units and the Netaian ship, and somewhere behind them, two of Stele's crewmen had to be hiding. As Brennen watched, one of the Carolinians sprinting toward the saboteur fell heavily.

"Drop your weapons," Brennen called, holding his crystace ready.

"You won't be targeted if you surrender."

A head popped out from behind Stele's little ship. Brennen activated the crystace and concentrated on that head. Blazer bolts would arrive at light speed, the moment he saw them fired.

He deflected a shot. Then another. He stepped closer. Where was his backup?

There! . . . Circling behind the Netaian ship. "Drop your weapon!" Brennen shouted again, holding the Netaian's attention until the Carolinian could line him up. The Netaian fired once more, and then the Federate guard dropped him.

Brennen whipped around in time to see the saboteur stand close to the bulkhead and start firing. Once, twice, three times. A horrible sucking sound filled the landing bay.

Brennen sprinted across its surface toward the saboteur. *Come on*, he urged the Netaian covering him. *Show yourself.*

He felt him before he saw him, alongside a blocky charge unit. "Behind Unit Six," Brennen shouted as he readied the crystace. This Netaian must've seen what the crystace could do. He hesitated, probably waiting until Brennen looked distracted. That gave Brennen time to get between him and his partner. Then he turned his head aside, pretending inattention.

The Netaian fired. Brennen leaped aside. The Netaian's shot felled his compatriot. An instant later, another Carolinian got him.

Now Brennen felt the ominous wind. "Repair," he shouted. "Breach in panel . . . four-eight-six," he read off the prominently labeled bulkhead. The landing bay held enough air to keep everyone inside alive for several minutes, even with several small leaks; but minuscule holes could spread, open cracks, and destroy huge sections of the hull. Even the ship itself.

Brennen breathed slowly and deliberately.

Two maintenance men dashed up, steering a cart laden with metal sheets and flexible adhesives.

Leaning into the wind, Brennen strode back toward the inner airlock. Stele stood bare chested, with both hands in wrist restraints. On the deck lay several white packets, sections of cobalt blue fabric, and dozens of short, multicolored detonator wires. One security tech held out a packet to Brennen. "Smells like Glyphex," he said.

Brennen didn't recognize the substance. "Well done. Take it down to Armament for analysis." Then he met Stele's eyes again. "So you were the sacrificial victim," he said coldly. "Did they order you to suicide because of Veroh?"

Stele's shoulders shifted. He was probably trying to pull his wrists free.

Brennen would've felt thoroughly disgusted, except for one thing: Dorning Stele, a commanding officer, would yield up everything Brennen needed to know about those critical undersea bases.

"Take him to sick bay," Brennen ordered. "Suicide watch."

The security team led away its new prisoner. Now, Brennen realized, the fleet must disarm Netaia right down to its last metals manufacturing plant before Admiral Danton could consider a surrender offer.

He no longer dreaded the battle ahead.

CHAPTER 10

SURRENDER

con brio
with vigor

By the time Brennen rejoined Vanidar on the command deck, Netaia's navy had launched all remaining ships. The Citangelo quadrant's defenses fell back before a punishing main attack, but on the dark side at Claighbro and the Bruggcman Gap, fewer Federate ships faced a fierce defense.

An alarm clamored. The frame on *Horizon*'s dorsal status screen turned from blue to orange. A voice pealed in his ear, "Topside attack, *Horizon*! Twenty marks, point-zero zero heading, range nine-seven-nine. ETI two-point-four minutes."

As if piloting his own fighter, Brennen first checked the cruiser's energy shields. Vanidar barked, "Full assault power to topside shields and gunnery." As others relayed the order, Brennen touched an interlink control. "Delta Flight, this is *Horizon*. Major Kirzell, can your quadrant spare the flight to defend the cruiser?"

"Yessir," snapped a familiar voice in his ear.

Brennen clenched a fist at the screen. Withdrawing Delta Flight from the battle to subdue Citangelo might cost more downside lives than it would save up here. Even with the intelligence he'd just taken from Dorning Stele, the Netaians' unorthodox tactics would only worsen their punishment.

"General Caldwell," came a new voice from a small speaker. "Gamma group over sea base three. We're badly outnumbered. I need more high support."

Brennen exhaled sharply and checked a grid for the sea base's newly acquired specs. A glance at the master screens showed his atmospheric forces already spread thin.

Brennen switched his link to Vanidar. "Redeploy Delta Flight to support Gamma group?" He wanted permission for this one, with *Horizon* in danger. As Vanidar gave it and Brennen relayed it, the corporal between them glanced up from her terminal. Sweat glistened on her forehead. Vanidar checked screens, then reached for the interlink board again. "Generator, draw power from all systems but weapons and life support to maintain energy and particle shielding. Status reports every two minutes."

The bridge fell eerily silent. Blinded by the loss of external screens, Brennen held his emotions under control and waited for a possible impact.

A minute later the lights flared on again, and with them the screens and a cacophony from the speakers.

"Take the link, Corporal," ordered Vanidar. The ordnance and shield banks had drained but were rapidly recharging, and the Netaian attack group was peeling away . . . twelve, thirteen, fourteen remaining. Then the group changed course. Brennen blinked. They'd lost thirty percent, but they were coming back. *Their commanders should be spaced!*

In three more passes, the suicide attackers were annihilated. Then Brennen could attend again to the atmospheric battle. The main force finally had neutralized Citangelo; over Claighbro and the Gap bases, the tide was turning again, in his favor. Relaxing slightly, he prepared to finish an unpleasant job.

Crown Princess Carradee Angelo watched tri-D monitors built into a catfooted marble table in her cream-and-gold parlor. On the night side of the world, lightning storms swept the skies. By daylight, tall buildings stood empty, industrial areas evacuated to an unnatural holiday-week stillness—except for outsystem attack ships that dropped in tight formations, destroyed Citangelo's remaining depots and factories, and sped off-screen. Terror strangled the mighty city.

She watched alone. Servitors attended her daughters, and underground somewhere in Citangelo, her husband supervised a communications network. Along the marble wall that separated their living suites, several receiving units had been set on a credenza to let her listen in on his movements, but one by one their voices had gone silent.

This cannot be! she moaned. *For Veroh and its forsaken basium mines we pay with our homeland? I've already lost a sister.*

The thought of Firebird brought tears. Carradee had tried to see Firebird in her proper light, a wastling who should be honored to pour out her life so young, so much younger than Carradee would be when Iarlet was ready for rule—

Well, yes, Firebird had that nonconformist streak. Carradee tried to smile. She would forgive that streak, given Firebird's fiery doom at Veroh and the way Phoena had tormented her.

The hall door opened without warning. A page in Angelo scarlet slipped in and shut the massive wooden panel behind him.

Hastily Carradee wiped her face dry with a silken hand cloth from her skirt pocket. "Don't you still knock?" she asked wearily. "We are at war, but the world still turns, and the Disciplines help it to do so."

The boy was gulping his own tears. "Pardon, Highness. Please, Highness. Her Majesty is dying."

"Dying?" Carradee cried. She scrambled to her feet.

"She said you'd have only a few minutes, Highness. Please hurry!"

Netaia's only remaining defenses were wheel-borne when Brennen sent reports to Admiral Danton, to General Frankin at Veroh, and to Regional command, then ordered downside silence. Netaia still hadn't officially surrendered. More deep-space forces would soon arrive from Ituri to reinforce this battle group, and Danton was bringing the *Corona* insystem.

Only one duty remained, and then he'd be able to rest. When he shut his eyes, he saw flames and explosions. There would be nightmares tonight.

The sentry at the ship's vault sprang to attention when Brennen stopped at his desk. "It's all over but the talk," Brennen said, "we hope. Item twenty-six seventy-six, please."

Three minutes later he sat on his bunk, examining the parcel. Through a fresh layer of clear wrap, fabric showed cobalt blue, and two ruby stars gleamed like smoldering sparks. Firebird, wearing this uniform at their parting, had bitten back a plea for her people—he'd read it in the cry of her emotions. He knew she would offer almost anything to buy peace for Netaia. Revealing her survival had already been named as part of the price.

He broke the seal and drew out the uniform. From its collar he unclipped the ruby stars, then laid them on a bunkside niche. He made a mental note to find a presentation box and send the rest of the uniform back down with a courier.

Gratefully he began to undress. He'd pulled off one boot when his interlink buzzed. Groaning, he reached for the tab.

"DeepScan transmission for you, sir. Switching on." For a moment the link crackled. "General Caldwell?" came Admiral Danton's voice. "We've been discussing staff for occupation forces. Since you're rather an expert on these people, we were wondering if you could see yourself as lieutenant governor. I need a strong second, someone to do my tough jobs while I work diplomacy. Temporary position. After you clean house, the diplomatic corps can move in someone else. Regional told me to push you, anyway. Want the job?"

Unbelievable. Lieutenant governor? Less than a month ago, he'd had only a flight team to call his own, and that only between intelligence assignments. *"When the fast track accelerates,"* he'd been warned, *"hang on!"*

He spoke to the pickup. "Sir, I accept. I believe I'm slated to assist you when they officially surrender."

"I want their surrender before I go planetside. Major General Mafis will do the honors. He's Diplomat Corps. You speak 'on behalf of the fleet commander,' and when papers are signed planetside, have Mafis announce both our names."

"Good, sir."

"I'll make an official landing soon after. But if they refuse to surrender, I suppose you'll have to convince them they should give up rather than take further losses."

Another strike? "Yes, sir," Brennen muttered.

As he expected, his sleep was haunted by circular dreams of a battle that couldn't end until he'd found every piece of a tridimensional puzzle. The following morning, ship's time, an interlink transmission woke him. "Sir," said an unfamiliar voice, "Major General Mafis has been delayed. We are holding a transmission from downside. He requests you answer."

"I'll be there immediately."

The corporal saluted as he arrived on the bridge. Resting one hand on the back of Vanidar's command chair, Brennen signaled for activation of the main reception screen.

A huge man's image appeared . . . Devair Burkenhamn, he knew from Firebird's memories, as well as Count Dorning Stele's. Accessing Stele's mind had been like bathing in sewage—arrogant, sensual, stifling—but informative. The marshal waited calmly, but Brennen read defeat in his posture. Brennen came to attention and nodded to the corporal. For the first time in sixteen hours, *Horizon* broke downside silence. "Sir," he said curtly. "Field General Brennen Caldwell, speaking for . . ." Yes, he'd been authorized. ". . . the fleet commander."

"Thank you for responding, General." Burkenhamn reached beyond the projection field to retrieve a long scribepaper. "I am First Marshal of Netaian Forces Devair Burkenhamn, authorized by the Electorate to offer complete and unconditional surrender, as you have demanded. When and where will you meet with us to discuss terms?"

Brennen warmed to his unexpected role. This wealthy world lay like a wounded beast on its back, with its military forces wiped out, and—for the moment—under his personal control. He could demand any of several humiliating conciliatory gestures. He felt almost giddy. This sensation must be the pride that corrupted, creating conquerors. He'd been warned to control his ambition, but he'd never guessed it would tempt him this way. "Citangelo spaceport is central," he reminded Burkenhamn.

"It is in ruins."

"I'm sure it's still adequate to handle one shuttle. Clear a landing pad. Meet us there at ten hundred local time. We require a representative from your military, one for the Assembly, one for the Electorate, and, of course, the Crown." That was it, the best statement of strength he could make. "We wish to speak with the queen, sir."

"And we will require—"

Brennen shook his head, aware that he was gloating. "The surrendering party will be treated fairly, but today's terms are not yours to set. Your day will come again, I assure you. The Federacy is anxious to establish normal relations. However, if Netaia tries treachery again, you will pay a high price."

Burkenhamn bowed his head and vanished.

During his next break, Brennen examined the new emotion. He'd made solid command decisions, and personally gathered the intelligence that made victory possible. No other living person could've performed those interrogations so well. Still, he'd been warned never to depend ultimately on his own abilities, but only the One. According to all he'd sworn, he was only a highly effective servant, and even that wouldn't last. Someday—many years in the future if he was careful—his starbred abilities would wane. Before then, he must learn enough wisdom to go on serving well.

So he mustn't let pride enslave him to himself. His people lived as exiles, torn from their home world, because their ancestors had lusted to rule. Now, from Netaia's West Reach to Kierilay Island, from the Cheitt Peninsula southwest to the fertile DeTar plain, Netaians must bury their dead sons and daughters and rebuild their lives. Imagining Thyrica laid waste, he tried to banish all sense of self-congratulation as he checked Vanidar's shuttle arrangements.

He settled for a deep sense of personal victory.

Three hours later, a saucer-shaped Federate craft settled gently on an area of Citangelo spaceport that had been dozed clear of rubble. Watching out a viewport near the main lock, Brennen saw that the spaceport was in fact largely unusable. Its main tower and outbuildings had been blasted into twisted, tottering shapes of metal and stone. Five rocket craters were dishes of jagged boulders, while its main terminal was glassy slag, framed by the fractured wreckage of a high-speed maglev system.

Brennen reviewed his orders. He would personally notify the Angelo family of Firebird's survival. He must be firm but respectful with Siwann, though he'd have liked to force access and make her understand, through Firebird's memories, how cruelly she'd scarred her third daughter. Grimacing, he straightened his tunic.

Twenty Federate pilots marched off down the shuttle's ramp into escort formation. Major General Clohon Mafis, the diplomat, had arrived on *Horizon* shortly after Burkenhamn's transmission. He followed the guards, carrying a silver scribebook. An albino soldier of the Dengii race from the Whorl's rimward-north quadrant, he stood nearly

two meters tall, with white hair brushed sleek and a scarlet tunic thick
with decorations.

Brennen came last, finally surveying firsthand the damage that had
been wreaked under his command. Unlike Veroh, Netaia had taken no
nuclear shelling. Precision bombing of military targets had left the
city's civilian skyline, a curious blend of ornate and angular, virtually
untouched, though its sun shone a bleary orange through dust and
acrid smoke. Less than a quarter mile from the spaceport's skeletal
tower, children could play in undamaged gardens.

The approaching Netaian delegates, more than had been requested, eyed him curiously. Standing beside the heavily decorated
Mafis, he guessed he looked like an honor guard. Thyrian regs still pro-
hibited him from wearing the honors he'd earned.

Scanning the Netaian group, he abruptly realized Siwann wasn't
there. He did see Carradee, standing between two burly House
Guards. Both relieved and disappointed, and wondering what consequences must be demanded for Siwann's refusal, he stepped forward
with Mafis and let his epsilon shields diffuse. Intimidation by position,
his masters had taught him, could control a crowd without overtly
menacing anyone. This crowd, however, felt subdued already.

With a long pale hand, Mafis activated a recall pad on a cart brought
up by one guard, and he introduced himself and Caldwell to the Netaians. Marshal Burkenhamn faced Mafis as chief of his own delegation,
regarding Brennen with unconcealed curiosity.

Brennen guessed Burkenhamn knew the uniform. Firebird had recognized his star even as a cadet.

Mafis spoke. "The terms of your surrender are as follows. Martial
law will be enforced. The Regional council has appointed Admiral Lee
Danton of the Second Division to be your governor. His official landing shall take place at this time tomorrow. Governor Danton has se-
lected Field General Caldwell, Special Operations, as his lieutenant
governor pro tem." He motioned aside, indicating Brennen. "The Netaian Assembly, the Electorate, and the Crown shall hold authority
under the planetary governor. Netaia and both its buffer systems shall
remain demilitarized. The Planetary Navy is disbanded until further
word, as shall be the Assembly and the Electorate. You shall hold new
elections in one month."

Brennen spoke next, quoting lines Danton had written for him. "Because the Federacy has no provision for holding a conquered state, Netaia with her subjugate systems will constitute an independent Federate protectorate, roughly equivalent to the Veroh system." That ought to sting. "You will have no forces of your own, but we will not leave you defenseless." He felt their surprise. Apparently they wouldn't have protected Veroh if they'd taken it. Disgusted, he restored his shields.

Mafis continued. "This document, as we directed in our communiqué, shall be signed by four Netaian representatives. I summon you four to sign the instrument of surrender."

Three men . . . and Crown Princess Carradee . . . came to the cart, their steps raising small dust clouds. The men signed the recall pad first.

Firebird's oldest sister was surprisingly tall, in her late twenties, and still slightly heavy from her recent pregnancy. She held her head and shoulders regally. As Brennen passed her the stylus, he asked so only she could hear, "Was the queen unable to come as we directed, Highness?" He would know if she lied.

"I am now the queen, Excellency, Carradee Second."

Startled by her news and the way she'd addressed him, he eyed her more closely. Her pale gray eyes looked red and puffy; her hands worked nervously at the hem of her fitted brown jacket. "My—our mother, Her Majesty Queen Siwann, left Netaia in our hands two nights ago," she added. She signed neatly, without flourishes, and stepped away.

His private conference would be vastly different from the one he'd anticipated. He caught her elbow. "Your Majesty, I am sorry. May I speak with you alone?"

"Is this something our sister, Princess Phoena, cannot hear?" Carradee turned toward the watching Netaian delegation.

Firebird had loved and trusted Carradee. He resolved to be tactful. Phoena, however, would be a hostile witness. Plainly dressed for once, she glowered over the proceedings.

Trying to manage the throne, was she? Maybe Phoena already was addicted to that conqueror's pride. "Alone, Majesty," he whispered. "For a moment. I mean you no harm. I have news for you to hear first."

Carradee nodded. They walked together through the circle of Federate pilots, away from the shuttle toward the edge of the bulldozed area, followed at a discreet distance by Carradee's House Guards and one uniformed Federate. Back at center stage, General Mafis began to address the crowd and media representatives. He'd written an instructive speech for the occasion, and Brennen had asked him to take his time about finishing.

CHAPTER 11

MAXSEC

tempo I
at original tempo

As Mafis's voice faded, Brennen cleared his shields again. "How did your mother die?"

Grief and anxiety blurred Carradee's mental state. "She took poison, sir, when it became evident to her that she had led us to a dishonorable defeat."

"Somnus?"

"Yes," she said bleakly. "In no other way could she save her honor and satisfy the Powers."

That gave him his opening. "We've dealt with that poison before, Your Majesty." He drew the tiny presentation box from a pocket of his belt and handed it to her. Suspicious, she held it at a graceful arm's length. "Nothing deadly, madam." He took it back, opened its lid, and returned it into her hand. Ten clear, marquis-cut rubies flashed in the morning light.

As she examined them, he studied her face. Men might kill for Phoena, but Carradee's attractiveness was subtle, touched with humility at the eyes and sadness at the mouth. She would be exactly the kind of queen Netaia needed, if she could hold on to power through these transition years.

Carradee eyed the goldwork on the back of one star, then replaced it on the box's velvette liner. "These are Netaian rank stars, General, as you surely know. Why are they in your possession?"

"They belonged to your sister Lady Firebird." He watched as his verbal missile exploded. Carradee pulsed with grieved dismay, then delight, then confusion.

She gripped the box. "We were told she'd been killed in action, but if that were true, these would have been destroyed."

"She is alive, Majesty."

For a compassionate instant, she let herself smile, but then she drew the inescapable conclusion. Firebird, now her subject, would be a grave concern. "Where is she, General? How is she being treated? Was she . . ." Her already pale cheeks lost all color. ". . . interrogated?"

Brennen glanced toward the crowd. Mafis droned on. He needn't hurry with Carradee. "She is under protective custody, at Regional command on Tallis." A single intercept fighter swept low over the sky-line, following the Etlason River toward its midtown confluence with the Tiggaree. "I assure you, she is well treated. But, yes, as a military prisoner, naturally she was interrogated. It was humanely done."

He felt panic replace her concern.

"Your Majesty, that is not the only reason why we were able to take Netaia without prolonged warfare and great loss of life. But may I suggest that many of your people were saved by her capture, and Count Stele's."

She wouldn't be diverted. "She was taken at Veroh, then?"

He related Firebird's suicide attempts and how they'd been thwarted, then her capture and questioning, without mentioning his own role. He'd need to be able to work with Carradee.

She frowned, still plainly displeased with Firebird for revealing vital information.

He asked, "Have you not heard of Ehretan mind access?"

"What is that?"

"I'll show you." She was watching his eyes, and he trapped her easily. She quailed and stepped back, and then, caught, she stood blinking. He probed only enough to confirm that Siwann had truly died and wasn't in hiding. Carradee had stood at her side at the last, silently sorrowing, terrified of the future.

He released her, catching her hand to steady her while she regained her balance. "That is very simple access. Your sister's memory was taken much deeper. I assure you, she did not cooperate."

The line of her lips became hard. "Those who did so should be punished."

He who did so, Brennen observed wryly, *will never recover*. "You'd rather hear that she had been tortured for information?"

Carradee stepped back and studied the dusty ground. When after a minute she spoke again, her words came in a toneless voice. "We would rather have gone on believing that Firebird died well, and is now beyond all of the suffering life dealt her. You and your kind are dangerous, Excellency. You surely will be a powerful lieutenant governor."

He wished he could. "I'll only oversee the establishment of our military governorship and the peacekeeping forces. We Sentinels are allowed to use those abilities only under a few circumstances. You'll see little of them now. The Federacy wishes to help your forces keep order, in the best interests of all concerned."

"Perhaps you mean, 'restore' order."

He detected a grudging respect as she closed her hand around the little box, snapping it shut.

"Many will be glad to hear that Firebird survived," the new queen went on. "She was popular among the people. We . . . I, too, wish her the best. However, the Electorate will be deeply concerned. We do not allow extraneous heirs, sir."

That again! "And your sister Phoena will be unhappy, I think."

Her gray eyes widened.

"We learned many things from Lady Firebird's mind," he said, "on several levels."

Carradee glanced over her shoulder. Phoena stood at the edge of the circle of guards, openly ignoring Mafis's call for unity, still watching Brennen confer with her sister.

Carradee turned back to him. "Be that as it may, General, she must know. I will tell her."

"Of course. Majesty, don't be afraid to contact me if you need to work with the Federacy. You've just been handed an awesome responsibility."

"Thank you," she said, "but that will not be necessary."

He honestly wanted to help her, but they must both follow protocol. As they walked silently back toward the circle, Mafis finished his discourse. Two guards let them through the cordon directly beside Princess Phoena.

"Good morning, Your Highness." Brennen gave Phoena a slight nod.

She raised one eyebrow, coldly looked him up and down, and then turned away.

Exactly as Firebird remembered her . . .

Brennen bowed toward Carradee Second and left them to settle their family affairs.

On Firebird's fifth day on Tallis IV, Captain Ellet Kinsman arrived early at the minimum-security suite where they'd locked her away for safekeeping. Its bedroom and anteroom were small but comfortable, with a magnificent view of Tallis's capital city, Castille. Sitting at a two-seat servo table in one corner of her anteroom, Firebird pulled a pale green audio rod from the player she'd requested. Ellet had kept her under a full news blackout. Determined to stay mentally active, she'd taken up a new field of study: Federate music.

Ellet's midnight blue tunic looked crisper than usual, and Firebird spotted thin lines of brown on her eyelids. Something was up.

"What was that?" Ellet nodded toward the rod.

"A Luxian art song." Firebird hoped Ellet would feel her amusement. The blackout had, at least, forced her deep anguish to lie down and rest. "It came with that assortment from the tower library yesterday morning. The melodies are gorgeous, but the harmony has me baffled." She set the rod back into its case. "Why are you early?"

"You have a meeting with the Regional council uplevel in half an hour. Just an introduction, I believe. They have little time to waste."

"Regional council?" This was a shock. Why would they bother with her now? Surely they'd won their war.

Ellet turned back to the door. "Half an hour."

The tower, where both had been assigned security rooms, was called MaxSec. Ellet had explained that stood for Maximum Security. Eighty stories tall, it was a self-contained fortress, with offices, laboratories, security apartments, and shops, and a sec system developed by the finest minds in the Federacy. Escape would've been impossible. Firebird had examined the broad, gridded window and had even given it a suspicious touch the moment Ellet left her alone. The stun pulse had left her arm limp for an hour. Within a day she'd learned to identify several classes of local aircraft. Traffic flowed steadily in and out of a parking bay above her.

Why the council, today?

News from the war, maybe. *It's over*, she guessed. *What's left of my home?*

Half an hour later, she preceded Ellet from the security lift into a long, lofty chamber. The pale gray ceiling rose three stories, vaulted by pure white stone arches. Air moved freely. They crossed an expanse of silver-flecked stone below empty spectator galleries, then ascended three wide stairs onto a platform large enough to hold a full choral orchestra.

Behind a long, curving table sat the ruling septumvirate of this half of the Federate Whorl. Three civilians sat at the table's right side. One had rough brown skin and sat in a mobility chair, bent nearly double by his hunched back. The white-robed woman at center looked oldest. To her left sat two men and a woman in military uniforms. A blank panel hung over their heads, probably a translation screen.

Ellet stepped forward. "Members of the council, I present to you First Major Lady Firebird Angelo of the Netaia systems."

Firebird made the formal half bow Ellet had suggested, but she felt awkward wearing gray shipboards. This was a full-dress occasion, with people who might eventually set her free.

The robed woman stood. "Good afternoon, Captain Kinsman. Lady Firebird, you are welcome on Tallis. I trust you have been treated well?"

"Yes. Thank you, Your Honor."

"I am Tierna Coll, formerly of the Elysia system. May I introduce Admiral Madden of Caroli, Admiral Baron Fiersson of Luxia, General Voers of Bishda." As she continued, she turned to indicate the civilians on her other side. "Mister Lithib of Oquassa, Madam Kernoweg of Lenguad, and Doctor Gage of Deng."

Firebird repeated her bow. *Coll, Madden, Fiersson, Voers,* she repeated silently. *Lithib, and . . . oh, squill.*

"Our news must be conveyed with sympathy," said Tierna Coll. "First, Netaia has surrendered to Federate forces."

Firebird bowed her head.

"We received that word late yesterday." Tierna Coll's voice was pleasant and commanding, like that of a well-trained alto. "The second news came only an hour ago. Your mother has died, Lady Firebird. She committed suicide. We are sorry."

"Thank you, Your Honor." Firebird couldn't summon up any other reaction. Her emotions seemed dead. Given the surrender and Netaia's traditions, this didn't really surprise her.

Admiral Madden, second from the left, seemed to see her awkwardness. He stopped stroking his blond beard and spread his elbows on the table. "We've been advised that the survival of our patrol holding Veroh resulted in part from a warning you gave. I am certain you have been thanked, but please let us add our sincere gratitude."

She made another small, polite bow. *Madden of Caroli*, she reminded herself. Caroli, Veroh's governing world, could afford magnanimity now.

Madam Kernoweg sat as straight as any military officer, with a strong brow ridge and close-cropped hair. "We have hoped for some time that your home world would covenant to the Federacy, Lady Firebird. Poorer worlds would benefit from its resources. Wealthier systems would carry lighter assessment burdens, while Netaia itself would reap significant rewards. This council has ordered our forces to demonstrate tact and respect in dealing with your government."

Firebird inclined her head, though she doubted Madam Kernoweg would get any positive result if the Federacy ever caved to the Netaian Electorate. Any show of weakness would only encourage defiance. Hadn't they learned that at Veroh?

At Tierna Coll's side, General Voers stood. Gold stars sparkled under the Federate slash on the breast of his coal black uniform. "Lady Firebird, we have before us a report submitted by Field General Caldwell of Special Operations concerning your government's weapons research. The . . . 'Cleary/D'Stang/Parkai Project,' " he read off his recessed terminal. "Is this a special concern of your family, Your Highness?"

Could she assume Brennen had survived another battle to submit that report? No. He would've sent it from Veroh. She restrained her urge to correct Voers' improper address and answered his question. "Princess Phoena sponsored that research, Your Honor."

"It also was supported by the late queen's electoral council, was it not?"

"Yes, sir."

"You were, I understand, a member of that body?"

"Yes, General Voers. An honorary member," she explained, "but with voting rights."

"General Caldwell's report states that you did not support the research. Why not?"

How could she answer without denigrating her family?—which she mustn't do, not here. "Your Honors, I have little official status on Netaia, and I am not authorized to speak for any of its governing bodies. But for myself, I must express my regret for this situation. I am a career military officer by choice, but I was born to the Electorate. I have . . . reservations about some of its decisions." In this bright, alien environment, even those carefully chosen words sounded like treason. If the Powers truly existed, if there actually was life after death, she might spend all eternity in the Dark that Cleanses.

"My lady." Mister Lithib's low, gasping voice seemed appropriate to his deformities. "This report indicates that you might be willing to consider—consider, I say—making a home among Federate peoples. We would find that heartening, after what you've endured. Would you confirm that report?"

Distracted by his appearance, Firebird forgot to worry about her eternal destiny. Lithib's dark, sad eyes were set unnaturally wide. On Netaia, severely deformed newborns were humanely put down; yet this man had risen to interstellar authority. She must rethink still more of Netaia's laws and traditions. "The standard," she said, "by which I've been taught to judge any policy has been, 'Is it good for the Electorate?' Your broader standards are hard for me to grasp." *Especially showing the Netaian regime respect!* "I do not understand how so many peoples can coexist as you claim. But I would like to believe it.

"And yes, I have been treated well here. I can consider remaining. It is difficult, though, to consider forsaking my home and my people."

Voers raised one eyebrow and frowned. She flinched, wondering how she'd offended him.

Tierna Coll spoke again. "That is a decision you need not face for some weeks. The public files of the MaxSec library will remain at your disposal, as will governmental newscans issued to Captain Kinsman, when she has finished reading them." She glanced down at Ellet, who nodded.

"Thank you," Firebird exclaimed.

Tierna Coll barely smiled. "Eventually, we hope to be able to accord you more freedom of information and movement without jeopardizing your safety. Please bear with our protective custody for a time."

Some inflection in Tierna Coll's voice, maybe her use of the royal "we," reminded Firebird suddenly of Siwann. Apprehensively she waited for the deep, dull chest-ache of grief that she always felt when remembering Corey.

It didn't come. She felt only relief tinged with regret, and amazement at having survived her mother after all.

"Lady Firebird, we thank you." Tierna Coll inclined her head.

Firebird imitated the gesture. Ellet touched her arm and led her away.

CHAPTER 12

PROTECTORATE

l'istesso tempo
although the meter changes, the beat remains
the same

Citangelo's day burned out in a sunset still fiery from atmospheric dust. Inside his office on the newly constructed occupation base, Brennen watched a transport decelerate toward the new spaceport north of a rebuilt control tower and new Memorial Gate. It returned Federate goods and gilds for a load of Netaian exports. He wondered who'd bought those first exports—exotic produces, fine arts, military souvenirs.

He turned back to his bluescreen. Like most of his office furnishings, the viewer had come from Caroli. Federate engineers had built the base out of military-depot rubble. Now it was a particle-shielded foothold on this conquered world. His wall shelves held an array of Thyrian pieces—pseudo-Ehretan reproductions, multicolored seashells, holo cubes that depicted Thyrica's vast western rain forest—none of them his own, but furnished to provide a Federate dignity to match the native aristocracy.

That aristocracy's tentacles were everywhere. It had ruled and still controlled manufacturing, research, and commerce, patronized music and the other arts, and had ordered the military. The nobles ruled as tyrannical benefactors, but also, to his distaste, as priests. They represented the nine Powers to their people.

He'd tried to untangle that concept of Powers. He'd thought they were a supernatural pantheon, and evidently they were still considered godlike, but during the isolated years of Six-alpha's space storms, the Netaians' loyalty to their gods had been sublimated into loyalty to the state. Perfect citizenship became its graceless religion. Conformity to the expected Charities and the written Disciplines bought a soul's way to paradise, the afterlife being the only truly "religious" aspect that remained in their religion. If a Netaian didn't make the minimum offerings, the financial base for their welfare system, or keep those laws correctly, a terrifying purgatory awaited.

So for three centuries, the semi-deified nobles had controlled almost every public function. Enforcement Corps officers imposed harsh penalties even for minor violations—recently, passing "seditious" information about offplanet trade had resulted in imprisonment for one offender and a reduction to servitor status for his children. The system still smacked of an older martial law. Governor Danton had decided quickly that disenfranchising the noble class would lead to chaos, so the Electorate had been given back the right to meet, under Federate supervision.

Brennen leaned away from his desk, refusing to sink into self-righteousness. His people had their own dark history. His first genetically altered ancestors had tried to seize power from their nongifted elders. The older generation had fought back. Family by family, they destroyed each other and their world. One priestly family fled rather than fight, taking fifty-one orphaned starbred children onboard.

Some contemporary Sentinels called that faithful remnant's survival a proof that in time, the Eternal Speaker would reveal himself openly again, in a prophesied messenger who would bridge the chasm to eternal peace for all of flawed humankind, on every world.

The prophecy interested Brennen keenly and personally. This messenger, this Word to Come, was to rise from a small Ehretan family that had been known as Carabohd, "honorably called."

If you will it, Holy One.

Netaia needed such a messenger. Firebird needed that peace. He couldn't give it, though. She must find it herself.

Or you must find her. Please.

He adjusted his bluescreen's brightness and checked his day's agenda. Two items remained. A man waited in the hall outside, with his secretary, another aristocrat for scan evaluation. It would be merely a surface emotional check. Brennen had avoided using deep access except in extreme cases.

Already he'd examined the former marshals and several electors. Unanimously, they longed to throw off Federate rule. Meanwhile the low-common class, held down by that penal system, itched to rise against the electors. The high-common majority was caught between and desperate for peace. Most lived in physical comfort, content to endure their less oppressive lack of rights because their co-opted religion and rewritten history had taught them to dread civil chaos. Thanks to those historic invaders and Sabba Six-alpha, even the elected Assembly deferred to the Electorate.

Civil war—the worst threat they feared—was distinctly possible, with so much unrest among low commoners with little to lose. Netaia needed several calm years to begin to see the Federacy as an ally and a stabilizing factor, to ease power away from the nobility, to equalize the distribution of resources.

High-common and noble Netaians cherished their independence—he'd heard some of the traditional stories and songs, listening fascinated while performers' fierce nationalistic pride radiated through his downed shields.

But though the Federacy offered stability, it never would stifle independence. Every Federate cultural unit, whether multiplanetary or single-continent, kept its local government and was represented in a Regional senate. His home world answered to Tallis, but Tallis rarely influenced Thyrica's day-to-day affairs. Personal and media contact with other peoples, such as the aristocratic Luxians, would demonstrate this to the Netaians, if the Federacy could bring peace and two-way communication.

That, he reminded himself grimly, was how his disobedient ancestors had justified creating telepathy. They'd hoped unrestrained communication would create complete understanding.

They'd forgotten greed. *Thank you for covering our faults, Holy Father and Speaker. Hasten the day when you will remove them.*

He pressed his touchboard to signal his readiness, and then he dropped all epsilon static, the better to read his subject.

Count Tel Tellai stepped into the office's far end. The count's small size and soft features made him look even younger than his eighteen Netaian years, which made him twenty-one, Federate. He wore the blue sash of office—father deceased only last year, according to the file glowing on Brennen's bluescreen—extensive agricultural lands, children's hospital. Otherwise dressed hat to heels in black, Tellai walked with measured steps. His antipathy created a nagging unease in Brennen's unshielded senses. "Please take a chair, Count Tellai."

Seated, Tellai looked slightly taller. He brushed dust from velvette trousers and pulled off his narrow-brimmed, fashionable hat. Short, fine boned, and effeminate, Tellai looked the consummate aristocrat.

Projecting the allowable calming assurance, Brennen began. "The purpose of this interview is simple, sir. We need to know your underlying attitude toward the Federacy. Naturally you wish us elsewhere, but for the present we must work together for the good of your people."

He'd repeated the lines several times already and recorded his subjects' responses. Here in private, he could scan conclusively. He could also place a subject under voice command if any tried to attack him.

Tellai didn't seem the attacking sort. Brennen pulled a stylus from his cuff and held it lightly between his hands. "Can you recall, briefly, your feelings toward the Federacy before this crisis set us against each other? Be honest, please. You are in no danger if you tell the truth, even unpleasant truth, but I can recognize deception."

Tellai's long, dark lashes fell closed, and Brennen was startled by a sudden resemblance to Firebird. Was there—? He glanced at his screen and touched for additional data. Yes, the connection was close. Tellai was her second cousin.

The count took several breaths. "I thought very little of the Federacy, Your Excellency. I had my lands to administer; I have been re-landscaping my primary residence . . ."

Brennen focused not on the words but on Tellai's underlying emotion. He caught a brief rise of regret, washed out by resentment. Not so different from the others, and Brennen didn't sense the inner strength that might've made him dangerous—unlike the queen's sister.

He'd heard rumors that Phoena stood behind most of Danton's electoral troubles. For the second time, Brennen toyed with the idea of suggesting to Carradee that she ask Phoena to leave off her agitating, leave Citangelo for a while, take a long vacation.

Tellai finished speaking and sat still, blankly apprehensive. Brennen rested his elbows on the desk and said, "In five years, the Netaian systems will be eligible to rise from this occupied protectorate status to full Federate covenance, probably including representation on the Regional council. That covenance would be tremendously beneficial to your defenses and your economy. Free trade would take Netaian goods to many other systems and return substantial wealth to a growing trade class. Assuming for the moment that this came to pass, how would you envision your role in such a society?''

Tellai's slender fingers curled around the hat brim in his lap. ''Never in our history has such a thing happened, sir, and it never, never will.''

Brennen had to admire the young dandy's sincerity, though fear of how Brennen might retaliate wept in both their minds.

This was no ringleader.

Restoring his epsilon shielding, Brennen shifted his stylus to a writing grip. ''Thank you, sir. You may go.''

Tellai blinked, opened his mouth—shut it—then scurried to the door. Brennen pressed the key to let him out, then made a line of shorthand notes.

The return of emotional silence felt coolly quiet, but he knew it wouldn't stay pleasant. Since Veroh, solitary spells had gnawed at him. This was the price of having touched absolute connaturality without bonding it, without even telling her how powerfully she attracted him. Blessed Word to Come, how would he say that?

Not as a lord over her people! As he'd created and amended his administrative duties, the conqueror's pride had almost lost its ability to tempt him. The better he knew the conquered Netains, the more he empathized with most of them.

A message remained on his Crown channel, saved for day's end and a possible follow-up. Carradee Second might reign chiefly as figurehead and standard bearer, but the nobles deferred to her so insistently—in public—that Danton hadn't ordered her to appear for an interview, nor even her troublesome sister Phoena. Danton meant to comply with Regional's orders to show the Crown respect. That would make occupation a tightrope walk, but eventually, it might shift the nobles' attitudes. In three standard years, occupation-moderated free elections, open to all four social classes, would determine whether Netaia joined the Federacy.

He called up Carradee's message. His bluescreen cleared, then filled with pale letters.

Lieutenant Governor Caldwell, greetings.

You must be aware by now of our tradition of heir limitation. For the present we are willing to accept the Federacy's injunction outlawing the issuance of any new geis.

However, previous to the establishment of your Protectorate, younger scions of noble houses often were granted expensive education and training and the wherewithal to make for themselves a most honorable end. This was considered an investment in the eternal nobility of our homeland.

Our sister Lady Firebird accepted such gifts, but took gross advantage of our investment and reportedly lives now under Federate protection. We and our Electorate deem it reasonable to request that the Federacy repay the house of Angelo the following expenses incurred anticipating her contribution to the homeland's glory, which apparently were squandered. . . .

Brennen gaped. Siwann's electors, still meeting as Carradee's, meant to bill the Federacy for three years of Academy education, all jet and laser-ion fuel thereby consumed, uniform allowance including jeweled rank insignia, and a thirty-million-gild tagwing fightercraft?

Half smiling at the absurdity, he stretched his legs. Federate policy respected others' viewpoints. To the Electorate, the request might seem appropriate.

He checked her request against the governor's reparations budget and decided to defer the matter to Danton, the diplomat. Danton might make a token payment for the sake of Carradee's good feelings. Brennen couldn't have it intimated that he'd asked the Federacy to buy Firebird's freedom.

He would, though. He'd give her all he owned. His life, his hand for protection, his future . . .

But would she take freedom, or forgiveness, as a gift? Did she even know what they meant? Did any Netaian, raised in this merciless mindset? He corralled his emotions and thrust them back down.

The message's postscript astonished him. The tone changed, implying a different author, and suggested the Federacy reduce Firebird to servitor status to pay that debt herself.

Unquestionably Phoena's touch.

He inserted "Can you believe this? See budget 12-C" after the postscript and keyed it onto Danton's agenda for the following morning. Then he shut down his viewer and waved off room lights. Evening was his, to settle another matter. Rumor had just reached him that Vultor Korda, whom he remembered with little respect, lingered in Citangelo. On his own time, he would start a different kind of investigation, to satisfy himself . . . and the Code of Exile that governed the starbred.

Sweating from a packing frenzy, Vultor Korda stowed his last load into a skimmer the electors had given him for his services. "Cheap slugs," he muttered as he buried a roll of Federate gilds in the toe of one shoe. "You could've afforded air transport, but, ah, no, save a little credit for Nella Cleary's lab work."

Exhaust from traffic below his apartment block congealed in chill air. Korda slammed the side trunk and ran back up to his studio for a last plunge into cabinets. Breathing hard, he paused in the doorway. He couldn't see his rented furniture anymore. It lay buried under a jumble of discarded belongings.

"Caldwell," he fumed. At least Phoena had come to warn him. "Why did they have to send that eight-pointed goody-boots?"

"Not a friend of yours?" Phoena lounged in the single unladen chair.

"Not exactly." He reached for a package of jelly wafers. It slipped out of his hand onto the yellow tile floor. One end burst, splotching a chair with purple confection.

From all others at Sentinel College, Korda had hidden his fantasies of power, biding his time. Then one day, by chance, he'd met Brennen Caldwell—already a fully vested Sentinel, at an age when Korda had only begun epsilon-turn training. The next day Korda had been called for reevaluation.

"Question of inappropriate ambition" had been the examiners' verdict, and Korda had been expelled, sentenced to report every tenday Thyrian *dekia* to be treated with epsilon-blocking drugs, to keep him from misusing what skills he'd already learned.

Scorch Caldwell and his ninety-seven harmonics!

Temporary blocking drugs, fortunately. Only radical cerebral surgery could disable the ayin, the genetically engineered complex of brain regions where a starbred's power rose. After five years of intolerable drug treatment, he'd fled. They would cut him or kill him if they caught him now, but his abilities had returned. Korda lived without static shields. That kept him attuned to all that transpired around him and saved his energy for occasional bursts of shallow access (he'd never mastered voice-command), without distracting his spirit from the destiny he still pursued. It wasn't for nothing that common people shuddered at the fate of lost Ehret. Knowledge still equaled power.

Indolently Phoena peeled a pale green banam fruit. "It sounds as though you love him the way I respect my young sister. I wish there were a way to get to Tallis. I'd love to show her she can't escape her duty to the Electorate."

"Do you mean that?" Korda stopped midfloor and stared into Phoena's hard eyes. He felt her hatred, and yes, she would pay almost any price to see her sister obey her geis order. "Highness, I could get one of your agents offplanet easily, if you have a suggestible acquaintance on the Interplanetary Travel Committee."

"I have several men and women in key places." She wriggled her shoulders and gave him a sweet smile he read as very false. "You'd do it for me, Korda?"

"When the time comes, give me the name of your ITC contact. He'll see a face other than your agent's, no matter who he expects."

She pursed her lips. "You'd go too, of course. To Tallis."

Korda blinked. That had *not* been his idea. "Not to a Federate world," he said flatly. "Sentinels aren't kind to informers."

"You're not an informer." Phoena raised one eyebrow. "You're a turncoat."

He tried not to sneer. "In your service, Highness."

She laughed. "Good. Then you're now my agent. You could get to her, when others couldn't."

He considered. It would be delicious if he, a mere trainee, could slip past whatever Sentinel they'd told to guard Firebird. Surely they'd use a Sentinel.

But it would be terribly dangerous. "What about you, Highness? Don't you want to see it done? Correctly?" With a high-ranking escort like Phoena, it would be easier—safer—to slip through channels to his former student . . . and escape.

Phoena buffed her nails on one sleeve. "I do, but I cannot leave

Netaia. I'll find another to keep an eye on you, someone with a particular . . ."

She was always doing that, trailing off before he could catch her thought. He dropped onto a hassock. "Grudge?" he prompted. "Against Firebird?"

"Actually, no." She smiled with one side of her mouth. "Perhaps it would shake your Sentinel compatriot in our lieutenant governor's office if we sent someone Caldwell thinks he's beaten. That could give us a psychological victory."

Korda frowned, shaking his head. "Caldwell has been bedimmed careful. He hasn't 'beaten' anyone yet that I've heard of."

"He'll have to, fairly soon," Phoena said placidly. "I have several men working quietly to get rid of that occupation base. The first time one of my men is caught, we'll move quickly. Can you get one more man offplanet?" she pressed.

"Highness," he said with a mock-deferential nod, "if you'll arrange my groundwork, yes. I can. I also want hazardous duty pay and privileges."

"Naturally." She glanced at the door. "You'd better leave. Leave the mess, too. His Excellency will probably come looking for you."

Korda swept out an arm and motioned her to precede him outside.

She strolled toward a servo instead. "No, I want to make calls without using a palace line. This suits me perfectly. Good-bye, Korda. We understand each other. I'll contact you at the house in Gorman when the time is right."

He dashed back outdoors and plunged the skimmer into traffic, steering toward the northerly highway.

Alone on her anteroom's tattered green lounger, Firebird grieved over a Federate newscan. Netaian networks weren't linked to any Tallan informational agency, so all her news came from this unsympathetic source.

Her own knowledge had helped engineer a disaster. A tear trickled toward her chin as she read the grim roster of destroyed facilities. She'd trained at Sitree, near the equator, vacationed at frozen Arctica, refueled at most of the other sites, and these very memories had given Brennen's forces their targets. Citangelo, Claighbro, Dunquin . . .

She stopped and read the long list again, frowning. Had she missed something?

No, it wasn't on the list: Hunter Height, just over 2,000K north by northwest of Citangelo, where the Aerie Mountains joined the Flenings, was one of her family's vacation homes and a fortified last-effort retreat. The ancient stone house sat over a tunnel complex on a granite mountainside, overlooking its own airstrip. It wasn't listed.

She sat upright, making the lounger creak. So her resistance hadn't been completely in vain. By focusing on other sites, she'd hidden one minor air base from Brennen.

Much good it had done.

Centered atop the glimmering page was a row of images: Brennen, Carradee, Siwann, a man named Lee Danton, and . . . Dorning Stele? She skimmed the account for his name. He'd been captured trying to sabotage the Federate command ship under the pretense of surrendering. Then, imprisoned and interrogated.

She thought she could guess who'd done the questioning.

The article credited Stele's extensive knowledge of Netaian facilities with providing the key for a quick victory.

Firebird threw back her head and laughed. Stele deserved this! The article didn't state where he'd been sent, but she found deep satisfaction in imagining him on board a Federate cruiser, locked into a tiny holding cell, wearing servitor's coveralls.

She touched Siwann's likeness more soberly, shaking her head. She'd never see her mother again. Siwann was dead by her own hand, killed by her own conscience, for the ruin she'd brought to her homeland. She ought to offer a prayer. *Powers grant you bliss, Majesty. Mother.*

Firebird rescrolled the newscan. Evidently Phoena, co-instigator of the invasion, hadn't suffered similar remorse.

But Carradee . . .

An odd thought struck Firebird. Staring out the window, she let it run its course. By tradition, Siwann should've eventually suicided once she judged her heiress fit to rule. Firebird had always suspected Siwann was expending little effort preparing Carradee. Siwann had intended to hold power for many more years. Now, gentle Carrie was thrust into a situation she couldn't control. Electors would be jockeying around her for the power the Federacy had already given back, in part.

Poor Carrie.

A week later, a lumpy packet arrived return-marked Citangelo. It had passed the censors unopened and was still slightly rolled from traveling in a message tube. A brown ID tape had been mounted on one corner. Below that, the packet was lettered, Personal. Security I.

Trembling, she carried it to her inner room, sat down on the edge of her narrow bed, and slit the seal. Inside she found three sheets of scribepaper and a scanbook cartridge. One paper was tightly folded and heatsealed, addressed in Phoena's flowery script. Another, unsealed, she recognized as Carradee's writing.

The other sheet was covered with an unfamiliar masculine hand. Though deeply surprised, she chuckled when she saw the formal letterhead atop the page. Brennen had learned quickly how to impress Netaians. It read:

Office of the Lieutenant Governor
Citangelo
Netaian Protectorate Systems

Mari—
There is a lull in affairs today. Please believe that I've written at the first available moment. My title is "Lieutenant to Governor Danton"—actually, I am his bodyguard, chief of enforcement, and mentor. We are impressing people with our knowledge. Despite their isolationism, they're good people, and some are truly noble.

We've met with hostility, but attitudes seem to be softening as Assembly elections approach (I've applied for transfer back to Tallis immediately afterward).

I had words yesterday with both your sisters. The palace is full of your presence. I spoke briefly with an elderly butler or some such servant, who spoke of you as I walked through the portrait gallery. He gave the impression that you were respected on Netaia. Is that part of your problem with Phoena?

Firebird blinked at the gray inner wall. In fact, it was—particularly after the late Baron Parkai had commented within hearing of both of them that "it was a shame about the birth order in that family." Phoena had scarcely said a civil word to her since that day years ago.

I may not be able to communicate again, and I didn't feel it was wise to prepare a personal recording. For the same reasons, don't answer this letter. Expense aside, I don't entirely trust the messenger service, even with an ID tape for security.

The cartridge should answer most of your questions.

Yours,

B.

P.S. The portrait is lovely.

Carradee's message was warm, if officious. She asked after Firebird's treatment, warned her to maintain her dignity, and reminded her to avoid the low-born. She promised "appropriate" clothing to follow. Phoena came directly to the point:

Firebird:

So you have betrayed us all. If I ever see you again, I shall personally remove you from the succession.

Phoena Irina Eschelle Angelo

Another postscript had been added in Brennen's hand, despite the heatseal on Phoena's paper:

Not if I have anything to say about it. I apologize for even including this, but it's important for you to know exactly how you stand with her. If it's any comfort, she would do the same for me.

B.

Shaking in her excitement, Firebird loaded the cartridge and scrolled down its table of contents. It contained dozens of news stories, all citing Netaian sources. They covered the Federate invasion and its aftermath, public reaction to occupation and other current topics . . . and she spotted a lengthy series on the Angelo family, with Siwann given a substantial tribute.

This should answer her questions, all right. She touched up the much shorter entry, "Captured at Veroh."

Her own commissioning portrait appeared on the viewer. She stared, wondering how she ever could've looked that self-assured. The entry itself was unemotional: the burned tagwing, the assumption of death, the Federate revelation. It didn't mention, didn't even suggest, her interrogation. After several readings, she decided that the entry's tone was mildly positive, which was more than she'd dared hope.

Exhaling with deep relief, she scrolled again and was amused to find an entry titled, "Reconsidering the Powers."

"Thank you, Brennen," she whispered up at her gridded window. This was truly a treasure.

She read and reread the personal letters as daylight faded, startled by the change in her feelings toward Brennen Caldwell. He'd stolen her destiny. He'd humiliated her and made her an exile, but only as his orders demanded. Since then, he'd acted with almost unconscionable mercy. He'd taken the trouble and expense to send news from her beloved home world, and he'd written, "They are good people." For that alone, she could almost call him a friend.

What had taken him to the palace? Had he advised Carradee, addressed the electors, or attended a social function?

Carradee's promised parcel arrived within a day, and in it a treasure: her clairsa, padded with clothing and detuned for travel. She caressed the intricate carvings in the leta-wood upper arch as though greeting a lost friend, and then set about restoring the tuning.

When Ellet brought the latest pocketful of aging Tallan newscans, Firebird offered a short concert. "I only play for enjoyment these days." She supported the long, thin, arched triangle in her lap with her left hand. "Not in public anymore."

Ellet smiled tolerantly. "I have a brother who plays a similar instrument."

Firebird ran her index finger along the strings, tweaked the tuning, then played a rolling arpeggio to warm her hands. A tinkling, resonant major chord climbed the ladder of strings in two swift strokes and hung in the air while metal strings rang out. She damped them before the chord faded away.

Crossing her ankles under the stool and leaning one corner of the small harp on her shoulder, she freed both hands and spun off a rollicking dance tune, the kind of music a young aristocrat learned as part of her well-rounded education.

"More," Ellet insisted. "Obviously you're not the casual player Labeth is."

Gratified, Firebird began the difficult etude she'd so recently memorized. *And Netaia,* she thought wryly, *is not the barbarian backwater you thought it was, Sentinel Kinsman.*

CHAPTER 13

ROGONIN

sotto voce
whispered, in an undertone

To Brennen, even the outbuildings of the Rogonin estate looked magnificent. Fronted with white marble, their corners and doorposts were carved with fruiting vines. The central residence was a monstrosity, rising three stories to a blackened metal roof and spreading long wings in each direction. As Electoral Ministers of Trade, the Rogonins had amassed an estate that would support some Federate space colonies.

It couldn't compare, though, with the Angelo fortune. Firebird had been raised with wealth that staggered him, in a palace larger and grander than this villa . . . almost as large as the Sentinel College, filled with more treasures than Tallis's Museum of Culture. Carradee had insisted, as they walked through the portrait gallery after an electoral meeting, that all Netaians owned that palace and its contents, just as they all took vicarious pride in Crown activities.

"*All?*" he'd asked cautiously.

For a moment, she'd hesitated. Then she'd repeated firmly, "All."

He eyed Rogonin's hedges for possible assailants. He'd brought two guards, one a tall woman in Tallan ash gray and the other a young Sentinel, but he led up the curving approach himself. A support craft hovered silently over the riverfront grounds.

An execution yesterday had done little to improve his mental state. One Federate ensign, kidnapping one Netaian girl, might've undone all the rapport Danton had worked to build these two weeks. As the "strong second," to appease an outraged high-common class, Brennen had been obliged to access the soldier, confirm his guilt, escort him into a public square, and witness his death. Brennen hadn't slept that night. Trained and experienced though he was, his nerves insisted that to execute in battle or self-defense was one thing, in cold blood another.

Vultor Korda, furthermore, had vanished from Citangelo. Brennen had run a complete data search and even checked public places for flickers of epsilon energy, but as he'd feared, both proved fruitless.

Four stairs rose to Rogonin's carved, ebony-framed door. He took them quickly and knocked. A girl's face appeared on a tri-D panel that had been invisible on the white background. "Yes?" she asked.

"I wish to speak with His Grace the Duke, miss."

"He is out, Your Excellency. Didn't the gate man tell you?"

Even in holo he could see she was lying, just as Rogonin lied when he'd claimed to be too ill to return to the occupation base for questioning. "This is government business, miss. Please ask His Grace to come to the door."

The image vanished. Behind Brennen, his guards watched the grounds. After a moment he extended a probe inside the door. He recalled the stale, musky savor of Rogonin's presence from his brief scan interview. When he felt it approach, he steadied himself for a struggle.

The screen lit again, this time with Rogonin's jowly face. "Your Excellency." The eyes widened—an attempt at surprised innocence. "How may I help you?"

"I must speak with you in person, sir, regarding a matter that concerns you closely."

"Excellency, that is out of the question. I am in my chamber. I do not feel well."

Brennen angled his hand and focused epsilon energy into the door's opening circuits. As it slid aside, he shifted his focus and caught Rogonin in command.

High ceilings rose above the unmoving nobleman, and ornate white-upholstered furniture stood along the broad entry hall. Two servants flanked the duke, staring in alarm.

"Take us where we can be alone, please, Your Grace," Brennen said.

His movement made awkward by the compulsion of voice-command, Rogonin shuffled toward a door on the hall's left. At Brennen's nod, the Tallan guard swept the room with her stare and then came to attention in the doorway.

Antique weapons hung on the study's walls over indigo leather furniture. Only one exit, only one window. Secure enough. Brennen waved Rogonin to a deep armchair and dropped his hand.

The duke hung back, clutching the wings of his chair. "Sir, this is the House of Claighbro and you have no right to force entry. I shall speak plainly with the governor about this intrusion."

"Governor Danton has issued me a warrant. Evidence has been given us that suggests this house conceals a store of weapons."

The duke glanced at several swords that hung on his study's walls. "If this is a problem," he said sarcastically—

"Tactical weapons," Brennen interrupted. "Please sit down, sir. My greatest desire at the moment is to see you cleared from suspicion, but I can do so only by searching either the grounds or your memory. Mind-access will take less of your time and demand fewer of your resources."

Rogonin remained standing.

Brennen motioned his Thyrian guard forward. Rogonin's fury exploded through Brennen's static shields. He countered by sending a calming frequency. "He won't harm you, and we have no desire for unpleasantness. Please."

Rogonin opened his mouth and took a deep breath. He meant to shout. Brennen caught him again in command. "Sit down," he directed. The duke complied. "Please don't force me to have you restrained in your own house, sir. I only want to clear you."

He let the command slip a little. Rogonin rose halfway out of the chair before Brennen could reestablish control.

He exhaled sharply. "I'm sorry, Your Grace. You leave me no choice." He nodded to the Sentinel guard. Carefully balancing his energy with the other's, he relinquished control. The moment transfer was accomplished, Brennen turned inward for his carrier, modulated it, and thrust it at Rogonin.

The duke's pain and rage sizzled, but Brennen held the carrier steady, probing quickly and hard for a flaw in the natural defenses of the nobleman's alpha matrix.

Rogonin had no idea how to resist. Brennen breached him in a second. His point of awareness plunged into heavy, distasteful pressure: strange voices, alien images, Rogonin's struggle to reassert his will, and a hatred as bitter as clemis root.

"We spoke of weapons," Brennen said softly.

Vision cleared. He seemed to stand in a dim room. Crates lined two walls, oblong cases of energy rifles and smaller, blocky metal boxes that might hide anything from handguns to photo-enhanced warheads. Filed with the image was its location below the villa's main floor. The interrogation lasted only a few seconds.

Brennen opened his eyes. Rogonin sprawled in the chair, almost convulsed in useless physical resistance. Brennen signaled his aide to let him go.

"Very well, sir," he said as the duke composed himself. He hated to arrest the man, which would scandalize the nobility, but inaction could mean violence. "I'm afraid you must come with us to the governor's office, to answer additional questions."

"You have no authority," the nobleman fumed. "I'll see you—"

Brennen angled a hand but did not command.

Rogonin shut his mouth and stood up. The guards stepped to his side. The Tallan woman caught one of his wrists in a restraint, touched his shoulder, and marched him out.

Unhappily, Brennen followed.

Three data desks, two secure interlinks, and a full-time recording apparatus had turned Princess Phoena Angelo's second parlor, in the palace's private wing, into the headquarters for a covert resistance operation. Soon it might threaten the Federacy, with or without Carradee's support. Burly House Guards watched her door in case the Federates suddenly altered their hands-off policy. Phoena might be gravely inconvenienced if they searched her rooms.

Phoena and her mother had often talked privately about the need for strong leadership, and of Carradee's reluctance. Those talks had led Phoena to hope that Siwann meant to quietly dispose of Carradee before stepping down from the throne.

Now Phoena must lead secretly, without recognition. *But only for Netaia and its rightful rulers*, she reflected, smiling with dignity. Deadly endeavors, she believed, were justified to focus power where it could be wielded. All her life Phoena had served that ideal—more sincerely, she felt, than any other member of her family. It grieved her to see Carradee display weakness.

Well. Her inconvenient older sister Lintess had met an untimely end. Her father Irion, who'd privately confronted her about Lintess's death, had been thrown from a startled hunting stallion.

Now—nearly midnight, two days after Muirnen Rogonin's arrest—a message light pulsed over Phoena's secure cross-town link screen. She glanced around the parlor before seating herself. She still lacked the equipment for disciplining her own people and any spies they caught: She wanted more monitoring devices, certain pharmaceuticals . . . and for emergencies, a restraint table.

She touched a key. Vultor Korda's pasty face appeared on the CT screen. "There you are," he said. "I got your roster. Did you find a ship?"

"Of course." She glanced over her shoulder. Earlier, she'd held a meeting of heirs. The suite had emptied, except for her private staff. One burly House Guard stood just inside her richly carved door. "Are you ready?" she demanded.

Korda nodded. "The diplomatic codes were hardest to get. You owe me for that one."

She shrugged. "You're sure we can get Rogonin out of lockup?"

"No trouble," he insisted. "His guards weren't any problem before." Yesterday, Korda had escorted her to Muirnen Rogonin's prison cell, at a midcity police facility occupied by the Federates. At three guard stations, she'd been ignored as if she wore a cloak of invisibility. Korda had used his powers to make the Feds look right past her. "You sure he's mad enough to cooperate?" Korda demanded.

"Oh yes." She'd only told Rogonin, "I've found a way to strike back." With his grounds violated, their weapons seized, and his brain made a Sentinel's picking grounds, Rogonin would've volunteered for almost any mission to embarrass the Federacy.

"False transponder for the ship?" she demanded.

Korda nodded again. "Ready to install."

"Diplomatic credentials?"

"We'll be as welcome on Tallis as Danton himself. With the transmission lag, by the time Tallis can double-check with Danton, we'll have struck. Now, you *promised*—"

Phoena stretched her long legs and signaled her personal girl to bring a cool drink. "Yes, I promise. If Tallis grabs you, I'll have you freed within weeks, or less." Unless that endangered her cause, of course. Korda was a unique and valuable servant, but to save her home world, she'd sacrifice him if necessary. "Enough money," she explained, "can buy almost anyone's loyalty for ten minutes . . . or ten years. Isn't that right?" she asked, lading her voice with sarcasm.

The Thyrian traitor touched his forehead and made a mocking half bow.

During three dull weeks, Firebird had rarely seen a smile wrinkle Ellet Kinsman's clear oval face. Gradually, Ellet had let their conversations—obviously manipulated to familiarize Firebird with the Federacy—touch on her own people.

Firebird leaned against the wall nearest her anteroom window, careful to avoid the security grid, simultaneously watching Ellet on the lounger and the free, outside world. Tiny clouds mottled the afternoon sky.

"What's the main difference between a Sentinel and a Master Sentinel, then?" she asked, continuing a piecemeal inquiry. "Is it a matter of degree, or a different set of skills?"

"Both." Ellet touched her four-rayed star without relaxing her tutorial stance. "The line of eligibility isn't drawn at any arbitrary point on the Ehretan Scale. Some ordinary potentials also influence trainability. Focus, for example, is a function of any mind's power to concentrate. Other potentials are solely our own. I could levitate a fairly massive object if I could rest afterward. General Caldwell could control his own rate of fall, a more subtle and difficult skill."

A passenger shuttle swooped past Firebird's window. She ached to be outdoors. "Is it—a physical center in the brain, then? A—Ellet, this is an awkward question. I was taught that your people are genetically altered. Who created the epsilon abilities? And why? Didn't they know, didn't they guess, there could be trouble?" *A whole world, depopulated.*

"There is a physical region, involving several brain structures." Ellet's brows came together over her shapely but prominent nose. "As for our origins and history, you may read about those in the MaxSec library."

"I have," Firebird admitted, "but I think those chapters were written by non-Sentinels. I've studied some science. I'm amazed that the . . . chromosomal engineers achieved so much."

"And so," Ellet said stiffly, "you wonder if your own scientists might duplicate the feat?"

"Ours only work on plants and animals. Human research is considered immoral."

"That also was true on Ehret." Ellet's voice dropped, and she looked away. "We believe we were exiled for our ancestors' disobedience, in creating those gifts. But only the few, the obedient survived to reenter galactic society." She lifted her head. "There are reasons beyond ourselves."

Ellet's superior mannerisms made Brennen's kindness shine by comparison. Firebird folded her arms across her chest. "I'm only curious."

"You are too curious. Every people has racial secrets. You must learn to respect them."

"I do," Firebird insisted. "But tell me about those reasons beyond yourselves. Who do you serve . . . above the Federacy?" Ellet's absolute emotional control had started to irritate Firebird. It made Ellet aloof, untouchable—whereas Brennen's gave him a comfortable steadiness.

"We serve the Eternal Speaker, who created space and time."

Firebird straightened, bemused. These people didn't bother with small matters like Strength and Valor. "Space and time?" she echoed.

"Yes."

"Then this . . . Speaker would have to exist outside of both."

"Exactly."

Firebird frowned, unable to imagine so transcendent a being. Something Brennen had said sprang into her mind. *You intended to die for something you don't love?* She eyed Ellet. "Do you love that Speaker, Ellet?"

The Sentinel raised an eyebrow. "You are overstepping."

Yes, but it had seemed relevant. "Why are you so reluctant to display any feeling, Ellet?"

Ellet laughed, a puff of breath and no more. "Consider it yourself. Among telepaths, broadcasting emotion is boorish—performing private functions in public. We restrain ourselves because some of our colleagues can send well but shield poorly."

Evidently Ellet would rather discuss her people than her god. "Why?"

"Talents vary."

"Range, then. How far away can you sense a person's emotion or send the carrier wave?"

"That too varies with Ehretan Scale. There are exceptions under unusual circumstances, but generally, the width of a large room is the range of a solid epsilon carrier."

. . . Just as Brennen had probed her across Twinnich's war room. The experience had been an infuriating public humiliation, but actually, the sensation itself hadn't been as unpleasant as Korda had led her to believe—nor had the long personal sessions.

Her thoughts slipped out in words. "Between a starbred man and woman, are there . . . experiences others don't have?"

"Yes." Ellet drew up tall on the lounger and delivered the word like a slap.

Though startled by her vehemence, Firebird pressed, "Such as—"

"The subject is not your concern." Ellet flushed deeply. "I think I've talked long enough. I wish to listen to you now. Play your clairsa."

Well. She'd touched a nerve at last. Firebird knelt to pick up the narrow instrument, took a stool, and sat down.

The sonata she chose came mechanically at first because it took her a minute to erase Brennen's face from her mind, but as the composition moved from minor to modal, its chords swept her back toward the Netaian frame of reference. Her links with her past, with her deep sense of self, had weakened as she studied the Federacy. Netaian music made her strong again.

Ellet broke into her reverie. "I must go."

"Come soon," Firebird said absently. Ellet locked the massive door behind her. Firebird finished the sonata, then softly plucked out an old ballad, humming as the strings rang brightly. It was a servitor song, a plea for freedom.

Maybe this powerless sense of imprisonment was how servitors and low-commoners felt about their lives. She certainly could relate to the lyrics in a wholly new way.

You intended to die for something you don't love?

The words echoed in her memory.

Reconsider your deities.

There's a higher call on your life now.

We serve the Eternal Speaker, who created space and time.

Firebird held the silent clairsa against her chest. Compared with the Powers she'd barely even understood, that concept seemed unbearably grandiose. Could any mere human grasp it?

She tried for half a minute, shrugged, then replaced her hands on her clairsa strings and played an old love song.

Several days later, Ellet brought unsettling news. Preparatory to the Assembly elections, Netaia's reorganized Electorate had sent an embassy to the Regional council. They were petitioning for a gesture of cooperation.

"What are they asking for?" Firebird asked uneasily. She and Ellet sat on opposite ends of the green lounger.

"You tell me."

Guessing was no challenge. "They want to take me back."

"Correct. To quote, 'The surrender of First Major Lady Firebird Angelo, reportedly captured at the battle of Veroh.' "

Firebird considered. On Netaia, now officially governed by the Federacy, she might be legally safe . . . but it would take more than Federate law to change the heirs' deeply held convictions, and only one recalcitrant (or faithful) heir to kill her. "I suppose they're still waiting for news of my suicide. They'll never forgive me for surviving to be interrogated, and it wasn't my fault."

Ellet gave her a sharp glance, as intent as any of Brennen's.

"Not my fault," Firebird repeated. She stared through the wall, seeing Rendy Gellison before he died in his groundcar, killed by falling debris. Accidental death—maybe. "I don't want to go back," she admitted. "I've gotten used to the idea of living."

Ellet rose. "I'll convey your wishes to the council. They'll be considered along with the Netaians' petition."

"Why is the Federacy negotiating with them at all?" Firebird demanded.

Ellet raised an eyebrow. "Politics. Some highly placed people seem to think Netaia's resources will fall into Federate control if its rulers are treated . . . delicately."

"That's greedy," Firebird murmured. "If the Federacy wants to impress the Netaian people, it should show honor and patience and strength."

"Some forces in the Whorl would like to see the Federacy show weakness. They have agents on Tallis. SO exposes their spies when we find them."

"That sounds like an easy job . . . for you people."

Ellet hesitated, looking as if she wanted to speak, then strode out.

Later that evening, she returned with a startling escort: His Grace Muirnen Rogonin of Claighbro, and—incredibly—Vultor Korda, who looked pasty-faced in tight black shipboards. As the men preceded Ellet into the brown permastone anteroom, Firebird rose from her lounger, where she'd sat comfortably curled around her clairsa. Two burly Tallan guards followed Ellet. Firebird came to attention, glad she hadn't yet undressed for bed. Silently she berated Ellet. *You could've warned me!* Brennen would've shown that courtesy.

"Gentlemen." She tried to sound cordial. "Come in, sit down." She motioned them toward the lounger. One guard came to attention beside her door, the other at the room's opposite corner. It was good to see Tallis take "protective custody" seriously.

Rogonin settled his bulk on the lounger, hands on the knees of his black sateen breeches. Korda joined him. Ellet walked behind them to lean on the windowbar.

Rogonin's soft green eyes absorbed every detail of the bare little anteroom and rested finally on Firebird, who stood near the door, feet apart and hands clenched at her sides. "Suns, Firebird, this is no place for a lady of your house. Aren't you ready to go back?"

Rogonin had left the title off her name, which he never would've done back at home. Clearly, she was in disgrace among her own class. She sent Ellet a questioning glance.

"The council," Ellet informed her, "has tabled the Netaian request until your period of temporary asylum ends, in six weeks."

Firebird nodded.

"But they did allow us to speak with you personally," insisted Rogonin, "and to convey their assurance that if you chose to return with us, they would guarantee you safe passage to Netaia."

"I see." Firebird envisioned a return on their terms. She would step off a Federate ship, leaving behind a Federate guard who'd seen her safely home. The redjackets would wait below.

Beyond her glasteel window, streams of cars flowed along wide avenues to an arc of low hills, then climbed to the passes and vanished. A little higher, wing lights blinked on atmospheric craft. Higher still, the nearest stars looked brighter, noticeably colored, and shifted to new positions.

"No, Rogonin," she said quietly. "I've chosen to stay."

"Then you must settle matters here," he answered. "Yourself."

Her cheeks warmed.

"Your electoral colleagues sent a last gift. It was taken away." He glared at one big Tallan guard.

"What was it?" she demanded. She probably knew.

Ellet confirmed her guess. "Dagger. Very ornate. Poisoned," she added.

"A quick one," rumbled Rogonin. "In the hope you retain some sense of honor."

Korda leaned forward. In the presence of Ellet, who had completed training Korda had only begun, she doubted he would try any Ehretan tricks on the guards, but she watched him closely.

"I have a message from your sister." Korda's strident voice became singsong. "Your people are shamed. The treachery you have dealt us will not be undone in many lifetimes. You would be wise to return and end the bitterness with which people speak your name."

He didn't say which sister had sent the message, but the words, calculated to sting a proud wastling soul, struck home. Where was her Valor, her Fidelity? She wavered. Could she go back?

As she glanced aside, she saw Ellet's eyes widen, focused on Korda. The Sentinel opened her mouth as if to speak, then shut it in a tight line.

What was this?

Firebird cleared her throat. "I want to go back," she said firmly, "but I don't feel this is the time. Thank you for calling on me, though."

"I think you're mistaken." Korda leaned forward, hands almost touching his feet.

Firebird tensed. That was an odd gesture. She shook her head and stepped backward. "It's not time," she repeated.

The quick probing of his fingers inside his boot top put her on full alert. It was the old game of stick tag, only this time, it was no game.

Ellet's jaw twitched. She blurted, "He's got a weapon!"

Korda whipped out a tiny rod. Firebird feinted left to draw his fire, then threw herself hard to the right.

Korda's first shot grazed her left shoulder. As she crouched to dodge again, she recognized the Vargan stinger, no longer than a stylus, but deadly if one of its energy bolts struck a vital area. Its little power cell could deliver four more shots.

But Korda toppled, stunned by a guard's shock pistol. Rogonin struggled to his feet. "How dare you?" he cried. "That man has diplomatic immunity."

"He just lost it." Ellet gripped her empty holster. "Or so I hope. Get up. I'll take you back to your quarters."

Rogonin thrust out a finger. "Your immunity is just as temporary, Firebird. Netaia will have you back, if the Federacy wants peace with us. No invader can hold our world for long."

One guard carried Korda, whose breath came in wheezes. Rogonin followed, and then the other guard.

"Are you hit?" Ellet asked.

Firebird fingered the scorched fabric. "Just grazed," she said, shaking her head. As blood rushed to the burn, it started to sting.

"I'll send a med." Frowning, Ellet strode out.

Firebird drooped on the lounger. *Ellet!* her mind cried. Ellet was her friend, her teacher!

But plainly, Ellet had realized—even before Firebird—that Korda had somehow brought a weapon past MaxSec scanners. And Ellet had hesitated to speak for several seconds, a lapse that could've proved deadly.

Why?

CHAPTER 14

ELLET

simile
as previously noted

Tel Tellai had visited Hunter Height before, when his father briefly had been a guest of the Angelo family, but never under these circumstances. This time, he came as Phoena's personal escort, leaving the concerns of his estate and holdings with his employees.

He shifted his ankles on the edge of a huge octagonal bed in the Height's uplevel master room. Occupying most of the top story, this room was oddly shaped, almost pentagonal, with windows curtained in drab brown. They commanded a 120-degree view to the north, east, and southeast of its mountainous environs. Although bare by his standards and devoid of fine art, the wood-floored room's spaciousness suggested grand possibilities—and the bed on which he sat had once been occupied by his royal granduncle and a previous queen.

Phoena, gowned tonight in brilliant green velvette, stood at the bed's foot, fists clenched in graceful strength on her narrow hips. In a high-backed wooden chair across from Tel, looking profoundly uncomfortable, sat a House Guard Tel didn't know by name. "Only their diplomatic immunity got them off Tallis," he finished explaining. "And a Federate account of the incident reached Citangelo on the same shuttle with them. Danton detained them on Base, this time."

At least they were back! Tel had been deeply relieved Phoena hadn't sent him to Tallis. He would've gone, as his duty to his class, but Federates terrified him, and particularly Sentinels.

"With Stele?" she demanded. "Same detention area?"

"Evidently not. And they've drugged Korda. Some kind of injection that keeps him powerless."

Coals of temper gleamed in Phoena's hot brown eyes. "So he can't even tell us which guards can be bribed."

"Not for eight to ten days, Your Highness."

"Then it's time to push Carradee." Phoena glared. "If she'll release them into my custody, I'll promise to keep them locked up. Here. Out of harm's way," she said bitterly. She swept the rustic master room with her gaze. "Actually," she muttered, "this is almost perfect."

"Beg pardon?" Tel asked.

"Do you know," Phoena said, "if—you," she snapped at the House Guard. "You're dismissed."

He made a full bow and hurried to the lift, which opened directly into the master room.

Phoena took up her thought again. "If we could move others of like mind here, quietly, we could expand our operation. The head maid insists no Federate has ever come here. I don't think they even know it exists. And downlevel, there would be room for a research laboratory. We could even restart our real work."

Tel pressed his palms together. "Brilliant, Highness. With the airfield and tunnels we could accommodate plenty of traffic. But would Carradee object?" He shifted his seat again, giving the rustic master room a more careful appraisal. "I can't see her giving permission without informing the Federates."

"She did suggest I come here. She wants me out of her way. I'll cut a deal with her. If she can convince Danton to send me Korda and Rogonin, I'll come back here and I'll stay."

Tel arched an eyebrow. "What about Stele?"

"I'll ask for all three, then back down on Stele. I don't trust him." Phoena sat down on the bed foot and arranged the folds of her gown with a slender, bare arm. "Hundreds of other naval officers were put out of work by demilitarization, and the Enforcement Corps is in turmoil." She scowled. "A select few could constitute a small defense force here. If any can bring military craft that survived the invasion, or weapons, we—"

"Yes," Tel exclaimed. "All the marshals, naturally, are absolutely loyal to Netaia. And nearly the entire upper echelon of our naval forces." At last, those tiresome military discussions seemed relevant.

Phoena pursed her full lips. "Tel, would you compose a message to be delivered quietly to—say, twenty of the best of them? Don't take them all off the top. They'd fight for the privilege of giving orders. Choose four marshals, then have them select their most loyal subordinates. A core, that's all we need for now. For now," she repeated, stroking her leaf green skirt. "After tomorrow's *elections*," she added, pronouncing the word with distaste, "we'll know better where we stand."

Tel rose and bowed. "I would be honored to serve you, Highness." He strolled toward the chair the House Guard had vacated. Stark and simple, it seemed almost lost on the wide wooden floor. "Of course, the master suite must be made over to suit you. So much could be done with carpeting, fine art pieces, flowering plants. It could be made a lovely place, and still efficient."

"Yes, and data desks . . . and there's room up here for a police operation."

Tel ran a hand over the unadorned chair's back. "If only we didn't need to hide our effort from the queen. If only . . ." He gazed at her glowing face. "Phoena, it should have been you."

She sat down in another chair. "Siwann thought so, too," she said earnestly. "It will be me, one day."

"Highness, I didn't mean . . ." Tel hated the tremble in his voice. "Carradee . . . and her little daughters? You wouldn't—"

"Never mind." She crossed her bare arms and shivered prettily. "It's cold here, Tel. I don't think they've adjusted the heat for autumn yet."

He stepped away, searching the nearest wall for a climate control board.

Phoena laughed softly and rose out of the chair. "I didn't mean that, Tel. Won't you serve my royal person and leave Carradee to her own fate?" Her voice faded to a whisper.

She couldn't mean what he hoped. "Phoena, I . . ."

Phoena stretched out both arms. "But you dishonor me if you refuse."

"Oh no, Phoena! Highness . . ." Tel's face flushed with scarlet heat as he stepped toward her. "I mean you no dishonor."

When Ellet returned to Firebird's cell several days later, the sky outside her gridded window was dark gray, as stormy and bleak as Firebird's feelings.

They pulled stools to the small servo table with a pot of kass Ellet had brought. Firebird drew a deep breath and steeled herself to ask questions that would probably alienate a woman who might have become her friend.

Ellet read her tension with the ease of natural ability and thorough training. "Go ahead, Firebird. You're in no danger from me."

Firebird wrapped both hands around her cup. "You spotted that stinger before I did."

"Yes."

That was a relief. At least Ellet would answer honestly. "Didn't you put them through a weapon scan?"

"I certainly did. It picked up Rogonin's dagger. It should've pinpointed the stinger, too. Korda must've fuddled the circuit. I certainly had no wish to access him."

"Explain."

"Vultor Korda is a traitor to my people. Worse, a partially trained traitor. You know how deeply people fear us."

"Oh yes."

"We found out too late that Korda's alleged diplomatic immunity was forged—as was Rogonin's. He was evidently under arrest and shouldn't have been allowed offplanet at all. The communications lag worked against us. Korda obviously abetted him."

"I see. But why didn't you speak sooner?"

Ellet gave her a wry look. "I had reasons for wanting to get Vultor Korda in custody. So long as he didn't commit certain crimes, I couldn't touch him. By our codes, he is the worst kind of criminal. He deserves death." Ellet studied her interlaced fingers. "Firebird, we police ourselves to keep the Federacy from turning on us. It fears us, as it should. The Sentinel who abuses epsilon skills sheathes a crystace in his or her heart. That's the first vow we take, even before training."

"So you wanted to catch him in an offense, but it had to be extremely serious. Such as . . . murdering a prisoner under protective custody."

"Or attempting it. You were anxious to die not long ago, in a good cause." Ellet looked up, eyes afire. "We've won the Federacy's trust. If we lose it by misusing our abilities, there'll be another war of annihilation. And this time, we will not survive." She shook her head.

"But no, I couldn't let him attack you. I considered provoking him to attack me. In the end, I simply let the guards do their job. My responsibility is to protect you, under General Caldwell's orders, and I will do so."

"Until you decide to bait another trap."

"I did not bait a trap. I recognized the potential of that situation. It proved unusable."

Firebird kept her emotions bland, thinking only, *Maybe Sentinels really aren't worthy of trust.* But a person could try to stay within their good graces. Aloud, she said, "I don't intend to lodge a complaint. I just want to hear, from your mouth, what you have against me." There had to be more to this than Vultor Korda's past offenses.

Ellet refilled her kass cup, sipped, and then leaned back her chair. She exhaled deeply before she spoke. "Someone," she said, "had better warn you that Brennen Caldwell is interested in you, and I don't mean politically."

"What?" Firebird slid her elbows off the table. "What do you mean, not politically? He respects me, and I . . . respect him. Considering the circumstances, he has been almost a friend."

"He wants to be more."

Firebird stared. No decent man ever wanted a wastling for more than a friend. "General Caldwell? That's ridiculous."

"Is it?" Ellet paused. "Brennen has his eye on the High command at Elysia. He could make it too, one day, if he didn't get thrown off course by such as you."

He'd been decent and merciful. Nothing more.

But he thought she had a future. Even Corey had never dared to plan beyond their geis orders.

Still, she protested. "You're not talking about—"

"Don't worry, he'd never force a relationship on you. He's a gentleman." Ellet's lips crinkled. Obviously, she thought Firebird was vastly beneath Brennen's attentions. "But if you let him get close to you, you'll never get away. I'm giving you a chance to prepare yourself."

"What do you mean, never get away? Mind control?"

"Of course not," Ellet snapped. "If we were allowed to control others' emotions, I'd have altered yours long ago."

Nevertheless, Firebird envisioned a line of women eased out of Brennen's life by Ellet Kinsman, and suddenly, all Ellet's actions and hints seemed clear.

"I'm warning you," Ellet went on. "A man with Sentinel training will have found ways to please a woman without ever touching her, just as you guessed: ways that will leave her changed, unable to forget or go back. It's permissible if she has encouraged him. I don't think you'd be capable of resisting. So unless you're interested in marrying the officer who interrogated you, you'd better step carefully. We don't waste much time on courtship. And that leads to the subject of pair bonding."

"Pair bonding?" Firebird echoed. Changed . . . unable to forget?

"When a Sentinel marries, he—or she—enters a permanent mental-emotional link. You can't resist; you can't escape. It affects the deepest level of existence. Oh, you'd keep your identity, but you'd never be the same. It's tough on outsiders, which is one reason we starbred families have maintained our separation. Another is that we can't let our genes be diluted. There are other telepaths, too. Renegades. We are the Federacy's only defense against them. We have to keep the families strong."

Can't escape? Suddenly Firebird wanted to be alone. "I see," she declared. "You have plans for General Caldwell yourself. Don't change them."

Ellet silently arched one black eyebrow.

"I have no designs on your Master Sentinel, Ellet. None whatever." The very notion of a long-term relationship stunned her.

Ellet slipped off her stool, picked up the empty pot, and ambled toward the door. "Don't forget that I can read your emotions, Lady Angelo." She pronounced the name with a sneer.

Stung, Firebird balled a fist on one hip. "Do not mock my family, Ellet Kinsman."

Ellet hooted. "Your family? Compared to his, yours is—" She halted wide-eyed. "That," she growled, "was more than I should have said. You'll mention it to no one."

"Don't worry." Firebird glared back.

"Ask him about it, though. If you dare." Ellet paused with one hand over the lock panel. As she looked over her shoulder, her voice became polite again. "Though I didn't get Korda in custody, I am glad you weren't hurt. I am sorry we can't be friends. Perhaps it's better not to even try, until that other matter is settled."

Firebird stood up unsteadily. "Thank you. I'll think about what you said."

"Try to be objective. And think quickly. They've sent out his replacement." She left the room.

Firebird turned from her door, deflated. So these were the feelings Ellet had hidden from her, all these weeks!

Brennen Caldwell, lieutenant governor of her conquered people, thought of her in that way? What had Ellet seen or felt in him—and in her—to make her believe it? And was there no privacy with these Thyrians? Obviously, Ellet hoped Firebird would be so taken aback by her warning that now she'd avoid Brennen entirely.

And she might. Surely the Federacy had other minimum-security detention areas. She could ask to be moved. The notion of mental bonding—deeper than the level of thought?—of never emerging unscathed—made her shudder.

Yet something else Ellet had said made her suddenly wistful: the concept of an indissoluble link, where before she'd possessed nothing lasting. For all her self-reliance, she'd been denied so many ordinary attachments—a family's loving nurture, the honorable intentions of good men, even the friendship of all but the other wastlings. She'd never even kept a pet, fearing its torment at Phoena's hands after she died. Buried beneath her pride, she knew she hid a dark, aching loneliness.

But—mental bonding? She barely knew the man!

Oh, but he knew her. To the deepest depths of her memory.

And still respected her? Even, if she dared to think it . . . loved her?

Torn between dread and delight, Firebird walked to the tattered lounger. She mustn't take this as a profound compliment, but as a warning. More than ever, she understood why some Federates distrusted these telepaths, even though they were sworn to Federate service. Entangling herself in their personal affairs—accidentally!—had landed her in a precarious situation. She recalled how Brennen had told the Verohan guard, *"I apologize for deceiving you, but it was done in the best interests of the Federacy."* When juxtaposed with Ellet's actions and cautions, those words took on sinister overtones. Might Brennen deceive her, or sacrifice her, "in the best interests of the Federacy?" In the best interests, maybe, of a man seemingly destined for the Federate High command?

How could she extricate herself without offending or angering him, and so putting herself in new danger?

And who were those others . . . the renegades, who'd take the Federacy if they could?

Firebird seated herself on the lounger and picked up her clairsa, clutching its carved frame to steady her fingers. She tuned automatically and defiantly began with the Academy anthem, "Beyond Netaian Skies." But that reminded her sharply of Corey, who alone had given and received her wholehearted support. Despite her resolve, a quick mental jump took her from Netaia, and Corey, to the battle of Veroh and all that had happened after.

She stared out at the dull sky. If Ellet was correct—if she could dare to believe such a thing—at what point had Brennen Caldwell seen her as a woman he wanted? What had he found, deep in her mind, worth his . . . his love? Was that truly what Ellet had meant? Because she did . . . respect . . . no, like . . .

What did she feel toward that man?

She clung to the clairsa, letting her emotions tumble, and listened with her heart for the music they would bring. A melody came, and she shaped it. It rose in a steady, stable fourth and a fifth, fell scalewise, then turned upward with a questioning minor third. She laughed uncomfortably. How could so simple a phrase betray so much turmoil? A pair of descending scale arcs fell into the second phrase, ending on a leading tone that begged for resolution. But it wouldn't settle yet. That was all that came. She played it several times to set it in her memory.

Ask him, if you dare.

Her fingers fell limp. Did Brennen also come from a powerful family?

Laying aside her clairsa, she keyed up the MaxSec library.

An hour's search gave her no clue. None of his listed ancestors were politicians. None had won acclaim in any of the fields known as Sentinel strongholds: intelligence, medicine, diplomacy. It looked like a very small bloodline.

She drummed her fingers. There must be some person, some

source, that could inform her before Brennen returned.

Special Operations? Two weeks ago, she'd sent a political query to that floor. They'd turned her down, "restricted to civilian resources."

Staring out the window, she combed through her memories of every dealing with Ellet.

Here was a thought. The Sentinel had left early one day, to attend a religious observance. The "chapter room," she'd said, was somewhere in the tower.

If that haven accepted visitors, maybe Firebird could convince a MaxSec staffer to take her there.

Think quickly, she reminded herself. *They've sent out his replacement.*

Abruptly, Firebird remembered the melody of her ballad for Queen Iarla, and a lyric started to flow for the stubborn second stanza. She seized her recall pad.

Stepping off a shuttle into the main-floor MaxSec garage, Brennen took a deep breath of warm wind. Home—the only home he'd known in ten years. He'd earned the month's leave, this time. He tossed his duffel to a porter, then headed for the Special Operations floor to check mail and messages.

Inside the broad, sunlit clearing room, a plump secretary bent over her data desk. Beside her, reading a governmental newscan, stood the very person he wanted to see first, Ellet Kinsman. He opened his shields to greet her.

She switched off the newscan. He caught a shielding blast of epsilon static. Through it, too strongly to hide, flickered a clear picture of Firebird and an alarming fight-or-flight reaction to his greeting.

Stricken, Brennen raised his own shields. What had he *not* been told about the Korda incident—or was this something else?

He glanced around the clearing room. The secretary ignored, or hadn't seen, their exchange. On her left, the door to a small conference room lay open. Brusquely he pointed toward it, then followed Ellet inside. Just short of the black conference table, he turned and leaned on its surface. The door slid shut automatically, closing them both into half-light.

Drop the shield, Ellet. You promised a full report.

She sank into a chair, glaring. "Brennen," she said, "you may have accessed Lady Firebird Angelo, but there are too many things you don't know—"

"Captain Kinsman," he said tightly. Dread grew in his mind.

Ellet shut her mouth and subvocalized. *There was an attempt on her life several days ago. I—*

He should've listened to his instincts. He should've sent someone else. Anyone. "Drop the shield, Ellet, or you are insubordinate."

"Very well." She tossed her head and stared up at him. "I have broken neither law nor custom, and you would do well to follow that example."

Her static cloud dissipated. Gingerly he swept across the outer emotional matrix of her mind. Jealousy, frustration, grim satisfaction: tasting her emotional state only whetted his shocked fury.

Fury? He'd lost affective control. He struggled to regain it, then bluntly requested memory access. She gave sullen permission. In the space of an instant, all her dealings with Firebird were transferred to his awareness.

. . . Looking through Ellet's eyes, he ushered Korda into Firebird's cell, felt Ellet's indignation at his coming, saw his inordinate attention to that left boot. Bringing a weapon into this cell wasn't the capital offense it would take to keep Korda in custody, but attempting to murder a prisoner would be! With one stroke, Ellet could rid the Sentinel kindred of traitorous Korda and a rival for the place beside Brennen in the exiles' perilous genealogy.

Ellet had held that thought for less than a second, then thrust it aside. Being tempted was no crime.

But only yesterday, she'd gone back to Firebird and deliberately poisoned any casual fondness she may have felt for the starbred—for himself—with fear, and entombed it in suspicion. Only yesterday.

He stopped the carrier flow roughly, deliberately shaking Ellet, wishing he were free to disrupt her epsilon center with a burst of his own power. "You'd better leave," he whispered. "I'll speak with you later, after I see just how much damage you have done."

"That woman," Ellet muttered, "serves false gods. In case you've forgotten."

Absorbed in misery, he didn't watch her go.

CHAPTER 15

BRENNEN

cantabile
as if singing

Leaving her MaxSec escort at the Sentinel chapter room's door, Firebird tiptoed inside. It had proved surprisingly easy to come here, but one glance spoiled her hopes. She didn't see a data terminal, a scan viewer, or even a historical tapestry.

Still, the silent peace drew her in. A hand-sized flame burned against the far wall, and an odd scent hung in the air. Incense? Overhead, a broad, bowl-shaped gold lamp hung from three metal chains that joined near the ceiling.

Under the flame lay a long, low table covered by brocade cloths of staggering beauty: red, blue, and green, with shimmering highlights and rough shadows. On the wall behind it hung a meter-high Sentinel star, with its sword-points haloed by countless fine gold wires. Two ornate, leather-bound books lay open on the cloths. Firebird glanced over her shoulder. Seeing no one but the MaxSec staffer, she stepped up to look. One book displayed an illuminated verse:

Lift up your heads, O people of light,
And rejoice before the cloths of the altar,
For He spoke His commandments that we might be led,
Holy is He.

The Eternal is One, His commandments are righteous,
From dust He made us to live with Him forever.
Lift up your heads, for your home will be with Him,
Holy is He.

Bless the Eternal One, people of light,

Confess your transgressions and receive His mercy,
For vast is His mercy, and it is forever,
Holy is He.

Distracted from her search, she glanced left at the other book. To her surprise, it was written in an unintelligible language.

She blinked. Almost every world in the Whorl, even Netaia, used Old Colonial. Curious, she leaned closer, then hesitated. Maybe she shouldn't touch it.

She called to her escort, "Would they care if I looked through this?"

The man shrugged. "This is a public place. If they didn't want it touched, they'd have put it under glasteel."

Still, she handled its supple pages carefully. She reopened at its beginning to find what looked like a table of headings: *Negiyah Zamahr, Cahal, Siach* . . .

Not one familiar word. These people had secrets, and they meant to keep them.

She stepped back to the right. That book's pages were also soft and heavy, but she found readable headings. *Confessions—History—The Prophecies and The Wisdom of Mattah—The Voices of Exile—Adorations.*

Carefully she paged back to the verse that had lain open, Adoration 29, and left the book as she'd found it. She didn't think she'd find Brennen's mysterious family in here. She sidestepped to a chair and sat down, disappointed. There wasn't even anyone in here to ask. Still, she didn't want to go back to her two-room prison, and this place didn't feel truly empty.

She'd been taught as a child to pray silently to the Powers for guidance. If telepaths claimed this Speaker, this Eternal One, then he shouldn't object to mental prayers. *Hello . . . Your Honor*, she thought into the eerie dimness. *Whoever you are, whatever. What was that about mercy?*

All the guilt she'd felt since Veroh oozed out of the hiding places where she'd contained it. She'd been torn loose from all she'd hoped to achieve. She'd accepted a treasonous asylum and refused to carry out her geis orders, both capital offenses, besides the matter of Alef and Jisha.

The Powers forgave nothing . . . if they even existed. They justified Netaian law, but also its oppression of nearly a quarter of Netaia's population by fewer than one percent.

Her chest ached bitterly. Was there actually some higher cause than the unfeeling state, some kinder authority than the holy Powers? A personal deity might have human feelings, maybe even a starbred empathy.

No, it would be even more cognizant than that.

She bowed her head. If there were a deity whose mercy was "vast" and "forever," what would it take to buy one guilty traitor free from her well-deserved retribution? She'd worn masks of courage and service for so long. Who was she, behind them?

Her next thought terrified her. Brennen Caldwell had probed the depth of her mind. Did he think she was a hero, a guilty traitor, or something utterly different from either?

Hearing a soft whoosh, she spun around. A gray-haired man wearing a Thyrian uniform walked in. Not wanting to explain her roiling confusion to a stranger who probably felt it, she stood to leave.

"You don't have to go," he murmured. "Stay, if you'd like. You won't bother me."

Years of social training brought her masks back up. As the intruder, she should offer a compliment. She gestured toward the low table. "Those altar cloths are lovely."

"Yes." He glanced down into her eyes. "You feel drawn," he observed. "I won't disturb your search. Please stay."

She flushed. This place had called strange thoughts out of her subconscious. She'd never guessed that she yearned for cosmic mercy.

"We're forbidden to seek proselytes," he continued, touching her shoulder with an open palm, "but you're being called. Otherwise you wouldn't be here."

Evidently he thought she'd come seeking spiritual truths. Flustered, she turned back toward the door.

In that moment, a surge of awareness flowed over her. Gone as quickly as it had begun, it carried the unmistakable tenor of Brennen's epsilon touch.

Was he near, or was this some other phenomenon? She stood still for a few more seconds, but the sensation wasn't repeated.

She glanced at the stranger. He seemed not to have sensed whatever she'd felt. "I need to get back," she murmured. "But thank you for making me welcome."

"Always," he said. "Come again." He took a seat and then faced forward, politely ignoring her.

She drew a deep breath. Brennen's arrival, and the untangling of feelings and events that it would bring, could be moments away. "I'm done," she told her staff escort.

Back in her quarters, she glanced nervously around the anteroom. Everything was tidily placed, except the answers she'd hoped would be tucked neatly into her mind before she ever saw him again. What would she do; what should she ask . . . or tell him?

Closing her eyes, she recalled the nuances of that surge of awareness, trying to make it flow again. It had suggested Brennen's strength, but not as she'd battled it over Veroh. She'd sensed a hesitancy this time, almost a tremble, as though he were afraid.

Of her?

An hour passed, but it felt like three or four, before her entry bell sounded. The MaxSec staff never rang before entering, and Ellet hadn't returned, but there wasn't the keen awareness she'd felt an hour earlier.

She walked to her door. "Yes?" she called, wishing she had a hall-monitor screen.

The door slid open. Dressed in ordinary civilian clothes, Brennen stood a long pace back. Field General, Master Sentinel, intelligence officer . . . and what else? She hardly knew him. He met her eyes from the distance. Undoubtedly, he was reading her feelings, but she felt no command, no pressure, no compulsion.

"Hello." His smile, too, seemed hesitant. "May I talk with you?"

"Of course." She stepped aside.

Brennen didn't move. "May I come in?" he asked.

What charming formality. "Come in," she answered, standing aside. "Welcome back."

He walked straight to her corner servo table and took a stool. Baffled by the change in him, she shut the door and then joined him.

He didn't look at her but at his hands, which lay open. Reminded sharply of the surge she'd felt, she blurted, "Was that you, about an hour ago?"

His startled expression delighted her. Whatever he was, he wasn't all-knowing. "Yes," he said when he'd recovered. "I was trying to read your emotional state before I came down. I thought I was being subtle. Few people can sense a quest pulse."

That felt wonderful. "I was several floors up," she admitted, "and I wasn't doing much, just thinking. You . . ." She groped for words that wouldn't say too much. "You seemed worried."

He pushed back from the table and stared. "I . . . the first person I met when I got to MaxSec, fortunately, was Ellet. My friend," he said bitterly, and the label became an accusation. "She showed me what she'd done. All of it. I could've choked her."

She could almost feel him seething. Thank the Powers, his anger wasn't directed at her. "As to the matter of Korda," she said, "I've almost forgiven her. I understand loyalty to a cause."

He gripped the table's edge, whitening his knuckles. "I'm going to find it harder to forgive. She'd have gladly seen you killed." His anger dimmed somewhat, and the hesitancy returned. "Then she tried to frighten you with concepts you must've found incomprehensible. She was brutal. I intended to explain, in the right time. Now I'm forced to begin with the end already known. Maybe it's better that way."

So he denied nothing. While she'd barely accepted his friendship, this fast-track Fedcrate hero wanted her for his own. Thanks to Ellet, he feared he'd already lost. "Wait," she said. "Stop."

He paused, looking puzzled.

She'd be spaced in slip-state before she'd let Ellet Kinsman defeat him. "I have to be honest. I've . . . missed your company."

He set an arm on the table and brushed hair from his forehead, caught off guard again.

Staying one jump ahead of Brennen felt like playing stick tag with Corey, and winning: exhilarating!

"You've been at Citangelo with me," he said softly, "because my memory is vivid. If I'd had a clue, though, that Ellet would've treated you this way . . ."

Firebird shrugged. "I wasn't injured." That graze didn't count.

"Those offplanet clearances should've landed on my desk. I hope Korda is questioned. Then we'll get to the bottom of this."

"Yes," she murmured.

"Korda must be stopped, but not by risking your life. Our laws are strict, and harsh to traitors, but the intent is life, not death." He shook his head slightly. "I can only be glad Ellet didn't frighten you as badly as she intended."

"I don't scare easily." Firebird hesitated, remembering how plainly he would sense her feelings. "Well, she did scare me," she admitted, "but she could've misinterpreted. Exaggerated. I'd rather hear this from you."

"Shall I be plain?"

Powers help me now. She braced herself, then said, "Please."

He looked directly at her eyes. "I'll explain all you want to know, soon—as soon as possible—but first I have to tell you one thing." He extended a palm across the table.

Firebird slid only her fingers into it. Even as he curled his larger hand around them—a new sensation, warm and provocative—part of her still didn't believe.

"I do want you, very much," he said softly.

She sat motionless, struck dumb by those few simple words.

"I have," he went on, "since I first took you under access. Do you recall my saying how deeply I was impressed by your talents, and how I was angered by your wastling insistence on dying?"

She nodded, still unable to speak. She'd remembered those words during the hours since Ellet had spoken, but she'd invented other ways to explain them.

"Even earlier, I sensed our connaturality. Noticing that without specifically probing is unusual. But I couldn't tell you anything, back at Veroh. You considered yourself already dead."

"True," she admitted, finally finding her voice.

He still gripped her fingers, though gently. "You had a long turning ahead, even toward the decision to live. And you despised us—the Federacy, my people."

She nodded again.

"You needed to deal with your prejudices before you could face any personal feelings." He leaned toward her. "I never meant to deceive you, Mari. I've just gone slowly. Sentinels enter quickly and young into lifetime commitments because we can read one another. I haven't asked that of you."

"We don't waste much time on courtship," Ellet had said. "That's true," Firebird answered. "You haven't."

"You fear me, though."

Look what you are, she wanted to cry. Instantly, she realized she might as well have shouted. "Why should I believe you'll let me change my own mind?" she muttered. "If I even want to."

He sighed. "So Ellet succeeded. You dread the very ways I would've hoped to please you. Now I'm afraid to show my feelings."

"I'd be helpless, unable to back out, to . . ."

"To get away?" He echoed Ellet's phrase scornfully. "I'd never try to coerce you, overpower you, or trick you." Those glacial-ice blue eyes pleaded. "I want to be accepted for myself, not for my epsilon skills. If you fear them, I'll do nothing to please you that another man couldn't."

Irritation flashed through her, ignited by a fresh realization. She'd worn her masks for too long. She'd obeyed the Disciplines while aching to do other things—to show forbidden compassion, to sing illegal songs, to insist that she had a right to exist. She shifted her hand to grip his. "Don't you dare diminish yourself. Be what you are and I'll do the same." Then she pulled her hands away and clenched them in her lap.

Brennen rested an elbow on the table, leaned on it, and then straightened again. "That's more than I'd hoped for, Mari. I was prepared to be sent away. Thank you." He pulled in his feet and rocked forward, ready to stand. "You're upset. Shall I go?"

"No." Firebird drew a deep breath. "Tell me how things are in Citangelo."

Relaxing, he looked aside. "Not good," he said softly, "though it's not openly bad. Your government is frighteningly unstable."

She thought she could guess what he meant. "It's certainly not fair to everyone."

"More than that, Mari. If it's not reformed soon, Netaia is ripe for a major class revolution."

The words chilled her. How many ballads had she heard that pled for freedom? "Might your occupation government stabilize things for a while?"

"It's trying. The Assembly and the queen seem to be accepting many small changes in your legal system, but the Electorate holds too much judicial power. If we alter a sentencing protocol, the courts redefine the offense. We can't eliminate the electors without disrupting the entire system, so nothing goes smoothly."

"The electors," she snapped, "believe they were born with divine rights. But Carradee is a good person. We've always been friends." She flicked some hair behind her shoulder. "But can I assume Phoena is still. . . ?"

"Still what?" he asked gently.

"Agitating," Firebird suggested. "Making everything as difficult as possible."

"We suspect she's behind a number of problems. Probably even Korda and Rogonin's attempt on your life."

"That wouldn't surprise me," Firebird muttered.

"She has a new little moon-shadow. Count Tellai."

"Tel?" Firebird choked. "But he's a child."

"He's old enough, and he's willing enough to dive into deep trouble for that woman. They're on vacation now, together. Anywhere but Citangelo."

"Did you ever see . . ." She hesitated. It hurt to ask. "Daley Bowman or Delia Stele?"

"Daley hasn't contacted you?"

She blinked. "What?"

"He accepted asylum." Brennen shook his head. "The last I heard, he'd bought passage to Caroli. Advanced mechanical school."

She managed to say, "That's wonderful." Daley had lacked his twin's boldness. Given a chance to vanish, Daley must've seized it. Someday, maybe, he would feel safe enough to renew old acquaintance. "Good for him," she added mournfully. "He should do well. And Delia?"

"She died at Veroh. I am sorry."

Firebird slumped and shook her head.

Brennen walked to the window, checking the time on his wristband. She saw him catch a glint from inside the glasteel panel, lean close, and examine the honeycomb-patterned security grid. It cast odd shadows on his even features.

She sighed. Unlike Daley, she would never be able to vanish. But could she ever go home? And to what?

Brennen turned away from the window. "At least now I can take you out of this cage. I've had a Cirrus-class racing jet for four months, and I've been so busy since Veroh that I've had no chance to take it through its paces. I'd enjoy your company." He nodded toward her clairsa, which she'd propped in a corner below the windowbar. "If you'd bring that, I'd consider myself well repaid."

She straightened, brightening. "Oh, Brennen. You have no idea how much I'd like that. Or . . ." She shrugged. "I suppose you do know."

He frowned. "And I know you won't forget Ellet's intimidation. Can I give you some promise that I'll respect your will, give you room for your own decisions?"

Why should she believe any claim of restraint? She'd experienced what he could do, and the memory still stung. Unable to think of a stronger vow by which to bind him, she said, "Give me your word as a Sentinel."

He didn't hesitate. "You have it."

"Then I'd love to get out of here."

"Tomorrow? Early or late?"

"Early!" The thought thrilled her, but she felt oddly disappointed. After such a tumultuous meeting, they'd parted with respect on both sides. Now they had nothing but careful, distant talk for each other? She didn't dare drop her guard, but she was treating him as less than a friend. Surely he felt that tension too.

She stepped toward him and laid a hand on his shoulder. "Welcome back, Brenn." Pulling closer, she gathered her nerve and gave him a quick, awkward squeeze.

He drew away, eyes glinting. "Thank you," he whispered. "I said it before, and it's true—you have courage."

CHAPTER 17

AIRBORNE

ad libitum
at the performer's liberty

The deserted parking bay felt comfortably cool, full of swirling air currents, in the last hour before dawn. "There she is." Brennen pointed.

The small jet at the western end looked like a silver dagger. Gleaming, back-curved wings tapered to join a knife-edged chine that protruded from the fuselage, sweeping like a blade from its nose to twin atmospheric engines. The pilot in Firebird leaped for joy.

"It's pretty," she said as casually as she could. "What'll it do?"

"I mean to find out." He opened the passenger entry. Seating was side-by. On her seat Firebird found a combat type, five-point flight harness. The Cirrus racing class, whatever that specified, rose a notch in her expectations. She adjusted her harness as he laid a duffel bag and soft flask in the cargo area, then her clairsa case, and secured all with a heavy net. "I'll be just a few minutes," he said, then made a thorough walkaround.

"How many standard g's are you qualified for, without a gravity suit?" he asked as he climbed into the pilot's seat, so close that their legs almost touched. She laughed inwardly when she realized his flying leathers were the same kass-brown as the craft's interior. Both were trimmed in forest green.

"I don't know. Netaia doesn't use your standard g's. Two-thirty-seven pressure units, however that converts. Five-eighty with a life suit."

"And you don't scare easily." He ignited the engines, then handed her a headset.

She clipped it on before answering. "That's right."

Smiling, he got flight clearance and then slid a throttle rod forward. The Cirrus glided out over the city.

Out, she was out, she was out! Buildings and greenery changed angles every moment. Through a glare-shielded cockpit that afforded almost 360 degrees of vision, she feasted on the growing sky glow, the jagged skyline of the capital city, and its ring of green hills.

As soon as they left the outer city's slow-zone, Brennen maxed the accelerator and pointed the jet's sharp nose for the clouds. Thrust pressed Firebird back and down into her seat, and she reveled in the sweet, familiar feeling. She'd breakfasted lightly, hoping he didn't intend to fly conservatively. He climbed at battle speed until the sky started to darken. Surely he was relishing her feelings, if he sensed them at all.

He stalled over the top in thrilling weightlessness, and then set a lazy, downward spiral.

"She seems to handle well." He reversed the spiral. "But this really doesn't demand much maneuverability."

Firebird sighed. "This civilian racer climbs faster than our tagwings. No wonder we lost the war."

"This isn't entirely civilian-equipped." As if to prove that, he tightened the spiral, accelerated the dive, and they dropped like a spinning leaf, reversing again and again. His hand moved confidently on the rods and touchpanels, barely tightening, mostly relaxing. It was a tawny hand, fine boned—neither long fingered and slender like Phoena's, nor broad like her own, more typical of the Angelo line— but strong looking and—

Stop! she commanded herself. *He's reading your emotions!*

He turned to her, and though his voice stayed casual, tiny smile lines around his eyes confirmed that he'd read that emotional flicker. "Are you game for some fast low-level? That'll give me a chance to test her gravidics."

"Sure. You seem to know what you're doing."

"Then hang on."

The next few minutes were breathtaking. He dove into a black-stone badlands area of spires and canyons and skimmed the ground at near-attack velocity, barely clearing boulders, cornering at dizzying speed and doubling back with somersaulting accuracy. A natural arch loomed ahead. The Cirrus shot through before Firebird could check his setup vector.

They soared again. "No problems?" he asked as they burst through a cloud.

"That was great," she cried. This man could fly! All the same, she touched the snugging control on her harness.

"All right, then. One more thing."

He nosed down and pushed the throttle forward.

Acceleration squeezed her up into her seat. The rugged ground rushed closer. Suddenly her mouth went dry. She tried to swallow but couldn't. Her legs, as if possessed with minds of their own, braced against the fore bulkhead.

He leveled out. "Too much," he said gently.

"Wait," she cried. "No, don't abort. Do what you wanted."

"Too much like Veroh?"

He'd realized it before she had: That had felt exactly like her attempt to crash her tagwing. A bitter, metallic taste poisoned her memory.

She tore her stare away from the horizon, met his questioning look, and tilted her chin. "If you feel this ship can handle what you wanted to try, do it. I know you're not suicidal."

"You're sure?"

"Yes," she growled.

He hesitated only a second, then took the jet into a long climb. "If you want me to stop, just shout."

"I will," she said, then pressed her lips together.

He nosed over again. She forced her limbs to relax, averting her eyes from the upracing ground, watching the intensity on Brennen's face instead as he waited, waited for the right moment . . .

Trebled gravity drove her hips into the seat. He took the bottom of the turn through the stone arch and soared skyward again. She whooped. "I'd've thought that was impossible!"

"And I'd've thought," he answered, "I would never know a woman who would enjoy that." He straightened out and steered for a broad, striated mesa. "I think the compensators pass inspection. Let's give her a rest."

He made a casually perfect landing on dark stone and cut the engines. Firebird climbed out onto the silent plateau. Hot, dry wind whipped her hair around her face. She gloried in the lifting, falling feeling and stretched kinks from her limbs, gladly breathing the scent of unseen flowers and faraway thunderstorms.

Please, please don't take me back to MaxSec.

Brennen strolled to the rim of the tableland and peered over at a glimmering yellow desert. In civilian clothes, out of the cockpit, he seemed a different man. Not a telepath, nor an enemy officer, just a man who . . . who wanted her, who had her alone, kilometers from anywhere. Sensitive skin tightened at the back of her neck.

He pulled his hand from his coat pocket and pointed downward. A hunting bird soared far below, its markings almost the same as a red-tail kiel's. Seven to eight hundred years ago, the first colonists had used similar terraforming stock throughout the Whorl. By the time they reached Netaia, their science had blossomed into a high form of art. It had vanished during the Six-alpha catastrophe.

The bird swooped beyond a hillock. Brennen turned. "Would you like to fly it now?" He inclined his head toward the silver racing jet.

Delighted, she sprinted back across the tableland.

He caught up as she boarded. "The control panel is totally different from a Netaian display. I'll show you."

He adjusted the seat and footbars for her and went over the display several times. When she felt satisfied that she'd unscrambled the board, she fired up the engines and gently took it off the mesa. Concentrating hard, she dropped into the badlands at half Brennen's speed and cruised along their contours, mounting small ridges and dropping into adjacent watersheds. A half-eight through and over the looming black arch bolstered her confidence. Gradually she accelerated through twisted canyons, pulled into a climb over the mesa, and watched the badlands disappear behind. The mountains far ahead were shadowy green, rich with summer.

"Find a place to eat," Brennen suggested.

"It's not time yet, is it?"

He touched the panel. "If that's how closely you watch your instruments, I'm surprised you passed flight school."

She chuckled.

"Actually," he said, "you are a good pilot, for such a new one. The NPN was foolish to waste you."

"Despite the fact that I couldn't crash a fightercraft properly when I was supposed to?"

"That," he said bluntly, "was my fault."

The green mountains rose to jagged, tightly folded ridges. Firebird crested the first ridge, then decelerated. Her chest squeezed tightly again. Finally, she found the breath and the courage to ask, "It was you, that day. Wasn't it?"

His voice murmured in her headset, "You needed to know. Can you forgive me?"

She nodded, swallowing hard. War had risks. Wastlings died, and she couldn't grieve Corey continuously. Still, she spoke lightly with an effort. "Yes. How much landing room will we need?"

"I'll talk you through." Near the divide of the second range, they spotted a round lakelet nestled in a cirque amid old-growth forest. She set down below it in a long meadow. As she climbed out, Brennen pulled out the clairsa and lunch packet and swung them over one shoulder, then held out a hand to her. "Watch your step. Tripvine."

"Is that what's blooming?" Though she'd tried to thrust Corey out of her mind, she ignored Brennen's hand. She felt dirty, disloyal. She bent down to examine the tangled ground cover. From under a round leaf she picked a blossom with a shape like a tiny purple trumpet. She held it to her nose. "Yes, that's it."

"They export the extract for perfume, but the stems are as tough as docking cable. I'm not exaggerating." He offered his hand again. "I would bring him back if I could," he added. "I give you my word on that, too."

She looked up into kindly eyes. The electors, not Brennen, had sent her and Corey to die.

She took his hand. Carefully they walked up the vine-covered field to the lake, where water and leaves riffled in a fragrant breeze.

"Over by the water, on one of those rocks?" she suggested. He changed direction without comment, and they scrambled over fallen trees and stones to the tallest boulder, well over twice her height.

He boosted her to his shoulder level. She found a good toehold and scrambled the rest of the way up the lichen-mottled stone. Brennen tossed her the bags and then jumped to the top, holding her clairsa case.

She gulped air.

"Does that disturb you?"

"No," she lied firmly. It was about time he relaxed and let himself play. "Do something else."

Turning toward the shore, he lifted one hand. A glacier-smoothed boulder rolled into the air and landed with a slurping splash.

There it was. In or out of uniform, he was a gene-altered Ehretan.

"We don't flaunt our abilities." He sat down beside her and stared up at the rocky skyline. "They cost energy and wear us down. And," he added somberly, "we've survived by controlling ourselves. If the Federacy ever decided we were dangerous, we wouldn't last. There are too few of us."

She slid off the uncomfortable dress shoes Carradee had sent, then knelt and helped him spread out the lunch parcel. He'd packed dark bread, thinly sliced; a fish spread and a tub of soft, pale, sweetish cheese; and a bag of spiky green fruit. They ate silently for a while, discussing only the food. Finally, Firebird raised the obvious subject again. "I suppose it took a lot of work to learn those skills, though."

"It did. Sentinel College is grueling."

She poured clear red liquid from his flask into a pair of squared cups and offered him one. "Did they teach other things, too? Arts, science?"

"My education was slightly strange. They took me to college for Sentinel training before I'd finished junior school."

"Which did you finish first, then? Your master's training?"

"Yes. Then a year after that—"

"How old were you?"

"Seventeen," he admitted. She tried to imagine a seventeen-year-old youth, trained as a Master Sentinel. They must've utterly trusted him.

"After another year, I finally finished Academy," he said.

"Why did you pick the military?" She envied the choices he'd had.

"Desperate to fly," he admitted, "like you, but we weren't well off. This was the only way I could afford to get into a cockpit. By then, I was getting pressure to take a second degree, in politics. I ignored any courses that might've fit anyone else's plans. I wish I'd broadened. I would've had time."

She nodded. Graduating precociously, he'd have had plenty of time.

"What about your Academy?" he asked.

She sipped the tart, cool fruit juice. "It must be the same everywhere. Flight. Dynamics. Slip physiology. Weapons, navigation, strategies." She slowed, trying to recall what had kept her so busy for so long.

"Interrogation and resistance."

She glanced up sharply. He was smiling. Very well, she could make light of it if he could. "Not enough, though."

"Poor instruction." He offered a small yellow disk. "Have you ever had citrene?"

On her tongue, it melted to a puddle of sour sweetness. "Oh, that's good. Are there any more?"

He dropped several into her palm, then repacked his dishes and scattered the crumbs over the edge of the boulder. Firebird wrestled momentarily with an urge to tell him about Hunter Height and its airstrip.

Corey wouldn't have told him.

Stop, she commanded herself. *Corey's gone. You're alive, and you shouldn't be—wouldn't be, except for Brennen!*

She ate the last citrene and pulled her clairsa from its case. Hunter Height could wait a day.

She played several classical pieces. He sat close, knees pulled tightly to his chest. Encouraged by his unblinking attention, she closed with the theme and variations she'd just composed. She didn't introduce it, but his eyes closed as she began. She let her feelings melt into her music, and when she finished, he sat without moving.

"Did you write it?"

"Yes."

"How long ago?"

There'd be no deceiving him. "After I'd spoken with Ellet."

He took a long, deep breath. "Mari?"

"Hm?"

"May I touch your mind?"

Yes? No? What should she answer?

"Only a touch, Mari, only a feathering. As you've just touched me."

Her neck hairs prickled again. Ellet had warned that she would never be the same, never get away if she ever let him approach her. But she had good powers of resistance. He'd admitted that publicly. *And I played that suite to impress him. Maybe,* she conceded, *just this once, and I could still escape.*

But her voice trembled. "All right."

His eyes reflected the sky. He didn't move or speak.

Past the surface of her awareness blew a sensation of approval so deep, so complete, that she wanted to shout aloud for sheer joy. Someone knew her completely, all her strengths and her flaws, and was neither intimidated nor ashamed. Laughing at herself, for her fears that hadn't come true, she set the clairsa back into its padded case. "You know what I need most of all, don't you?"

"I could help fill that need in you, Mari, for as long as I live."

Only then did she appreciate Ellet's warning. A person who'd been loved in that way would never settle for anything less. Glowing inside, she leaned away from him and hastily changed the subject. "Could you really free-fall?"

He glanced down, and when he looked up again, his eyebrows had arched. "Yes," he said. "It's well within my grasp if I'm rested."

"And if I jumped?"

He shrugged slightly. "I could land you. Do you want to try it?"

What perverse impulse had made her choose that subject? *But I might never get another chance,* she told herself. "Yes, I do. If you're rested."

He grinned and pointed toward a high ridge. "We could launch from that ledge."

After a thirty-minute climb, they stood high on the broad, windy ridge. Far below lay dark forest and the silver Cirrus, dropped like a giant's dagger on shimmering green meadow. The gale made it seem ten degrees colder up here; it tugged her hair forward, whipping her face.

"Brennen," she said abruptly, "something's been bothering me."

"Yes?"

"It's crazy, it—seems like a contradiction. You Sentinels are trained in emotional control. You have to be, to face the barrage of others' feelings. Ellet explained that. But then how . . ." She scuffed a stone with one foot. "How can a Master Sentinel fall in love?"

"We have hopes," he answered, "as personal as anyone's. If we release our emotions, we love deeply, maybe more deeply than others. We don't forget the wonder of finding and winning."

Gazing into the hazy distance while trying to contain her hair with one hand, Firebird nodded. It was time. "Then what's pair bonding? You promised to explain."

He sat down on a large flat stone. She took one just downwind, slightly sheltered by his body from the hair-lashing blast. "I wouldn't think it was as 'rough on outsiders' as Ellet wants you to believe, though few of us marry out." He took a long breath. "It's a deep, permanent link that manifests in the emotions. Each feels with the other, anytime the other is near."

"The way you can read my feelings now?"

"No. Deeper, more certain, and eventually the awareness blends with the other senses. There's an adjustment period, but for my married friends, it wasn't long. I'd guess a few weeks for you—but less for me, because of my training."

"But an outsider wouldn't be taken over?"

"Absolutely not," he insisted. "Only . . . uncomfortable, for a time. A little confused."

She studied the rocks at her feet, flaked fragments of a disintegrating sedimentary layer. "I'd like to believe you. But it's easy for you to make that statement and impossible to prove."

"I've met nongifted people who married my kind," he argued. "They were distinct individuals, even decades later."

She shifted to a more comfortable position on her rocky seat and asked casually, "Your parents are pair bonded?"

"They were." He sounded wistful. "They were very happy. After my father died, it took my mother two years to recover enough to go back to her work. That's a powerful argument against your having me, by the way. In my profession, it's possible I'd leave you a young widow."

He hadn't bristled when she asked about his family. "They were both Sentinels?" she pressed.

"Not military. But both came from starbred families, and both trained."

"Then Ellet . . ." She hesitated. "Are you and Ellet connatural, Brenn?"

"Marginally, I think."

That confirmed Firebird's guesses. She plunged ahead. "She all but dared me to ask what's unique about your family."

His eyebrows came together for an instant. He covered his mouth with one hand. "I'll tell you what I can," he finally murmured, "if you'll let me make sure you tell no one else."

"You mean, do something to my mind?"

He nodded soberly.

Squill! She'd asked for it! But surely he couldn't do any worse than what she'd already experienced. "Go ahead," she insisted. "I want to know."

He touched her forehead with one finger, holding it there long enough that she almost wished she'd backed down. Then he drew his hand away. She'd felt nothing. "It's a very old family, Mari. It's always been small. But my brother and I, and his children, are the only heirs to an ancient . . . religious promise."

She'd heard the Ehretan survivors called "mendicants." "Yes? What is it?"

He flushed. "I'm sorry. That's all I can say, even now. I'm under command myself."

He'd compelled her to silence for that? She almost laughed, then guessed, "Is the secrecy meant to protect your family?" Ellet had mentioned renegade telepaths.

After a long hesitation, he said, "Yes. There's no wealth involved, no personal benefit. I'm sorry. I truly cannot say more about that."

Obviously, to him this was no casual matter. She picked up a smooth brown rock and hefted it, watching him, waiting to see what he'd say without prompting.

He said, "I would hope to have my own children someday. Soon, actually."

Children! He'd said it softly, and obviously, he meant it just as seriously as poor Corey had meant it. Admitting that hope made him vulnerable. But . . . children? Immediately?

"I was a wastling," she answered, stalling while she tried to picture herself as a parent. It was only slightly less difficult than trying to imagine an eternal being. "I wasn't supposed to have children, and I didn't try to want them." Her voice softened as their eyes met again. "The . . . altered genes don't make this impossible, do they?"

"No. We're all mixed blood now."

Yes. Korda had said that. "And you know that I come from a long line of daughters."

He frowned. "I saw that in the portrait gallery. Why?"

"There hasn't been a male born into the succession in over a hundred years. Not since the last time an Angelo prince married against the Powers' will, out of the noble families."

"I suspect that could be cured, whatever causes it. How has the surname survived?"

"Since Prince Avocin's time, the men who've married us have taken the name as a matter of rank and pride."

"I would not."

She opened her hands. "Of course not." A gust of wind caught her hair and tossed it wildly. She seized it again.

Brennen folded his hands around one knee. "Here is a secret I can tell you, Mari. The ayin—the complex of brain areas that gives us our abilities—ages slightly each time we use it. Over time, we lose our powers."

She didn't miss the fact that this time *he'd* changed the subject.

He stared at his lightweight boots. "Here's another. My people have lived as exiles for almost two hundred years. Everyone outside the kindred builds walls against us. They either give us more honor than we deserve, or fear and suspicion that we have to understand. We feel it. We do inspire fear.

"So you see, few people know me. If you did, the way I know you from access, you'd understand how well we complement one another."

But they were worlds different in blood and allegiance, right down to their little cultural habits. Her mind echoed with words he'd spoken in other places: "A matter of Federate security" . . . "I'm sorry to have deceived you" . . . "You could still be a great help to us" . . .

"Ellet said I could cost you the High command."

"That's true." Shrugging, he shifted his feet.

"Why?"

"My single-mindedness would be suspect," he said dryly. "You're not starbred. You're not even Federate."

With the rank he'd achieved at his age, he could have taken a shot at the top, where waning powers might matter less. "No, I'm not Federate. At this moment I have no home at all. At least you have Thyrica."

"And something even deeper. I hear that you visited our chapter room."

Cosmic mercy ... "Do people from other backgrounds worship your god, Brenn?" she blurted.

He raised his head, and the light in his eyes became keener. "Yes. Many do. Grace and truth aren't limited by home worlds."

"On Thyrica, then?"

"And at Tallis, Caroli, Luxia. Wherever we've lived in numbers, we've drawn inquirers."

Firebird heard a note of utter confidence in his voice. She envied it. Whatever he believed, he gave it all his heart and mind. She hadn't felt that sure of the Powers in years. "But you don't push your beliefs on other people."

"That's forbidden."

"Why?" she demanded. "That's strange to me."

"I know," he said softly. "It's our greatest pain and our deepest regret. The powers our ancestors gave us came from their immoral experiments, on their own children. We live with the consequences, good and bad. Until we redeem ourselves by serving others, we've forfeited the spiritual rights we were promised, especially the right to proselytize. We're under divine discipline. Someday," he added wistfully, "that will change. But . . . because we tried to force ourselves on Ehret, we live as exiles."

A hereditary racial guilt?

"Someday," he repeated, "we'll be released to actively seek converts. That's another promise, another prophecy. But for now, it's a terrible irony. We have much to offer. We're in an era of collective pen-

itence but individual mercy. At least we can point the way, when outsiders inquire."

Mercy... Again the ache pressed on her heart. Could a divine ruler
demand utter obedience but stop short of punishing the guilty? And
what did he mean, "redeem themselves"? Her head whirled with questions.

No, shrieked her conscience, *stop!* She stood close to committing
fresh treason. For someone born to her position, acknowledging any
authority higher than Netaia was deadly apostasy.

She mustn't ask. Tossing her stone over the side, she looked at
Brennen steadily, knowing he would read her feelings all the more easily through her eyes. "Let me tell you how I feel, Brennen. I won't
refuse you, but I can't commit myself, not yet. Not to any person, and
certainly not to a strange religion."

His eyes flicked to each of hers in turn. "You'd like to," he murmured.

She felt her cheeks flush. "Who wouldn't?" If such a transcendent
being could exist! She forced her gaze to stay on Brennen's. Her longing for understanding had momentarily overcome her need to keep a
distance.

"But you still don't trust me," he said.

"I'm afraid to trust anyone."

"I understand," he said gently. "Because you're valuable to the
Federacy, you suspect my intentions. You have that right." He took
her hand and massaged it. "I don't know what I would do if I had to
choose between you and my people. And I can't put you above my
God. There must be one highest priority in your life for which you'll
give everything—your possessions, your rank, your hopes, even your
life—or you're not a full person."

"Don't I know it." She'd given everything for the Powers, the
electors, and the Angelo family. She slid her hand out of his. "And what
do you do when that highest priority fails you, Brenn?"

"You find a higher."

If only it were that quick and easy. Higher than the Angelo family,
there'd always been Strength, Valor, and Excellence; Knowledge, Fidelity, and Resolve; Authority, Indomitability, and Pride. Higher even
than those, in her heart: truth, justice, and love—not the sweet warmth

of human affection, but her searing, self-sacrificial love for Netaia and its people.

Could Brennen's higher master return that to her?

He stood and brushed rock dust from his leathers. "Meanwhile, would you trust me enough to jump if I went first? It is the easier way down."

She snorted, appreciating the paradox he saw. She would trust him with her life in free-fall, because the worst that could happen would be a fast, fatal landing. But if she let him get too close, the worst that could happen might be . . .

Unfathomable.

Shivering, she scrambled to her feet. What if she bound herself to a Sentinel, and then one day he turned on her? How deep could that misery run?

But if they were truly bonded, heart and mind, could he ever do such a thing?

She stepped up to the cliff they'd climbed and peered over its side. The ridge was nearly as tall as the MaxSec tower, and here it was just as sheer. "I hate climbing downhill."

"Good. We'll jump." He eyed the cliff's distant foot as if picking a landing spot. "I'll go first. Once I'm down, give me a minute to rest. You'll feel it when I take a good kinetic grasp on you. Then don't wait too long, and be sure to jump outward."

"Like tower jumping." An Academy skill she'd enjoyed.

He walked to the other side of the ridge. She stared, still not quite sure he meant to do it without a parasail, an anchor line, or even a cushioned landing pit. Then he started to run. After six long strides, he leaped onto—nothing. Her heart pounded as she watched him drop. His shadow rushed to meet his feet. Seconds fled. . . .

With knees bent and arms outstretched, he alighted, absorbing the impact with loose-legged grace. He dropped to his knees, resting, then got up, turned and raised an arm. She felt something invisible take tingling hold of her.

Hesitating, she almost lost her nerve. That was ridiculous. She'd wanted to fly since she was four, and Ellet had insisted it was easier to control another falling object than one's own body. Brennen had just proved he could do that. She walked back ten steps from the edge, sprinted forward, and jumped.

Her hair whipped behind her shoulders and upward from her head. Chill mountain air tugged her outstretched arms. The hilly horizon lifted itself, and it was glorious—like the swell of an orchestra. When she blinked, the falling feeling went on, and on, like a dream. But she had to watch.

Brennen stood below. Time expanded, stretching every half second into a minute. Treetops clutched for her feet but couldn't catch her.

At last, Brennen's arms opened to receive her. She slowed almost to a stop, caught the glitter of his eyes, and then fell the last meter against his chest. She clung there and laughed herself breathless.

He held her close. One of his hands slipped up into her tangled hair and curled around the back of her head. Enraptured, she shut her eyes. A hesitant kiss warmed her temple. She tilted her head back, abandoning caution.

As he kissed her lips, her insides turned to fire. She'd never felt this kind of heat. She wanted to bathe in this warm, incense-filled sea . . . no, to drown in it.

Suddenly alarmed, she struggled for breath. His arms fell away, and a rueful expression clouded his eyes. "Don't be afraid," he whispered. "I'll never try to hurt you, or dominate you. And I'll never take advantage."

"I . . . I know," she stammered. She pressed her head against his shoulder, then pushed away and headed downhill toward the Cirrus jet. How could she explain that she was terrified, not by his feelings, but by her own?

CHAPTER 18

STEADFAST

mezza voce
in a subdued voice

When on leave, Brennen tried to stay as far from Special Operations as possible. He preferred to sort hard messages on the SO floor rather than having them sent up, though, so on this blustery morning, after a thorough thousand-K check of the Cirrus jet, he concluded with a stop at the clearing station.

The pileup was diminishing. After two scrolls of the main screen, he flipped through a stack of correspondence. There were routine messages, advertisements, and pleas addressed to him but which should be handled by Special Operations, and an innocuous-looking brown packet with a return marking that caught him by surprise: a private correspondence from his sponsoring master, Shamarr Lo Dickin. More than a Master Sentinel, Dickin was the spiritual hierarch of Thyrica. Brennen tucked it into a jacket pocket.

Several minutes later in his seventy-fourth-floor apartment, he pulled it back out.

Brennen:
   In the power of the Word to Come I greet you, in our vows of service I join you, as my son of promise I embrace you. Stand firm in truth, for today's path determines eternity, and beware the subtle arrogance of self-sufficiency.
   Is it true what Sentinel Kinsman has written, that your heart leans toward one outside our kindred? The thought gives me no joy, yet I can guess only one reason for it. Without absolute connaturality, any bonding would bring you pain, and because of your epsilon intensity it could be crippling. You need not protest that you've bonded no wife already for this reason. Life with an out-

sider, though, could be even more difficult. Hold steadfast. Be certain of the woman and yourself, and remain willing to refuse her.

Yet realize that you could bring her to salvation. More than that I will not say, except that you are in my awareness and surrounded by my hopes.

> In steadfast love
> Your father of ceremony
> Dickin

A breath whistled between Brennen's lips. Ellet, interfering again! But hoping to draw the Shamarr's reprimand, she'd won him an expression of trust and support.

That sobered him. He understood what he was considering. His family was ancient, the promise sacred. His people's customs had kept the Ehretan genes from dissipating.

"Life with an outsider . . ." Yes. Just to start the questions, where would they live? Could Firebird make a home on Tallis, Thyrica, or—in time—Elysia? Would her epsilon inability wear on him, or could they work out their own ways of communicating?

And how would they resolve their spiritual differences? Even for her sake, he must never disobey the strict codes of exile. He hoped she'd understood that, when they talked on the high ridge. Fully accredited prophets, consecrated to speak for the Eternal Speaker himself, had delivered those codes. The clause she'd questioned stated that the starbred must never again force their will on other people, and so they couldn't even speak of their faith unless they were asked.

Brennen didn't fully understand the Holy One's reasoning, but because of that clause, he couldn't assuage Firebird's fear of eternal torment, of that terrible myth of the Dark that Cleanses. Not yet.

Intermarriage wasn't forbidden in the Exiles' holy books or by the Shamarrs. Their community was too small to survive without bringing in new genes. But with his heritage, could he join himself—heart, body, and mind—with a woman who wouldn't worship alongside him? *One highest priority*, he reminded himself. Setting down Dickin's letter, he stared out his window. He imagined how terribly his spirit might be torn if she tried to pull him away from the Holy One.

But if they were truly and deeply bonded, could she do such a thing? Any pain that she caused him would shred her own soul.

The prophecies added even more responsibility. If he might father the messenger, the Word to Come, could an unbelieving woman help raise Him?

Tarance has children, he protested. *He's the eldest. Let him fulfill the prophecies.*

That didn't wash. More was at stake than his personal desire.

Wasn't the universe's Creator capable of changing one woman's heart?

Of course. But He would not. He gave every soul the perilous freedom to choose, based on the information He led them to find.

Brennen covered his eyes with one hand. *Are you telling me I must wait until she chooses?* he asked, dreading the answer.

In a quiet corner of his heart, he felt a loving but firm touch, not an answer but an assurance. He was known; he was loved. He would find the right way.

Forgive my doubt, he prayed, and he knew he was instantly restored. He stood up and stretched stress out of his shoulders.

At least she'd started to question her assumptions—and to wonder what anchored him in eternity. *She'll ask again*, he told himself. *She has the inquisitive mind.*

Holy One, make it soon!

For the first time in her life, Phoena Angelo had worked a morning with her hands—and she'd found herself enjoying it because she labored for a great cause.

Swirling a conical flask with one hand, she added enrichment broth to a murky soup of dark green algae. Across the granite-walled laboratory, Dr. Nella Cleary stood hunched over her bluescreen. Cleary's laboratory coat was splotched with browned algae, front and back. Phoena glanced down. Her own coat was spotless.

Delicately, minding her freshly tinted fingernails, she filled her autopette with broth and started treating the next flask. The strain, developed by Cleary on Veroh, was safe to handle in this phase. When grown in a basium medium, though, it would produce deadly toxin. If exposed to hard radiation, it would bloom prodigiously. Three or four dozen *Chlamydiminas clearii*/basium warheads would fill a habitable world's oceans with poison within days.

A bell chimed beside Cleary's desk. The stoop-shouldered woman touched a button. "What?" she growled. Cleary often was cross. She'd hoped to tempt Netaia into buying out her family's basium mines, never guessing that the Electorate already meant to unify Netaia's social factions and spur its economy by annexing another buffer system. It wasn't Phoena's fault Dorning Stele had made Veroh open-air uninhabitable for the next three lifetimes. Cleary ought to be grateful. Despite Netaia's temporary embarrassment, Cleary now was wealthier than she'd ever dreamed.

From Cleary's desk came a voice. "Count Tellai to see Her Highness, Doctor. Is she available?"

"Tell him yes." Phoena set down the autopette and flask and wiped her hands on a towel. "This should be word from the Electorate."

Cleary tried to bow as Phoena shed her lab coat and dropped it on the floor. "Thank you for your assistance, Your Highness."

Phoena hurried up the stone accessway and stroked the palm lock of a huge metal door. This east branch of the tunnel system had been used in the past for medical projects, and Cleary seemed satisfied down here. She almost never came up into daylight, though Parkai and D'Stang had grumbled about working underground like burrowing tetters.

Phoena would sleep better after Carradee sent Korda and Rogonin to Hunter Height. She couldn't imagine why it was taking so long. *Soon*, Carradee had promised. *Any day now.*

Tel waited uplevel in the master room, pacing a deep new carpet in bright-eyed excitement. Phoena enjoyed being worshipped by such a sincere believer. She met his welcoming embrace and accepted a long kiss before pulling away. "Well? Tell me, how went the vote?"

His round young face crinkled with smile lines. "It passed, Phoena, despite Carradee's new electors. The mission will go ahead as we planned—through channels this time, as we should've tried before."

"Whatever works, Tel. Who will they send to get her?"

"This is the best part." He seized both her hands. "Captain Friel of the electoral police, to represent her class and her family, and Marshal Burkenhamn, the very officer who administered her commissioning oath. Everyone knows what that commission meant to her. I'm certain your sister will do the honorable thing if confronted honorably."

Phoena snorted. She sent a sidelong glance out the windows toward Hunter Mountain's towering triple peak. "The girl's utterly selfish, Tel, and I believe she has fallen to heresy. If I'm right, you'll see. She'll do everything she can to avoid the highest honor we could give her. She has no hope of bliss anymore."

He lowered his eyes, and his long, dark lashes fluttered. "I . . . I do feel sorry for her, Phoena, sometimes."

He admitted weakness! Phoena seized her opportunity. "Tel, your nature is noble, but in this case your sympathy is unbefitting a nobleman. Firebird was raised a willing wastling," she said patiently. "She is a traitor now, a Federate informer. She will not suicide. So to salvage her reputation, and for the sake of her eternal destiny, we must bring her back. The electoral police will take charge of her, as is their rightful office. They will honor her by doing so." Phoena stared past Tel's shoulder toward the portrait of Siwann they'd brought to dignify the Height. That last strong queen would have approved this mission.

For if Carradee were too weak to rule, Firebird had a perverse inner strength. Phoena had known all her life—or at least guessed—that this wastling was strong enough to seize power, to destroy the ways of the Charities and Disciplines, to tear the very fabric of Netaian society. In Firebird's position, Phoena wouldn't have gone willingly to a noble death!

"You won't see her imprisoned at the palace," Phoena declared, as much to the image of Siwann as to Tel. "The redjackets have detention quarters at their Sander Hill station. They'll hold her there—question her—until arrangements can be made for a proper, public trial, with all the pomp our House can afford. Not even the governor will interfere, if the Tallans bind her over." Phoena gave a long sigh and returned her gaze to little Tel. "As much as the notion pains me, they must punish her as an example. What would become of our ability to steer the economy if every wastling scattered his family's resources?"

Tel nodded sadly. "You're right, Phoena. You're absolutely right."

She shut her eyes. In her mind, the climax would occur at the Naval Academy's amphitheater, near that redjacket station. Just as when Liach was executed, there'd be a grand procession down the broad main aisle, a few final words, the fatal signal. Breathing a little quicker, Phoena decided to order a suitable dress for the occasion. She would observe from on stage. "The family will be shamed, of course, but it is for the good of our people, Tel. You must understand that."

"For Netaia," he whispered. "For our people."

When Firebird learned that Brennen had access to physical training facilities in the MaxSec tower, she jumped at his offer to take her there early in the morning. She'd had little exercise since leaving Netaia. For a week they politely ignored one another on training time. On the sixth morning, though, as she struggled to master one machine, Brennen abandoned his own station and paced toward her. "Stop and rest for a minute. Your effort is so loud in your mind that I can scarcely think."

She forced herself to relax and finish the set before looking his way again. He'd settled onto a nearby bench, breathing hard. His arms glistened, and his skin-thin white training suit clung to his muscular shoulders.

She managed not to stare. "It must be hard," she guessed, "for outsiders to maintain any privacy on Thyrica."

"No," he insisted. "The major part of our training is the Privacy and Priority Codes. When we're allowed to use our skills, when we're not, and when we must. Memorization and then thousands of hypothetical cases, two hours a day for three years."

She wiped her forehead. "Three years?"

"The death penalty is enforced for 'capricious or selfish exercise of Ehretan skills.' "

She thought of Ellet and Vultor Korda. "So I gathered."

"The moral testing before acceptance for training protects us, as well as our society."

That made sense. "I'd suppose your religion creates a moral grounding for most of you."

His eyes came alive. "That's right. Not all those we train are walking the Path."

"That's what you call your religion?"

He virtually leaned into his smile. "What do you want to know about it, Mari? What can I tell you?"

"Only one god. Correct?"

"Absolutely."

"Then wouldn't you say that all 'Paths' lead people to Him?"

"No," he said flatly. "It's a Path, not a highway."

"Hm." All her life she'd attended state services in Citangelo—and, later, those electoral Obediences. She'd offered her life. But for what? "We serve the state," she said. "But we can see it. It's governed by written laws, by people we can look in the eye. How can you imagine a person who created time and space just by speaking?"

Brennen spread his hands. "Actually, in the original tongue the term means *sang*. One of our names for Him is Zamahr, the singer. 'He sang, and time began.' "

She liked that idea. A well-crafted song could have incredible power. "That sounds like a quote. Is it from one of those books in the chapter room?"

"It is. His Voice, His Word, and He himself are co-equal creators. He is *Shaliyah*, the Three . . . but the Holy One. Our Father, the Eternal Speaker."

Baffled by too many names, she flashed back to her attempts, as a determined three-year-old, to memorize all nine Holy Powers without knowing what most of them meant. "And you believe He exists outside space and time."

Brennen nodded solemnly.

She frowned. "I still can't grasp that, Brenn. If I don't, will that come between us?"

He dropped his small towel and clasped his hands. "Mari," he said gently, "you have a fine mind. I think that in time, you'll comprehend."

"I probably could." But did she want to?

"I shouldn't marry outside the faith," he finally answered, "and yet already I'm torn."

She felt stung, vaguely offended.

"I shouldn't, because of those promises to my family," he went on, speaking quickly before she could interrupt, "and because that is my highest priority. But I couldn't walk away from you now."

She refused to be manipulated. "I could respect your beliefs. Your . . . Path." She flicked a strand of drying hair off her forehead. "Couldn't you accept mine, for now?"

He raised his head, looking more deadly serious than in the war room at Veroh. Several seconds passed before he answered. "You told me yourself that you obeyed the Powers, but you didn't truly believe in them."

"Unfair," she mumbled. "You'd just been inside my memories."

"But it's true. You doubted them already."

She fell silent, too paralyzed to think any further. She saw herself standing at the edge of another cliff, almost . . . almost . . . ready to leap. But would anyone catch her this time, or would she destroy herself?

"Faith is foreign to you." Brennen spoke softly. "But sometimes it takes only a glimpse of His majesty. Eventually, true reverence—real worship—compels a seeker to learn more."

Majesty. One familiar word. She shook her head slowly. "That's too complicated. Perfect obedience was easier to understand." Even if it was impossible to give.

"If you truly believed, you'd want to obey."

"You know that from experience?"

"Yes."

She envied that. She had to know just one more thing, today. "What about . . . death? I died once," she said solemnly. "At least I thought I'd died. What do you people do to earn . . . bliss? Mercy?"

"It's not earned. We can only honor Him for all that He is."

"No obedience clauses?"

He smiled with arched eyebrows. "He's given us codes and commandments. But also mercy, in life and death."

"Brennen, it's too much to hope that eternal pleasure would come without your . . . Speaker demanding something. How do you qualify?"

This time he frowned and looked aside. He took several deep breaths before answering. "You're right," he admitted, speaking slowly. "There is a price."

"What?"

He bowed his head and looked up into her eyes. "A life."

"You mean a death, don't you?" she demanded. Not so different from what she'd owed the Powers, after all.

"Not in the way you think. Not at all."

But obviously, he didn't want to explain. Not yet. Confused and deeply troubled, she paced back to her machine.

Brennen picked up his towel and swatted his bench with it. He'd said both too much and too little, even after so many prayers for guidance. He should've simply asked her to declare herself an inquirer, before she so pointedly ended the conversation. Then he could've spoken freely from now on. But until she asked again, he'd have to show his respect for her and the One by keeping silent.

Ask soon, he pleaded silently toward her retreating back. Those shoulders had felt so good, so right, locked inside his arms in the high mountain cirque, but he ached for a far deeper union.

Even before leaving Veroh, he'd felt trapped by his memories of interrogating her. Now he'd given himself too deeply to back away unscathed.

Some fates will find you, Dickin had told him. Did the Holy One intend to refine him through Firebird's struggle toward faith?

He begged for wisdom, and mercy . . . for both of them.

CHAPTER 19

HERESY

risoluto
resolutely

One afternoon shortly after that troubling discussion, Brennen stopped by Firebird's rooms. He remained near the door, in uniform again. Had his month's leave ended already? "Mari," he said, "I must tell you something that you'll like as little as I do."

She'd given up wondering why he still called her that. It was simply something they shared with no one else. "Come in, then. Tell me."

Stepping forward, he said, "You have a day," then he halted. He started again. "Two ambassadors arrived yesterday from Netaia. They want to take you into custody."

She stared. She'd felt safe here. Protected. Now her worst fear sprang out of a corner where she'd half hoped it had quietly died. "They can't do that," she insisted. "There's a week left on my asylum."

"The council . . ." Anger lines formed on his forehead. "They're going to conduct a hearing."

"A trial? For what? They're not going to send me home . . . are they?" she protested, backing away. His silence frightened her. "Brenn?" she urged.

"Not a trial. But a hearing. Remember how badly the council wants Netaia to covenant."

"They have to show strength, Brenn—"

"I know. I agree. This wasn't a unanimous decision. There could be other forces at work, trying to weaken the Federacy. SO and Thyrica's Alert Forces are . . . concerned. But that won't help us tomorrow night in the council chamber. I can't use my abilities to influence anyone there, though I'll want to. That's our law. I must let events take their course."

Speechless, she nodded.

The line of his shoulders softened. "I'll do all I can, though. I've just come from recording a prehearing report—everything you've shown me about the Netaian mindset, and all I learned while I was there, that might be relevant. Three councilors want to renew your asylum. They'll be as prepared as they can be."

"Thank you."

He spread his hands. "But I must warn you. Even they are more concerned about maintaining order, and broadening their trade base, than . . ."

"Than with protecting me," she finished the thought. "That's not comforting."

"Don't give up." He stepped toward her. "I won't."

She slept poorly that night, and in her dreams, redjackets chased her through the back streets of a surreal Citangelo. The following evening her door slid away on schedule to reveal a pair of guards in flawless white. She'd dressed in a finely tailored blue tunic from Carradee's parcel. She took a deep breath to calm herself and then stepped out between them. Three councilors wanted to renew her asylum, three of seven. She must convince one more. Which three? Which one?

The guards took her back to the high-arched council chamber, cleared again of observers. Four other principals already stood at the other end, silent as she walked the long aisle. She recognized the tall Netaian delegates from behind. Captain Kelling Friel wore his red-jacketed police uniform, black cap tucked into his belt. Several steps from Friel, flanking a space evidently meant to receive her, waited an even larger man, First Marshal Burkenhamn. Knowing from his plain gray shipboards that Netaia was still demilitarized, and so he couldn't wear the cobalt blue, and remembering his fairness and sense of honor, she felt a traitor. What if these men could've read her recent thoughts?

She reached the stairs. One guard touched her arm. He nodded toward Brennen and Ellet, who waited opposite Friel and Burkenhamn at the right side of the wide steps. She wondered if Friel or Burkenhamn recognized Brennen as their former lieutenant governor. Probably!

"Stand with them," the guard directed.

She took the space between the Thyrians and glanced left. Captain

Friel looked incongruous here in his finery, but the sight of that gold-edged crimson-and-black uniform reawakened an old, disquieting response: grudging but automatic submission to his authority. The electoral police represented everything she'd been raised to revere. What she thought, what she wondered didn't matter. She'd been trained to obey.

Brennen and Ellet seemed so alike in stature and their relaxed, easy bearing that she felt out of place between them. If they didn't dominate the chamber, they were comfortable here.

Tierna Coll's white robe rustled as she rose. Once all eyes had turned to her, she spoke. "We are assembled to consider the disposition of Lady Firebird Angelo of Netaia, which has become an issue of sufficient magnitude to warrant this council's attention."

Her amplified voice reverberated from stone walls and high ceiling. Firebird thought again how beautiful she looked in her dignity.

"The Netaian government shall speak first, as the body to which Lady Firebird is responsible. We then shall hear Field General Caldwell, the guarantor of her initial asylum, and Captain Kinsman, who served as temporary guardian under General Caldwell."

Ellet turned slightly to study Friel and Burkenhamn with her keen black eyes. Netaia had sent an imposing pair.

Tierna Coll went on. "Following the guarantors, any councilor who wishes to recommend shall speak. Then, as it is her own fate we decide today, Lady Firebird shall take the final position of influence and honor. Are there any objections to this order?"

No one commented.

"Very well. Which of you shall speak for Netaia?"

First Marshal Burkenhamn stepped forward as Captain Friel placed both hands on the hilts of his ceremonial sword. Firebird's breath quickened at the gesture that censured a defendant, though no one else in this chamber—except possibly Brennen—would recognize it.

"Your Honors," Burkenhamn began in his rich baritone, "the Crown and the electoral council request that Major Angelo surrender herself or be surrendered to the government which, by birth, she does represent, and which she serves under solemn oaths. She is called to appear in Citangelo and answer charges pertaining to her conduct as an officer of the Netaian Planetary Navy. As a sovereign government under the protectorship of this Federacy . . ." The marshal glared at Brennen. "We do insist that our internal laws be respected."

Then he did recognize Brennen. Firebird widened her stance to make sure she didn't sway. The Netaians' prudence worried her. They'd based their demand on the key Federate practice of self-government.

The dour General Voers stood to speak. "Marshal Burkenhamn, perhaps the Netaian delegation would postulate the whereabouts of a merchant vessel called the *Blue Rain*. It left Twinnich nine days ago with a shipment of basium concentrate and has not arrived at its destination, Ituri III."

Cleary, Firebird realized. *She's at it again!* Shock washed over her even as Burkenhamn's sharp intake of breath betrayed his surprise. He exchanged glances with Captain Friel before answering. "Your Honor, we have not been authorized to treat on any subject but the surrender of Major Angelo."

"I believe we were speaking of honoring internal law," Voers replied, but he sat down without saying more.

Tierna Coll motioned to Brennen. "General."

He stepped forward. "Your Honors, some time ago I offered a place among us to Lady Firebird, on behalf of the Federacy. I ask that the choice remain hers, to live among us if she so desires. We created the situation that makes it impossible for her to return to her home. For that, we owe her support and protection."

"General," called the head of the council, "do you make a recommendation as to her choice?"

One of Brennen's hands clenched down at his side. Firebird reminded herself that she still scarcely knew him. What was he thinking? "Let the Federacy remember that this is a person of talent and intelligence," he answered, "whose life should not be wasted. We owe her protection," he repeated.

"Then, do you recommend, General?"

Like a knot untied, his hand straightened. "The decision should be hers." Still looking forward, he stepped back into place.

She'd learned to respect that note in his voice. He couldn't say more. Perhaps his own highest priority stood on trial.

"Captain Kinsman?" Tierna Coll turned slightly. "Do you recommend?"

Brennen's head turned toward Ellet, and Firebird intercepted his cautioning glance. "No," Ellet answered blandly. "Let the council decide."

"The council," she'd said. Not "her." Very diplomatic.

"Colleagues?" Tierna Coll swept the arc with her gaze. Firebird searched for sympathetic faces.

Mister Lithib straightened on his deeply padded mobility chair. "Let the lady choose," he wheezed. "It is her destiny of which we speak."

Firebird smiled at him, although disappointed that he'd said no more. In the ensuing silence she heard a faint, rhythmic tapping. Captain Friel stood drumming his fingers against the red leather of his sword's sheath.

"Any others?"

General Voers stood. "My colleague speaks of destiny." He nodded toward Mister Lithib. "But one's destiny often lies in the hands of others. Furthermore, we follow a strict noninterference policy in local affairs. By trying to alter Netaian civil law, we may already have meddled in this situation more than is appropriate."

Firebird started. Were the Federate policy makers divided over Netaian reforms? Did those freedoms they enjoyed make it difficult to govern other peoples?

At the moment, that didn't matter. She must win one councilor, without losing any of the other three. "Any others?" Tierna Coll asked again. Firebird braced herself. It was her turn.

No, Madam Kernoweg had stood. "Colleagues, honorable delegates," she intoned. "The inequity among our worlds' resources has long been a source of contention for my people. We of Lenguad carry more than our share of levies to support other Federate citizens. We understand the Netaians' reluctance to involve themselves in federation, which they might perceive as a drain on their resources. We wish to assure them that they would be received by us as equals, perhaps by honoring their request today. At some junctures, my friends, practicality must take precedent over principle. One prisoner's fate must not outweigh the thousands who would benefit from Netaian covenance

. . . on Netaia, as well as other worlds. We must not preempt Netaia's jurisdiction over a Netaian citizen." She sat down.

Captain Friel's fingers drummed a little faster. Dread knotted Firebird's stomach as she waited for Tierna Coll to motion her forward.

The white-robed woman beckoned graciously. Facing her and ignoring everyone else, Firebird stepped out from between the Sentinels. She spoke slowly, as she'd been trained to do. "Your Honor, General Voers speaks the truth when he says that my destiny lies in the hands of others. I am alive today because of words and actions of others here present. And while living here, I've learned that the rights of each individual citizen of a Federate system take precedence over all corporate rights." She glanced guiltily at Madam Kernoweg. Truly, thousands of Netaians would prosper if Netaia joined the Federacy. *Later*, she promised herself. *I'll do all I can for them—someday!* But first, she had to survive. "Therefore I ask to be heard as an individual, Your Honors. If I'm given the choice, I wish not to be sent back to stand trial."

Voers' dark baritone voice rang out, "But you are not an individual citizen of a Federate system, Lady Firebird. Consider, if you will, a hypothetical situation. Suppose we could not justify continuing this protective custody. If we could offer you only a dignified, private death rather than that public trial, what would be your preference?"

She started. Could the Federacy execute her, rather than continue her asylum against Netaia's wishes? Brennen had never hinted at that possibility!

"Hypothetical," he'd said. Maybe it was a rhetorical question, asked simply to establish every degree of preference . . . or convince one wavering councilor.

It did force her to declare herself. She couldn't choose to be publicly executed for treason. "Your Honor, if it came to that, without any other honorable choice, I would rather die here." She glanced down, then backed into her place.

"Well spoken, Lady Firebird." Madam Kernoweg lowered her prominent eyebrows.

Tierna Coll seated herself. "Colleagues, let us judge."

Now that it was too late, Firebird wished she'd said more. She watched the councilors confer in silent privacy, speaking via screens and touchboards. The chamber seemed cooler than it had been only a few minutes ago. They were taking considerable time with their decision. Whether that was a hopeful sign, she couldn't guess. General Voers looked more solemn by the moment. Madam Kernoweg ran a hand over her closely cut hair.

One councilor, she pleaded silently. *Just one.*

"General Caldwell?" Tierna Coll beckoned him to Admiral Madden's board. As he walked around the far end of the table, his hair—sun-bleached from weeks planetside—caught a stray gleam of light. He eyed the screen intently, glanced at Tierna Coll, then reached for the board. Firebird didn't think he looked pleased.

Not a trial. Not at home. A traitor's death wouldn't be as quick or as comfortable as Liach's firing squad. Netaia had grim ways to execute traitors.

General Voers stood. Firebird composed herself to stand steadily. "Lady Firebird. It is on record before this council that you would prefer to remain on Tallis, even if it means your death, and not return to Netaia. Please confirm that statement for our recording."

Powers that Rule! Had she lost?

No, no. They were following protocol. "If I returned to Netaia it would surely mean my death, Your Honor, in complete humiliation. Here, though I die, I've had a choice."

Voers returned to his touchboard. To Firebird's surprise, the seven councilors turned to Brennen.

He gave a slight nod and soberly touched a single panel.

Tierna Coll rose to her feet and beckoned regally. "Lady Firebird, come forward."

As Firebird slowly mounted the broad steps to stand at the center of the table's arch, Tierna Coll continued. "Worthy delegates, we now declare the following salient points. One, Lady Firebird has sought and been initially granted asylum among us. Two, Lady Firebird was taken by the Federacy as a prisoner of war, during an act of undeclared aggression initiated by the then-independent government of Netaia. Three, Lady Firebird is yet a Netaian subject."

As she emphasized those final words, Firebird's courage melted. She glanced at Brennen. He stood with his eyes closed.

"Legally, then, the Netaian delegation is entitled to demand her return. However, the attempt on her life here on Tallis has led us to believe that she will not be granted justice on Netaia. Honorable delegates, do you wish to respond?"

Firebird didn't turn aside, but she knew Burkenhamn's voice. "She will have a trial, Your Honor. Justice will be done."

"We assume that your verdict has already been delivered, Marshal Burkenhamn."

Only silence answered her.

"Very well. Lady Firebird, we wish a lasting relationship with your people. If that required your death, you would choose to meet it here?"

Again! Back at Veroh, it had seemed logical to ask for death. Now she choked on the words. Retreating into the role she'd played for so long, she raised her masks back into place and avoided looking at Madam Kernoweg. "Yes, Your Honor. If you so order, I will ask only for privacy and a well-sharpened blade."

"We do not order that, my lady." Tierna Coll nodded to Brennen.

Firebird kept her eyes on the council table but felt him walk slowly behind her. After an interminable moment she heard a high, keen note.

Aghast, she spun around to face him. He had drawn and activated his shimmering crystace. His eyes were clear, and his face determined, as he swept up the blade that was easier to hear than to see. He halted it a hand's breadth from her throat.

Had they ordered him to execute her, out of mercy—to keep her out of Netaia's hands?

"Face the council, Mari." Brennen's low voice allowed no objection. She remembered he'd said, *I question what I'd do if it came to a choice. . . .*

Obviously, he'd decided in favor of his people.

But he'd claimed that he cherished her!

She turned her back on him and on hope. Ellet's eyes shone. The chamber was as still as death, except for the singing crystace.

"Worthy delegates," said Tierna Coll, "you have witnessed the thrice-confirmed choice of this prisoner, to die on Tallis rather than return to Netaia for public trial. We request now that you acknowledge our authority to rule thus."

Kelling Friel sounded far away. "This is irregular, Your Honor. Lady Firebird's noble birth, and the offenses with which she stands charged, demand one of a few specific death protocols. If you will not give her over to custody, we demand that she be given the means to dispatch herself in a traditional manner."

Firebird breathed slowly, deeply, cherishing each lungful of air.

"We have been advised of Netaian suicide customs, Captain, but Lady Firebird does not stand on Netaian soil. Our decision hangs partially upon your answer. Marshal Burkenhamn, do you bow to our ruling?"

Firebird's ears rang as the sopranissimo blade hovered. How close?

Burkenhamn hesitated. To anyone raised outside the Netaian legal system, any death might suffice, but to a Netaian, ceremonial precision was almost half of justice. The Powers had decreed it so.

Powers? Firebird's mind raced. What were they? Dissociated attributes of gods who might never even have existed? Even if they had, even if they still did, what did they care for one young woman's fate? Or for anyone else, for that matter? Had they interfered at Veroh, when Dorning Stele slaughtered civilians?

What claim did the Powers have on her life, after she'd tried to die for them? She had nothing else to offer.

"We abstain from voicing, Your Honor," Burkenhamn said at last. "Her fate should be decided by Netaian custom alone."

Firebird clenched her fists. Her heart pounded in her ears as she struggled to put words together. Before she died, she would give Kelling Friel something to remember.

But Tierna Coll called, "Then we declare our decision in full." Her ringing voice softened. "Lady Firebird, do not be afraid. You are free to die here, a Netaian subject—under *our* custom—or to return with these officers, if such is your choice. However, you need not choose either. This delegation refuses to acknowledge our right to give what they claim to want, which is your life. Therefore, we are not obliged to allow them to take it. You may remain on Tallis."

Firebird's mouth fell open. She snapped it shut.

"We will impose one condition, however. Would you indicate that one day, you might choose to become a Federate transnational citizen, as an example to your people? Under the duress of this moment, we cannot ask you to make any decision, but we do request some assurance that you could seriously consider transnationality."

Firebird blinked, forced her mind clear, and struggled to understand. The council had forced the Netaians' hand. Tierna Coll had made Burkenhamn refuse to endorse her execution, if it happened here. Then, surely Brennen wouldn't have . . .

Twisting her shoulders, she glanced back at him. Behind the atom-edged blade, his lips remained firm but his eyes pleaded. Was he play-acting this role? Would he strike, if they ordered it?

It didn't matter. Her destiny had been given back to her, and this decision had nothing to do with Brennen Caldwell. Could she consider taking Federate transnationality?

Absolutely. As a priority, the government she'd been raised to worship had utterly failed her.

She flung off her masks. She wrenched free from the roles she'd tried so hard to play. Why, why, why die for a government that had deliberately corrupted its people's faith? . . . And how, knowing all she now knew, could she sacrifice her life for an electoral cartel that "protected" her people by oppressing them? Serving the Powers had created an insane dishonesty at the core of her being. She wouldn't serve them one minute longer. Not even if by dying in this chamber, she might have regained her chance at instant, eternal bliss.

As an example to your people . . .

Feeling almost light-headed, as if she'd shaken off a heavily armored helmet, she came to attention. She spoke the words that would damn her in her own family's eyes: "Your Honors, I will take Federate citizenship here and now, if that might bring our peoples closer together."

Tierna Coll's eyes widened for a moment, and then her cheeks twitched into a quick smile. "Lady Firebird, we demand no such commitment. In fact, we generally give citizenship candidates several weeks of instruction. But," she added, glancing at Friel and Burkenhamn, "we could make an exception in this issue. If you swear allegiance to us now, you will do so without duress and in full view of these Netaian representatives. Are you so willing?"

No second thoughts! Forget Friel, forget Burkenhamn—forget Brennen, too, if need be. This would be her first step toward finding a new, higher priority, a new set of truths. She would formally forsake her determination to die for a lie. "I am," she said.

Behind her, the crystace's hum snapped off.

Tierna Coll touched several panels and met Firebird's eyes again. "You will take this oath, then."

"Solemnly I swear this day," Firebird repeated after Tierna Coll, "my unwavering allegiance to the authority of this Federacy."

"I do acknowledge," intoned Tierna Coll, "that Federate trans-nationality supersedes any citizenship, affiliation, or rank that I hold under any local government."

Firebird glanced left. Captain Friel clenched his sword hilt. Marshal Burkenhamn shook his head, disbelieving, grieved.

She took a deep breath and tried to ignore him.

"Go on," Brennen encouraged softly.

But she struggled a moment longer. Besides her loyalty to Netaia and the Electorate, she had an aristocrat's pride in herself, in her own strengths. She'd hoped to win glory through utterly indomitable obedience.

But where had it brought her? The electors already believed she was of no further use to Netaia.

At last, she realized how badly that hurt. She'd have served her people with complete devotion, if only they'd let her. She steeled herself to step across an invisible line into an incomprehensible future. "Your Honor, would you repeat that clause?"

She finished the oath in a steady voice. Tierna Coll slipped a paper from her transcriber and turned it on the tabletop. Firebird picked up a stylus and firmly signed away her former life.

In her class's eyes now, she was worse than dead. An apostate, a heretic. Unable to look at either Friel or Burkenhamn, she rode with Brennen back to the minimum security floor.

Brennen stroked the palm lock. "Please let me come in," he said urgently.

"Come," she muttered.

As the door slid shut behind him, she flicked on the lights. "Shall I order kass?" she asked, taking refuge in meaningless hospitality.

"No." He stood close. "Talk to me."

"You talk to me!" She sank onto the raised end of her lounger. "Was that a trick, to trap them into letting me stay here? And why you, with the—the crystace?"

As she raised her hands to gesture, he grasped them. "It was Voers' idea, based on my prehearing report. We maneuvered them, but they made the critical choice."

"We? Did you know they were going to—"

"It was only a hope. You had to win one councilor. You convinced Admiral Baron Fiersson. Then I was ordered to go ahead. As guarantor of your asylum, I was the logical person for the role the council ordered me to take."

"But—"

"Voers and I were certain your people would demand to see things done their own way. And I was certain . . . enough . . . that you wouldn't choose to go back with them."

She pulled back her hands. "But it could've ended that way."

"If you'd asked to go home, the council would've sent you home, this time. You're dealing with a bureaucracy, Mari. An idealistic one, but a bureaucracy that includes Madam Kernoweg and many others like her."

"But if Marshal Burkenhamn had consented . . . to let you. . . ?"

"You don't think he could have. Neither did I."

"I don't know," she whispered. "He's gruff, but he's a good man. I probably broke his heart in there."

"Are you all right?" He peered down at her.

"I will be."

"You were magnificent, Mari. I'd never dared hope you would do that."

"I made an important decision," she said. "I should probably thank you." But she didn't want to. For all his explanations after the fact, he'd terrified her.

"I frightened you," he said, as if he'd read her thoughts.

"Brennen." She had to ask. "Would you have killed me?"

"How can you even ask?" he whispered, frowning. He held down both his hands to her. "I know exactly what it meant to you, taking that oath."

She shut her eyes, heartsick. He hadn't answered.

"Mari," he whispered from the distance. "Mari, I love you."

She squeezed her eyes even more tightly shut. "Sometimes," she said, "you have strange ways of showing it." Feeling him move closer, she looked up.

"I showed it," he said dispassionately, "by saving your life."

Truly, he had. Twice now. And she didn't doubt she'd made the right choice, swearing allegiance. "Sorry," she murmured, "but I'm too full of adrenaline to be rational."

Grasping her hands again, he drew her to her feet. She stared up into his eyes. She'd never felt such turmoil. "You never answered. What am I to think?"

His eyebrows lowered. "I would have died," he said flatly, "before striking you. Ellet would've had to execute us both."

She bowed her head and pressed her forehead to his chest. Salty puddles gathered in her eyes.

She felt his fingers lock behind her neck. She raised her chin, and as the puddles overflowed down her cheeks, he lightly kissed her lips. The smoky-sweet presence touched the edge of her mind again, warmer than before, and stronger.

Recalling the overpowering sensation of mind-access, she suddenly understood how much power he was holding back, and she glimpsed the magnitude of what pair bonding might involve. Appalled, she pressed her palms against his chest.

Once again, he instantly loosened his arms. She slapped the tears from her cheeks, pressed her head against his chest, and circled his waist with her arms, trying to release all thought and tension. She felt shattered inside.

"I'm sorry," he murmured. "I'm sorry. I'd hoped you would trust me. But how can you, when everyone else you've trusted has been destroyed . . . or else tried to destroy you?"

At any rate, now it was done. She no longer had any hope for eternity. This life, as long as it lasted, would be all she could hope to receive.

So be it.

"Oh, Mari," he whispered. He sounded as if he were close to tears himself.

She would have stood holding him that way for an hour, pressing her ear close to his beating heart, but abruptly she remembered Voers' words to Marshal Burkenhamn. "Brennen," she said. "That ship that vanished—the *Blue Rain*—I'm sure Netaia has it. They've got to be working on that basium project again."

She lifted her head and added, "And I think I know where."

CHAPTER 22

RETURN

intermezzo con accelerando
interlude, becoming faster

He pulled a little farther away. She felt his scrutiny where a moment before there'd been only sympathy. "Go on."

"You probably don't believe me."

"Of course I do."

"I'll show you, if you'd like. Access, I mean."

"I think that would be wise." He motioned her back to the lounger. As he settled beside her, she reminded herself that this was the first duty of her new citizenship. She offered her eyes, then her memories of Hunter Height.

Brennen stood up before she'd completely refocused on her surroundings. "Come with me," he said. "We may be able to speak with Tierna Coll before she retires for the night."

The moment Firebird finished explaining to the tall woman in white, the outer office door slid open once more and admitted Ellet Kinsman. The Sentinel strode in without a word or glance to Firebird or Brennen, or even explaining why she'd come. "Your Honor, forgive me for intruding."

"I am glad you are here, Sentinel Kinsman." Tierna Coll motioned Ellet to take a seat. "Perhaps you can clarify an issue for me. Lady Firebird has just confessed to having concealed data from Master Brennen under interrogation, data which if genuine could require our immediate attention. In your opinion, is this possible?"

"Her?" Ellet sounded incredulous. "Your Honor, this woman is no match for Brennen—in any way!"

Firebird flushed.

"You've held her under access yourself?" Brennen glared at Ellet.

"I have not. But I know you, Brennen. I know your strength, and your training, and the heritage of your family. You seem to have forgotten who and what you are." Ellet turned back to Tierna Coll. "Your Honor, Firebird Angelo of Netaia could never have deceived Brennen under access, not then. But maybe, now that she's had opportunity for learning to work around his abilities—"

"Your Honor, I would know deception." Brennen's face darkened. "And, Ellet, if you know my strength, you know that, too. There's a grave danger to the Federacy. I've offered my services to avert it."

Firebird bristled, too. "I'm not inventing this, Ellet. Access my memory, if you must." The notion made her cringe.

The head of the council conferred with her touchboard for a minute longer, then shut it down. "This is sobering, General. We must investigate, but without showing overt disrespect to the Netaian government at this delicate moment. Lady Firebird, thank you again for your transfer of citizenship. Still, a case could be made to support Sentinel Kinsman's suggestion. These weeks you have spent in General Caldwell's custody do suggest a possibility of truth."

"I'll give her access," Firebird said again, "if you feel she'd be more objective."

Tierna Coll glanced at Ellet, then Brennen, then smiled mildly. "That won't be necessary. In the morning, I will dispatch a message urging Governor Danton to investigate this locale. His staff should have answers for us within a few weeks, or immediately, should they feel the need to strike. We must walk a careful middle ground, without showing weakness. Thank you for your concern, Lady Firebird, and your counsel, Captain Kinsman. And, General, your offer is appreciated, but your services are needed here on Tallis. Please return Lady Firebird to her quarters."

Firebird's door closed behind them as she stumbled toward the table. "Kass now?" she offered wearily.

"Please." Brennen took a stool and stared at the table.

"At least she promised to investigate. Immediately." Firebird pulled a pair of filled cups from the servo's cubby and set one in front of him.

"Yes," he said slowly. "But you saw that she doubted my word. That has never—*never*—happened before."

"Maybe she doubts because you're a Sentinel."

"They do," he whispered. "They all do. Even those who respect us. I'm certain now." His misery showed in the set of his jaw and the lines between his eyes. "No wonder none of us ever reach the High command."

Firebird wanted to ease that misery, but she couldn't think of anything to say that might help. "Do you think," she said reluctantly, "that Danton will move quickly enough?"

He looked up. "No," he said. "Danton is first a diplomat." He bowed his head over folded hands and sat motionless, except for his shoulders' slow rise and fall.

Brennen's thoughts boiled. He must step out from this nexus. But in which direction?

Hunter Height, as Firebird had just recalled it for him, could support weapons research. Phoena Angelo, "on vacation" from Citangelo, was as determined as her distant ancestors to throw off "out-system invaders," and just as likely to use violent means. The *Blue Rain* had carried basium, and the wealthy Angelos still owned ships that were capable of piracy.

Could he draw any other conclusion?

No. If the weapon were deployed before Lee Danton proved it existed—a small but disastrous possibility—millions, even billions, could die.

The Sentinels' Privacy and Priority Codes demanded that he step into danger when innocent others were at risk, "if he plainly possessed the resources to defuse that situation in a timely and appropriate manner." With Special Ops, he'd completed covert operations of exactly the sort he was considering.

But could he disobey a direct order? His people longed to put a Sentinel on the High command, where he might live out their codes and beliefs in plain view. Many sincere seekers might step onto the Path because of such an example. He had the abilities and the ethics to bring honor to the position.

But was some higher plan in motion? Maybe even his family's sacred hope?

Tonight, he must make only one correct decision.

If he went to Netaia covertly, against orders, he'd have to set aside his lofty military goal. Insubordination must carry severe consequences. He might be demoted, even forced to resign from Federate service, though he could hope that Regional would only reprimand him if the outcome justified his decision. But he'd never achieve the High command. Someone else would rise in his place.

He clasped his hands tightly. *Holy One, I need wisdom more than ever. Which way shall I turn, and how far must I leap?*

Then he silenced his mind and listened intently for the Holy Voice.

After a time, Brennen got himself another cup of kass, downed it standing, and tucked the cup into the sterilizer. "Get some sleep if you can, Firebird," he said firmly. She heard an odd, brave note in his voice. "I may be back, but don't wait up." He left without explaining.

She stumbled to the back room and fell fully clothed onto her bed. *"Firebird." How long has it been since he called me that?* Did it signify new respect, or rejection?

The next she knew, he was pulling her back to her feet and pushing another cup of kass at her. Trying to stand steady enough not to spill the bitter brew on herself woke her completely. He vanished into her freshing room. In a minute, she peered in. All her personal things had disappeared, and he was closing a small black duffel kit.

"What are you doing?" Blinking sleepily, she smoothed the wrinkled blue dress tunic she'd worn to face the council.

"I want to take you to Hunter Height. Will you help me?"

"Tierna Coll changed her mind? How did you do it?"

"She did not."

Firebird leaned against the doorway. "You mean to go without her orders?"

"Against them," he corrected calmly.

"Brennen!" She shook her sleep-fogged head. "What is it you want me to do?"

"Get us in. Identify Cleary and her collaborators. Help me stop the research. Then get us out, if you can."

"But Tierna Coll said—"

"If we go, if we're wrong, the Federacy can disclaim all responsibility." He handed her the kit. "But if we're right, your basium people have had too much time already since the *Blue Rain* disappeared. That gives them a head start."

"My basium people?"

He snorted softly. "Sorry. But we can't wait for Danton."

"Right. But the council—the High command . . ." Was he throwing away all hope of promotion?

Handing her the duffel, he spoke slowly, as though he were making sure he believed every word. "I must follow the vows I made when I was vested as a Sentinel. This woman Cleary is developing a way to foul an entire world, if you understand it right. It could be Caroli, Varga, Tallis."

There it was again, that highest priority. Those Sentinel vows, and his god. "Tallis," she suggested. "Phoena would like that."

"Knowing that Netaia will be eligible for full Federate covenance in three years?"

"There are Netaians who won't ever want that."

"That's true," he said. "Mari, if Phoena's project is finished and deployed, and if you're right, Tallis could be attacked in weeks, or less. Danton wouldn't win any support for the Federacy by sending missiles into Hunter Height, even if he did investigate instantly. Two of us, though, might destroy the project without taking other lives. We have to keep Netaia from striking. For Netaia's sake, and others.' "

She straightened.

"Will you help me?"

"Of course." Firebird seized two extra pairs of gray shipboards from her open closet. "I'm ready."

In the gleaming Cirrus jet, they soared out to the Fleet's primary spaceport, where she'd first stepped onto Tallan soil. An attendant took the Cirrus into his charge at the gate of the massive clear dome, and Brennen watched apprehensively as the young lieutenant slid into the pilot's seat with undisguised glee.

Firebird watched Brennen's gaze follow the Cirrus to a storage hangar. She laughed silently in sympathy. If she owned a jet like that, she'd worry too. Then he led onto the base proper, past rows of parked atmospheric craft and streamlined dual-drive ships that were equally maneuverable in vacuum and atmosphere: interceptors, transports, gunships, shuttles. Her eyes widened at the display of Federate striking power, gleaming under lights.

Inside a stuffy arms depot that smelled like institutional disinfectant, Brennen picked up a black drillcloth pack and gave her a peep inside at a load of miniature explosives—sonic, incendiary, and others she didn't recognize and he didn't explain. Three stylus-shaped recharges for his blazer vanished into the pack's side pocket.

"I know the night sentry fairly well," he said softly as they zipped into high-g acceleration oversuits. "SO people often pick things up at odd hours. It's how I got a ship, too, and how we'll get offplanet."

Dozens of near stars shone through the arc of the dome, though the sky had started to brighten toward dawn. They stopped at a parking row near the dome's edge, and there she looked up at a thirty-meter craft with minor atmospheric adaptations. Its enormous stardrive engine dwarfed the slim, upper cabin compartment. "It's a DS–212, a Brumbee, designed for clandestine message delivery." He examined its rounded surface and talked his way down its length. "They've pared it down to absolute essentials for long-distance slip. It'll maintain acceleration and deceleration at several g's past what normal translight drives will give you." He straightened and grinned. "In other words, it rides like a missile."

Firebird jumped for the security handle, got her balance on the door plate, and released the entry hatch. Brennen followed her in and secured the hatch behind him, plunging the cabin into darkness. Feeling her way, she slipped into the left chair. Brilliant blue striplights glimmered on above her. Brennen squeezed between seats and into the pilot's, then started rearranging controls on the slanting display. "Would you stow the pack?" he asked. "There's a bulkhead compartment behind you."

Atmospheric engines thrummed, responding to their lasers, as she closed down a magnetic seal. Returning to her seat as he finished his checkout, she slipped into her flight harness.

"If we should get into a scrap," he said, "you shoot, I'll fly. Here's the ordnance board." He touched a rectangular orange panel at the console's center. She studied it while he raised the ship and set it in motion.

A vast, wedge-shaped sky hatch loomed ahead, a pale slice of sapphire blue edged by luminous strips. He confirmed clearance for take-off, flipped the last levers, then killed the striplights. The atmospheric drive roared to full power. Brennen released the ground brakes and they shot through the wedge.

The stars of the Whorl glowed brighter and more intensely colored, moment by moment. As Brennen had predicted, they weren't challenged, but she felt uneasy. She'd committed high treason, there in the chamber. Now she was helping Brennen flirt with insubordination.

His Sentinel vows, he'd declared, took precedence over the Federacy's orders. *As Ellet's interpretation of those vows took precedence over his orders*, she thought with a sudden chill. One Sentinel had betrayed her. What really, what now, were his intentions toward her—for this mission, and after? Uneasy, she wriggled in the deeply padded seat.

"Ten seconds to slip," he said.

"Ready." She snugged the harness, took a deep breath, and consciously relaxed every part of her body. First the odd vibration of the slip-shield took hold, and then the pressure hit. Even wearing a high-g suit, it was worse than she'd ever experienced. She pulled in a slow breath, and gradually, the messenger ship's gravidic compensators caught up with thrust.

Finally, she managed to lean forward and look around. The stars on their visual screen had vanished. Brennen seemed unaffected. "I checked the conversion factor for Netaian pressure units. That was six-seventy, perceptible. Almost twenty percent over your rating, but our suits are more efficient."

She took another deep breath, glad he hadn't slowed the mission to make it easy for her, but assumed command as a colleague.

Colleagues. She could accept that, for the moment. She released her harness and yawned.

"You're done in," Brennen observed. "It's been a long night." He brought the striplights back up and dropped one of a pair of broad shelves from the curved overhead compartments. "Here are bunks. Across the way—watch your head—is the galley servo. If I complain about the food, it's only overfamiliarity. I've been through the menu too many times."

She examined every part of the cabin. "How long do your psych people think a human can travel in a compartment this size and not go off balance?"

He let down the second bunk, little more than a black-blanketed pallet. "We have life support for two for just over a month."

"You're joking."

"No. These ships were designed to make the Tallis-Elysia run. The messenger service uses this model, and I've spent more time in one than I care to remember." He rolled his eyes at the recollection. They shone deep blue under the striplights.

Exhausted, she stared at those eyes a little too long. She could almost feel the power behind them.

She flushed. *Colleagues!* she rebuked herself. *He has proved he won't force himself on you.* Still, she couldn't bring herself to trust him entirely. He was a man, a stranger. Potentially dangerous.

Yes, and she was a traitor. Apostate. And if Phoena won the next round, soon they both would be dead.

Why did it still seem important to keep him at arm's length? He'd offered an honorable relationship.

What *would* it be like, to love him?

He leaned against a bulkhead, waiting for her to speak.

Her cheeks warmed. "Ellet admitted, that is—well, she said that you people had ways of . . ." Words stuck in her throat. She sat down carefully on the lower bunk.

He walked as far away as he could, to the pilot's chair.

Was he still trying to prove she could trust him? And was she being cruel, pushing him to answer such a personal question before she'd settled her mind about his faith?

But she had to know this. She found her voice. "Ellet said Sentinels could please one another in ways outsiders can't. Is it like—the way you touched me the day we took out your Cirrus?"

He nodded somberly.

His gentle-eyed respect seemed a priceless gift, particularly tonight, when she felt stripped of all honor. "Is it permitted to show me? Just a little," she added.

"As long as I don't touch you."

No wonder he'd retreated. "Please," she said. A tingle of apprehension heightened her longing. She could no longer pretend she didn't want this.

Brennen looked deeply into her eyes, and the tingle of access-beginning brushed through her. This time, though, he called up neither memory nor emotion, but sensation: a caress of the soul, like feathered wings beating against her heart.

She tried to look away. Immediately his strength flooded her, warm and reassuring. He would do nothing inappropriate. Gradually, the urge to struggle left her until she felt only Brennen's enfolding, accepting presence.

Then he drew back the tendril of epsilon energy, though she sensed a lingering glow. He'd relaxed sideways on the pilot's seat, and the beveled star on his shoulder caught the blue striplights, reflecting sparks that dazzled her eyes.

"Pair bonding," he said softly, "is created when two connatural minds join in a contact like that, only closer—to the total interweaving of emotional fiber. That seals the physical marriage. For life." He folded his hands. "Only the connatural can endure such a close approach. That's why only they can pair bond. But connaturality alone isn't enough to make a union. There must be love. Shared goals. And trust." He stressed the word a little sadly. "Each bond mate remains an individual. Each one can please or devastate the other."

"Brennen." This hurt her pride, but she had to say it. "You realize, don't you, that I'll never be able to do . . . what you just did . . . for you. Is that fair to either of us?"

He answered without hesitating, "Yes. I would feel your pleasure, and my enjoyment would pleasure you. It would echo between us. It wouldn't matter how it began."

An echo, a resonance of tenderness. "Do you still want that with me?" she asked.

"Yes," he murmured; then he added, "I've never asked anyone else."

She pressed her spine against the cold bulkhead. "First, we have a job to do. If it doesn't come off . . ."

When she didn't finish the sentence, he nodded. "Even if it does, the other masters could rule that I misjudged in disobeying orders."

Wouldn't that be amazing?—outcasts, both of them. "Better us in trouble than both our worlds."

He rose out of the pilot's seat, stepped onto the foot of her bunk, and climbed into the upper. "You're right." His voice came down to her, accompanied by rustling noises. "We'll talk about it later, when we're both awake again."

Awake? How could she sleep? Echoes of Brennen's touch ricocheted through her memory like laser fire.

Ellet had spoken truly. She would never forget.

Carradee Second stood alone in an ornately appointed sitting room that had been Firebird's. Only the furniture looked familiar. Servitors had archived Firebird's personal possessions when her death first was announced.

I will never bear a wastling. I could not take the anguish.

She'd talked with Danton for an hour today in her day office. He'd insisted—again—that Netaia was ripe for rebellion, and that the Federacy wanted to help the noble class prevent bloodshed by smoothing the change to a more equable system.

She couldn't concentrate on that, with Firebird in jeopardy again. What would happen if Friel and Burkenhamn succeeded and brought her back to Citangelo?

Sunlight streamed through high, white-curtained windows, giving marble walls a soft sheen and setting off dark wooden furnishings. More keenly, Carradee noticed things that no longer were there. Scanbooks full of pictures from distant worlds didn't clutter the dark fayyawood end table. The coat-of-arms crested desk had been cleared of Academy trophies and ribbons. No flight jacket was flung over the brocade desk chair.

Burkenhamn would report to her, Friel to Phoena, whether their mission succeeded or failed. Soon, within days. They'd taken a fast craft.

She strolled into the adjoining study. This room had been stuffed with musical paraphernalia. Gone now. Sold, all but the clairsa, to pay those education debts. Firebird's portrait, removed from the gallery after Lieutenant Governor Caldwell drew her attention to it, hung on the inner wall.

Carradee touched its gold frame. She'd grieved for Firebird, really grieved, and storing this portrait in darkness would've been too much like consigning her to a mausoleum. Carradee had hung it here herself, in the music room where Firebird always had seemed happiest, if she were on the ground.

If they brought her back, must Carradee put her on trial? Even more terrible, must she arrange her execution and burial? Plainly Firebird wouldn't suicide, and with heir limitation outlawed, they couldn't touch her for geis refusal. No, it would be treason. A terrible death.

That was hard to imagine. Of all people, Firebird had kept the high laws so passionately. Her rebellions had centered on minor matters. Commoners' concerns, palace protocol . . .

Siwann had kept a healthy distance from the fire-haired imp, but not Carradee.

Surely, though, the Federacy would keep her on Tallis. Carradee stared at the diadem the girl in the portrait wore proudly—if a touch off center. Could the Federates let Firebird be punished for becoming the key to their victory? Perhaps it was hope, asking that. Phoena's hopes were different. Phoena's ideological retreat would be well under way now, free from Federate intrusion, as Carradee had promised.

Hunter Height—Carradee loved the place. She shut her eyes, basking in the pleasant sadness of her small martyrdom. She would stay in the bustling city, while Phoena and her friends enjoyed the majestic old Height. *At least Phoena will cherish it, and it won't stand empty. The lieutenant governor was right, though: The city is quieter without her.*

Carradee studied the portrait's impish smile, comparing it to the sad courage in her eyes. That artist had captured her sister's nature perfectly.

Could I attend Firebird's trial?

As queen, she must not only attend but preside. And she could not veto an execution order if the Electorate handed it down.

"Please!" she whispered to the unseen Powers. "Keep Firebird on Tallis!"

On their last day in slip, Firebird and Brennen finalized plans, talking through every level of tunnels under the Height, each spur, and the worrisome possibility of fumigation. He'd requisitioned oxygen sniffers and lightweight chem suits; he'd explained the different types of explosives. Finally she rose from her bunk, opened the galley servo, and stared at its contents. She'd stuffed her brain with plans and information. It wouldn't hold one more detail.

"Mari?"

Turning, she caught a wistful look in his eyes.

"What will they do with you if you're caught? Have you considered it?"

Why did he want to know? Could he intend to abandon her, use her as a distraction? "Kill me, of course," she answered, considering as abstractly as she could. "Any faithful Netaian would now. But I suspect—I think—they wouldn't shoot to kill on sight if they recognized me. Phoena has to be there. She sponsored Cleary's research from the beginning. If I know Phoena at all, she'd love to create a spectacle. Parade me around. Make it sting."

"And if they took me?"

"How could they?" she scoffed.

"It's possible. What might she do?"

Firebird leaned against the servo counter. It had never entered her mind that Brennen might falter, whatever he tried. The image of Brennen powerless in Phoena's hands appalled her. "That's hard. She'd want to hurt you, to punish you, but she'd want to make everything 'proper.' Are you—"

"Afraid?" he asked softly, completing her thought. "More than I have ever been. Afraid to have come this far but to lose what you and I could have had."

"You'll come through, Brenn. With your resources . . ."

"I'm not invulnerable."

"I suppose not." Only incomprehensible sometimes, such as in the council chamber with that eerie weapon—"Brennen," she said sharply. "May I look at your crystace?"

He flipped the bunk up out of sight, groped inside his left cuff, and drew the slim, dull gray dagger hilt. He laid it on his palm and held it toward her. Near the wide handguard she spotted a small, round stud. It was just as Korda had described.

Brennen shifted his grip, held the crystace at arm's length, and pressed the stud. Instantly, the piercing resonant frequency sang in her ears, and the blade appeared. It caught the monochromatic cabin light and reflected scarcely visible shades of green, blue, and violet. He swept it around to stand upright between them and eyed her through the shimmering crystal.

Korda had described the blade's edges as of one atom's width, and she finally believed him. Wonderingly, she reached out a hand.

Brennen gave it to her. She made a tentative swing in the air. It was lighter than it looked but exquisitely balanced. "What is ehrite?"

"I don't know. I'm no chemist."

She swept it side to side, across her midline and back, and traced a few tentative fencing parries she'd learned long ago in school. She was no swordswoman, though. Afraid she'd damage something, she handed it back.

He took it and pressed the stud. "Are you hungry?"

She chose the stew, variety number three, spicy and warming. Brennen ate without comment, preoccupied with a map he'd spread on her bunk.

Soon they sat at their stations, g-suited again, strapped to the acceleration chairs. The final seconds counted off on the break indicator, and then the little craft's engine reversed with a roar. Pushed painfully against the black webbing, Firebird glimpsed Netaia's majestic arc as Brennen leaned forward to correct their course. He'd assured her that the transponder codes he'd secured would take them past any Federate surveillance satellites. They approached from the south, over the vast polar ice, speeding toward the South and North Deeps, as far as possible from any population center. One swirl of cloud frosted the Great Ocean.

The cabin heated with atmospheric friction as they crossed Arctica. She watched hungrily, more homesick than she'd ever felt. She could never call this beautiful white-frosted blue globe home again. Never. The thought made her chest ache, as when she'd lost Corey.

Still decelerating hard, Brennen dropped the craft to low-level and skimmed the flat, icy continent as predawn light began to glow. Then the Aeries raised their magnificent shoulders. Like a hovercraft on open sea, the ship rose and fell with high passes of that ice-locked range, running south.

"There it is." Firebird spotted two familiar peaks. League Mountain, separated by a short ridge from Hunter Mountain, filled the horizon. Both continued to grow as Brennen decelerated hard, dropping the ship on a snow field as near that ridge as the slope's pitch would allow. He cut the atmospheric engines. Silence rang loudly in Firebird's ears.

They unbuckled and stretched. Brennen moved aft, which was now downhill. From the cargo area, he pulled two dark gray suits and handed one up to Firebird. "Thermal controls on the left wrist."

She turned around, slipped out of her gravity suit and shipboards, and stepped into the heavy gray pants. After struggling with the shirt, she joined the pieces at her waist. The suit didn't hang too badly. The shirt collar fit high and snugly, and the sleeves ended in flexible gloves. She touched a wrist panel and immediately started to shiver. Obviously, that wasn't what she wanted. She touched a different corner. Warmth flowed through her hands, feet, and body.

"Have you figured it out?" Brennen came up beside her and eyed the wrist panel. "Comfortable?"

"A little too warm."

"Leave it that way."

She slipped back into her boots, then buckled on a gun belt. Brennen opened the outer hatch. Frigid air swirled into the cabin. They'd need no stepstand; the Brumbee's hot skin had melted a trench in the ice and snow. It still settled slowly.

She hoisted the drillcloth pack and jumped down, then waited in calf-deep surface snow as Brennen sealed the hatch, perching on the tilted door plate and clinging one-handed to the security handle. Gracefully he leaped down to her side and took the pack.

"I'll spell you carrying that," she offered.

"The best way to work as a team is for each of us to do what he—or she—does best. I'll haul."

He reminded her suddenly of a teacher she'd almost forgotten, one who'd urged her to study music and forget the military. "Go ahead. But I'm not along for the scenery."

He smiled. She headed upslope, trying not to break through a thin crust into deeper, older snow. It made for slow going, particularly for a man carrying a pack as heavy as that one.

"We're leaving tracks," she observed.

"We won't have to worry about it, going down the other side. Southern exposure."

"And what about the ship?"

"Danton's people aren't watching this area for anything so small."

True. They weren't watching this area at all.

He passed her and plodded ahead, breaking trail. Her heart pounded with the altitude and unaccustomed exercise, despite her recent weeks of training. They skirted the summit just west of the ridge, where the wind roared stiffly. Here, even the old snow had been blown away. They made faster progress on rocky ground. The view south into staggered lines of distant foothills raised her spirits, but they dropped down quickly to avoid presenting recognizable silhouettes to any watching eyes.

About ten meters below the ridge, Firebird stopped for a breath. Behind her, Brennen whistled softly.

Hunter Height lay below, on a stony knoll. The house, built of Hunter Mountain granite, was designed like a small hexagon atop a larger one. From the southern foothills, an ancient, winding road approached, and from the north a switchbacking lane led up from a box canyon, which ran east and west and concealed a sizable airstrip. The knoll was ringed by a venerable stone outwall—etched, as Firebird remembered it, by lichens and the wild mountain weather—and inside the wall lay informal grounds, often battered by blizzards, sheltered somewhat by Thunder Hill's forested shoulder.

"From orbit," he murmured, "it would look like part of the mountain."

Firebird smiled smugly. "That's why your recon flights haven't picked it up."

CHAPTER 20

HUNTER HEIGHT

crescendo poco a poco
gradually becoming louder

In MaxSec's bustling thirty-fifth-floor hallway, a man in Thyrian blue saluted Ellet Kinsman. Briefly puzzled, she returned the gesture. He looked familiar. He must've gone through college either before her (he was built older, tall, and well muscled) or after (but the face was so young).

"Captain Kinsman." He shone a cordial smile. "Air Master Damalcon Dardy, Thyrian Alert Forces. I'm looking for General Caldwell, and the secretary sent me to you. Is he on a security assignment?"

He was older, then, and he ranked her. Ellet kept her static shield thick. "Is there something I can help you with, sir?"

"I've just checked in from following up a Shuhr incident, and I'm only passing through. I wanted to introduce myself. However—" He touched her arm. Both pressed against a wall to allow a man steering a service cart to pass. "Since this obviously isn't a place for private discussion, would you join me for lunch in the officers' lounge?"

"Sir, the MaxSec lounge is expensive."

His even-toothed grin softened her reserve. "Then I'll take it out of my vital contacts budget."

He did precisely that, presenting his ID disk to the host and insisting on a private booth with a north view. For half the hour, while she savored a salad of genuine Thyrian shellfish, he asked only about her interpretive work, and she found herself warming to him.

"Caldwell, then." He spread garnetberry jam on his roll and switched to silent subvocalization. *I mentioned him at the SO office, and I was given the impression Regional has been overloading him, hoping he'll break or resign before they have to promote a Sentinel up to High command. What's wrong? Where is he?*

I don't know precisely, she responded tightly, and it was enough of the truth to pass. *He has gone with the Netaian woman, Firebird Angelo.*

Dardy set down his roll and leaned across the booth. "What do you mean?"

Ellet remained stoic. *When he turned up missing from duty, I put in for med leave to cover him and made a check at the depot. He took a ship, but they seem baffled too.*

Dardy tapped a finger on the tabletop and eyed the hilly horizon. *Well, they wouldn't have asked him any questions*, he sent back. *SO is SO. Have you reported him?*

"Not yet," she said aloud. She clenched her folded hands against the table.

"You're not telling me everything about this Netaian woman."

"No."

Ellet sensed a slight apprehension.

She's connatural with him? he asked privately.

For one moment Ellet wished for the long, slow period of making acquaintance that outsiders experienced. No one but another Sentinel would expect to be shown so much, so quickly and intimately—but that was their way. It had made the starbred a people who couldn't easily be divided or fooled. "Apparently so, sir."

"That's too bad." Dardy made a wry face.

She kept her response as stony as she knew how to make it. "This is not the end of the matter."

Dardy picked up his fork, speared a last mouthful of smoked fish, and chewed thoughtfully. The lounge quieted briefly as Mister Lithib rode in on his mobility chair.

"Tell me, then." Dardy laid down his fork and pushed back his plate, now entirely sympathetic. *How much do you know about where they've gone?*

She frowned. *Firebird's people aren't taking occupation well. She raised Brennen's suspicion that certain action needed to be taken there on Netaia, although Tierna Coll herself ordered otherwise. She played on his pride and won.* Ellet raised her head to meet the air master's eyes and sent the painful admission. *She won, sir.*

Counter to orders? Dardy looked—and felt—stricken. *Express or implied? Can the codes justify his action?*

Express orders. I saw them given. As to our codes, I can't say. That's for the masters to judge.

Dardy shifted his muscular shoulders to lean sideways in the booth. "It might not be too late to make him stand back and think the issue through. Could they be intercepted?—The woman apprehended for escaping custody and Brennen called back for questioning? Or . . . is there someone there on Netaia who respects our kindred but might hold the woman there at home, to pacify the regime?"

"Governor Danton." Pleased with the idea, Ellet sipped her kass. "He worked well with Brennen and wouldn't want to see him in trouble, but Danton's also close to the royal family. I'd assume that the queen wants her back." Ellet felt no compulsion to tell Dardy what that return might mean to Firebird.

"Perfect," he said. "Regional could alert Danton by the next messenger ship." *And we could maintain Thyrica's hopes to get a Sentinel on the High command,* he added silently.

Despite having found a genuine supporter, Ellet felt a pang of loss, for Brennen's actions had declared his choice: Firebird, unless she refused him. Holding her emotions under tight rein, Ellet raised her kass cup.

Firebird was glad for the thermal suit and stiff teknahide boots as they picked a way down slick, frosty rubble and scree toward the woods. Underfoot, little alpine plants clung to pockets of soil, turning red and brown with the onset of cold weather. Many glistened, edged leaf by leaf with delicate frost crystals.

Just above the evergreen forest, Brennen stopped and waited for her. She'd slowed her pace to scan the Height again before they entered the trees. "There." She pointed with a gray-gloved hand. "By the south wall. And another beyond the back gate."

He followed her gesture with his eyes.

"And there's another, walking along the west end of the grounds. See them?" she asked.

He nodded. "Three guards on morning duty."

"And infrared scanners we can't see. I think we'd better try that side tunnel first. It's farther to walk, but the house is well covered."

"Lead on."

Another hour's trudge took them up onto Thunder Hill, but at the entry site Firebird remembered, they found only a huge jumbled pile of stone.

"Squill," she exclaimed softly. "They've blocked it. Recently, too." She eyed the crushed vegetation, still green. "Can you . . ." She swept out her fingers as if levitating the rock pile aside.

High above her, Brennen peered down from the top of the pile. "That would take too much time and energy." He step-jumped down to join her.

"And we'd better save our explosives for the laboratory. Still want to try the kitchens?"

"Infrared alarms fail sometimes," he said. "If I can shoot one out over the service doors, we might have time to get in before they reactivate it."

"We'll have to get close. These are tiny ones."

He dug into the pack and handed her two energy cubes, and she chewed them dry. "Here." He dropped two more small, hard lumps into her hand.

Citrene! She popped both onto her tongue, then drank a gulp of water from his bottle. He shouldered the pack again and turned back down the hill.

They walked in silence, just to the right of a chute scoured bare of trees by avalanches. Woodsmoke faintly perfumed the air, and the afternoon sky over the treeless swath was purest autumn blue.

As she watched a hunting kiel soar on rising air currents, a roaring silver streak sliced the sky. She ducked into the trees.

Brennen joined her, hands on her shoulders. "It's an active place, all right." Peering back, she saw him smiling. His apprehension must've run its course. He looked almost eager.

In a copse of barren, prickly bushes they rested out the afternoon, and they moved down at dusk. The high wall, once worked elegantly smooth, now wore the cracks of antiquity, and here and there stones had fallen, affording Firebird all the footholds she needed after Brennen boosted her. Lying flat atop the wall for a few seconds, she spotted house lights through the trees, warm yellow in the lower windows and dim blue above. A scent of roasted meat made her mouth water. Convinced no one was near, she slipped down inside, rested her feet on the heavy iron handrail that circled the wall's inner surface—installed centuries ago by an elderly inhabitant—and then jumped backward down to the ground. Brennen followed.

When they reached the manicured tip of the forest, Firebird could see clearly into the kitchens. Lights still burned, and white-gowned cook staff hurried back and forth in front of southwest windows. She turned to Brennen, who stood in deep shadow behind another evergreen tree. He made no sign.

She looked up, startled by the almost starless twilit sky. Netaia was a splendid recluse at the Whorl's end. The brightest points of faint, familiar constellations winked down as she hid and waited. She spotted Tallis in the rising Whorl. Tallis looked somehow different now. She'd lived under that star as a sun.

The kitchen lights went out. Firebird shot Brennen a quizzical look.

He shook his head, and they waited in stillness a few minutes longer. Slow, even footsteps approached. A guard passed, vanishing around a broad corner.

Brennen flung himself prone and steadied his blazer on one hand. Firebird held her breath and averted her eyes from the energy pistol's muzzle.

He took a deep breath. Then another.

Then he touched the stud. A single flash fled out the corner of her eye. She waited a moment longer, until Brennen led out at a run.

She came close behind. As Brennen tried the handle, she flattened herself beside the kitchen door. The iron latch clicked as it released. He started to open the huge wooden slab, but before they could steal through, it ground on its hinges. Brennen froze.

Firebird bit her lip.

He pressed up and pulled the door outward a little farther, then motioned her inside.

The great kitchens stood empty, lit only by cracks below inner doors. Firebird followed the outside wall left a few meters to the kitchen store.

Brennen zipped the gloves off his suit, then knelt and pressed an open hand to the lockbox at waist level. Firebird watched, intrigued. In a moment, she heard another soft click inside the mechanism. Brennen pushed the door open. They squeezed into the pantry and closed the heavy panel behind them. A dim, pale green light sprang up beside her, Brennen's pocket luma. The tiny cube illuminated a ghostly green sphere around them as they threaded their way between shelves of foodstuffs and cooking equipment.

At the end of the pantry, a palm lock guarded the cellar stairs. Brennen dropped again to his knees.

"Wait," Firebird whispered. She pocketed her own gloves and pressed her bare right palm to the panel.

The door slid away.

Firebird smiled and murmured, "Well. They haven't changed the locks."

She led stealthily around the wedge-shaped stone steps that she remembered so well. They widened into the tunnel system, where cool air made her face tingle. After circling once, she could see an orange glow beneath. Brennen pocketed the little luma. She steadied herself with her fingertips on the left wall. In a few steps more she came out in an alcove that led to a cross tunnel. Its left branch passed eastward, toward the area they'd agreed to search first for Cleary's laboratory, but Firebird recalled a large chamber at the center of the system. It would have to be crossed if they traversed this level. Brennen motioned her to remain in the stairwell. He'd drawn his shock pistol. Stealthily he walked forward into what seemed an unnatural brightness, then disappeared left.

She edged along the right wall to the end of the shadow, drew her own pistol, and waited. Brennen returned, shaking his head. She pointed the other way. They scurried down the right branch, then made another quick right turn, down into darkness.

After they'd spiraled down another stone stair past the second level, he stopped. "She's here," he whispered.

"Phoena?"

"Yes. There were men in the main chamber, talking. They mentioned both her and Cleary."

"As if we had any doubt. That chamber would've been risky to cross anyway. Let's go without light, as long as we can still cover ground."

Edging downward in total darkness, Firebird found his firm hand-
hold reassuring. The wall vanished beneath her skimming fingers.
"Here," she said softly. "Eastbound."

Firebird led now. As they drew on, a yellow glow grew stronger.

At last Brennen whispered, "Stay here," and crept on alone. She
watched in dim light, a little aggravated at being left behind. He
paused, listening with some epsilon sense, then went on.

Straining her ears, Firebird heard footsteps from the west.
"Brenn!" she called in a penetrating whisper. Before he could join her,
she drew and aimed toward the steps. Her tiny red targeting beam
showed movement. She fired. There came a surprised shout from up
the corridor, and then silence. An afterimage of her weapon glowed
faintly in her eyes.

"Quick!" he said. "There's a guard up ahead. He's sure to have
heard." They sprinted back westward, as silently as two people wearing
boots can run.

A north-branching corridor left the straight hall. "Here," breathed
Firebird. She turned right in the dark and plunged downward only moments before laser fire lit the passage.

This tunnel's floor was more broken. Brennen tripped after only a
few steps. She heard the scuffle as he caught himself, then the luma
sprang back to life. Again she pushed herself to a run. The faint green-
ish glow made her bare hands look sickly and pale but sped their progress around the long curve east toward the main northbound tunnel.
Several side passages led off into blackness. Their shadowy depths
mocked the intrusion of light, faint though it was. Here and there,
mineral crystals caught the emerald light and glittered eerily.

Once the curve had been put behind them, protecting them from
following fire, they stopped to rest.

Panting, Firebird leaned against a smooth spot on the wall. "Unfortunately, now they know someone's here. If they split up they can
have us like slinks up a tree."

Brennen was listening again. "No one's coming."

"He's reporting, then. Now we worry about fumigation."

"We have chem suits and sniffers."

"There's also that spur up under Thunder Hill. I was here once
when they gassed for rodents, and I remember they talked about how

heavy zistane vapor is, and how it sinks. The spur might be safe for a while. But it's a dead end."

"I do have an idea—" He killed his luma. "Get down."

Firebird dropped onto the hard stone and rolled against a wall, fumbling blind for her shock pistol. Nearby, a stealthy step broke the stillness. Then another, quieter yet. She held her breath. Then rocks, pistol, and Brennen gleamed crimson as he fired.

She heard him breathe deeply, and then the luma shone out again, held high in his left hand as he aimed his blazer steadily up the tunnel. Cautiously, she got back to her feet.

"I felt something alive back there," he whispered.

No sound flowed down the shaft toward them. Brennen slipped her the luma and backtracked warily up into blackness.

When he came back, he shook his head. "There's no body. But I don't feel it anymore."

"Something from down one of those side passages?" She shivered.

"Does anything live down there?"

"I don't think so. But the staff used to tell us monster stories that kept Carradee awake for nights on end." She moved a step closer, and he reached for her hand. "Let's go," she urged, stepping out.

"Wait a minute." He pulled her back.

"You said you had an idea."

"It's risky," he whispered.

"It couldn't be riskier than waiting to be fumigated. What is it?"

"To split up. I'd like you uplevel, out of the danger of gas. We have to find the researchers' main data base. You'll recognize the scientists."

"Yes. But—"

"If Phoena fumigates, the researchers should evacuate uplevel, especially if they have ground-floor offices. I'll suit up and keep working."

She stiffened, suspicious. "This is something you'd thought of already, isn't it?"

"Yes and no. It was always a possibility, but I hoped we wouldn't have to try it. You'll be in particular danger if we separate."

"I can take care of myself. I know Phoena pretty well, and the Height even better."

He drew her shock pistol and blazer from their belt holsters, checked both charges, then handed them back. "Can you kill, if you have to?"

"Not with this." She holstered the shock pistol on her right side, for an easier draw.

"They're deadly at point-blank range," he reminded her, "but the blazer is better. You could have to kill in self-defense. Can you?"

"Brenn, of course I—"

"Face-to-face?" He pressed her hand. "Even from a cockpit, you tried to put down the Verohan interceptors, not the pilots."

"I see your point. I—" She still dreamed sometimes about the pilots she'd shot down at Veroh. She did hope they'd survived. "To save my life . . . yes, Brenn. I think I could. If I'm careful, I won't have to." Finally, it hit home: "Phoena would kill me now, if I gave her the chance," she realized aloud.

"Remember that," he said.

"Yes." She wrested her mind back to their plan of attack. "The only real trick will be getting into the tubes."

Shipboard, they'd discussed the Height's hydraulic network, drilled through granite walls in a previous century to carry solar-heated water into freshing rooms, kitchens, and lower-level labs. As a child Firebird had found the abandoned hollow system, far wider than the pipes it held, and explored it over a series of summers. It had made an ideal hiding spot from Phoena, something she frequently needed. Painstakingly she'd cleared away obstructions until she could negotiate the entire system, and she'd kept it her own secret in this carefully guarded place. Assuming she hadn't changed shape too much as she matured, she should still be able to use it.

"Listen, then," he said. "If those researchers have data desks uplevel, destroy them. Any way you can. A shock pistol can fatally surge a main drive, too."

"I suppose it could." She wondered what kind of situation he'd survived to bring back that trick.

"Give me an hour to lay charges, then half an hour to get clear enough to detonate them. When I'm away, I'll send off a quest pulse homed on your feelings, as I did on Tallis."

She nodded.

"If you've destroyed the uplevel offices or confirmed there aren't any, and gotten off the height, concentrate on something strongly pleasing when you feel that probe. I'll touch off the charges."

"Off the height," she repeated. "Airstrip?"

"Perfect. Get a plane ready while I'm on my way. But if you're not clear when you feel me call, answer with fear. I'll feel it. I'll come for you." He opened a side pocket of the black pack while he spoke. "And here's one more thing." He handed her a palm-sized touch activator card. "I'll carry the explosives close to the lab and arm them before I do anything else. Blow them if I don't call."

She touched the card with one finger, shaken by his trust. He was putting himself at her mercy. "But you might be close. Surely it won't come to that, Brenn."

"It could. Could you do that, too?"

"I . . ." She swallowed. "No."

He slipped the card into her hip pocket. "I'd make it an order if I were your superior officer. Think. If it comes down to that, I want you to. The activation sequence is V-E-R-O-H."

"I won't forget that," she murmured.

"We can't let them devastate another world."

Abruptly she realized he carried his ancestors' world on his conscience, just as she carried Veroh. She nodded.

Within minutes, they cautiously approached the main tunnel north to the airstrip. Firebird peered out into its breadth. Everburners gleamed, imbedded in glossy black walls. Its floor recently had been scored by vehicular traffic. Even Brennen sensed no one nearby.

She met his eyes for one last time. "Thank you for everything, Brenn. I hope it works."

He took her in his arms. "Go with His protection, Mari." He kissed her, started to draw away, then reached for her again. She clutched him, wishing uselessly that their paths had crossed in peaceful, trustful times.

He stepped away. "Start timing now. An hour and a half."

He turned back down the side passage, and Firebird headed upward at a quiet jog. The paved lane was as still as a tomb, and she knew it could soon be hers, if something went wrong.

Where she reached the first level, the tunnel ended in a chamber just east of the main hall. She remembered a maintenance hatch in there, the nearest hydraulic access. Drawing her shock pistol, she stepped out into the chamber and listened hard. Elevators pulsing, a distant shout, her own heartbeat: She heard nothing immediately threatening, so she took half the ten meters to the opposite wall at a dead run.

Bootsteps clattered off to her right. She dropped, rolled, and came up shooting. A red-collared figure fell heavily. She dashed to the floor-level access panel, knelt down, and started popping out tracker bolts. The smooth rectangular slab loosened in her fingers. Meticulously she slid one edge outward, lifting as she moved it, leaving no mark on the black stone floor. Then she squeezed herself into the hollow beyond. Two white polymer pipes ran up and down along one side of a shaft that could've held eight—had been intended for eight, she guessed. It was snug, particularly at shoulders and hips, but she fit. As she pulled the panel home, voices echoed out in the chamber.

Extending her arms, she grabbed one pipe, wedged her feet against opposite sides, and shinnied upward in utter darkness.

Thick stone dampened all sound above her, below, and on all sides. Not even the occasional scuttering of small trapped creatures livened the hollow tonight. She wrenched herself upward another three arm-lengths, then rested a minute. Now that the first claustrophobic minute had passed, she felt safer in this dark sanctum than she'd felt since leaving Brennen.

Brenn. She twisted her arm and checked the time-lights on her wristband. She'd already used fifteen minutes. She had to hurry.

But the tube was slow going, particularly after she wriggled over into a horizontal cross passage. At one point it narrowed so tightly that she shimmied back a meter, eased out of the heavy thermal shirt and pants, and pushed them ahead of her, shivering and collecting scratches from the cold granite, until she passed the constriction. After that, she struggled back into the garments but left them unfastened, and soon she was glad she had. Three more times, she needed to shed every millimeter.

Finally, scraped and stinging, she judged that she'd nearly reached the safest place to pass into the house. Another five minutes' creep put her at the end of that hollow with an upward passage directly overhead. Once, it had held the feed tube to the collectors. Trying not to stir a deep pile of dust and small skeletons at the bottom of the drop, she worked herself up into a standing position, then patted the wall for a remembered crack between wood and stone.

After a minute's search she located it, and then the widest prying spot, two hands lower than she expected. She'd grown since first finding it. Cautiously she wedged two fingers inward. Gripping the wooden panel, she pushed it a centimeter. Then she waited. Watched. Listened. Just past this wall had been a walk-in wardrobe used primarily by staff. No light came through the opening. She pushed gently again and met squashy resistance. Linens, she hoped. She gave it another shove.

The wardrobe was silent, but shouting and heavy, running steps echoed in the halls. Cautiously she squeezed out of the hollow into a dark north bedroom.

Movement caught her eye, the hall door slowly opening. She dashed across the room toward the inner wall and pressed behind the door's path of swing. A shadow cast by the hall light appeared on the floor. Another House Guard slunk toward the open wardrobe.

She drew her shock pistol. One silent shot left him senseless and Firebird armed with another Netaian service blazer. She tucked it into her gun belt, then eyed the unconscious guard. She didn't think he'd seen her, but she didn't want to take the risk. She dragged him into the wardrobe and barricaded him in with the heaviest-looking chair in the room. Then she crept out into the yellow-lit hall.

The sound of footsteps sent her dashing for a utility room on the inner wall. Someone passed by and out of hearing. She tiptoed on, zigzagging between inner and outer rooms. What luck Phoena hadn't thought to reprogram the palm locks against her! Undoubtedly the House Guards thought they'd secured this hall already. Even Phoena hadn't expected her to come back.

Behind the fourth outer door she heard Dr. D'Stang and Baron Parkai, arguing loudly about having been dragged from their down-level beds. She smiled grimly. If they'd gone to sleep without complaining, they would've been harder to find.

She pressed her palm to the slick black panel and heard the latch release. Then she secured her grip on her shock pistol and elbowed the door open wide.

CHAPTER 21

GEIS

agitato
agitated, excited

One shocked face turned to Firebird as she placed a silent stun burst. A man fell across a bed.

She sensed movement and whirled around. An older man stood behind the door, raising a blazer. Startled, she fired. He crumpled.

She secured the door and leaned against it, breathing hard. Then she dropped to her knees beside the man she'd stunned at close range: Elber Parkai, Baron of Sylva and DeTar. *Stunned?* she begged, checking his wrist and then his throat. No pulse. He wasn't breathing either.

He was dead, just as Brennen warned.

Struggling to inhale, Firebird pushed away from his body. *He meant to murder millions of Federates,* she reminded herself. Still she stared. She'd only meant to stun him. . . .

She stood up, hands trembling. Beyond the rumpled beds she spotted three windowpanels with their slatted filters closed, and a windowless outside door. That, anyway, was perfect. No outdoor guard would peer in and see her.

A quick circuit of the room proved it was used only for sleeping, not research. She searched the nightrobed bodies and found no data chips, rods, or disks.

Disappointed, she muscled Dr. D'Stang into another large closet. *What about Baron Parkai?*

She couldn't leave his body in plain sight. She felt like a butcher, dragging it into the closet and dumping it beside his stunned fellow-worker. This wardrobe had an ancient two-way lock. She unscrewed the inner knob and then secured it from the outside. Sighing, she steeled herself to slip back out into the hallway and search out Dr. Nella Cleary.

Wait. A voice from her training spoke up. *Never leave weapons behind enemy lines.* She spotted Parkai's dropped blazer near the inner door. *Can't leave Phoena's forces any additional arms,* she reminded herself. *Not that they seem to have any shortage of these.*

She stepped to the outer door, slipped through, and glanced around outside. All the outdoor lights burned fiercely, casting sharp grass shadows on the north leg of the outwall and obscuring the stars. Cold, still air stung her face. Judging from shouts echoing off stone, the hunt was up—far downhill and to the south. Someone must've spooked a brownbuck and mistaken it for a human intruder.

Near an untended flower bed, she spotted a pile of rotting grass clippings. She sprinted over, plunged Parkai's blazer deep into the decaying pile, then roughened its surface to hide the hole she'd left. Then she pulled the guard's blazer out of her belt and stuffed it too into the compost. She only had two hands. Better not to carry extra weapons that could be turned against her.

Now to look for Cleary.

She hurried back inside and cycled her shock pistol to a fresh charge.

Then she stole out into the hallway. Halfway to the next room she heard running feet, both ahead and behind. She sprinted toward the door, switching her pistol to her left hand so she could palm the panel quicker. The footsteps behind her pounded.

Someone grabbed her shoulders. She spun toward her assailant and instinctively kicked as hard as she could. A strangled cry and a thud sounded behind her. She wheeled away from the runner ahead and hit an inlaid wall, grinding her nose and cheek against it. Rebounding, she tripped on a flailing arm and fell.

Instantly there was a knee on her back and sharp pressure against the base of her skull. "Drop the gun," ordered a shaky voice above her. "Then take your hand away."

She could do nothing else. Reluctantly she let her shock pistol go and lay still, breathing quickly. The knee shifted. A well-kept, slender hand descended into her field of vision and removed her weapon, and then she felt it fumble at her holster. The weight lifted. Footsteps retreated across the passage, and then she heard the voice again. It sounded vaguely familiar.

"Now. Get up. Slowly."

She complied, facing the ornate wall.

"Hands on your head."

She locked her fingers and waited.

"Turn around."

She came slowly around to face him—them. Two men stood glowering at her. The smaller—young, dark-haired, and thin, wearing a noble's blue formal sash, held her own blazer trained on her. Beside him, the portly Duke of Claighbro, Muirnin Rogonin, stood shaking and seething, obviously in pain.

How had he gotten himself out of lockup?

Suddenly Rogonin's expression changed to utter confusion and supreme embarrassment. "Your Highness?" He shook his head. "I beg your pardon! Why are you—"

"No," his young partner interrupted. "That's not Phoena."

Then Firebird recognized him, too: Phoena's "little moonshadow," Count Tel Tellai. She stood motionless, eyeing Tellai's firing finger, wondering if she'd have time to sprint for freedom while they stood baffled.

But Rogonin smiled. He wiped his palms on his white lace shirt front. "Well, Firebird. You came back after all. Call your friend uplevel, Tellai."

As Rogonin drew a shining blue-and-gold blazer, blatantly ornamental but just as deadly as the gunmetal gray service model Tel Tellai had taken from her, the young count hurried to the next room. She heard his voice. "Phoena, love, you'll never believe it. We've got her." Silence. "Well, someone you've been hoping to see. You're going to be—yes, it's she. Shall we—of course. Oh yes. Right away."

On a deeper level of awareness she felt Brennen's sudden, distant touch. He knew she was caught, then. She tried to assure him he didn't need to worry but should finish his job . . . quickly.

Tellai strolled back into view, beaming like a praised pet. Firebird glanced from Tellai to Rogonin, weighing her chances of escape— slight at the moment. She decided to play along. Brennen would need some time yet.

Tellai rocked on his heels. "Uplevel, Rogonin. Her Highness's room."

"One minute. I think we'd better spoil your sash first."

"Why?"

"Tie her."

"Surely you don't need to do that. This is a new one—a gift!" The slight young noble crossed his chest with one hand and smoothed the glowing fabric.

"I know this lady. Do you want Her Highness down our throats for losing a prize catch? She'll thank you for sacrificing that sash."

Tellai yanked it off. Rogonin improvised a tight wrist restraint, winding the excess up Firebird's forearms with an additional knot that strained her shoulders. Firebird submitted, willing herself to stay calm.

Her flash of fear had torn through Brennen. He dropped all shields, to be able to sense her—or the presence of guards. Leaning against rough stone, he sent off the quest pulse and let her feelings flood him. Defiance flamed through her emotions.

Caught, then. Recognized, but not yet threatened, and apparently not tempted to buy her life by betraying him to Phoena. Those had been his only earnest fears—that she'd be killed before they knew whom they'd taken, or that some old habit would revive her former loyalty, even though that would cost her life. She *had* hidden Hunter Height from him. Shouldering his pack, he headed up to search out the laboratory.

Five minutes later he reached the main lane and paused to quest-pulse again. Firebird remained fearful, but was even more controlled now. He drew his shock pistol and jogged up the lane, following the way she'd come. Where it ended in the bare chamber he turned left, hurried up a short passage, and stopped dead.

In front of him rose a three- by five-meter guardwall, its edges sealed to stone. Light from an everburner behind his shoulder reflected off a satiny surface that looked incongruously modern in these antique shafts. Above its locking panel, a sign warned: DANGER. No Unauthorized Entry.

He turned inward to focus a probe, then sent it on his epsilon wave behind the locking panel. Humming circuitry surrounded his point of awareness, a sensation that prickled like insects attacking. Up one course he found the resonating chamber of an alarm horn. A little farther on, a high-voltage conduit connected back into the palm panel's outer edges. It would deliver a killing shock were the wrong person to touch it.

Cautiously he traced the tangled circuitry into the confirmation box. At that point, a proper palm print would be recognized, an improper one rejected. He gave the point a nudge of energy.

The monstrous wall slid aside. Brennen stepped through the opening. Another pulse closed it behind him.

He looked around, gripping his pistol at loose ready. The corridor curved right, walled in old stone. Along the left waited several doors, all closed.

Brennen paused beside the first door, out of sight of anyone inside. Still feeling no warning presence, he opened it, then peered into darkness. Cautiously he slipped through. Using the tiny luma, he located a light switch.

A glass wall gleamed halfway across the stone chamber. Beyond robotic controls, claw-fingered metal hands drooped in mechanical sleep. Past them lay a long, fat metal warhead. With a tendril of epsilon energy he probed its circuits. At its heart, it was one of the outmoded nuclear killers. What then made it such a reputedly formidable weapon . . . the basium?

Dull sheets of Verohan metal lay stacked alongside the half-plated bomb. Inside the woefully inadequate protection of that hardened glasteel wall, a layer of basium could be wrapped around the warhead and sealed in place by mechanical arms. He didn't understand—neither the basium nor other changes in the warhead's circuitry, because this wasn't his expertise—but he would remember and report. The warhead itself was smaller than he might've expected. Undoubtedly, the key to the weapon's threat value lay in a sealed launching compartment near its nose. Something would be released with detonation.

Brennen slid off the backpack, thinking through an operation more delicate than he'd anticipated. Setting off the wrong explosives, too near, might detonate the monster and any of its kin in other rooms, atomizing the granite mountain and sending a radioactive cloud into the atmosphere.

In the second room he found an office setup, its bluescreen left on. From a safe distance he fiddled with its circuitry, but it wouldn't tell him any secrets in the little time he could spare. Using his shock pistol, he surged all its networking circuits. If he were caught and his work halted, that stroke alone would slow Cleary.

Then he moved on.

The third chamber held a stack of huge, shielded crates, a shelf lined with desiccator jars and several flasks of green liquid. The air smelled oddly marine, reminding him of Thyrica. He stepped back into the corridor and laid his pack on the ground.

At that moment the shriek of a whistle tore through the tunnel. An alarm—why so late? A signal to evacuate? Firebird's distress came through more urgently when he quested now. *Protect her until I can get there!* he prayed.

His empty pack lay like a rumpled black pillow at his feet. He shook out and donned the thin chemical suit, then turned back to his work. Deftly he armed every charge, as he'd promised Firebird. Then he distributed them: nothing into the rooms containing nuclear materials, an incendiary onto the office chair. In the hallway he eyed the stone supporting walls, and then, charge by slim charge, he created a hidden line in one natural crack that would bury the access under meters of blasted granite. He laid a second line up the other wall, securing each charge with a small lump of flexible adhesive. Applied dry, flexid would hold them almost indefinitely.

Firebird had stepped off the lift between her captors into the spacious master room on the Height's top floor. Loud, excited talking suddenly stopped.

The master room's odd shape had always fascinated her, but there'd been changes made. In contrast with the utilitarian tunnels, Phoena had made this room glitter, from springy red carpet to crystal-tiered chandelier. Even the black marble communications console and a long, bare metal table shone like mirrors. Below a row of formal portraits stood almost twenty people: older sons and daughters of the ten noble Houses, a few servitors, several House Guards and redjackets—and Vultor Korda, who stood under a long window, all but licking his lips with anticipation, tiny eyes narrowed to slits. Firebird's stomach curdled. Somehow, Phoena had freed both Korda and Rogonin. Was Dorning Stele here, too?

Phoena herself, in a flowing gown of brilliant yellow-orange, parted the line of people and walked regally toward her. Yes, Firebird admitted, that graceful, long-limbed (hateful, haughty) woman with the knot of chestnut hair was a beauty.

"You!" The scornful word rang in the room. "What are you doing here?"

Firebird stood silent, unmoving, eyeing the nearest redjacket, who gripped a twinbeam blazer.

Phoena glowered at Rogonin. "I just had a second report from downlevel. Parkai is dead, D'Stang stunned."

Behind Firebird, a woman squealed, "No!" Firebird wondered if she looked as guilty as she felt.

Phoena folded her arms tightly against her chest. "Yes. Was she armed?" Tellai stepped up and handed Phoena the blazer and the shock pistol. "Ha," she said. "You searched her, of course?"

"No, Your Highness." Firebird heard a note of chagrin in Tellai's voice.

"Do it now," Phoena commanded icily. "Do it right. And if she moves, strip her!"

Grinning, Rogonin moved in. Firebird's flesh crawled as he started to pat down the thermal suit. She clutched the fabric tying her wrists, diverting her mind from Rogonin's examining fingers and the burning urge to kick him again. She knew Phoena well enough to believe in that threat.

Once Tellai and the nearest House Guards saw that she stood still, they approached too. Each groped into a pocket. Tellai found the touch card and showed Phoena. "What's this?"

"Explosives," she hissed. "I should've expected as much." Phoena seized the card. "You have a friend downlevel, I assume?"

Firebird didn't speak. Brennen could have armed those charges by now, though Phoena wouldn't risk destroying her precious laboratory by trying a touch pattern. Touch card, weapons, and her Federate-issue gun belt made a tidy evidence pile on the long metal table.

"It's time to carry out your geis, wastling. Loose her." A guard cut the sash from her wrists. Phoena smiled without warmth as Firebird straightened her thermal suit with all the dignity she could muster. "First, let's discuss your escort. I'll make it easier for you if you cooperate. Who brought you? Is he here now? Or is it a *she?*" she asked with a side glance at Korda. He must've told her about Ellet Kinsman.

Firebird stared back, not even tempted to answer, working warm blood back into her hands. Evidently Phoena hadn't yet heard what happened at the Regional council hearing. Firebird must have beaten Friel and Burkenhamn back to Netaia, but by how long?

Phoena slapped her face with furious strength. Firebird reeled away. Rogonin seized her shoulders and thrust her toward Phoena again.

"Who brought you? Where are they?" Phoena repeated.

"Don't you believe I could get here myself?" Firebird challenged her. Every minute she distracted Phoena was more time for Brennen to finish their real mission.

Phoena slapped her other cheek.

Vultor Korda spoke up. "Your Highness, would you like me to examine her? Her mind should be fertile ground by now. She and I have a score to settle over a certain encounter on Tallis." He took a step forward. "I would enjoy serving you, Highness."

Phoena sniffed. "I see no point in that, Thyrian." Firebird would've smiled if she'd dared. "This is obvious enough. She has always opposed me on this project, and she's here to destroy it. Guard— clear the tunnels. Get ready to gas them and run the new security unit. In one minute. I have no time to waste."

Firebird started, amazed that Phoena hadn't fumigated already. Was the basium project so close to completion that they were rushing toward deployment?

The guard hastened away as Phoena spoke on, running a fingernail along the inside of her own arm. "Do you know what this means to me, to be able to have you executed? We can even do it at first light." She stopped pacing. Rogonin's grip tightened on Firebird's shoulders. "This is for our family's sake, you know. In fact, just to show that the honor of the family comes first—to me—I'll give you a blade now . . . if you ask. But not poison. That would be too easy. And you'll have an audience.

"You see—" She turned again to Korda. "We offer poison and peace to those whose time has come honorably. A blade for penance or last resort. And for the criminal . . ." She drew back to include Firebird in her stare.

Criminal? Phoena didn't know the half of it!

"It may surprise you, Firebird, to hear that we brought a full complement of D-rifles to the Height. In such a delicate situation, I wanted to be prepared for treason in the ranks." Smirking, she pointed at Firebird. "And here you are."

Rogonin stroked her throat with a damp palm, clearly enjoying her predicament. Someone along the wall whispered.

Phoena turned to the nearest House Guard. "Charge the rifles." He too bowed and hurried out.

Firebird clenched her fists. The narrow-band D-wave originally had been developed for surgery, but it had to be used with heavy anesthesia because the field built slowly, disrupting nerve cells before disintegrating them, crazing a conscious patient with pain. Netaia had adopted the D-rifle for one of its public execution protocols, for which a victim would be stripped to the waist of any metallic object that might distort the wave. If a criminal's legs and feet remained to be buried, all the better.

Still, Firebird didn't panic. First light was hours away, and as she'd anticipated, Phoena wanted to wait until then—long after Brennen would be ready to come for her, if he truly meant to come. If he did— if he returned, risking himself for her sake—she must never doubt him again.

Had an hour and a half passed?

Phoena seated herself at the long marble desk below the southern window and touched a series of panels. Rogonin maneuvered Firebird along after her, keeping his grip tight on her shoulders. Others, whispering, formed half a circle a few paces behind them.

Above the desk, six visual screens lit. Each displayed a three-dimensional image of a stone corridor. Centered on the left screen were the double doors of the elevator shaft. As Firebird watched, they slid open. A yellow cloud started to spill out, driven by the lift's powerful fans.

Phoena gloated up at her. "Last chance, Firebird."

Firebird pressed her lips together. Brennen had insisted he could deal with the gas.

Movement on another screen caught her eye. As the cloud billowed downward, a man in House Guard red and black dashed into range of the wide-angle pickup, eyes down, running hard, a blazer clutched at his side.

"Phoena!" Firebird gasped. "Shut it down!"

The princess shrugged. "I signaled that there was no time to waste. I can sacrifice one guard to make the others realize they must obey my orders. And actually, this is perfect. There's something else I want you to see and hear."

The runner stopped, finally noticing the yellow cloud. Raising horrified eyes to the surveillance lens, he raised an arm in entreaty and waved the other arm back down the passage.

Phoena sniffed. Pale and wide-eyed, Tellai laid a hand on her shoulder. Rogonin grinned beside him.

"Now, then. We're fortunate to have a subject in view." Phoena reached forward, dragging her sleeve over the black marble tabletop. "I ordered this from offworld. 'Soniguard,' I think they call it. Federate technology. Watch." Her graceful finger stroked a small, glossy panel below the screens. Then a second, and a third. An eerie howl rose underfoot.

On screen, the guard's eyes bulged. He flung both hands to his ears.

Phoena sighed. "You'll appreciate this, Firebird, with your musical background. Those three notes induce what I'm told is a ringing in the brain, as if the entire skull were a bell. What is it, an overtone? At any rate, it's quite paralyzing. Fatal, eventually. All the cranial arteries rupture, one at a time."

Firebird's throat constricted. The guard retched, convulsed, and then collapsed onto the stone.

Brennen had just turned back to the massive guardwall when the first blast knocked him to his knees. It paralyzed his thoughts for two long seconds, while the second and third tones entered in deadly harmony. Invisible hands squeezed his brain. As his body curled into a fetal tuck, he struggled for recollection. He'd been trained to endure sonics, long ago. He must shut down blood flow to . . .

The pain bore deeper, making thought difficult. His epsilon carrier began to disrupt.

Phoena withdrew her hand from the panel and glared at Firebird. "You're wondering if your friend is far enough down the tunnel to be safe from this, I'm sure. We've installed relays clear to the airfield. I'd hoped to be able to test it."

As the guard's body vanished into bilious fog, Phoena turned fully around. "In fifteen minutes, the system will be flooded. But there isn't a gas suit in existence that can keep out sound waves. Who is it, wastling? Did Lord Corey turn traitor at Veroh, too?"

Firebird lunged for the glossy panels. She managed to touch one off before Rogonin heaved her away.

Phoena reactivated the tone. "That's enough. Guards. Restrain her." Five burly uniformed men moved in.

CHAPTER 22

PHOENA

grand pause
a rest observed by the whole orchestra

Brennen blinked and pressed his temple through the chem suit's flexible mask. He knew he'd been stunned despite his effort. Silence blanketed the stone he lay on. His head pounded viciously. And the smell . . . foul . . .

He gasped. It made him retch.

Had he torn a leak as he fell?

Far above, he'd felt Firebird's fear mounting. He felt nothing there now. He didn't want to spend the energy for another quest pulse.

Poison gas! his own voice shouted, as from a distance. *You've been breathing it!* His fuzzed memory echoed, *tardema-sleep!*

It was a skill he'd learned for just such emergencies . . . but how deep should he send the cycle, to time his waking? How long until the gas cleared, and he could afford to breathe again? He turned inward and found his carrier. Another coughing spasm shook him.

Suddenly Firebird's emotions screamed, rousing all his instincts from a distance, just as she'd done at Veroh. Screamed—and then swiftly faded.

Horror-struck, Brennen opened one hand from the claw it had formed. He pushed it toward his pocket for the touch activator and worked out the first four letters of the detonation sequence. If he couldn't achieve tardema, then with his last effort—and one final touch—he would blow the lab.

They couldn't have killed her!

Yes, they could.

Battling the urge to breathe, Brennen turned inward for one more attempt to reach tardema.

Firebird had struggled frantically, but the guards caught her hands and dragged her to the metal table. One swept her gear onto the carpet and bent her backward over it. Another lunged for her feet and received a hard kick in the teeth in his mistress's service. The next seized both her knees and swung her around to lie flat.

An instant later she couldn't move, caught once again in a restraining field. She lay staring at the glittering white ceiling, her arms like immovable stone at her sides. The guards' hands pulled away. She lay panting, tears for Brennen streaming from her eyes.

"Nicely done," sang a female voice from somewhere she couldn't turn her head to see.

Close by, Phoena's voice held a note of deep satisfaction as she answered her friend, "This time she's ours, Liera." Then she spoke more softly. "Everything in one room, Firebird. Command post, secure sleeping quarters—and interrogation facility."

Something splashed into Firebird's face. It blinded her eyes and made her fight for breath. Brandy, she guessed from the piercing smell and the burning in her nose. She tried to spit, couldn't move even her head, and had to swallow. Phoena must've set the field on maximum range and strength. Only her eyelids responded, and her tongue, and she could slow her breath. Salty tears slowly washed away the stinging liquor.

When she could see again, a pink blur resolved into Vultor Korda's face. She averted her eyes.

"A toast!" shouted Rogonin's voice close by. "Netaia!"

"Wait," Phoena called. "Finn, bring glasses for everyone."

Firebird heard clinking and pouring as she blinked out the last of the fire in her eyes. Korda moved away.

"Netaia!" the shout echoed, followed by a wash of conversation.

Then Korda whined, "Highness . . . Your Highness, I sense a presence about your sister that I don't like."

The hubbub stilled. "Oh?" asked Phoena's voice, distant once more. "Explain yourself, Korda."

"I can't—quite—isolate the nuances. But, Highness, if she came with anyone at all, I think she did come with a Sentinel."

Cultured gasps and inhalations hissed on Firebird's left.

"You needn't be concerned if he—or she—was trapped in the tunnels," Korda explained, chilling Firebird. "But what if he hasn't yet entered the Height? They could be listening to us through her."

"They can do that?"

"Some can."

He was lying. He had to be.

"What do you recommend, Thyrian?" asked a low, menacing voice Firebird knew well. Rogonin.

"Kill her," Korda answered instantly. "Now. Or at least drug her. They can't touch or detect anyone who's unconscious."

"No, wait. Lock her up somewhere else," Tellai suggested. "Away from the command center. Alone, under guard."

Bless Tellai. Bless the little fop's cowardly heart.

"I don't want to move her." Light footsteps drew near, then Phoena's face. "Every second she isn't restrained, she could slip free."

"We could move the party," Tellai began, but another engine roar, flying low on approach, cut off his suggestion. Muttering voices clustered beyond Firebird's feet, probably near the communications console. She squeezed her eyes shut, trying to isolate the transmitted voice out of this commotion. Was it possible—had Governor Danton acted instantly on Tierna Coll's recommendation, after all, and sent Federate troops?

"No, no." Phoena's laugh sounded slightly giddy. "She's already here. I'm sorry you missed her at Tallis."

How could she laugh like that? She'd just killed at least one man. Maybe two . . . *Please, not two!*

The other voices finally quieted. Firebird faintly heard the static of an open line, then an answering voice. "We did not miss her, Your Highness."

Captain Friel!

"Explain yourself," Phoena snapped.

After a longish pause, Friel answered, "I'll be there momentarily. You say that you have her? Secure?"

"Absolutely."

"Alone?"

"So far."

"Do nothing until I arrive."

Whispers and muffled footsteps flowed away from the console.

Phoena's face reappeared. "What's this, Firebird? You saw Captain Friel on Tallis? Perhaps there's something you would like to tell me?"

"Only this." Firebird's words came slurred. "You will not win."

Phoena hooted, reached aside, and seized a drinking glass from one of her friends. Firebird shut her eyes again, barely in time. More liquor splashed into her face.

A whooshing door admitted Friel several eternal minutes later. Bootsteps hurried to the restraining table. "This is amazing," Friel declared.

Firebird stared back at him.

Friel turned to address the gathering. "The hearing on Tallis went against us," he announced. "We were denied custody of Lady Firebird."

"But she was there?" Phoena strode to Friel's side.

"Absolutely."

"This makes no sense," Phoena argued. "They should have relinquished her without a murmur. Netaia's jurisdiction extends to all citizens, wherever—"

"But she's here, Captain Friel," Tel's voice interrupted. "Already."

"We were denied custody," Friel said evenly. "Has she told you why?"

"No," snapped Rogonin.

Firebird had never heard Captain Kelling Friel chuckle before. "Look at her," he directed Phoena's assembly. "First Major . . . Lady . . . Firebird Elsbeth Angelo. Wastling and traitor. Less than a week ago, standing in front of the Federacy's Regional council, First Marshal Burkenhamn, and myself, this woman swore allegiance to the Federacy."

"What?" Phoena's shout rose above the other shocked protests. "Don't taunt me, Friel. This is outrageous."

"Ask her."

"Firebird," Phoena cried. "Is this true?"

What could Phoena do worse than she already planned?

There were still hours before first light, Firebird realized, and Phoena—who knew all her worst fears—had just bragged about her interrogation facility.

"Korda," Phoena snapped. "Tell me. Did she do this thing?"

Firebird shut her eyes tightly. Footsteps approached once again. Prickly nausea touched the edge of her mind, but she thrust it away. She'd resisted a stronger Thyrian, and a better.

"Well?" Phoena demanded.

He probed again. Recalling his instructions, she envisioned her boot heels. She meant it as a taunt, and he would know it. But would he dare to admit failure to Phoena? *There's no mercy in your new mistress, Vultor Korda.*

"Your Highness." Korda oozed shock and sincerity. "Your Highness, it's . . . it's true."

Unbelievably, Phoena laughed—first lightly, then viciously.

Powers help me now, Firebird begged, and then she caught herself. There would be no more help from the nine Holy Powers.

All other voices fell silent. Phoena laughed on, and on, until her breath came in choking, hysterical gasps. The door whooshed. Voices murmured, fading, clustering, leaving in groups. Phoena's laughter grew desperate.

"Here," Tellai's voice soothed. "Take this. Wash it down with a little brandy. You'll need a good night's rest."

More helpless shrieking—then a momentary silence, the sound of choking, and Phoena's frantic laughter subsided into a hoarse, hiccuping chuckle. "They're gone," she complained childishly. Whatever *take this* had been, it worked quickly. "Why did they leave? We could've had a good time."

"They'll be up very early, tomorrow." That was Rogonin, somewhere out of her field of vision. "Get your rest, Highness. The day will be glorious."

"Don't leave her alone," Phoena pleaded.

Tel's voice soothed. "There's a guard. Go to sleep, love. There. Shall I turn up the cover?"

Footsteps. The door whooshed again, and then silence fell like a curtain.

Firebird wrenched her eyes aside. A red-jacketed guard sat close by, studying a lap viewer. Phoena lay propped on a pile of gold-edged pillows, eyes closed, smiling even in sleep.

Sleep, Firebird reflected. She'd better rest. Phoena had guessed correctly: The moment they released her from the restraint field, she would spend every bit of energy she had left, trying to escape.

She couldn't shut her eyes, though. With Brennen almost certainly dead in the tunnels . . . or fled . . . the odds were enormous that she'd die at sunrise. Could she face an agonizing end bravely, confident that there would be no bliss, no Dark, no awareness at all beyond her execution?

If there wasn't, then her pain would end when the D-waves burned down to her major nerves. Then she'd simply cease to exist. Forever.

She shuddered. She couldn't summon enough faith to believe in an unending nothingness. Every instinct rebelled at the thought.

There had to be something beyond physical life, if only the echoes of death, fading into eternity. She couldn't expect help or mercy from the Powers. Her only hope must lie in something greater, much greater than even the Powers claimed to be. Something capable of forgiveness.

Had Brennen's people found the answer? A Speaker, a Singer . . . a composer-creator, a conductor of time's rhythms, who could punish her after her death for all her shortfalls and offenses . . . the life she'd just taken . . . or offer her mercy?

She desperately wanted that assurance, but she couldn't ask for it dishonestly. If she wanted death benefits, she felt she had to commit herself unconditionally, whether or not she lived past sunrise.

But I don't know enough to decide, she railed at the night. An answer came out of her memory: *Sometimes, it takes only a glimpse of His majesty.*

She lay still for several minutes, trying with all her might to imagine that kind of a person. She could picture huge, but not that huge. She could imagine old, but agelessness eluded her. And what about that hidden cost, that death Brennen had finally admitted as the final price?

She gave up. It was impossible. Unless . . .

Show me, she begged.

For an instant, nothing happened. Then an image flashed through her mind, of a vast, primal, and unending intelligence. It made a sudden music so incomprehensibly magnificent that the universe exploded into existence, every particle and energy wave singing praise at all frequencies, an exultant harmony that condensed into billions upon billions of brilliant stars and their attendant worlds. He was the ultimate otherness, the omniscience beyond any Sentinel's probing ability. He was the source of all life, and He was its goal, to which life would return enriched and ennobled. Strength and Authority were only the colors that robed Him, Valor and Fidelity His fingermarks on those who believed in His sovereignty.

Shocked by the image's richness, Firebird tried to seize and hold it, but it melted away like a symphony's last notes, too splendid for any recording to capture.

But even if she were too small to comprehend Him, He existed. He did!

Trembling inside, Firebird squeezed her eyes shut. She relaxed against the steely restraint table. *Take me, then. You are the one I have always wanted to know. Do what you will with my life and my death, even if that life can be measured in hours, and death comes hard. I'd rather die for you than the Powers.*

She listened, longing to hear an answer sung back, feeling tone-deaf compared to what she'd just heard. There was no voice, but her screeching fears had fallen silent, and now peace flooded her mind. If the Eternal Singer existed, who was Phoena to frighten her?

Exhausted, she plunged toward sleep.

Harsh human voices roused her to aching wakefulness and a terrible thirst, still constrained in a field that reeked of stale brandy. Footsteps hurried past. She opened her eyes and spotted several red-jacketed uniforms. The restraining field collapsed. Strong arms wrenched her up into a sitting position so suddenly that her vision dilated and almost winked out.

When it cleared, she saw four House Guards carrying weapons, standing close behind Captain Kelling Friel. It was Friel who gripped her shoulders.

This was no time to bolt. She'd have to wait for a better chance.

Phoena stepped through the line. "Ah," she cried, "you're awake." When Firebird saw what Phoena held in her hand, she changed her mind and flung caution away, springing up and aside. She almost slipped Friel's grasp before two others reinforced his hold.

Phoena laughed merrily. "Oh, you and needles. But I'm doing this for your sake. The more dearly you pay now, the better your chances of bliss . . . eventually." She drove a wicked silver spike through the thermal suit into Firebird's shoulder, between Friel's fingers, then injected a stinging fluid. Firebird gasped. By the time she caught her breath, she recognized the sensory overload. Tactol again . . . and something more, this time. Her muscles tightened suddenly and firmly. She would've tried again to fling off the guards if they hadn't tightened their grip.

"Feel better?" Phoena tossed the medical nightmare onto the metal table. "Your color's better. Now you'll experience the full thrill of this hour, as I will."

Although Firebird's scraped hips and shoulders throbbed and burned, she felt as if she could climb Hunter Mountain in one leap, throttle all five guards at once (now she understood why Phoena had brought up so many of them), or tear the restraint table to pieces with her bare hands. But the injection had also intensified her emotions, and the sight of one guard's misshapen D-rifle, heavy chambered with a ceramic point at the barrel's end, aroused an adrenaline thrill of absolute terror. Another guard carried a massive tripod.

She would momentarily be reduced to a target, then to a victim dying in agony. She tried to relax, to control her fear and seize back the uncanny peace she'd found last night.

She glanced out the east window. "This hour," Phoena had said, and the faint glow beyond distant hills confirmed that less than an hour remained before sunrise. Her pulse beat in her ear like distant parade drums.

Where was Brennen? Had they found him, and was he dead or alive? Maybe he'd escaped. He must have, he must!

So these were her true feelings, sharpened by Phoena's drugs to pierce all her masks and defenses. She trusted and loved him. Completely. Even if they murdered her, even if he'd retreated to save himself, she'd die easier if somehow she knew he still lived.

But with morning arrived and their timetable long used up, then if he hadn't come for her, then he must be—he could be . . .

Brennen! she shrieked mentally. *Brenn, are you alive?*

Beneath the glowing chandelier, Phoena spoke under her breath to Tellai. Her dresser had robed her in another splendid gown, one that fit closely through the body and billowed out in a long dark skirt, looking like the legendary phoenix rising from its ashes. Tellai, in soft gray brocaded with silver, paled beside his regal mistress. A sweet spicy scent drifted from a pair of gilt cups on Phoena's bed.

Firebird bent forward and rested a little weight on her pressure-sensitive feet. "May I have a cup of cruinn?" she whispered to Captain Friel. "My mouth is full of dust."

He tightened his fingers. "I think not. You won't be thirsty for long."

Brennen, oh, Brenn. All the chances I wasted.

Phoena lifted something dark and limp off the bed, crossed the vast room again, and flung it at Firebird. A thin black jumpsuit with zip-cloth closures landed at her feet, then a pair of flimsy night slippers. "Put them on," Phoena ordered. "And don't try anything, or I'll have you stunned and let you die out there naked."

The guards at her shoulders let go. Firebird turned her back and started to peel off her suit's bulky shirt. Her scraped shoulders, scabbed to its lining, felt as if they were being combed with knives.

Suddenly her spirit leaped. On the Height's north side, she'd hidden two blazers. If they hadn't been found . . . if she could stay free enough to dash toward them—

Another red-collared House Guard burst through the elevator door, saluting Phoena on the run. "We've caught the other one, Highness!"

Firebird gasped and went stiff. The guards grabbed her again.

Phoena splayed her fingers in the air. "Was Korda right? Is it one of *them*?"

The guard drew up even straighter. "Yes, Your Highness. His so-called Excellency, the former lieutenant governor."

"What? Not Caldwell," Phoena croaked. Tellai dashed to the lift.

"It is, Your Highness. And he's alive—barely. We took him in the east lab. But he's having trouble walking. I think he's harmless now. Korda should be able to tell us for sure. The rest of my detail is down-level, disarming and collecting explosives."

"Ha!" Phoena breathed. "Someone tell Rogonin!"

Firebird's emotions whirled as she finished zipping into the execution jumpsuit. Harmless? Not Brennen. Never! But . . . if he wasn't, then how had they taken him?

Phoena hurried onto the lift and held a hand over its closing circuit.

"Bring her. I don't want her out of my sight until it's over."

Yanked forward by her elbows and trying to exude meekness, Firebird boarded the lift.

In the living area, about forty people had gathered near the firebay, all wearing warm capes and coats except one. Brennen stood at an edge of the crowd, still wearing his boots and thick thermal pants but stripped of his thermal overshirt. Blinking as though barely awakened, he tottered from foot to foot. He didn't seem to see her.

Tellai bowed deeply and presented Phoena a priceless Ehretan crystace. She seized it and glared down her nose. "Good morning, Your Excellency. Welcome to the Height. We've planned a brief ceremony in a few minutes, and I'd be pleased—delighted—to honor you beside my sister. Your fellow citizen," she growled.

"Let her go, Your Highness." Brennen's quavering voice horrified Firebird. Finally he glanced at her, with eyes that looked like dull gunmetal. "Send her to Danton. He'll take her offplanet. She'll never threaten you again."

Phoena snickered. "If you're trying one of those Sentinel command tricks, it's not working." She tucked his crystace into a pocket of the cape Tellai offered. "Someone check that skinshirt of his for metal. Where's Korda?"

"Here, Highness." The crowd parted to let the pale little man step through.

Firebird had never pictured their meeting this way. Korda advanced as Brennen looked away, trying to avoid the traitor's eyes.

"Do we really have him?" Phoena demanded. "Or is he shamming?"

Korda thrust a hand into Brennen's face. "There's no trace of shields on him," he gloated. "We have him."

No, no, Firebird pleaded. *Brennen, come back!*

"Prove it," Phoena demanded. "Tell us one of his secrets."

Brennen tried to back away from Korda. A House Guard shoved him forward again. Korda's eyes fell closed, and a rapt smile spread over his face. Firebird wondered what forbidden pleasures he was experiencing.

"Hoo," Korda crowed, "here's one for you, Phoena. Your mighty

Master Sentinel really would rather die in your sister's place. He loves her!"

Hoots and suggestive glances answered Korda. Brennen glanced solemnly at Firebird, his eyes gray and yellow from the zistane gas he must've breathed. Then he dropped his chin and stared at the inlaid wood floor.

Captain Friel stepped forward. "Your Highness, that calls to mind something important. On Tallis, when Lady Firebird renounced Netaia, one of the Federates claimed she'd been living under Caldwell's guarantee of asylum. Furthermore—by the Nine, Your Highness—that oath of hers was taken at the tip of his sword!"

Phoena whirled around. "Yes," she crowed. "It all comes clear. I think we've found the *real* source of your intimate knowledge of Netaia, Your Excellency. Not poor Dorning Stele!" She stepped close to Brennen and slapped him, leaving crimson fingermarks on his pale cheek. "How dare you insult my house by trying to consort with its wastling?" She twisted her fingers into Brennen's hair and jerked up his head. "And you, Firebird. So this was the price of your treason. A lover. I should've guessed."

Firebird clenched her fists. Denying that charge would only remind Brennen how little she'd trusted him.

"The time!" Phoena exclaimed, swirling her cape onto her shoulders. "Tie her! Where's Rogonin? We can't wait."

One of the hallway guards moved in with a fat hempen rope. Brennen stared as the guard looped her wrists and then let her bound hands fall behind her back. The changing angle dug prickly fibers into her sensitized skin.

"Move," ordered Phoena. Firebird didn't dare try to bolt, leaving Brennen disabled in Phoena's hands.

Arm in arm, Phoena and Tellai led out the massive eastern doors, across the flagstones and left along the winding lane that descended to the airfield.

North, Firebird prayed. *Send them north.* She walked the paving beside Brennen and surrounded by guards. Her spirits sank further each time he stumbled, and every step jolted her tightly strung senses. Predawn cold flowed through her flimsy jumpsuit like ice water. She clenched and unclenched her hands to keep them warm as the road fell from the Height. Near the outwall, the procession turned left again onto the long northern field, where grassy, weedy terrain made slower going. Phoena and her friends dropped behind.

North. There still was hope. "Brenn?" she muttered.

He tripped once more, barely catching himself. "You woke me. Thank you."

Woke him? Had he heard her mental shriek, or her terror of Phoena's needle? How had he heard anything at all, if he was as helpless as Korda claimed?

Firebird glanced back over her shoulder. Phoena's people followed the guards by twos and threes, warmly bundled, few speaking. Two carried a long equipment locker between them. A rosy stripe glowed in pale gray clouds over the spot where the sun was about to rise. The glow hurt her eyes.

The guards had fallen back a few paces. "I hid two blazers," she whispered urgently, "in a pile of dead grass, near—"

She caught movement with one corner of her vision. The guards had caught up. Still, Brennen's quick side glance encouraged her.

Dew from the ankle-high grass soaked through her pant legs and flimsy black slippers. Side by side, they passed a stake driven into the ground. She guessed it at the customary thirty paces from the northern outwall. Four guards halted. She heard something clattering but refused to turn and look. Her stomach twisted painfully. *The D-wave*, she heard again, *crazed a conscious patient with pain . . .*

Only Phoena would think to add Tactol to that misery.

At the outwall, two guards knotted the ends of the ropes binding her wrists to the freezing iron handrail. Two others placed Brennen a meter away.

"Your hands are behind the metal," one of Firebird's guards said smoothly. "Orders. 'Fingerprints are valuable proof of decease,' " he quoted, almost capturing Phoena's tone of voice. "But this isn't so tight that you can't shift them to the front of the rail, if you'd rather have it done cleanly."

Cleanly. Without leaving any part for Phoena to manhandle.

Another guard finished with Brennen and reached for his black neckscarf. "Do you want a blindfold, Lady Firebird?"

She shook her head steadily. If this was the end, she wanted to face it. If not . . . if they still had a chance . . .

The guards sauntered back to join the firing squad, who stood at attention behind four massive tripods, between Friel and Phoena. The princess's gown shone like orange flame among the guards' red berets and the others' more somber attire.

Now they stood alone, to die together. She never would've predicted this, back at Veroh. "Talk to me, Brenn," she pleaded.

"The knot is in reach of your right fingers."

She fumbled for it. Sure enough, a loop, fat and loose, lay inside her left palm. She picked at it with cold, swollen, supersensitive fingers. "I didn't think you were . . . done." Blessed freedom! She stretched enough slack from the loop to draw both hands through.

"Every minute they wait, I feel less sick. If I can get those blazers, are you up to shooting?"

The peak of Hunter Mountain gleamed suddenly orange, and slowly, the sunlit streak swept down toward the outwall. Firebird eyed the rifle squad . . . and Phoena, whose hatred and ambition had placed them here. "Yes," she murmured. "They've given me a stimulant. Are you really all right?"

"No," he admitted. He closed his eyes. She guessed he was focusing all the epsilon strength he'd regained. Couldn't she stall Phoena?

Not if that meant trying to hold off the dawn. Tellai strode out in front of the D-rifle line and called for quiet. Phoena would want to announce their offenses, and then invoke the Powers to witness this event. The "brief ceremony."

"Ready, Mari?" His voice was soft and steady.

"Brenn?" she whispered.

He glanced her way.

She had to tell him. "Brennen. I love you."

CHAPTER 23

FIREBIRD

allegro con fuoco
fast, with fire

"Loyal subjects of the Netaian queen," Phoena shouted. "At this dramatic moment—"

The ground shook with a low rumble.

Phoena froze before she finished her preamble.

The rumble echoed off League Mountain. Startled, Firebird slid her hands free of the loosened rope. Had Brennen even kept a touch card? Everyone had underestimated him, including her.

Phoena spun toward her intended victims. Firebird couldn't hold back a smile.

Phoena seemed to fill with hatred and purpose. "Present!" she shrilled to the execution detail.

Firebird glanced over Brennen's shoulder. Behind the house rose a dusky, billowing cloud.

"Sight!" Phoena screamed. The D-rifles swung on their tripods.

Firebird stared up two ceramic-tipped barrels into somber Netaian eyes. She shivered, and not from the cold. "Brenn," she muttered, clenching her fists. "Now or never."

He stretched out both arms to the compost heap. The handblazers flew toward his palms, trailing a litter of brown grass clippings. He tossed one weapon to Firebird.

Now she could fight back! She dropped to one knee on the frigid, wet grass and sighted up the nearest D-rifle, crouching as small as she could behind her metal blazer.

"Fire," Phoena shrieked, "fire!"

Firebird aimed for the House Guard, squeezed her firing stud . . . and missed. Phoena's drugs made her wrists and elbows quiver. Several of Phoena's friends bolted toward the house.

Brennen extended an arm again, reaching into the gesture with his whole body. As the D-rifles started to thrum, his crystace sailed from Phoena's cloak pocket. Phoena grabbed for it, lost her balance on the uneven ground, and fell facedown in the weeds.

A weird, heatlike pain crept up Firebird's extended left foot. She yanked it closer to her body, behind that frighteningly small blazer, then fired again, aiming higher. She dropped the guard as Brennen caught and activated his crystace one-handed. To Firebird's amazement, he flung it away. It soared for the D-rifles. As Brennen, too, crouched to fire, it whirled through two rifle barrels, slicing off their ceramic points.

One of the disarmed D-riflemen lunged for a hand weapon the dead guard had dropped in the weeds. Firebird felled him as Brennen got the other man.

The horizon glowed. The light made her eyes water, but her clumsy-numb hands began to feel warm. She swept the scattering crowd with her sights for the ample silhouette of His Grace, Muirnen Rogonin. Had he drunk too much of Phoena's brandy to rise early?

So she happened to see Vultor Korda fall, twitching, and the satisfied expression on Brennen's face, and the crystace returning again to his hand.

A blazer bolt flashed past Brennen's shoulder. Forgetting Rogonin and Korda, Firebird returned fire. The redjacket swung his arm, and again she looked down a weapon's bore. Brennen's crystace swept in and deflected the shot. Firebird squeezed again. *Got him!*

With the last threats down or fleeing, Firebird relaxed her wrist. Then she spotted Count Tel Tellai across the tussocks of weeds, unarmed but bravely shielding Phoena with his body while she waved wildly at somebody else. The odds were still forty to two. Firebird's finger crept back toward the firing stud. *Should I?*

Down the shaft of her energy pistol Tellai drew up, stretched tall, and braced himself.

She hesitated. He *was* only a child. He'd been decent last night. She couldn't let herself become a cold-blooded killer.

She lowered the blazer.

Tellai gaped.

"Let's get out of here, Brenn!" Over the outwall, up the mountain . . . and then where? If Phoena kept her wits, she'd quickly lock down all vehicles, send Friel for infrared snoops, and hunt them down. How long could Brennen keep moving? Besides the gas, there'd been that hideous Soniguard attack. At least after an hour, when the Tactol wore off, she'd feel normal . . . if she were still alive.

The crystace's hum snapped off behind her.

Across the field, Phoena shouted to someone. Firebird caught the word "airstrip." Tellai and four others dashed down the field for the back gate.

"Brenn!" Firebird cried. "If they can put a fighter in the air, we're groundside targets!"

"Then we'll beat them."

She couldn't think of a better idea. Finally releasing her unnatural energy, she sprinted after Tellai. Each step jostled her spine. Before she'd taken ten painful steps, Brennen shouted from far to her left.

She stumbled to a halt. He'd headed for the northern outwall instead of the gate, running as if one leg hurt. She angled back to join him. The sun crept at last over the horizon, and she winced at the brilliance of . . . everything. At that moment he turned and shouted, "Drop!"

She plunged into prickly weeds that felt like small knives. A bolt of green light blew a stone from the wall, piercing the spot where she'd stood an instant before. Prone himself, Brennen fired once.

"This way!" He sprang back to his feet and started to climb hand over hand. "Hurry. I missed. It's Friel, in the trees."

He could've jumped that wall. His strength must be going. She hoisted a foot onto the handrail. As she did, she dropped her blazer. Another shot cracked a rock at her knee. She pushed up, caught the top of the wall, and peered back for her weapon.

"Leave it!"

She linked her hand around Brennen's wrist, clambered over the weathered gray top stones, and dropped with him onto the canyon's rim. Far to her right, five men sprinted in a group, halfway down the airstrip lane. Below on the apron lay four Netaian tagwings, golden darts glistening among shadowy private craft.

She bit her lip. If they couldn't get away, they'd have to hide here in the mountains. If only they could call Danton, for backup—

Brennen snatched her hand. He pulled her through rocks and bushes to the steepest point of the rim, directly over the tagwings. "Up!" he puffed. Before Firebird could protest that he was too weak, he swung her into his arms . . . and leaped.

She clung to his neck as the cliffs flew by. This time, the plunge made bile rise in her throat. "Can you fly . . . a second tagwing?" she demanded, gulping.

"If Burkenhamn can fit, we can. Barely."

Together?

The permastone apron rushed up. He released her at the last second. She landed hard, tumbling, then scrambled up, feeling as if she were covered with bruises. She glanced back. He was coming. Limping. She dashed up the apron for the nearest fightercraft.

The stepstand was gone, but she'd sprung onto a fore wing hundreds of times. She slapped the escape panel to raise the bubble, then jumped in. *Was* there room? She was small. Brennen wasn't large or tall.

He sprang for the cockpit and fell short. Firebird flung out a hand. She pulled him aboard as he leaned heavily on her arm.

"Ankle?" she asked, sliding the inclined seat to its maximum forward position, the way her crew chief usually set it.

"It's all right." He tried to struggle into the aft cargo bin.

"Too small back there," she realized. "Get up here on the seat. I'll sit in front of you." She stood up, leaned forward, and touched in a code sequence to ignite the laser-ion generator. Its roar rose to a hideous howl in her ears. Groaning, she covered them as Brennen settled onto her seat and locked it down at maximum-back.

"Can *you* fly?" he demanded.

She remembered the other time, and her all-Academy record. "If I'm angry enough," she answered, squeezing down onto the seat. It was tight. Too tight.

Brennen tried to pull the flight harness around both of them while she sealed the cockpit. "Too short," he gasped over the generators' roar. She looked for a helmet. Only a headset dangled beneath the display. Was she setting herself up for ear damage?

Better deaf than dead, she decided. She didn't want to talk to anyone here anyway. "I guess even Burkenhamn isn't this big around. Secure yourself and hold me." She hastily checked her controls. She'd done no walkaround. This could be a short, nasty flight.

"Wait." Brennen's right arm dug into her back, and then he handed her a lump of something sticky and gray. "Wet it," he instructed. "Wet it *well*, then put it in your ears."

She divided the lump, spit on both halves, then improvised a pair of ear plugs. When she sat back, Brennen's arms circled her waist. She barely had room to breathe.

Something moved away down the apron. The runners had reached the strip. One had raised the canopy of the far tagwing and was climbing aboard. Others had nearly reached the next ships. Firebird pivoted her fightercraft to starboard and fired its twin laser cannon down the row, enveloping the golden ships with scarlet lightning that made her wince and blink. Two men dove for cover. The nearest ship burst into thousands of metal shards. Then the second.

The third hull merely twinkled. "His slip-shield's up," Firebird cried. "I can't take him broadside now. But I don't think he'll oblige us by taking off first."

"We can't stay here." Brennen peered around her left ear. The other tagwing's engines glowed. "Get up fast if you want a good chance in a scrap. Do you know who that is?"

"No. But I hope he's a redjacket." *I am angry enough!* Firebird cut the brakes, raised shields, and careened off the apron onto the strip, accelerating at max before she hit the canyon straightaway. Seconds later, she pulled up. She banked hard starboard instantly to avoid being blasted from behind.

They skimmed Hunter Height, just clearing the outwall, where a large area of eastern slope had collapsed. Brennen had done it— enough charges had remained hidden and armed to bury the basium lab. But now her stern sensor board picked up her pursuer. The display showed that he'd dropped both shields, coaxing extra speed from his engines. Apparently the pilot was no amateur, and he meant to finish them quickly.

With double shields, she couldn't shake him. Spinning full starboard, she singled the shield. Projectile protection dropped away, and a surge of acceleration pressed her spine against Brennen's chest. *Let him leave those shields down,* she pleaded silently. *I wouldn't have to hit an engine port, I could take him with a side shot!* But his extra velocity kept him out of her sights, above and behind, closing fast to make the kill.

All right, then. We die trying. Save me a place in your choir, Mighty Singer. Simultaneously, she cut out her last shield, angled straight up, and laid into a fast roll. For a terrifying moment she passed directly in front of him. An energy burst caught the tip of her tail fin. The pitch threw her off her seat's edge. "Hold me, Brenn!"

His arms tightened.

Then inspiration struck. She wrenched the emergency blackout switch off her left-hand sideboard, cutting sensors and display to fly virtually blind, diverting the last erg of generator output into her engines. Totally inverted, her fighter looped back. The hillside spun crazily above the cockpit as she turned about, riding her instincts, pushing for the top of the tagwing's envelope.

Suddenly, incredibly, the other tagwing slid past the center of her cockpit bubble. She gripped a firing stud and reactivated her particle shield. A flash momentarily blinded her. Then the hull tinkled like singing metallic rain.

"We did it!" she cried, blinking. She righted the tagwing and cut speed to unload the generator. The horizon circled back down to where it belonged.

"Mari." Brennen exhaled the name like a sigh. "You are a Firebird. Well flown." His head fell on her shoulder.

"Well. With his shields down it was like hitting a radio dish. Easy." Wishing her voice had a little less shake, she wagged the damaged rudder. It seemed stiff.

Stiff, like Baron Parkai's body would be, by now . . . and she'd just disintegrated a Netaian pilot. . . .

Her eyes thickened.

"Easy," murmured Brennen. "You had to. You saved yourself. And me."

She drew a deep breath, and it calmed her slightly. *Phoena's drugs!* This was no time to grieve. "I don't suppose we'd better stay around."

"Probably not." She felt hair pulled back from her throat, and a warm kiss below her left ear.

"Don't," she begged. Nothing had ever felt so unbearably wonderful. "Citangelo, then?" She'd love to try that fast vertical roll again, with no one shooting. "Or should we pick up that messenger ship?"

"Citangelo. Danton can pick up the Brumbee before Phoena spots it. We should get offworld. Quickly."

"How?" Without that messenger ship . . .

"Citangelo," he repeated. "A drop-in with orders for Danton, and we'll pick up a ship with a little"—he flexed his left foot, sandwiched between hers and the hull—"more room."

One-fingering a long arc to port, she chuckled. "Orders? Who takes orders from whom, Brenn? You or Danton?"

"Call it news, then. Intelligence."

Laughing, she cried, "Hang on!" and sent the tagwing high into the morning sky, in the wildest victory roll ever negotiated over the craggy Aerie Mountains.

Then she soared southwest, staying low over the foothills of the Flenings, avoiding the central plain for as long as possible. Abruptly she pulled her hands off the controls. "Cleary!" she gasped.

"Dead, I assume." Brennen shifted one hand on the sideboard. "Just before they took me uplevel, I saw her in the chamber outside the basium lab, wearing a sniffer and hunting explosives—carrying several."

"Oh." She checked her altitude. She couldn't regret *that* woman's death. "Then here's one for Cleary!" She seized the stick. Again the horizon spun, but this time she didn't mind the dizziness. "What *was* she building?"

"Can you wait until I discuss it with my superiors?"

"Brenn?" She wriggled one cramped, slippered foot. "This time, I'd be glad to wait." She still felt supercharged, too full of emotion to speak rationally, to tell Brennen that she'd discovered how deeply she loved him.

He has to know, she reflected. *He must be choosing not to take unfair advantage.*

A softer kiss warmed the side of her throat. She leaned back her head and pressed it against his, ear to ear. "Thank you," she whispered. Again, his restraint seemed a priceless gift.

"Would you show me," he asked, "what happened after we separated?"

Access? Perfect. She felt awkward about trying to tell him what she'd seen and heard—and asked—lying on that restraint table. "Sure," she said lightly. "Go ahead. Just don't distract me from driving."

She relaxed into the warm, tingling sensation and watched memories speed past, as quickly as the foothills that slipped by below them.

They halted at the very moment when she'd imagined, and loved, One who'd sung in solitary magnificence; One who offered mercy and had given her peace, even such a small detail as a good night's rest.

"Mari," he exclaimed in a joyful whisper. His arms tightened around her middle.

"Maybe He helped us," she suggested. "Just now."

"Yes," he said hoarsely. She thought she heard his voice catch. "Yes," he repeated.

Half an hour farther south, as she crossed the Division River between the old town of Treya and metropolitan Kerrigy, a pair of elegant black Federate intercept fighters roared into escort position behind them and challenged over the interlink. Brennen reached for the dangling headset and answered in some kind of code. The other pilot sounded chagrined as he acknowledged Brennen's transmission. The pair peeled away as neatly as skin from a banam fruit.

She needed no warning to keep quiet herself. If anyone official found out she were here, she'd be instantly arrested, charged again with her crimes, and locked down.

The tagwing's roar slowly faded. Finally, she reached for one ear plug.

"Let me," said Brennen, and he carefully dug out both lumps.

She sighed and shook her head.

As she followed the Tiggaree into Citangelo, Brennen reached for the headset again. "Would you object to waiting in the tagwing while I talk to Danton? I'll hurry."

"No, that's all right." The familiar autumn colors of Citangelo's western outskirts swept beneath her. She was flying on visual and savoring the still-brilliant reds, golds, and browns. If her flight trainer had spoken over the interlink, she wouldn't have been surprised.

With another series of obscure-sounding transmissions, Brennen obtained landing clearance at the occupation base, then shut off the interlink and spoke softly against her ear. "You can still stay here if you want, Mari. This will always be your home world. I'm sure Danton would eventually untangle your legal status." He smoothed her hair over her shoulders. It made her tremble. "But you're welcome to go back with me to Tallis and face the consequences."

"Tallis," she said. "Of course. Do you think you're in trouble with Regional?"

"Danton will tell me. One way or the other." With words, she understood, or in ways only Brennen would notice.

She dropped the tagwing on an unfamiliar new breakaway strip and taxied, at Brennen's direction, toward an L-shaped stone and metal building with a tall viewing tower. As Brennen squeezed out, she stared at his face. It still was pale, but no longer yellow.

"I won't be long," he said. "You might want to keep your head down." He slid carefully to the ground and strode off, slowly, favoring his right ankle.

Tel steadied himself with one arm against a master room wall. He couldn't believe what he was hearing. Carradee jelly-bones was standing up to Phoena! After last night and this morning, he was almost glad.

"I told you," Phoena seethed into the tri-D pickup over her desk. "Caldwell was here—and with Firebird, like a mated pair! And of course it was a laboratory. You would've known that if you'd given it half a brain. Catch them! Don't let them offworld! She's sworn allegiance to the Federacy!"

"What were you building?" Carradee demanded. "You've played this secrecy game long enough."

Phoena clenched her fists. Her shoulders trembled.

"You'd better tell her," Tel whispered. "You may need her on your side."

"An ecological weapon." Phoena clipped each word. "Toxin-synthesizing algae, and a mechanism to make it bloom through an entire ocean system."

"To . . . to foul an entire living world, just as Cleary claimed."

"In days. The basium helps it along somehow. But they've destroyed the entire tunnel, my spore stock, the basium concentrate we just seized—"

"Enough!" Carradee's nightrobed likeness stood tall and imperious, and for one moment, Tel saw their mother instead of Carradee. "Phoena, as of this moment you are confined to your suite at the palace, and it will be thoroughly inspected before you walk in. We will send an escort for you, and if you value your safety, you will cooperate. We shall also send a team of engineers to see if the Height's understructure is reparable."

Phoena glared back. "The Federates should pay to rebuild it. They gave no fair warning, made no request—they just obliterated the east end. It'll take months to rebuild."

"If you rebuild that laboratory you will face sedition charges!" Carradee's passionate sincerity shocked Tel. Finally, Phoena had pushed too far. "You defiled the Height! You swore you were conducting a cultural retreat, and we trusted you. We—I took your word. I should have my head examined."

Tel glanced from sister to sister, alarmed. For the first time, he realized the Federates might take vengeance on Phoena, and—he swallowed—himself.

"Have you any more to say?" Carradee demanded.

"Don't let them get away, you incompetent! She's betrayed us completely!"

Carradee gulped air like a skitter. "If we find Firebird, we'll detain her. But if you break arrest, Phoena, then Powers help us, we'll send the redjackets after you, too!"

Brennen slipped into the governor's office without waiting for the secretary to announce him. Danton looked up from his bluescreen. He radiated alarm. "Caldwell! What in Six-alpha are you doing here? Tallis has asked me to detain you on sight." He set down his stylus. "So get out of my sight."

That was bad news, but Brennen couldn't bring himself to care. He walked forward as quickly as he could. His legs still felt weak, and his ankle throbbed despite his effort to numb it. He longed to lie down, to rest . . . preferably in Mari's arms.

"You had a tetters' nest up north, Lee," he said. "Hunter Height, a private estate—"

"Yes, I had that message yesterday from Tierna Coll, but we couldn't find the locale on any map. I put in a query to the queen's office."

Brennen reached for a map projection on the wall behind Danton's desk chair. "Here. They've kept it off maps, so I'm not surprised you couldn't find it. Phoena Angelo converted it into a nuclear laboratory. They were modifying bombs."

"That would be the height of stupidity," Danton objected.

"True. You'll want to send a mop-up crew, and a pilot to pick up a DS–212 Brumbee just over this ridge." He pointed again. "We left about fifty angry loyalists, probably armed. But they've no tagwings now, and no ordnance lab."

Danton rubbed his chin. "Bombs? But they signed a treaty."

"Dig it out if you want, sir. I'm leaving." He paused with one hand on a corner of Danton's desk. "What about Lady Firebird?"

"Caldwell, we have no idea where she is. None."

Brennen nodded thanks.

A small red light began to pulse beside a label on Danton's link board. It read "Angelo."

Brennen stepped backward. "If I were looking for me, knowing I might be in trouble, I'd try the Sentinels' sanctuary in the Procyel system." He offered a hand. As Danton clasped it, Brennen opened an unguarded corner of the governor's mind. *If that's Carradee, stall her.* Then he spun on his good foot and asked, "Would you clear an unidentified 721 for takeoff?"

"Consider it done." As the door closed, Brennen heard Danton's polite diplomat's voice ask, "Good morning, madam. May I help you?"

Brennen slipped out a side door toward the tagwing and glanced around. No one was in sight. Danton's doing, he guessed. He hurried toward Firebird.

She'd seen Him! And last night, she'd heard a music he'd never imagined in such heartbreakingly beautiful detail . . . and she'd watched it take effect. She'd been given a vision and a song by the

Speaker himself, a glimpse—as Brennen had predicted—of His majesty.

He slowed his stride. Some of his people would say he still mustn't take her for his own until she'd formally joined their community.

But she'd received that image with childlike delight and offered herself as the sacrifice. He couldn't wait to see and feel her response when she learned that other blood had paid the price.

Holy One, I'm only a man. All that I am is your gift, including these desires . . . and this certainty that someday, we'll serve you together.

He'd reached the tagwing. His pulse quickened.

Firebird helped Brennen check the five-seat shuttle for liftoff. Her ears still rang from flying unhelmeted, despite the earplugs. Instead of programming the course for Tallis, though, Brennen gave the computer liftoff instructions only.

Then she felt his awareness touch her senses again, a deeper access than before, a long, tender stare at her moment of vision. She felt calmer now. Phoena's drugs were wearing off. As Brennen's probe recreated the instant she'd tried so hard to stretch out, her longings rose with it. She ached to rest in that peace, that mercy . . . that music . . . forever. In life and in death.

Brennen glanced aside. That broke the feathery sense of access, but he turned back to her. "Mari?"

Now she must face it: He also knew that she'd discovered how deeply she loved him. She sat erect in her flight seat, steadying both hands against the control panel. Ready-lights flashed across the board.

"We don't need to slip directly back to Tallis," he said. "The intelligence I took from that laboratory will keep, for now. I want to take you to Hesed House."

Firebird reached forward and released the flight brakes. "Where's that?" she asked, but she guessed his intention. Her hand trembled.

"Hesed is a sanctuary of my people." Thrust caught them, and they lifted. "A retreat, like Hunter Height but more pastoral. It is our traditional place for wedding. I can't offer you pomp." He touched her hand on the console. "You know what I offer."

Yes, she knew. Though the idea of bonding still frightened her, he offered it like a gift. She'd been a fool when she fought him for the right to die.

So what kept her from accepting him? Was it Netaian tradition, or cowardice? She didn't fully understand him. That might take a lifetime. But she knew enough, loved enough, to embrace his mysteries—and his certainty—and to step out on this path, too. Again she heard, or remembered, a timeless harmony.

She straightened. "Brenn, if you're willing to take a Netaian, I can face your pair bonding."

He gripped her hand. Instantly, she felt the same gust of approval that had blown through her mind in the high Tallan valley. This time, though, it carried an undercurrent of assurance and joyous anticipation. Brennen's eyes shone under blue striplights. He entered the destination coordinates for a south-spinward slip.

Stars sprang one by one from the blackness of space as Netaia's horizon curved far below. Unconsciously she started to hum, and then she almost laughed aloud. Another melody had sprung into her mind, her ballad of Iarla, the wastling queen who'd triumphed over her fate. Though still unfinished, it swelled in her heart like an anthem. She suspected she'd be able to write the other verses now.

Brennen smiled. "Ten seconds to slip," he said.

"Ready."

Like fire kissing water, the ship winked out of Netaian space.

AUTHOR'S NOTE

Most fiction, including most science fiction and fantasy, begins by asking, "What if. . . ?" In creating a spiritual struggle for Lady Firebird, I asked one of those questions: What if God had created a universe without Earth, and a chosen people with a vastly different history?

If the culture prepared to receive the Messiah had been obliged to wait two or three thousand years longer, then before He was born they might have developed space travel. They could've terraformed other worlds and experimented with genetic engineering, playing out Israel's cycles of sin and repentance under the Judges on a galactic scale. A few children might have escaped God's wrath in an arklike generation ship, and even in exile, a faithful remnant might await His birth. The Jews of Christ's time expected a military deliverer; these exiles might hold a similar hope.

Though their history would be different, they would know the same truth. God would have sent prophets to teach them that personal salvation rested on an atonement that was only symbolized by their ancient sacrifices. Their highest commandments would be to love the One God with all of their hearts, minds, and strength, and to love—to serve—their neighbors as themselves.

Our Lord's family tree includes people who were no more priestly than Lady Firebird Angelo, and at least one woman who wasn't born Jewish. Many, though—like Brennen Caldwell—knew the prophecies. I wonder how many men and women looked down into a cradle and wondered, "Could this be my King?"

Intriguing possibilities, but only speculation. The Firebird series isn't a spiritual allegory, but only an extended—slow-motion—parable of conversion. God actually sent our Messiah into a small Jewish household two thousand years ago, on an exquisite blue-and-white planet that He spoke into existence.

Kathy Tyers
Montana
September 1998